OLD GORGE ROAD
A KENTBURY MYSTERY

To Victoria —
With much love to
someone who knows the
"real" Kentbury. Thank you

CHERYL NUGENT

for your friendship all these
years — where does the
time go?
Cheryl Nugent xox00
2014

(and share with Martha!)

iUniverse LLC
Blooming[ton]

D1213344

OLD GORGE ROAD
A KENTBURY MYSTERY

This is a work of fiction. All of the characters, names, incidents, organizations, and dialogue in this novel are either the products of the author's imagination or are used fictitiously.

iUniverse books may be ordered through booksellers or by contacting:

iUniverse LLC
1663 Liberty Drive
Bloomington, IN 47403
www.iuniverse.com
1-800-Authors (1-800-288-4677)

Because of the dynamic nature of the Internet, any web addresses or links contained in this book may have changed since publication and may no longer be valid. The views expressed in this work are solely those of the author and do not necessarily reflect the views of the publisher, and the publisher hereby disclaims any responsibility for them.

Any people depicted in stock imagery provided by Thinkstock are models, and such images are being used for illustrative purposes only.
Certain stock imagery © Thinkstock.

ISBN: 978-1-4917-2125-4 (sc)
ISBN: 978-1-4917-2127-8 (hc)
ISBN: 978-1-4917-2126-1 (e)

Library of Congress Control Number: 2014901191

Printed in the United States of America.

iUniverse rev. date: 02/04/2014

For Mary Ann Vitale DeMaio, a beautiful lady,
special friend and constant inspiration.

Sincere thanks to fellow wordsmith Dara Oden, for encouragement and good advice.

Thank you to Will Nugent, son and super critic . . . I love the input.

Special thanks to Jean McRae, who never ceases to amaze me with her enthusiasm and willingness to read for me . . . again and again.

For technical support I thank John and Patricia Subbe, who know Hunterdon County and its history so well.

Thanks to Wayne Kephart who sent me a link to wonderful old photos that helped in writing vivid descriptions of a bygone era.

And a big Aloha to friend and mentor, Teresa Webber, a gifted writer and the mom of the real Tuk-Tuk, a sweet little cat from Thailand, fondly remembered in these pages.

Finally, a very big thank you for my husband, Allen, whose love and support mean so much.

The cover for Old Gorge Road is by artist, Kathy Outersky Bonem, from her original work done in the style of Chinese Brush Painting. The artist and the author attended school together in the real Kentbury and this is their first collaboration. Kathy Bonem now makes her home in Florida.

ONE

It was cool for August. Gaffer White hugged a ragged jacket to his wiry arms as he carried the day's bounty up the steep climb to the cottage. A day working for Mrs. Newberry meant two or three days worth of groceries and, to top it off, the lady gave him a ride to Old Gorge Road where he now negotiated the narrow path through the woods to his home.

The music made by the birds and insects dwelling there was wasted on Gaffer. He took no pleasure in hearing the rhythm of water rushing over the rocks, splashing and falling into streams and pools on its way to Lake Raynard. The powerful beauty of the place did not give him pause or engender joy. The animals that shared the woodland with him were not his friends. The white tail deer, the raccoons, skunks, muskrat, beaver and squirrels; the snakes, turtles, toads and frogs were just there, like the trees. Gaffer did not trap or hunt; the creatures were not his prey. He missed the opportunity to interact with nature. He did not consider himself part of it. He did not consider himself part of anything. No one ever pointed out a beautiful flower to Gaffer, read him a story, asked his opinion or sought his advice.

The old stone cottage where he made his home was borrowed, which is to say, Gaffer moved in after a fire, never paid rent and no one ever tried to kick him out. *Uninhabitable,* the fire chief declared, and so it was thought until Gaffer moved in. The two top rooms were unusable and the roof was damaged in the front, but a makeshift tarp kept most of the rain out. The kitchen and two extra rooms downstairs were more than enough for the short, skinny man most folks considered simple-minded. Built into a hill, the fieldstone walls of the sad house made it cool in the summer and, with a kerosene heater, not too bad in winter. The owners of the 1840 cottage were city folks who never bothered Gaffer, which suited him admirably. He never wondered why. He did not know that the owner's son drowned in the ocean and the boy's mother lost her mind, the father killed himself and the part of their estate that was a little cottage off Old Gorge Road was stored in files at a lawyer's office in New York City.

The fire conveniently occurred about the time Gaffer's mother passed away, almost sixteen years ago. The Great Depression was on then. His choices, as far as he could see it, were to take to the road and live the life of a hobo, or find some permanent arrangement in the town where he was born and raised. The fire gave opportunity, something rare in Gaffer's life.

Gaffer scavenged the dump, mowed lawns, did odd jobs as they came along, happy to exchange his labors for a good meal, old clothes, or anything else someone could part with that made them feel charitable. His daily concerns were food and listening to his radio.

Gaffer missed his mother when she died. She was simple-minded too, or so folks said. When she became pregnant, sometime early into the century, everyone thought it was a disgrace, they even thought, but would never actually say—*rape*. When Weird Aggie, (the name most folks knew her by), gave birth to a sickly baby boy, they expected he would die; "*for the best*," folks said. But somehow Aggie managed and the baby lived. With uncommon kindness for the time, Aggie's employers let her stay on, baby and all. For the first six years of his life, Aggie called him *Baby*, which then became Bobby when some effort was made to send him to school. School was a disaster. At fourteen Bobby found work for himself. He dug graves, dug ditches, tarred roofs, carried bricks on house sites and someone gave him the name Gaffer. He was often the brunt of a crude joke, but since he never knew exactly what a joke was anyway, it provided little fun for his tormentors.

Right after Aggie died, people came around to offer their help, but since they didn't know what to do and Gaffer didn't either, the do-gooders went away. That was at Mrs. Logan's. He hated that house. He liked the big house where he lived for so long. But the people there died and lawyer people came and made Aggie and her son move to Mrs. Logan's.

Gaffer accepted his lonely existence, and friends were people who said hello or gave him a ride home from work. The women were usually nicer than the men. Gaffer never knew a woman, in the biblical sense, but he did see sex of sorts performed once when his fellow workers insisted he accompany them to the back of Bugler's Tavern. The act made no lasting impression. It did not stay in the boy's mind to provide dreams, fantasy or desire.

Thunder clouds were gathering; the summer light was fading. The trail to the cottage grew darker as the woods became thicker. Gaffer never wondered why he couldn't see as well as he used to or why his bones ached in cold weather.

No papers encumbered his life but, only two days ago, there was a real letter that came when he was at the Romano's. The man who delivered it wasn't anyone Gaffer knew and he called Gaffer "Mr. White." He talked about papers somewhere, but Gaffer didn't understand most of it. He wanted to do his job and he wanted the man to go away. He put the letter in his pocket but it was almost forgotten until he remembered there was money in the letter, so he kept it close, and when he showed it to one of the few people who were nice to him, they read it for a long time and said he shouldn't tell anyone, and maybe it was even a joke. He didn't think it was a joke. Maybe he would show it to Mr. Newberry since he was very smart, but for now he'd keep it all; the money could buy a new blanket, maybe a warmer coat and he'd hide the rest.

Gaffer might have wondered how the man found him or knew who he was, but Gaffer rarely wondered about anything. He never wondered about his birthday, who his father might have been or what it would be like to drive a car. He didn't wonder about the people he saw in the summer who came to The Gorge and Lake Raynard, thrilled by the intense beauty and primitive magic of the place. Trespassers might have bothered him if they found their way to his remote dwelling, but he never imagined it and could never imagine what he might do if such a trespass ever occurred. Local boys used to come to the cottage sometimes, yelling things at him, but that had not happened in years.

He could smell the cheddar Mrs. Newberry put in his bag. His imagining this summer night reached as far as a cheese sandwich. A movement caught his eye as he neared the broken steps by the front door. It was not like an animal movement but what else could it be? Hunger overcame fear. The smell of cheese spurred him on. A hearty sandwich beckoned.

Pain. The heavy stick that whacked him on the head drew blood. Blood was running in his eyes. The groceries scattered as Gaffer fell to his knees. Dragging. Someone was dragging him into the cottage. Gurgling noises, flaying arms and legs he couldn't move. It hurt. *Stop it!* They were pulling his pants off. Wrestling with his jacket! *Don't, please don't!* He could smell the kerosene and feel it soaking his legs. His hand met flesh as it scratched in defense of his life. He saw the person then. He thought he saw his mother. He longed for her. Wonder did enter his mind then and a great, screaming question formed there before it shut down forever.

Why?

TWO

S ix short years after the end of World War II, the Borough of
Kentbury was booming. The town revolved around the Tyler-
Sykes Iron and Steel Mill, in place since the 1700's when it made
cannonballs for the War of Independence. The mineral-rich hills of the
county were mined by early settlers and the Native Americans before
them. In the 1850's, the Jersey Central Railroad came to town, ensuring
Kentbury's prosperity as an industrial center surrounded by farming
communities. The population of 2,500 included the descendants of
expected Anglos and Scotch-Irish, as well as the early German and Dutch
settlers, the old names dotting the area for generations. But with each
wave of immigrants coming into Ellis Island, a few always seemed to find
their way to the rolling hills of Hunterdon County and to the Borough of
Kentbury, established 1722.

The colonial hamlet had a rich history, most of which was known
to the locals and anyone who had passed through the sturdy brick
schoolhouse where countless citizens learned the Three Rs from teachers
who seemed to be in place forever. An annual Thanksgiving play assured
the town's history would not be forgotten when Mrs. Bigley's fifth graders
re-enacted eighteenth century events for an enthusiastic audience. The
once heavily-forested area was home to the Leni-Lanape, later called
Delaware by the Europeans. It was not uncommon to find arrowheads in
local woods and fields. The town's founding family, the Kents, still had
a home within the town limits, although their estate was reduced from
thousands of acres to five, a once-grand house now in disrepair, and an
old car no one could drive. The two heirs to the once sizeable fortune
were a brother and sister said to be mad, to never wash, to possibly share
a bed and to eat any foolish child who might trespass on their land. The
ghoulish lore made for little intrusion on the private property, as well

as fueling delightfully creepy stories older children could pass on to the younger generation.

Because Kentbury's economy depended more on industry than on farming, the town prospered during wars. The Mill was cited for its contributions in every war America fought in and had its place in history for other things as well, like furnishing power shovels that dug the Panama Canal. The Great Depression hit hard, like everywhere in America, but a year after Hitler rolled into Poland, the President of the steel works, Randolph Tyler, sold several innovative ideas to the War Department, so by the time the Japanese bombed Pearl Harbor, the little town in New Jersey with the old iron and steel mill was out in front of its competitors and among the top producers on the east coast with lucrative government contracts.

Prosperity remained. Returning GIs came to Kentbury to find work and begin a life they fought for, dreamed of and believed in. Some were boys returning home, others were newcomers finding their way to Hunterdon County because of good jobs and affordable housing that began dotting the area on once-rich farmland. *Developments* they were called, and while they missed being the frenzied assembly-line homes of Levittown, they went up fast, provided construction jobs and more homes for all the new families moving in. There was talk of a four-lane highway going into New York City that would make travel back and forth a quick, one-hour commute. The railroad already had a steady stream of country-to-city commuters who didn't mind the long train ride that allowed them to have the best of both worlds—work with city salaries but the affordable charm and quaintness of the country to call home. Many celebrities had weekend or vacation homes in the area and even though no one would argue that it was, by all standards a "hick town," it offered beauty and clean air, good schools and nice people, safety and predictability. Folks rarely locked their doors. Crime was usually petty theft by several known characters. People talked about murders that happened thirty years earlier, but none in recent memory, and domestic violence was a hushed, behind-closed-doors problem that could, if it got out of hand, involve Kentbury's small police force.

In the spring of 1951, former Marine Sergeant, Terrence Andrew Kramer, began his career in Kentbury as Deputy to Police Chief Ernest Campbell, known either as Chief, which made sense, or Bull, which only made sense to those who christened him with the nickname some fifty years earlier. To his new deputy, he was Chief.

A returning war hero to townsfolk, Terry Kramer preferred to forget the war and his medals and why he was awarded them. The hell that he went through in the Pacific was private, he did not dwell on it, he did not find solace in a bottle like some he knew. The shrapnel in his leg did not remind him to hate, but rather was there to tell him to live. He had won, and he damn well better make the most of the life he had snatched away from the gaping void that swallowed so many of his fellow Marines. Of his original company sent to the Pacific in 1944, he was one of ninety-four survivors. Names and faces, sounds and sometimes smells returned, unbidden, usually in the night, but Terry managed. He knew he was lucky. He was alive. He came back to his hometown, he had a good job that made him want to get up in the morning, and he had a beautiful wife he adored.

The chief's version of coffee greeted Terry with the now-familiar smell of burnt socks. He had two cups of his own brew at home which, thankfully, was all he needed.

"Terry! Morning. Nothing much happening this morning," the chief said, sitting behind the old wooden desk in the large office that had served as Kentbury's police station since 1922. The chief's desk sat near the windows looking out to Main Street. Terry's desk was on the other side, near the bathroom, and down the hall was a door leading to the jail, a two-cell lockup which, happily, rarely had guests. The sturdy, turn-of-the-century building also served as the town hall, with offices upstairs and a small library run by the colorful Dolly Argyle, who took the job over from her mother who had been the town librarian/historian for almost forty years. Tuesdays and Fridays, before she went upstairs to open the library, Dolly brought in a bag of doughnuts for Kentbury's finest. The chief was enjoying one while he talked, letting Terry search the bag for his favorite cinnamon cruller he knew would be there. Both men were trying to give up cigarettes; the chief because his wife was convinced by their doctor that it was aggravating his heart condition, and Terry because Joyce didn't like it and bought him a pipe which she said was much more sophisticated. He was fighting the cigarettes but couldn't take to the pipe.

"Rupert Taggert threw his garbage all over Main Street again last night," the chief said, beginning the day's report to his young deputy. "His son picked it up and promised it wouldn't happen again, but I don't see how he can guarantee that unless he gets his old man to give up the booze. Oh, uh the road boys'll be tarring up on Old Mine Road today. I'll be running over to the county courthouse and I'm gonna grab a bite of lunch with Sheriff Zimmer, so we can meet back here this afternoon," he finished.

Some days were like that, quiet, even boring, but they also had their days of robberies, road accidents, husbands beating up their wives and kids that needed more help than the police could usually offer. Terry preferred the quiet days.

"Oh, yeah," the chief went on, "Ethel Barrow called a few minutes ago saying she saw a fire up in the gorge last night. I suspect she gets a good view from her place, but nobody else has seen anything. Still, it might have been some kids or something, so go have a check on that would ya?" he said.

"Sure enough, Chief," Terry answered.

"That thunder storm last night would've put out a three-alarmer, but you might as well go talk to her and see if she can give you some details. Ethel's old, but she's not silly," the chief said, using one of his favorite compliments.

The amiable police chief and his new deputy were getting on just fine. The fellow before Terry Kramer had been a disaster. Arrogant and self-important, the chief only agreed to take on Leonard Smith to appease some of the Town Council members when his deputy of four years moved to Arizona. This time they wanted a veteran. Leonard was a local boy who had been in the army, and even though Leonard only got as far as Fort Monmouth before the war ended, he came from an old Kentbury family. Small town or not, politics lived here as everywhere else and Leonard got the job. He lasted six months. By the end of his time on the two-man police force, he had alienated almost everyone, including his original mentors. By a strange irony, Leonard moved into Terry Kramer's old deputy job in the next county and rumor had it that he was just as stupid there as he had been in Kentbury. It was a move up for Terry to come back to his hometown, since Chief Campbell was planning to retire in a year or two and the deputy could expect to step into the job. Terry Kramer was a local boy too, a Marine who had seen action in the Pacific, been wounded, had a nice young wife, and didn't feel he had to brag or bully to do his job. People liked him and he was fitting in well.

The road to Ethel Barrow's house went down into a poorer section of town, into East Kentbury, past the steel mill and on around past Lake Raynard, into yet another part of town boasting elegant, older homes, a few picturesque farms and several historic houses where Hessian prisoners were kept during the Revolution. Terry knew the town history as well as anyone and was well-satisfied with life on such a beautiful August morning. He and Joyce made love before he dragged himself out of bed at six. Unlike most of the wives in town, Joyce did not feel responsible for her husband's breakfast, and Terry didn't mind. She was a city girl, used to a different life *"Getting up with the chickens,"* as she called it, was not in her wedding vows.

Joyce slept while Terry washed and dressed and when he came back to their bed to kiss her goodbye she had reached up to him, half asleep, letting him kiss her lips, her neck, her firm breasts. She pulled him down to her and while it would have been so easy to succumb to a few minutes of urgent lovemaking, he left her wanting him as much as he longed for her. Her scent stayed with him. He could smell her now and knew that his day would be filled with thoughts of her and when he did get home, supper could wait while they acted out the fantasies each had embraced all day. It was a rare day they did not make love, even after almost two years of marriage. It would change when children came. They both wanted children, but they were in no hurry and their life so far suited them. Terry's thoughts rambled on until he came to the paved drive leading up to the Barrow house.

Ethel Barrow was a widow who lived with her sister, Madeline Stone, also a widow. Both ladies were left well off by husbands who had shared a law practice in New York. When Madeline's husband died, five years ago now, she came to live with her sister in what had been the Barrow's vacation house near the lake. Set up on a hill, the views went for several miles, one side of the house facing the gorge.

As Terry approached the wraparound porch of the attractive Victorian home, he was met by the resident collie, Jimmy. The old dog did an announcement-bark only. Terry could tell the animal was friendly and spoke quietly to Jimmy, while offering him his hand to sniff. When his mistress finally came to the door, the dog was enjoying stroking and kind words from the visiting deputy.

"Good morning, young man. Bull said you'd be coming. Do come in. Madeline and I are just having coffee and biscuits, won't you join us?" asked Ethel.

Terry remembered the stories he heard about the Crisp sisters: Ethel and Madeline Crisp. They were contemporaries of his Grandmother Katherine and he grew up hearing about a way of life all but forgotten in the bustling modern world. Terry's Grandmother Katherine was a farm girl, married a railroad man and lived in the city for a while, but she had gone to high school with the Crisp sisters, being in the same class as Madeline, the younger of the two. When graduation day came, Terry's grandmother was busy planning her wedding, while Ethel and Madeline Crisp were preparing to sail off to Europe for their Grand Tour.

Within a year of their return, both sisters had married well and made their new homes in New York City, returning in the summers to their family estate near Lake Raynard. Most of the Crisp property was sold years before, but Ethel and her husband managed to keep several acres on a hilltop where they built their "summer cottage" which was completed in 1911. A small plaque at the front gate declared that it was indeed, "Lake Cottage," but Terry had to laugh at what some people considered a cottage. The two-bedroom house he and Joyce were renting could fit into Lake Cottage five times over.

Jimmy followed his mistress into the cool interior of the elegant home. Terry loved dogs and old or not, you could tell Jimmy was a champion of his breed.

"We'll do your walk later, Jimmy," Ethel said to the collie.

"We try to give him a walk every morning—he loves it but a good constitutional is good for us as well," Madeline said, and Terry was tickled at the word "constitutional," something not heard very often these days.

Terry readily appreciated good dogs as well as good houses, big houses, like the one he was raised in, and it was one of the things he and Joyce talked a lot about. They had no interest in the shoe boxes that the new developers were turning out. Even the house they rented was roomy. It was only two bedrooms, six dollars a month more than a three-bedroom they could have had, but they opted for some space and privacy, something they both held dear. Joyce was popping into his head again . . . he was slightly embarrassed by his thoughts when he realized Mrs. Stone was addressing him.

". . . now, that was your grandmother on your father's side, is that right, Deputy?"

"Uh, my grandmother Katherine, yes, that's right, Mrs. Stone," Terry answered, understanding that Madeline was asking about her old school mate.

"You know, I was at my son's home in Westchester when she passed away . . . what, two years ago now? I was so sorry when I heard," Mrs. Stone was saying.

Terry would occasionally see the Crisp sisters in town and last year, right after he got the deputy job, they came into the station to report someone abusing a dog, but this was the first time since returning to his hometown that he had occasion to call at Lake Cottage. As always, the ladies were demurely but elegantly dressed, perfectly coiffed, pearls adorned their slim necks and he was easily charmed by their superb manners, kindness and sense of humor. He was surprised to see Ethel wearing trousers, slacks Joyce called them, but she wore them well and still looked quite proper with earrings and pearls in place. He knew they had grown up with privilege, but had not been sent off for schooling like some of the town's elite, remaining to get their education in town but with a social life that meant they could reach well beyond Kentbury if they wanted to. If there was any snobbery at work, Terry never heard about it with the Crisp sisters.

As much as the deputy was enjoying the early morning visit and second breakfast of strong coffee and delicate biscuits with homemade preserves, he did remember why he was here and turned the conversation to the business at hand.

"Yes, dear," Mrs. Stone was saying, being among a select few who could address the police deputy as 'dear.' "Ethel called me out to the porch when I was getting our dessert. We finished dinner around seven, so this would have been perhaps seven-thirty or so, is that right, Ethel?" she inquired of her sister.

"Yes, Madeline. I think we mentioned the time because we wanted to catch Jack Benny on the radio. Yes, about seven fifteen to seven thirty. Come, I'll show you," Ethel said, getting up and leading the way to a side door.

The inviting wraparound porch was appointed with wicker furniture boasting colorful chintz cushions, several rocking chairs, and large and small tables, suggesting the ladies might occasionally take their summer meals outside. Ethel Barrow stood at the porch railing, pointing toward the rocky hills of the gorge as she explained what she saw the night before.

"We see much farther in the winter, of course, Deputy, but even with all the foliage I could see that smoke. I called Madeline and she agreed that it looked out of place. You know, not like campers or even a trash fire," she explained.

We weren't sure what to do. Call the fire department probably, but clouds were already gathering and in a few minutes we got that horrendous storm," Ethel said.

"Yes. And we weren't about to use the telephone in that electrical storm, you can understand, but with all that rain, whatever it was certainly would be extinguished, so we didn't feel it was actually an emergency," Madeline said.

"No, we didn't, Deputy, but we did think we should tell someone, I hope that's all right," Ethel said to Terry.

"Ethel, I think 'Deputy' sounds very impersonal. We knew this young man's grandmother, for heaven's sake. May we call you, Terry, dear?" Madeline asked, completely throwing out a new subject Terry was not prepared for.

"Oh, yes, certainly, ma'am," he answered, feeling a little foolish but not sure why.

"Yes, Madeline, fine. But I'm sure the deputy . . . Terry, needs to get on with his duties. Is there anything else you need to know?" Ethel asked.

"No, Mrs. Barrow. That's fine. I'll go on up there and check around. I'm sure if it had been any of the houses we would have heard by now, but it could have been kids up to something I suppose," he said.

"It was fairly high, you know, more to the left. I'm not sure there are any houses there, and I'm not sure who owns the property, Terry, but you might want to check that," Ethel Barrow said, referring to some privately-owned land that was part of the whole 600-acre gorge area.

"I can look into that, Mrs. Barrow, but we appreciate you letting us know. I'll check it out and thank you again," Terry said as he stepped off the porch and went back to the black Ford with *Borough of Kentbury, Police*, painted in gold letters on the front doors. Jimmy accompanied him to the car, getting a few good pats from the deputy before he departed.

THREE

Before the Marine Corps, before defying his family and joining up a year after Pearl Harbor, Terry was going to night school at the college in Trenton. He thought about becoming an engineer and had taken an introductory course in geology, passing with a B+. With the GI Bill, he could afford to go back, but he had Joyce to think about now and who would support them if he was in college? Joyce talked about working, but he didn't want to make that kind of burden for his wife. Night school was still an option and sometimes they did talk about that.

Even without a knowledge of the geological history of the gorge, it was a fascinating place. Everyone knew the Delaware Water Gap had similar beginnings in the natural phenomena that made the gorge, but one of the things Terry had learned that struck him every time he was here, were the similarities between Kentbury's tiny natural wonder and the majestic Grand Canyon. A miniature version, to be sure, but they shared the same secrets of creation, craggy outcropping of rocks eroded by water over countless centuries, caves where ancient peoples once dwelled, limestone, sandstone, shale and now an abundance of fish and wildlife.

As he negotiated the winding drive along the lake and came to the end of the paved area, Terry turned left at the T, onto the reddish clay dirt road that went for several miles through the picturesque area known locally as just The Gorge. Straddling the south branch of the Raritan River for almost three miles, the area would one day be part of the Parks Service, to be known as a Wildlife Management Area, with rules to protect it from pollution and misuse. But even now, the local citizens and visitors who came in the warm weather appreciated the unique beauty of the place. There were always a few who carelessly left their trash and couldn't respect what Mother Nature was sharing with them but, by and large, most were thoughtful of their surroundings. The pristine streams gave up their trout and bass to dedicated fishermen and nature lovers of all kinds, from bird watchers to historians, knew a good thing when they saw it. Terry used to fish. It had been years but maybe it was something he should take up again. He might interest Joyce in the sport. He knew plenty of secluded spots where they could make love. Would his city-bred woman like that? He hoped so. His thoughts were in bed again. He brought himself back to the present as he pulled into a parking area. The entire road was shaded and he left the windows down so the car would stay cool while he began to climb, looking for any evidence of the fire Mrs. Barrow had seen.

He never tired of being in the woods. When he was a boy, the house he grew up in backed up to a woods with a meandering stream where he and his younger sister would strip to their underwear to cool off in the summer heat. His sister now lived in Connecticut and his parents had, for a reason he could barely understand, retired to Florida. He hated Florida. He knew some of his dislike was unreasonable, but he couldn't help it. The tropics, palm trees, unrelenting heat, threw him back to the Pacific. Back to 1944. Back to death and carnage. He needed to be where he was. He needed green woods, season changes, cool-running streams.

Several summer homes sat amongst the woodland, most being further downstream, closer to the lake. He knew of only one that was lived in year round, and that was a mile or so farther along from where he was. Terry had to laugh at himself. Whether he liked it or not, he did seem to know a lot of the town history. He wasn't sure he had wanted to come back here when the deputy job opened up, but he was glad he did. There was peace and comfort in his hometown, and with Joyce, it was close to perfect.

Deer droppings were near the footpath and a large jack rabbit froze at Terry's approach, propelling itself into the air at high speed when he got too close. NO HUNTING signs were posted in the woods, but he knew some of the locals would hunt when and where they pleased, risking the fines to supplement their food supplies. Chief Campbell usually looked the other way, Terry was not sure he could.

Terry went back to the car and drove on another mile to a higher area. Even though the thick trees prevented him from an exact view, he thought it was a place that could still be seen from the Barrow's porch. He was beginning to think it was a waste of time, that it must have been kids up to some kind of mischief, or even someone trying to camp out when he recognized a spot with a well-worn path he had known as a teenager. He had almost forgotten about Gaffer White. It was a right of passage when he was about thirteen, to go up to the fire-damaged house and yell at the poor old guy. Terry had done it, like all of his friends, but he remembered that either Gaffer wasn't home or he just didn't react and, except for the rush of adrenaline Terry got from getting near the spooky place, it wasn't a very memorable occasion.

Gaffer was a familiar figure around town for as long as Terry could remember. He didn't recall ever having actually talked to the pathetic man but he had come this far, so he would continue on. He supposed the fire could have been at Gaffer's place. He would make sure the old guy was all right, check a few more areas, then go back to make his report.

The sun was soaking up most of last night's heavy downpour, but the trails in the gorge were still slippery and muddy in places. The rushing water was louder than usual as the streams swelled with summer rains. Terry heard an Oriole. It pleased him that he could recognize its call.

The house was a mess, but he knew it would be. It was a mess when he had seen it fifteen years ago, and nothing had improved it. Garbage was strewn around the path and animals seemed to have been at what looked like a loaf of bread and soggy baked goods. He would ask Mr. White to at least clean up around the place. The front door stood ajar. A strong odor assaulted Terry as he gingerly found a footing on the broken stone steps, calling out as he got closer.

"Mr. White! Hello! Gaffer White, Deputy Kramer here. Are you all right, sir?"

Terry Kramer was not prepared for what he saw on such a beautiful summer morning. The stench was a familiar one. Burnt flesh. The smell clung to him, crawled up his nostrils. His stomach knotted. Strawberry preserves and cinnamon crullers came back to his mouth. He tried to swallow, then rushed to the door in time to rid himself of both breakfasts.

He was embarrassed. There was no one to see, but he was ashamed of his fear. *Deep gulps of air. Joyce's face. Cpl. Toleski with his head blown off. Burnt corpses lying in the mud. Joyce's face.* Sweat soaked his shirt and ran down his neck. More gulps of air. Joyce's face, her voice, her smell embraced him, calmed him. He took his time. He breathed the sweet summer air and waited for the assault to pass.

Terry was fine. Racing down the slippery path to his car below, Deputy Kramer got on with his job.

FOUR

Terry was assigned the older of the two Kentbury police cars, but both vehicles were fitted with new radios last fall, and Terry urgently called in to Chief Campbell, catching him as he was about to leave the office. The chief was on his way. Even though there had been a road of sorts leading up to the cottage, Terry was not about to test the police car on the overgrown, pot-holed lane. He raced back up the narrow footpath to await his boss's arrival, and possibly the State Troopers. If he knew the chief though, he would want to have a look around first before calling in the Staties.

The flashback of terror he experienced passed quickly. Terry had been dealing with his war for seven years. He didn't think it would, or even should, go away completely, but usually he could handle it. This was so unprepared, such a surprise, the sights and smells sent him back without warning. He returned to the crime scene prepared to do his job, knowing it would be all right.

There was no way this could have been an accident, even a freak accident. Almost the entire bottom half of Gaffer White's body was burned black. His pants were halfway down, crumpled around his knees. Miraculously, from the waist up, there was singed clothing, some evidence of burning but nothing severe enough to have killed him. Strange. The blood on the corpse's face may be hiding other wounds, but he could see one large gash by the right temple, and at least one other. There seemed to be an unusual amount of blood on the legs and abdomen, visible even with the horrible burning. Terry wouldn't touch the body; he'd leave that to the coroner, Dr. Walsh. As horrible as the sight was, he had seen worse and his professional side took over as he looked for ways to explain just what had happened.

Terry heard the chief's car negotiating the overgrown drive. Somehow Bull coaxed the shiny new Ford through the weeds and bushes. It was just as well the big man hadn't tried to make the climb on foot, but Terry had a flash of insight about the chief's nickname. Maybe it came from a stubborn streak.

"What the hell have we got here?" Bull Campbell had seen his share of strange stuff in thirty-five years of being a cop, even a small town cop, and this would have to rank among the strangest. He had seen plenty of fire victims over the years, and the little bodies of burned up kids would be with him forever, but this was beyond comprehending. Who would want to kill somebody like poor old Gaffer, and why ever in such a cruel and horrid way?

"Here, Deputy, you can get pictures," the chief said, handing Terry the camera, flash attachment and bag of bulbs for the flash they used at burglary scenes and car accidents. "I want to have a look outside. I'll make a call to the State Police after we've had a good look around."

After almost an hour, Bull Campbell and his new deputy pieced together what they felt was a plausible scenario for what happened the night before. Mrs. Barrow spotting smoke from the fire gave them a good time frame, and the heavy rains that came with the summer storm put the fire out, preserving as much evidence as it probably washed away. To Terry, it looked like the killer was in a hurry, doused the area around the body, maybe not even meaning to throw kerosene on the body itself, thinking the flames would just grow, engulf the whole house and destroy evidence of any crime. A rusty kerosene can was in the corner and Terry looked at it carefully, leaving it in place. He took two pictures of it and wondered if the troopers would find any fingerprints. He wanted to be as thorough as possible. His dealings so far with the NJ State Police had been amicable enough, but he hadn't been involved in anything like this. Cops got awful sensitive and territorial, especially when something came along that was likely to make headlines. Would this make headlines? Maybe not. It was weird, that was for sure, but Gaffer White was just an old bum, so maybe his death, like his life, would go by with little notice.

"Crazy, isn't it?" the chief was saying. "If he'd been set on fire further into the room, the whole place might have gone up in smoke, but the old tarp blew off I guess, and with these holes in the roof and this broken window, the rain must have whipped in here like a flood. Look how wet the body is," he said, carefully feeling the old jacket that was only partially burned and damp to the touch. There were puddles on the floor and mold around a window that must have been broken years ago.

Terry had to agree with the chief. The scattered groceries outside, the drag marks on the floor in what was once an entryway, the head wound and bloody clothing meant someone hit Gaffer on the head, making him drop the groceries, then the murderer managed to drag him into the house. If the murderer was counting on the fire to cover his tracks, he was foiled by a storm that came up with little warning. Even he and Joyce had gotten soaked in seconds last night, as they raced around closing windows and doors and snatching up some records that were left on the floor by the phonograph.

"Why bring him in the house, Chief? Why set anything on fire?" Terry asked.

"Good questions, Son. I can think of a few things, but the big question is why the hell kill the poor bastard in the first place?" the chief said.

"Where'd he get the groceries, Terry? Gaffer made his living from selling old junk he got at the dump or getting paid in food by the folks he did odd jobs for. I don't think he hardly ever went to a store to buy things, so I suspect this food may have been from one of his employers," the chief said, pointing to a can of baked beans that had rolled down next to a tree stump.

The men were careful not to move things and not walk around more than they had to outside, but Terry did have a quick look around the rest of the house. Surprisingly, the room that served as Gaffer's bedroom was dry and reasonably clean. The kitchen had a small fireplace that looked like it was used and since there was no electricity, Terry supposed Gaffer did his cooking there. Then he saw a one-burner hot plate and an old radio. When he turned the knob he heard the familiar morning broadcast on WMCA.

"Yeah, I kinda knew about that," Chief Campbell was explaining. "Oh, it must be ten years now at least that Howard Shore, you remember him . . . . he was feelin' sorry for Gaffer that fall and thought he'd come see just what was left of the electrical wiring here. Nobody ever bothered after the fire 'cause nobody ever figured anybody would live here, but Howard workin' for the electric company did something, that's all I know. He did tell me once that the usage was so little nobody bothered with it, but that hot plate must be new. Now that would use a lot of juice I would think."

"Doesn't somebody read a meter?" Terry asked. "It's still got to cost something."

"Yeah. Howard sees to it. You might want to go talk to him. He's manager over there now," the chief explained.

The big burly Chief of Police was a softie underneath and everybody knew it. You would never want to be on the wrong side of Bull Campbell, but as a friend and officer of the law, he was loved far and wide. He'd had a little heart trouble a few years back and dropped some weight after his wife, Lou, put them both on a diet, but one reason Terry Kramer came back to Kentbury was because the chief had told him personally that he was going to retire early and take it easy. The ticker was a little off and he wanted to enjoy life. It was a great opportunity for Terry, but he was in no hurry to see his boss turn in his badge.

"Mrs. Barrow wasn't sure who this property might belong to, Chief. Do you know?" Terry asked.

"I seem to recall that we had to contact somebody connected to the Wexler family when the fire happened, but I'm not sure now. I might have something in the files on that. Funny, isn't it? I don't know how much land goes with the cottage, but it's a darn nice little place if somebody bothered to fix it up. Can't imagine just leaving it like this. That's another thing you could ask Howard Shore, Terry. He might know because of electric company records and the tax office of course. The clerk's office would know," Bull said.

Marvin Walsh, the part-time county coroner, came with the State Police and by the time the rescue squad arrived, rumors were flying high and wide. The volunteer fire department and rescue squad were the top in the county, in several counties. They consistently won praise and awards for their efficiency and had an impeccable record for service to the community. Because they were being sent to pick up a corpse, only two men came with the ambulance, but from the time they got the call to the actual arrival, rumors were circulating furiously. It was already known where they were going, who had died and some of the details, however inaccurate, were being repeated in the bank, the Pan About Town, the shops and by telephone to friends and neighbors. By lunch time, the story would be all over Kentbury and well into the surrounding towns. *The Kentbury Kaller* came out on Thursdays, the *Hunterdon County Herald* on

Wednesdays, and this was only Tuesday, so it would definitely make the papers.

It was almost three o'clock by the time things were finished up at the crime scene. Because it was a workday, and the house was in a remote area, there were not a lot of people showing up to have a look at the goings on. Terry suspected by the weekend there could be people coming though, and Chief Campbell said he could bet on it.

Gaffer's body was sent to the Franklin Brothers Funeral Home where the county coroner would do an autopsy, but the two detective sergeants who had examined the scene, agreed with most of what Bull Campbell and his deputy had already ascertained. Keeping a low profile, the chief and Terry observed quietly and let the state boys do their job. They had a police photographer along and weren't interested that Terry had taken his own roll of film, but that was fine. As the chief had expected, they would certainly do an investigation, but he could tell, unless something else came up, the murder of Gaffer White was not going to get high priority with the State Police.

Halfway through examination of the crime scene, Sheriff Zimmer showed up. With the murder taking place within the boundaries of Kentbury, the Sheriff, based at the County Seat in Flemington, had no jurisdiction here, but courtesy would prevail. He and Bull went way back. Clyde Zimmer got to see more murders than his friend Bull, but politics and friendship would see that the County Sheriff's Office was kept abreast of the investigation.

Before they left the property, Terry and his boss put up a barricade halfway up the grassy lane. It would deter most people who got that far, and since it wasn't seen from the road, it would not announce the location to casual passers by.

"Terry, I want you to go back to Lake Cottage and tell Mrs. Barrow and Mrs. Stone just what's going on. They've heard the rumors by now, I'm sure, but they need to hear from us personally. I'm going back to the station to get this report started, and then I've got to talk to the mayor and a few other folks," Chief Campbell said.

FIVE

Terry was starving. Not only had he lost his breakfast, nobody had gotten any lunch while they worked at the crime scene. Sitting on the shaded porch of Lake Cottage, Terry was more than grateful for the iced lemonade and turkey sandwich Madeline Stone insisted he have.

"You've been stuck up there all this time, dear, and it's because of us really. The least we can do is feed you," Madeline had said.

Between bites and small offerings to Jimmy who sat by attentively, Terry informed the ladies about Gaffer White, just saying he was killed but omitting any details. Ironically, it was Ethel and Madeline who were telling him all kinds of things he hadn't known about the deceased.

"My yes, Terry," Madeline Stone was saying. "His mother was working for the Wexler Family. Now, you probably don't remember that name because the Wexlers had two girls, and a son, Jerome, who was killed in a hunting accident. We didn't live here then, but of course we heard about it.

"Jerome Wexler was a handsome devil, Terry, but a bit of a rogue. He went to Princeton but did not actually graduate, did he, Ethel?" Madeline asked.

"I remember Mother warned us to avoid him, which was too bad. I think Magnus Wexler, the father, was a bit of a tyrant. We knew them but rather casually. The Wexlers all went away to school and we did not, so we didn't really know them that well. The sisters were quite a bit snobbish we always thought, and poor Mrs. Wexler seemed to be a sad woman as I remember," Ethel said.

"Margery Wexler married, but Lenore, who was quite a beauty, never did. She was a spinster living in Philadelphia the last I heard. In any case, the name died out here. Around . . . oh, when, Ethel?" her sister asked.

"I think it would have been sometime in the 1920's. I remember Margery getting married the summer we broke ground for Lake Cottage," Ethel said.

"That's right. Margery Wexler married Simms Dalton of the Basking Ridge Daltons," said Madeline.

"The Wexler Dairy in Califon, that's still run by the family, isn't it?" Terry asked.

"Oh, no. There were two Wexler Dairies, the other one was in Three Bridges, but the one in Califon changed hands shortly after Mr. Wexler died and became the Weller Dairy. The dairy in Three Bridges is some kind of government farm now I think," Madeline explained.

"Yes. And I remember that Mr. Wexler died the day the new phone directory came out, March of 1920, and it seemed strange that his name would be in there for a whole year, but no Wexlers lived here anymore," Ethel said.

"But no Wexlers lived here for years, is that right?" Terry asked.

"Yes, they moved to Philadelphia soon after Jerome was killed," Ethel answered.

"That's true. We weren't living here then ourselves, but our mother wrote us and remarked about the strange thing with the phone directory," Madeline said.

"Yes. They kept the house and had a phone there, obviously, but I think Mr. Wexler visited a few times a year, but no one lived there year round," Ethel stated.

Terry couldn't wait to tell Joyce about his bizarre day. The murder was one thing, unusual and horrible, but part of his job. Sipping lemonade and reminiscing with the Crisp sisters was something else again.

Although he did not disclose the gory details of his discovery to Mrs. Barrow and her sister, they heard some of it anyway. Confirming what they heard, he corrected some things, expecting the genteel ladies to be shocked and even frightened by the gruesome murder and was surprised to find they were neither. By the time he left, Terry had a different feeling about the man whose body he found, and a certain insight into the lives of Ethel and Madeline Crisp. He would ask the chief about a few things and it would be interesting to get Joyce's impression too. As soon as Joyce popped into his head, Terry's mind filled with images of what he hoped would be an evening of love and confidences. Thoughts of his wife were pushed aside with all that had happened today but they rushed back now as he drove past the steel mill, up into town and to the office. He was almost in the parking lot when the chief called on the radio to see when he'd be getting back.

"I'm back right now, sir," Terry said, pulling into his space in back of the town hall.

SIX

Terry called Joyce as soon as he got to his desk. As expected, she heard about the murder and understood how busy he would be. He was pleased to learn that Lou Campbell called her earlier, reassuring her about not only what the police would be doing, but to say that this was not a common occurrence for the peaceful town, and giving her advice on fending off people who would expect Joyce to give them inside information. Joyce promised Terry a good dinner and a few other things that made him hope none of the operators were listening in, as they were rumored to do.

It took twenty minutes for Chief Campbell to go over his report with his deputy. As the person who discovered the body, Terry would also be responsible for a detailed report that would go to the State Police and the Prosecutor's Office at the County Seat in Flemington.

While Terry filled his boss in on what he had learned about Gaffer White from the ladies at Lake Cottage, the chief generously poured his deputy a cup of coffee. Terry didn't refuse. Even the chief's evil brew was welcome after the kind of day it had been.

Bull Campbell knew some version of what Terry was now relating to him but every now and then would comment, pursing his lips and saying things like, *I'll be damned, No foolin'* and *That would make sense.* Terry assumed the chief knew everything there was to know about Kentbury and the people in it, but that apparently was not so. The puzzle surrounding this terrible crime was going to take more investigating than Terry could imagine, but that was the part of the work Terry loved. He was up for it.

"That's right," the chief was saying, "we moved here when I was about seven. My dad was working at the Epcot Farm for a while, then went on the line at Tyler-Sykes."

Terry knew the Epcot Farm, up Prescott Avenue then out Red Hill Road almost to the town line. It had been one of the biggest in the area at one time. Mrs. Epcot was his old Sunday school teacher and she and her husband still worked the lovely old farm even though they must be in their seventies by now. It sounded like the chief's father had been one of the hands there before getting a more lucrative job with the steel mill.

"I was only in grammar school and can't say I remember it, but you can believe it must have been a pretty hot topic, a real scandal for those days," the chief said, referring to the gossip that accompanied Gaffer's birth and stayed with him all his life. "But it sounds like you got some real inside dope there, Son," he observed after Terry told him what he had learned so far.

It seemed that Agatha White, Gaffer's mother, worked as a domestic for the Wexler Family, their fortune coming from lumber, dairy farms and leather goods, the latter a by-product of Mr. Wexler's partnership in a Newark slaughterhouse. By the turn of the century, that is 1900, the Wexlers, being among six or seven of Kentbury's wealthiest families, employed a house staff of four, several stable hands, a driver or two and a full-time gardener and his helper. Aggie White, or "Weird Aggie" as she was sometimes called, started working for the Wexlers as the all-around girl when she was just thirteen.

While Terry was visiting with Mrs. Barrow and her sister, the chief wasted no time gathering whatever information was on record about Gaffer White.

"Now, I couldn't find any record of birth for Gaffer, but Saint Michael's had a baptismal certificate for a baby boy dated April 14, 1901. Father Hanover says he remembers Aggie White and he remembers how there were some folks thought the baby shouldn't get baptized on account of being illegitimate, but he was just a young priest then himself and wasn't sure what was right.

"But Old Father Ryan was still in charge back then, and said it wasn't up to people to say who could go to heaven and who couldn't, so the boy was baptized right there at Saint Mike's," the chief explained.

"There seemed to be some question as to whether the baby might live. He was born sickly I always heard, and Father Hanover said Father Ryan wouldn't have wanted the baby to die without being baptized," the chief said, handing Terry the old church record.

The distinctive document was elegant. The heavy ivory paper was decorated with pictures of saints and angels and Latin words in gold lettering. Even the hand-written parts were beautiful, done with black ink, in full, flourishing letters.

"This looks like the original. I thought the family got that?" Terry asked.

"Oh, there was a note in the file, Father Hanover gave me," Bull said.

The handwritten note stated that Mrs. Wexler would pick up the baptismal certificate when it was ready, but he said it just never got picked up and stayed there all these years," Bull said.

*Baby Boy White was baptized at the Church of Saint Michael's, this 14*th *day of April, in the Year of Our Lord, 1901.* Terry couldn't read Latin, but he appreciated what it represented. It indicated that those present were Fathers Hanover and Ryan, Agatha White and Mrs. Antonia Wexler and Miss Lenore Wexler. Terry was surprised to see the document was for an Augustus Peter White and wondered if it was, in fact, for Gaffer.

"Oh, it's his all right. Father Hanover confirmed that and you wouldn't know this, but Gaffer's mother always just called him "Baby," until he was old enough for school and then somebody started calling him Bobby and that lasted until he was in his teens and began getting his odd jobs. That's when he got christened with Gaffer and that stuck," said the chief.

"1901, really? I thought he was somewhere in his sixties at least," Terry said.

"Gaffer had a tough life, lived rough; that takes its toll I guess. I don't know when it started, but for years now, everybody called him 'Old Gaffer,'" Bull explained.

The rest of the day went by quickly as the two police officers answered phones and took care of the people coming in to ask questions, among whom were reporters from *The Kentbury Kaller* and *The Hunterdon County Herald,* printed at the county seat in Flemington. Terry was happy to stay in the background and let the chief do most of the talking. One of the phone calls Terry took was from Leonard Smith, the man he essentially switched jobs with, over in Warren County.

"This is Deputy Smith. Listen, Kramer, I understand you're having quite a time there. From what I hear, it sounds like some damn kids might have been involved and I'd be happy to give you names that popped right into my head the minute I heard," he informed Terry.

Some guys were like that. No matter what they did, they could rub you the wrong way, but Leonard Smith seemed to work at it. He wondered how the chief put up with him for six months. He could well imagine that the former Kentbury deputy was feeling left out of what he would probably consider high excitement.

The last of the visitors were leaving and Terry handed the phone to the chief, then waited to hear Deputy Smith put in his place.

"Ah, Leonard, I figured you'd be calling. Now listen here, Deputy," the chief began, "I think we're doin' just fine. You'll no doubt get to hear most of what's goin' on but I'd appreciate you keepin' opinions to yourself. As far as kids doin' anything, you're out of line on that, Leonard. Think about how you're gonna feel when this is resolved and everything you've said so far is proved to be just a lot of horse shit. And by the way, is your chief there? Put Harvey on the phone, I'd like to talk to him."

Bull Campbell hung up laughing and shaking his head. "I knew Harvey wasn't there and that's why Leonard took it upon himself to call. Son, I'd probably be well into retirement, or else six feet under if you hadn't come along when you did. Poor Leonard. I don't mind so much that he's an idiot and a horse's ass, but that self-important stuff has no place here and it can be dangerous. Just keep an eye out for him, that's all," the chief said to Terry.

It was dark by the time Terry and the chief left the office together. Both men would be on call and both would be back early the next morning to begin a formal line of investigation. The State Police would also be doing enquiries and over the next few days there would be meetings and exchange of information . . . some information. If the State cops got the person or persons who did this terrible thing to Gaffer White, then good. But thirty-five years of police work, along with knowing his little town and its people, gave Bull Campbell lots of knowledge and insight, but this crime just didn't make sense. Still, he gave Terry a list of leads to follow and was happy to hear his new deputy already had a list of his own.

As he drove up Prescott Avenue to his comfortable old home on Silver Lane, the Kentbury police chief mulled over the day's events. An unbidden image of Gaffer White came to mind, a picture of a sad-faced little kid standing on the grass by the old schoolhouses. Bull was in ninth grade and this boy they called Bobby had wet his pants and was standing between the two old buildings that were long gone now but, in those days, elementary school was two rooms in one house, and high school was two rooms up and two rooms down in another house, with a green field in between for play and recess. Two sheds, or outhouses, were at the end of the grassy area but it looked like the boy wasn't able to make it that far and had an accident. The fourteen year-old-Bull, kind by nature, was about to offer the little kid some help when the boy took off like a scared rabbit, probably headed for home. It wasn't much of a memory, but it came to Bull because he remembered how sad and lost the boy looked. Over the years, the look more or less remained, just getting older. Funny how some people weren't allowed to have any happiness.

Bull reflected for a while on happiness and knew he had been lucky in his life. His daughter was grown and married to a good man and lived over near Frenchtown, so they got to see a lot of the grandkids. He and Lou were married thirty-eight good years so far. He didn't get to the war, the First War, but his younger brother had been on the last troop ship out of New York and was killed in France. Yes, Bull knew he was lucky. His heart acting up was probably his own fault, aggravated by too much work and long hours. But now he had Terry, and Lou had him on that damn diet. Generally, he was feeling better, but this murder was bad business. He was making a mental list of questions he wanted answered but knew he'd have to get it written out so he wouldn't forget anything. He was thinking about a hundred things at once as he pulled into the gravel drive. The lights were on in the kitchen where Lou was waiting supper. He could eat a horse. He hoped she wasn't going to give him fish for dinner again tonight, because he was in the mood for a big steak. To hell with what the doctor says!

SEVEN

"Honey, Terry, wake up! Terry, you're dreaming, wake up!" Joyce shook her husband gently until the moaning stopped. His nightmares no longer frightened her the way they did the first months of their marriage when, instead of waking him, her touch would send him flying out of bed, to crouch down, as if taking cover, or other times he might make a stand, holding an imaginary rifle, ready to do battle with the memories that haunted him. When he awoke there would be embarrassment, but explanations did not come easy. He knew the innocent girl he married did not need the horrors of war in her life, not that she could begin to understand, but they talked, and talking helped even though he told her very little. Joyce accepted the stories and learned that questions were not welcome. Now at least, efforts to comfort him did not prick every nerve and send him flying out of bed, but let him escape the tormented dream into a normal sleep. She said she understood, but she wasn't sure that she did, not all of it anyway.

Terry was strong, intelligent, handsome. His dark good looks were in direct contrast to her fairness and it pleased her that they turned heads wherever they went. He swept her off her feet when they met at a USO dance in New York. The bullet wound in his arm and a leg wound with a bit of shrapnel still there, had not resulted in an automatic discharge and he was toying with the idea of a military career when they met. He got his discharge in November and they were married the following April. Joyce told her skeptical mother that she would go anywhere with the man she loved but she had not been prepared for Kentbury. It was nice enough for a little town, but she didn't fit in. She thought if she could work again, do the designing she had gone to school for—work which she was good at, things would get better, but Terry balked at the idea. He wasn't unreasonable though. She expected that if she could have an avenue, do work at home, he would come around. He still talked about going back to college on the GI Bill and she encouraged that, as much for him as for herself, but he did like his police work and he was good at it. Kentbury offered a future, and probably a good one, but she didn't dwell on the prospect of spending her life in this place. Love would make it all work out, she was sure of it.

After finding that body today, Joyce wasn't surprised he had bad dreams—who wouldn't? He was sleeping soundly as she slipped out of bed for a glass of water. Their rented house had tall trees in the yard that kept it cool during the hot days of August, but still they kept a small fan on the dresser, it's steady hum droning along with the crickets and night sounds she was finally getting used to. The first year of their marriage they had a nice place in Flemington, in one of the big old Victorian homes converted to apartments. It was right in town and more than enough country for Joyce. Terry commuted to his deputy job in Warren County and Joyce could walk to the grocers, the county library and shop at some of the nicer stores not in evidence in Kentbury. With the enthusiasm of any bride, she was fascinated with her new life. Her role as wife and homemaker and the delicious excitement of making love nearly every day with a man who wanted her as much as she wanted him, had kept her from missing New York and the life she left behind.

It was only 10:30. Joyce thought about her friends from home, the places they might be going tonight. The city was just waking up. Sequined and lame` gowns hung in the closet next to the fur stole her mother gave her for an engagement present. It could have been in storage at Flemington Fur, but she kept it here, in moth balls, so she could take it out and look at it when she wanted to. If she wasn't careful, she'd wind up in mothballs too, and then she was ashamed of her thoughts. Terry was wonderful, she loved him desperately and things would get better. She even had a new friend.

Gloria Skinner and her husband Mike moved in around the corner. Mike worked at the bank and Gloria was from Montclair, almost the city, and the girls found they had a lot in common, including over-worked husbands who were in the war, and mothers who felt sorry for their daughters because they were stuck in a little hick town. It was funny really. Gloria was driving them to Flemington tomorrow to shop at the glassworks, have lunch out and pop in to some of the nice dress shops along Main Street.

Terry awoke to the smell of bacon and eggs. It wasn't Sunday. What had gotten into his sleep-loving wife?

"I thought it was the least I could do before you started out today. Oh, and I've packed you a few sandwiches in case you get stuck again, like yesterday," Joyce explained.

Joyce was wearing white shorts and a halter top, her blonde hair swept off her face with a blue scarf almost the color of her eyes. Watching appreciatively as she set the table, Terry found it hard to concentrate on breakfast when the cook looked like a pinup girl. Last night they had taken plates into the living room, having an impromptu picnic on the floor, with their old record player offering up Glenn Miller and Artie Shaw. Terry told Joyce about discovering Gaffer White, omitting his reaction and missing the chance to tell her it was her face, her beautiful, gentle face that helped pull him back from hell. He told her about the State Police coming, about Leonard Smith calling and Chief Campbell's handling of things, including the reporters who came by, and she was delighted by his description of the Crisp sisters and Lake Cottage. After they ate, Terry turned out the lights. They made love in front of the empty fireplace where Joyce placed candles, the small glow of their flame transforming the ordinary living room into a romantic grotto. The night air was warm and sweet and as they listened to the summer sounds filtering in through the screened windows, Terry was reminded of his earlier fantasy—making love in the woods. Later, with Joyce only half awake, he carried her into their bedroom where their lovemaking was less urgent, more playful and afterwards he talked again about his strange day, and she listened attentively, occasionally asking a question or making a comment until, exhausted by the day and sated in their desire, they fell asleep in each others arms.

This morning Terry did not remember his nightmare and Joyce did not remind him. Terry was anxious to start his day, but still managed a long kiss and sweet suggestions before giving his wife a playful slap on the bottom, then ducking the wet dishcloth she threw as he went out the back door.

It was a little before eight when he pulled into the town hall parking lot, but the chief's car was already there. Terry wasn't surprised. Everyone was getting an early start. A town like Kentbury was not supposed to have things like murder, horrific murder no less. That only happened in other places, not here. It wasn't true, of course. Murder happened where there was a murderer, and a motive. The chief was right . . . why would anyone want to kill a poor old bum like Gaffer White? It was the haunting question in everyone's mind, along with *Who*, and Terry got several calls last night from people giving their opinions, backed up with rumors and wild speculation, but no evidence. He suspected the Campbells had gotten even more calls from local citizens throwing out ideas and even relishing a story that was well on it's way to being part of local lore and legend. They were scared though, and who could blame them?

The chief was on the phone.

"Yup, that's it in a nutshell, Harvey. I do feel sorry for you, old buddy, not just for being stuck with that damn idiot, but because you lost the best deputy in five counties," the chief was saying as Terry walked in, catching the last words that he knew were about himself. Bull was talking to Terry's old boss, Chief Harvey Riggs. Compliments embarrassed him but he was pleased that Bull Campbell thought he was a good deputy. He thought he was too, but he would always do his best and look for ways to do better.

"He's walkin' in right now, Harvey, I'll tell him what you said, and thanks for the warning. Bye now," and he hung up.

"Your old boss misses you, Son. But you knew that. As per usual, Deputy Smith is makin' more trouble than he's worth. Thinks he knows some things about who might have murdered old Gaffer and made some inquiries he shouldn't have. If you meet up with anybody who mentions Leonard, just set 'em straight. He has nothing to do with this and nobody needs to talk to him. Harvey basically wants to fire him, but it seems Leonard's got somethin' goin' with Widow Thacker, the council woman, and so things aren't just black and white. Can you believe it?" The chief said, chuckling and shaking his head.

Terry believed it. Leonard wasn't bad looking; he was young and . . . yeah, he could believe it, and he told his boss as much before they got down to the more serious business of their murder investigation.

After exchanging information, mostly about the phone calls they each got at home last night, the chief gave Terry a roster of people to interview. The capable deputy had drawn up his own list, most of which agreed with the chief's, plus a few other names he added on as certain ideas came to him. Talking with the Crisp sisters (as he invariably thought of them), gave him some notions he was determined to check out. Some though, the ones that sounded a bit crazy even to himself, he wasn't telling the chief about just yet.

"That's fine, Deputy. You can start right away on your list, and I've got to meet with the State fellas. You understand they have the detectives and the resources for this kind of crime, but mostly they're good cops. They won't step on our toes, but we just have to make sure they know what we do. You can find me if you need me. See ya later," said Bull.

Terry had office duty until nine o'clock when one of the people on a short list of volunteers was coming in to keep the office open and man the phones and the radio. Usually, the chief or the deputy would be in the station, but not with a murder investigation going on. At five to nine, Terry was pleased to see Fred Browning walk in the door. Fred was a retired engineer and would always be their first choice when they needed a steady, no-nonsense fellow to help out. After a short chat, Terry left the station in Fred's capable hands and got started with what he hoped would be a profitable day of inquiry.

It was just as beautiful this Wednesday morning in August as it had been yesterday, but everything looked different. Yesterday, Terry had to pull his mind away from Joyce. Today, back in his car on the way to Gaffer's cottage, all he could see was a half-burnt body and his own terrible reaction when he found it. The body was gone now and he needed to look at the scene again. By this afternoon, they expected to have the coroner's report. The State of New Jersey had paid for Terry to take a two week course in forensics, so he knew a bit about what to look for at a crime scene and what they might expect to learn after the autopsy. While a two-week course taught only the most basic things about the science of forensics, he did come away appreciating how much you could learn from an autopsy if the doctor knew what to look for.

The barrier was in place. Terry hoped any ghoulish sightseers would have been deterred by the official police sign. Still, with school out, he thought some of the town's kids might find their way here, yet nothing looked disturbed.

It was too early in the day for swimmers and picnickers, and the few campsites people used were actually over the town line into Lebanon Township. Sheriff Zimmer had jurisdiction there but Chief Campbell was also planning to check any campers . . . see who they were or if they might possibly know something. In the meantime, Terry's list of inquiries began with Mrs. Newberry, very likely the last person to see Gaffer alive. She called the chief at home last night to say Gaffer had worked at her place all that day and she had given him a ride home. Terry was headed over to see her as soon as he had another look around the old cottage.

EIGHT

Raymond and Mabel Newberry lived on Prescott Avenue just before the two-lane macadam road became County Route 513, going past the state park and on to other small towns and hamlets, eventually meandering over the state line into Pennsylvania. Prescott Avenue, known locally as The Hill, began at a crossroads near Main Street, winding its way up to one of Kentbury's nicest neighborhoods comprised of older homes with generous green lawns, well-kept gardens and backyards with swing sets and sandboxes. A good mix of families with toddlers, or with older kids to do chores and babysit, and enough old-timers, husbands and wives, widows and widowers, gave it a steadiness and stability Terry admired. The whole town was more or less like that, but except for an aunt and uncle he seldom saw, his family was gone from the area. Neighborhoods like the one on The Hill, with families that went back almost to the town's beginning, made him feel good. Houses here rarely came on the market, but he had dreams of moving to a neighborhood like this with Joyce one day. The house they were renting in East Kentbury was not exactly in a neighborhood but sort of an area, with more houses rented than owned. It was nice enough, but closer to the Tyler-Sykes Mill, with the old row houses and gin mills nearby, something not even heard of on The Hill. Terry came onto Prescott Avenue the back way, from Old Gorge Road, reminding him what he loved as a kid . . . the town was full of circles. He used to traipse all over the place, usually with a few of his buddies and his old dog and he knew most of the roads and lanes by heart. Coming back after so long, it was a comfort to see that little had changed.

The Newberry's attractive stone house, appointed with dark oak and lots of glass, was built sometime in the 1930's, and considered by many to be too modern but Terry had always liked it. Raymond Newberry was waiting in the large living room and greeted Terry from a wheelchair that sat near French doors leading out to a walled garden. Mabel Newberry offered iced tea that was waiting in a crystal pitcher, which sat on a silver tray that rested on an antique table. He felt awkward as his heavy rubber-soled shoes sank into a thick oriental carpet twice as big as his whole living room.

With some effort, Terry declined the cigarette Raymond Newberry offered. He had a pack of Camels in the car and had two since yesterday, but he was still making an effort to quit.

After accepting a tall glass of iced tea and after polite questions about their respective families, Terry learned that their daughter, Sharon, was married to a doctor and living in Princeton.

"Oh, and they live just a few streets away from Albert Einstein, Terry. Sharon's actually met him!" Mabel said.

"Can you imagine, my little girl having Albert Einstein for a neighbor?" Raymond added.

Terry agreed that was pretty impressive.

Sharon was two years older than Terry and he wondered what her parents would say if they knew he had a crush on their daughter all through high school, but Raymond Newberry brought him back from the reflective thought, turning the conversation to the reason for Terry's visit.

"It's a hell of a note, Terry, when a nice town like Kentbury has something like this happen. We've heard the rumors about kids, but I doubt it. The War changed things, we know that . . . you know that better than most, but kids, even delinquents, don't do that kind of thing," Raymond said with more conviction than Terry might have had, but in this case he agreed.

"It wasn't kids, Mr. Newberry, we're pretty sure of that, but if you could just tell me about Tuesday and anything that might have struck you as odd or unusual . . . anything, we'd appreciate it," Terry began.

Raymond Newberry was President of the Kentbury First National Bank until his retirement four years ago. A hunting accident had left him with a shattered tibia and while he could walk with a cane, at home he spent a good deal of his time in a wheelchair where he was looked after by his wife and their day-lady, Ona Birch. Mabel Newberry enjoyed working in the garden, but for extra help and odd jobs they usually employed Gaffer White.

"That's right, Terry. He showed up here about eight o'clock and Ona always gives him some kind of breakfast. I was in and out, grocery shopping and running a few errands but Raymond was here all day," Mabel explained.

"Mostly I was reading and catching up on letters I owed friends. We had Gaffer digging up an area out back Mabel wants for some boxwood and after lunch he helped Ona get rid of a pile of junk we had in the garage. Clean-Up-Day is supposed to be on Saturday and Gaffer was coming back to get it all out by the road in time," Raymond said.

The borough had its own sanitation department and several times a year there would be a Clean-Up-Day when anything and everything could be put out in the trash pile. There was a junkman who came around with his sons in a decrepit old truck, bells jangling, announcing that he would take almost anything too, and if you were lucky, he might even pay a few cents per item, but since he gave no warning of his visits, most people took advantage of the town's regular service to clear out basements and attics. The majority of trash made it to the town dump where characters like Gaffer White picked it over, and some treasures only got as far as the house of the garbage man who saw it first, but either way, people got to rid themselves of unwanted things and start all over again.

Terry learned that Gaffer had been working for the Newberrys for almost ten years. There was no real schedule but he would show up with the season changes and they always found something for him to do. He might work for them for a day, several days in a row, or as much as a whole week, then move on to another job. Terry would be talking with others in town who employed Gaffer, but the Newberrys came first.

"Oh, I suppose we over-paid him a little and I always made sure he ate when he was here and then Ona packed some kind of bag for him to take for his supper, but he was such a sad fellow and his work was fine," Mabel was saying.

"No ball-of-fire, Terry, but Mabel's right. He did his job and we'd pay him two dollars, per day, sometimes more, plus feeding him, of course," Raymond added, managing to sound magnanimous.

Terry made notes for future reference but nothing jumped out to point any fingers in one direction or another. Good police work was a lot of plodding, he knew that, but this was no ordinary case, so he was having a hard time trudging along with ordinary information.

Mabel Newberry told the deputy in detail about Gaffer's work there the day before. On the way out a side door to view the area in the backyard where Gaffer had been working, Terry noticed several photos in silver frames sitting on a small table. One was Sharon Newberry's wedding picture and another showed a little girl in a white dress holding a white kitten. Sharon was a cute little girl who grew into a beautiful, elegant-looking woman.

Mabel Newberry was understandably upset. Several times during their interview she touched her eyes with a white linen handkerchief. She always struck Terry as a bit stiff, a bit fussy, but she could have had some affection for the dead man, and anyone would be upset by this kind of death in their safe little town. Terry looked at the garage Gaffer cleaned out, resisting the impulse to ask about two old cane chairs that caught his eye. The chairs looked like they were going to be thrown away but he couldn't bring himself to mention it. It would be unprofessional, certainly, but he also wouldn't embarrass himself by asking about something the Newberrys obviously considered trash. Terry thanked the Newberrys, promised to let them know about any funeral for Gaffer, then went on to the next person on his list.

Ona Birch lived in a small rented house two miles up the road, where Prescott Avenue turned into Route 513. Mabel Newberry told her to stay home today, so Terry was on his way to her house to do a routine interview. He doubted she would know anything, but she was one of the last people to see Gaffer White alive.

Terry knew that Ona only came to Kentbury about a year ago from Somerville. Her husband was killed in the war and there was expected sympathy for the widow who quickly found employment as a house cleaner, cook and sometime caregiver, but began working for the Newberrys full-time when they elevated her to a cook/housekeeper which seemed to suit her and Mabel Newberry as well.

Terry remembered a call to the house last winter for a domestic dispute called in by Ona regarding one of her neighbors. It turned out to be not much more than a loud family argument and embarrassed the neighbors who said Ona was a busybody. Terry held judgment but she didn't seem the most pleasant woman. She thought she was though. She thought she was a proper lady, full of lots of rules and made-up social protocol, but there was just something irksome about her. She might have been attractive, but was a little heavy, wore her hair short like a challenge and took pleasure in looking down her nose at others when she could get away with it. Terry thought the chip on her shoulder showed on her face. Ona worked almost every day for the Newberrys who were quite happy with her. She did work hard apparently, cooked well when they needed it, and Terry suspected Ona saw herself on a par with her employers, distancing herself from hired help like Gaffer White.

Ona never talked about her dead husband, but most people were trying to put the war behind them.

"Well, it's not something a lady likes to think about, Deputy," Ona was saying when Terry began the interview about Gaffer's murder. Ona was one of the last people to see him before he was killed and Terry thought her shock and horror were a little overdone. Like everyone else though, Ona said Gaffer White was a sad figure, but she couldn't help conveying a certain belief that "people like that" were somehow more susceptible to meeting a bad end.

"Why is that, Mrs. Birch?" Terry wanted to know.

"Well . . . you know . . . living like that, going through people's trash, never going to church," Ona said, quite confident no one could argue with such logic.

Ona had gone to the doctor's yesterday afternoon but fed Gaffer a lunch of egg salad sandwiches, then left about one o'clock for her appointment. She had no idea and, refreshingly thought Terry, no opinion about who could have done it. Even in the kitchen, even after some twelve months of working together on and off, Gaffer had little to say beyond compliments for her cooking, she told Terry. Ona did mention one thing that got Terry's attention though. Sharon Newberry, now Mrs. Phillip Hamilton, had been visiting her parents that weekend, but left Monday afternoon. It hardly seemed worth interviewing her about the events on Tuesday, but Terry surprised himself by looking for an excuse to do to just that. Two of the names on Terry's list were people who lived on Church Street, and he headed down that way after his interview with Ona Birch. He gave in to the Camels sitting in the glove compartment and took two long drags before throwing the damn cigarette out the window. It was an expensive way to quit but he would keep trying.

Church Street was so named because of not one, but two churches which stood on the tree-lined avenue that ran between Main Street and Prescott Avenue. Four other streets connected to the wide thoroughfare, all with large homes, many prime examples of early Victorian architecture. Some of the large houses, older still, displayed a definite colonial style with dates going back in the town records to 1790. Kentbury's third church, Saint Michael's, was on Main Street, not far from the police station. Growing up, Terry's family attended the Dutch Reformed, a beautiful stone structure at the bottom of The Hill, on the corner of Church and Prescott. He and Joyce had been once since moving to Kentbury and he knew they weren't likely to go a lot, but probably at least Christmas and Easter. Two doors down from the simpler, but very pretty, Methodist Church, was the Potter House, and Terry stopped there first.

Neither the Potters nor the Romanos had anything they could add to the investigation, although George Potter did his best. Gaffer had been at the Potter's a week ago, then went on to the Romano's but neither family had any schedule for him to return soon. They did give Terry a few more names of people in the neighborhood who used Gaffer from time to time and Terry would eventually check them all. He got back to the station at one o'clock to find the chief reading the preliminary coroner's report, the remains of a Pan About Town lunch on his desk. Grabbing a Coke to have with the sandwiches Joyce packed for him, Terry was enjoying his lunch while the chief filled him in on the autopsy results so far. It wasn't exactly lunchtime reading, but Terry was hungry and he would look at the report but save the pictures for later. "Seems Gaffer was hit twice," the chief was saying. "Report says a blunt wooden instrument, possibly a log or tree branch. Bits of wood in the hair and tissue. Gives blood type. No other type in evidence. I guess they mean the murderer might have left blood somewhere. Uh . . . bumps and bruises from the dragging. Third degree burns on ninety percent of the lower half of the body. Seems it could have been worse but that storm whipped up and put out the fire. At least that's what Doc Walsh thinks, and I tend to agree with him. You don't want to look at these pictures while you're eatin', Son, but I'll leave everything here for you. I'm going up to see if Dolly's back from lunch. There are a few things I want to ask her about. You want to know something about the history of Kentbury ask Vera Bigley over at the school, old families like the Crisp sisters, or ask the librarian," the chief said, going out the door.

"Oh, and, Terry, have another look around for a murder weapon. If it was just a big stick from the woods, the rain probably washed away any evidence, but give it a try, please," Bull asked.

"Did that this morning, Chief. Nothing apparent at the house or in the woods, and I checked along the road too, just in case," Terry replied, to which Bull said he should have known and to keep up the good work.

Joyce's sandwiches were delicious. Baked ham, sharp cheddar, lettuce, and lots of mustard from a deli she liked in New York. Her mother sent care packages every few months, as if they were living in the jungle somewhere. Never mind, the mustard was great.

When Terry got around to reading the autopsy notes for himself and looking at the accompanying photos, he learned little else about the crime. Cause of death was blows to the head. A hand-written note from Dr. Walsh said he would call when he had the final results, hopefully some time this week.

NINE

For the next two days, Terry and Chief Campbell questioned anyone in Kentbury who might have something . . . anything . . . to tell them about the murder. Sheriff Zimmer and people in his office made inquiries in their own jurisdiction, and information was exchanged with the State Police detective doing his own investigation. People were obliging and eager to help, but the few leads they uncovered led nowhere.

Had anyone seen a strange car? Of course. This was summertime. Folks from all around came to Lake Raynard to swim, have picnics at the gorge, fish, go hiking.

Did you personally know Gaffer White? Of course. Well, what do you mean by personally? Everyone knew the poor old guy.

Notice anything strange? Anybody asking directions to Gaffer's place? What do you mean by strange? The damn gypsies were around sellin' their furniture. Gypsies can be strange, everybody knows that.

Every summer, people who were known as gypsies came in a large open truck with heavy wooden chairs, benches, tables and other odds and ends they crafted which made for sturdy, long-lasting outdoor furniture. They already talked with Alphonse, the head of the clan everyone considered gypsies, and learned they had been in the Lambertville-New Hope area most of August. The group usually showed up in Kentbury in May or June, working their way through the towns of several counties before going to their permanent home in the Watchung Mountains after Labor Day. They doubted the hard-working family had any knowledge of the town murder. Still, it was good police work to get that out of the way and cool off the small minds that worked overtime on pointing a finger at anyone a little bit different.

The *Hunterdon County Herald* was out yesterday and *The Kentbury Kaller* came out Thursdays, today. Bull Campbell was pleased to see his interview appeared more or less the way he wanted it to in the *Herald*. The front page story had a picture of Gaffer's cottage and another with a shot of the gorge and was all together a good piece, factual and honest, with the bit of information Bull could share.

The Kentbury Kaller, or just *"The Kaller"* to everyone in town, was something else again. The chief and his deputy were enjoying Dolly Argyle's cookies and trying to decide who would be talking to who, and what kind of schedule they needed for the weekend, when Dolly herself came from the library on the second floor, to give the chief and Terry the latest edition of the weekly paper.

"For chrissakes! Excuse me, Dolly," the chief said as he and Terry looked over the article. "I know everybody says that woman writes well, but I always said she was a little dizzy, now I know it!"

"That woman," the chief was referring to, was Etta Marx, the special lady friend of Nelson Hunt, the owner and publisher of *The Kentbury Kaller*. Divorced years ago, Nelson Hunt was still considered a good catch and even though Etta Marx had caught him, in a way, rumor was that it was Nelson who wouldn't tie the knot and make it legal. They maintained separate homes and it no longer caused raised eyebrows if Etta's car was at Nelson's house all night. Etta and Nelson had been an item for about three years, but she started working at *The Kaller* only a year ago. She did a cooking column, covered charity events and flower shows, and occasionally did a special piece on something historical about the town. The chief was surprised when she showed up instead of Nelson to do the interview about the murder, and when he commented about it, Etta reminded the Chief of Police that Nelson was attending his daughter's wedding in North Carolina and would be back next week. He thought her manner was even more superior than usual, but he was not prepared for the license she had taken with the article and with his comments, not to mention her own tidbits that made everybody sound like they were in some damn soap opera!

"Listen to this!" Bull said, reading aloud to Terry and Dolly.

Chief of Police Ernest Campbell confirmed that it was his new deputy, Terrence Kramer, an ex-Marine recently returned to Kentbury, who found the burned and mutilated body of 50-year old Gaffer White. Kramer stepped into the deputy job when former deputy, Leonard Smith, moved on to a law enforcement position in Warren County. While not prepared to confirm or deny that Deputy Kramer may have unintentionally moved or harmed certain evidence at the scene because of inexperience in this kind of terrible crime, he did confirm that some two hours passed between the discovery of the body and the arrival of the seasoned State Police detectives and the County Coroner, Dr. Marvin Walsh.

Both men were scowling as the chief continued reading.

The State Police were not prepared to name any suspects in the murder, but certain sources have suggested the crime could be the result of local youths who have already demonstrated a propensity for violence and have had previous run-ins with local law enforcement.

I'll tell you who that sounds like! If Leonard Smith hasn't got his big nose in this, I'll eat my hat," Bull said.

"What the hell's the matter with that woman, Chief? And it's not *ex-Marine*, it's *former-Marine*," Terry said, unable to hide the disgust in his voice. He didn't like being in the newspapers to begin with, yet he knew a certain amount of that went with the territory. But being in the papers and being painted as incompetent was not only unfair, it could undermine the investigation.

"I can't believe Nelson will let her get away with this. Hell, I've known Nelson Hunt since he came here fifteen years ago. He can be a little uppity sometimes, but he's a decent reporter, always got things right. And why the hell would he want to piss us off like that? Sorry Dolly," the chief said, once again apologizing to the librarian for language he wouldn't normally use around a lady.

"Now listen to this," the chief said, reading again from the front page article with the Hollywood headline.

Murder Most Foul On Old Gorge Road.

In interviews with local residents, the sad life of Bobby "Gaffer" White came to light with the sensational history of the wealthy Wexler Family linked to White and his mother, Agatha. Agatha White, sometimes known as "Weird Aggie," worked for the Wexlers at the turn of the century as a char girl, one of a dozen servants manning the twenty acre estate in East Kentbury. Born to the unwed Agatha White in 1901, much speculation prevailed as to who the deceased's father might have been, especially in light of Agatha White and her illegitimate son remaining at the Wexler Estate until the death of Magnus L.

44

Wexler in 1920. The estate was maintained by the Wexler family although there were no permanent residents after the family moved to Washington, D.C. in 1912. Jerome Wexler, the only son, was killed in a hunting accident in 1910 at the age of 28. From 1930 to 1937, the estate was used in the summer months as a camp for underprivileged children, and in 1939, after two years of standing empty, the once-grand mansion was partially destroyed by fire. The property remains in the Wexler family, but the current owners were not available for comment on the recent events.

Dolly was shaking her head. At 5'11" with a statuesque figure, the large woman carried herself with a manner Bull always thought of as regal. Soft-spoken, with a pretty face and creamy complexion, Dolly took after her Dutch-descended father, Aubrey VanHaven. Dolly's mother, Mary, petite and pretty, was the town librarian before her daughter, and no one more than Bull Campbell appreciated their friendship.

"That's really terrible, isn't it?" Dolly said. "Some of that is absolutely wrong, you know. But the innuendo . . . the suggestions there, and that patronizing tone."

"Damn. Whether Nelson Hunt is here in town or on the moon, shouldn't mean the paper turns into a gossip rag because that idiot woman is in charge!" the chief yelled.

"Tell me what's wrong with it, Dolly? I mean aside from the stupidness and nasty tone, and insulting everyone including myself and Terry here," the chief asked, calming down.

"First of all, the Wexlers I know of were living in Philadelphia, not Washington, D.C. I'm not sure what the exact lineage is, but since the son died and the girls never had children or maybe one had a son, but he might have died too, so I'm just not sure who those Wexlers would be. And I could be wrong, but I don't believe there were ever a dozen servants there. Oh, and "char girl," I'd like to know if Etta Marx even knows what that is. And I'd say the Wexler's had a big house, but it certainly isn't what you'd call a mansion," Dolly said.

"It was a mighty big house, I do know that, Dolly. What makes a mansion, anyway? But whether she's got all the facts straight or not . . . and she certainly does not as far as what she's saying about this office, I can't believe anyone would be so insulting. Hell, if I were the Wexler Family, I'd sue the pants off the woman!" Bull said, becoming less agitated the more he talked.

"Is that right on Gaffer's age? He's a lot older than fifty, isn't he?" Dolly asked.

"Terry asked the same thing, Dolly. Gaffer surely looked old but . . . yeah, that's right," Bull said.

"When's Nelson Hunt getting back?" Terry asked.

"On Monday, I believe," said Dolly and the chief agreed that's what he also heard.

"Don't worry, Son, he'll be talked to but I've a mind to send you there right now to talk to Etta and ask her where the hell she got this picture," said the chief, pointing at a very old photo showing Gaffer White at about age ten or twelve, with several other people standing on a lawn with a large house in the background.

"Oh, I know where she got the picture, Bull. It's one from my mother's own files. But that's not the best one. Mother has several others. She told me Etta came around to ask for one of Gaffer and Mother gave her that one. She doesn't care for Etta much but she's going to care for her a lot less after this story. She certainly had no idea Etta was going to write such an awful piece. From what Mother said, this was going to be more of a sympathetic story about poor Gaffer and it certainly is not that," Dolly said.

"Now, how did she come by these old photos, Dolly? I think we should have a look, don't you?" Bull said.

Dolly explained that not long after the library moved to the town hall, late in 1935, several large boxes of old photos, tin types and daguerreotypes were earmarked for the trash. Dolly was in high school at the time, two years ahead of Terry Kramer, and remembered helping her mother rescue the old pictures and her mother's indignation that no one but herself seemed to realize the interest and historical value of such a record. Over the years, Mary VanHaven catalogued the pictures and tried to get them all identified before everyone who could tell her about them would be gone. It became a sort of hobby and not many people knew about Mary's rescued treasure, but apparently Etta Marx did.

"I knew Mary and a few others studied the history of Kentbury, and I know the newspaper might run some old time photo and give credit to your mother, but I didn't realize she had such an extensive collection. I'd like to have a look at it," Bull said, the keen interest showing on his face.

"You choose, Deputy. Etta Marx at the news office, or Mrs. VanHaven," the chief said.

Terry didn't have to think about which woman he wanted to interview. He was afraid that if he saw Etta Marx in his present frame of mind, he'd forget to be a gentleman and only make things worse. Besides, he had fond memories of Mary VanHaven and was more than curious about the photographic collection she had. Talking to her actually fit in with his ideas about seeking out town historians as he looked for pieces to fit into the puzzle of finding Gaffer White's murderer.

Mary was a widow who lived in one of the historic houses near Lake Raynard. Built in the early 1700s, the house first appeared in county records in 1749, and was well-documented as keeping Hessian prisoners during the Revolutionary War. Set in a shady glade with its own pond and stream, it was only a few miles from Lake Cottage. Terry imagined that Dolly's mother would be a contemporary of the Crisp sisters, but he had a vague idea that she wasn't originally from around here, and he didn't know her maiden name. The VanHaven name went way back, and everybody knew VanHavens from here or over in Warren County.

The first memory he had of Mary was when he was in eighth grade and had to do a report on Thomas Edison. The school library had some material but Terry found his way to the town hall and the four-room library on the second floor. Instead of reprimanding him or making him feel foolish, like some teachers liked doing it seemed to him, Mary VanHaven welcomed him enthusiastically, making a big deal about issuing him his own library card and even helping him find extra information and illustrations for his assignment. When his report was handed in to the imposing Mr. Langford, his history teacher, Terry got a surprising but well-deserved A. For Terry, it marked the beginning of a new attitude about school, learning and books, and libraries in general. Mary retired when Terry was in the Marine Corps and he was excited about seeing her again after all this time.

Cats. He remembered Mary VanHaven liked cats. A big, beat up-looking orange cat used to occupy a chair by Mary's desk at the library and no one ever seemed to object. What was that old cat's name? Dickens? Mr. Dickens, that was it. Several large, over-fed tabbies were dozing on the porch as he parked under the trees in the gravel drive.

"Terry! How nice to see you. Don't you look wonderful!" the retired librarian said. Dolly called her mother to say Terry was on his way and, like almost everywhere else he went, he was offered homemade refreshment. Mary had a pitcher of lemonade and sugar cookies waiting which she brought out to the porch, all the while asking him questions about his family, about coming back to Kentubry, and about his wife. Scooping up a small grey cat from a wicker chair, Mary offered Terry a seat, then took one herself, sharing her chair with the large orange cat already in residence.

"That's not Mr. Dickens is it, Mrs.VanHaven? Terry asked.

"For heaven's sake, you remember Mr. Dickens? My, no. Mr. Dickens died years ago, but this is probably a relative. His name is F. Scott, but usually I just call him Scotty," she said.

Terry could well imagine that all the pets had literary names, and even though he was curious, now wasn't the time to talk about cats. He wanted to ask Mary VanHaven questions about Gaffer White and the Wexlers and look at the old photo collection.

Twenty minutes of catching up and reminiscing passed quickly though, and finally Terry followed Mrs.VanHaven into the large, two storey house. He remembered coming here once on a tour in fifth grade when, for a ten year old boy, it brought the Revolutionary War to life. Actually standing in a house that existed back then, imagining the redcoat prisoners, seeing saber marks on the floor and then hearing the inevitable ghost stories, made for a never-forgotten history lesson. The thick stone and stucco walls kept the house cool even on such a hot day. Mary led the way down the wide hall to her own private library, an inviting room with floor-to-ceiling shelves full of books, an old roll top desk and a few well worn, comfortable looking chairs, one of which was presently occupied by a large black cat that looked up when her mistress came in, then promptly went back to the serious job of napping.

"I should have known better, I suppose. Etta Marx is a bit self-centered, I'm sorry to say, but she's used some of my photos before. Not for anything like this, of course," Mary VanHaven said as she scanned a long row of albums taking up several rows of shelves. "I specifically asked her not to use my name as credit for the photograph. At least she honored that. Probably expected to keep on the good side of me. I'll tell you though, this is a wonderful excuse for me to tell her to get lost if she has the nerve to come here again asking for pictures!" she said, surprising Terry with her anger and what would be considered slang for her. She had every right to be angry though. She had been used and nobody likes that, but it sounded like it wouldn't happen again. *Good going, Etta,* Terry thought with satisfaction.

While Terry was enjoying his informative visit with Mary VanHaven, Chief Campbell was confronting a somewhat nonplused Etta Marx. The auburn-haired Etta was sitting at Nelson Hunt's desk when the chief strode into the office of *The Kentbury Kaller*, two blocks away from the police station. While he had not thought out all that he wanted to say to the idiot woman, (as he readily thought of her now) he did know the things he was not going to say. If he said what he wanted to, he'd only bring trouble on himself and maybe have a heart attack besides. Using his most professional tone, the larger-than-life chief nodded to the few people at their desks in the outer office then, without knocking, entered Nelson's office, pointedly closing the glass door behind him.

"Miss Marx, I'd like you to explain some of this to me," Bull said, holding out a copy of the Kaller toward the surprised Etta.

"It seems you are privy to some information the police need to know about. In addition to that, there is not only misinformation in this article you've written, but there seems to be enough innuendo and bad-reporting that I wouldn't be surprised if Nelson Hunt won't have a law suit on his hands!" The chief borrowed *innuendo* from Dolly, but it was a good word and probably surprised Etta Marx that he used it at all.

It took a few seconds for Etta to compose herself. The chief couldn't be sure which part of his speech got to her the most, but he thought it might be the *bad reporting* part. Etta wore a yellow cotton dress and grabbed a matching sweater from the back of her chair, throwing it over her shoulders. It certainly wasn't cold, so the chief thought she was using it for protection.

"I'm sorry, Bull, I didn't think there was any bad-reporting there. Are you suggesting my sources are wrong? I can't reveal my sources, you know. And of all people, you must know the First Amendment rights," she said with a certain bravado.

"First of all," the chief began, "you can call me Chief Campbell, not Bull. Second, don't give me that First Amendment stuff. The Freedom of the Press is alive and well in Kentbury and I don't think I said anything to the contrary, and you don't have to reveal any sources to me, but the next time you talk to Leonard Smith you better be sure he knows what he's talking about. As far as my deputy goes, Terry Kramer is the best deputy I've ever worked with, probably the best deputy in the whole state and your suggestions about his inexperience are downright incorrect. Not only that, loose talk like that could affect our investigation and I could hold you responsible for wrongful interference. Think about that. Oh, and it's former-Marine, not ex-Marine. A good reporter would know that. Please tell Nelson to come by and see me when he gets back," the chief said. As he turned and went back through the little office toward the front door, he nodded politely to the people at their desks, all trying to look uninterested. He felt good. Etta wasn't even that pretty. *What the hell did Nelson see in her anyway?* he wondered as he walked back to the station.

TEN

An hour went by like ten minutes. Terry was surprised and pleased to find several photos of his family—one of his grandmother on a float for the Fourth of July parade, his father in a high school photo of the baseball team and one of the Methodist Church with the inscription, "Methodist/Episcopal Church."

"I didn't know that," Terry said, referring to the church that was now only known as the Methodist Church.

"Exactly, Terry! It is just this kind of thing that makes these old photos worth saving. So much to tell, and they are worth a thousand words. Look at those unpaved streets, the horses, the houses and old shops, the clothes and styles way back then; and the foundry—that's history at it's best, I'd say!" Mary stated.

Terry was taking notes as he listened to Mary VanHaven's stories about the town as they went through the photos, many with writing on the back, imparting even more information about bygone Kentbury days. Terry found himself fascinated with not only the wonderful old photographs in the extensive collection, but with the wealth of information Mary had in her head. Unfortunately, it was easy to get sidetracked from the police business he was here for.

Terry promised to come again soon and yes, he would love to bring Joyce to meet Mary. As soon as he got to the car, he radioed in to the station.

"Deputy Kramer," Fred Browning began, "I have two messages. The first is from Miss Lester, asking if you could come have a look at her back door. She thinks somebody was trying to get in last night— again." Minnie Lester, a Kentbury character, lived in a world of treasured memories and imagined dangers. Terry or the chief would always make time to answer her calls, but they were not usually in the middle of a murder investigation. He'd find time though, to at least go reassure her.

The second message was from Dr. Walsh, the County Coroner. Terry wasted no time in getting over to Franklin Brothers, the funeral home that was used on the rare occasions when a Kentbury body required an autopsy. Bobby Franklin greeted Terry and pointed him to the room where Dr. Walsh was working.

Terry's emotions were in check today. Poor old Gaffer lay on a steel table, a sheet covering him from the waist down. Even in death, the old fellow looked sad.

"Terry, here, have a look," Dr. Walsh instructed. "This is the blow that did him in," he said, gently turning Gaffer's head so Terry could see the huge gash going from his right temple to a few inches along the right side. "I'd say this was the first blow, to the back of the head. That knocked him down. He probably was thrown to the left and his right side was exposed, looking up to the assailant, and that's this harder blow that got him. He likely was unconscious when he was dragged into the house—why do that? Don't know, and mercifully, there was no smoke in his lungs, so I'm saying he was already dead when the fire was started.

"Now this is strange: these deep gashes and cuts in the groin area. They were done post mortem, so there was no reason other than some motivation I wouldn't begin to guess at," the doctor explained.

"God Almighty," Terry said in hushed tones when he looked at the terrible wounds. "What the hell is that about, Doc?" he asked.

"There are eight stab wounds around the scrotum and a huge slash that almost cut it away all together on the left, and I don't know what the hell it's about Terry, but this murderer isn't just about killing," he said.

"Meaning what, Doc?" Terry asked.

"I guess I mean you might need to talk to an expert in these things, someone from the State Hospital in Trenton. I've got an old friend who practices psychiatry if you want to talk to him, but I don't know if that would help," he said.

Terry wasn't sure about pursuing this strange lead but appreciated knowing there might be help out there if he needed it.

"Oh, now this is interesting, Dr. Walsh went on. "I am guessing poor old Gaffer was done in by a baseball bat. The wood splinters are ash and they seem to have a varnish."

Terry was impressed.

"Are you sure, Dr. Walsh?

"Well, we make new strides almost daily in forensics and there are comprehensive files now in labs all over the country where you can look up all kinds of things from paint chips to fabrics, metal filings . . . wood chips! They catalog it all so there's a point of reference for comparisons. Yup, it's pretty impressive but the best sources right now are at the FBI in Washington, sometimes the Smithsonian and once in a while some of the universities can help us out. They need to have one place for all of this and maybe they will some day, but I got my suspicions confirmed by a colleague at Rutgers, drove it down myself. It is ash, it did have a varnish and that makes a baseball bat a likely candidate for the murder weapon. Not a hundred percent sure, Deputy, but a good guess I'd say," Dr. Walsh concluded, satisfaction evident on his face.

"No defensive wounds?" Terry wanted to know.

"The poor fellow was waylaid, that's obvious, and I'm guessing he was knocked out enough with the first blow that he didn't have a chance to put up any kind of defense, I'm afraid," the doctor said.

"Dr. Walsh, can you tell me anything about the murderer? You know, height maybe weight based on the angle and depth of the blows?" Terry asked.

"Ho, we've got a Sherlock Holmes fan I see. Good questions though. I'll tell you what I can, Terry.

"Ok, then. Gaffer was 5'6" tall, weighed only 134 pounds, but he was wiry with fairly good muscle tone for his age. Teeth were not bad considering he'd probably never been to a dentist. A bit of arthritis, probably some rheumatism, but nothing really remarkable.

"Now, I'm guessing at this. I tend to think the killer was taller than 5'6", but suppose they were standing above him when he was hit? Or, what if they were somehow a little lower, but they were tall enough to whack him in the back of the head so that the blow struck him coming down? It was a blow from above, not below, that much is clear" the coroner explained. "As to weight . . . I'd say it would be someone fairly fit, but it runs a big spectrum—you could have a slight woman with good muscles, or a big man with flabby muscles," the doctor concluded, a half apologetic grin on his face.

Terry could see nothing much was coming of this, but he appreciated the effort.

"Oh, there is another thing. Probably nothing, but I'm turning this over to you, Terry. You know, the State Police detective hasn't even contacted me yet. I've sent them the report of course, but I discovered this just before I called you. This was inside the right pocket of his pants," Dr. Walsh said as he handed Terry a small manila evidence envelope.

Inside was a 4"x 3" triangle of heavy paper, Terry said looked like the left corner of a letter envelope. Dr. Walsh agreed. Another, smaller piece of heavy paper was inside, that could be part of a letter or other document and while intriguing, would hardly be called a case-cracker!

"What's this, Doctor?" Terry asked, examining the tinier of the two bits of paper.

Ah, yes. Well, appears to be a typewritten letter "c", the doctor answered.

After some discussion, both men agreed it could have been part of some kind of letter with the "c" standing for "copy," but that hardly led anywhere. Armed with all the evidence to be had for the moment, Terry left, thanking Dr. Walsh and taking one last look at the victim. "I'll do my best for you, old fellow," Terry said to himself.

Bull Campbell was at his desk when Terry got back to the office. It looked like he could get home a lot earlier tonight, and he asked his boss if he could take a few minutes to run down to The Flower Pot on the next block, before they did the recap of their day, and before the little garden shop closed.

"You go right ahead, Son," the chief said with a little chuckle. It pleased him that his deputy still acted like a newlywed. Well, only two years married, he was still a newlywed.

Terry returned shortly with a large bouquet that he put in the bathroom sink while he and the chief exchanged information.

Terry began with the visit to Miss Lester. He reassured the lady, which is all she usually wanted. It did bother Terry a bit that if she ever really did need police assistance, it might not come as fast as it should, but he hoped they would always be able to respond. Bull thanked him for his patience and appreciated his deputy's kindness. Leonard Smith always referred to Minnie Lester as "that cuckoo clock on Taylor Street."

Bull had little to add to information relating to Gaffer White's murder, but Terry did learn that his boss and Chief Harvey Riggs were on the same page where Deputy Smith was concerned. Chief Riggs agreed that Leonard Smith was probably the source of the bad information reported in *The Kaller,* and apparently even Sheriff Zimmer thought, based on his dealings with Leonard, that the eager deputy needed reigning in. That was all well and good, but Leonard was warned and there were a lot more important things to worry about.

Sheriff Zimmer also imparted information to Bull over lunch about the State Police investigation. After the initial examination of the crime scene, some mandatory reports and liaison with the Prosecutor's Office, the state enquiries would rely on the Kentbury Police Department to handle their own crime. They did have resources available when needed but the murder of Gaffer White, while cruel and horrific, would take a back burner to other crimes being investigated throughout the county. The detective assigned to the case met with Bull Campbell briefly the day the body was discovered, but he was already busy working on other offenses, including a double murder in Stockton. The victims there were prominent citizens and while no one would ever say it, Gaffer's death was quickly eclipsed by the higher priority/higher profile crimes needing solving throughout the county.

"Hmm, this is pretty interesting, isn't it?" the chief said as he examined the two small pieces of paper Dr. Walsh found in Gaffer's pocket. "Surprised the fire didn't get it, but glad for that."

"I asked about that too," Terry was saying. "The fire burned the bottom half of the body pretty badly, but I guess that rain happened in time to leave this intact and it was actually protected in that pocket. Dr. Walsh said there was something sticky in the pocket. I think the killer grabbed the envelope, not realizing or not caring that a little corner was left."

Bull and Terry discussed at length just what the tiny pieces of paper meant.

Heavy bond, something official written on it. Gaffer hardly had a mailing address and probably never got a piece of mail in his life, so was this something for him or did he find it somewhere? If it wasn't anything, why would his killer make a point of taking it? Or is it just a big nothing?

They were intrigued with the little clue but both men agreed they would start afresh tomorrow. Bull said he would lock up and Terry could get home to his pretty wife.

"Don't forget those flowers. They're beauties, she'll like 'em for sure!" Bull said.

ELEVEN

Terry was in early this Friday morning, glad to beat his boss for a change and be able to make the coffee. The phone was ringing as he unlocked the door and seconds later he was sprinting to the parking area just as Chief Campbell was pulling in.

"Chief! You'll want to come with me! Nancy Romano just called with some very interesting information that could explain the paper in Gaffer White's pocket. I'll tell you about it on the way," Terry said as he jumped into the passenger seat of the chief's car.

The Romanos lived in one of the gracious colonial homes on tree-lined Church Street. A few doors down from the Dutch Reformed Church, the large white house had beautiful grounds, the backyard especially attractive in August thanks to Nancy Romano's green thumb. As he had done at the Newberry's, Gaffer was here on the Saturday before he was killed, helping clean out the cellar and garage for the upcoming cleanup day. While her parents were out shopping, Cathy Romano was at home and it was Cathy the police wanted to talk to now.

The terrible murder was a main topic of conversation in Kentbury at the moment, and it was no different at the Romanos. Up for an early breakfast, Cathy told her mother about a man she saw talking to Gaffer White on Saturday and had forgotten about it. While it probably wasn't anything, Nancy Romano did not hesitate to call the police, just in case.

"What did this man look like, Cathy?" the chief began.

A cute, bright girl going into tenth grade, Cathy explained that she had been reading in her room and looked out the window when she heard voices. She did not know the man talking to Mr. White. Both the chief and Terry were impressed with such nice manners, to hear Gaffer referred to as mister.

"Well," Cathy began, "he was taller than Mr. White, dark hair, a plaid jacket, but no tie. He was kind of thin. Oh, he had on sunglasses and a summer hat. You know, one of those with holes on the sides."

"How old do you think he was, Cathy?" Terry asked.

"Well, I thought he was kind of cute, so I guess he was youngish," she explained. Terry found the teenager's criteria for age pretty funny, but it all added to the description.

"Cathy, did you happen to hear anything that was being said?" the chief asked.

"Oh, well . . ." Cathy looked to her mother. Eavesdropping was not nice, but her mother reassured her that in this case, it could be a good thing.

"I just heard a few words, Chief Campbell. Mr. White looked very uncomfortable, but the other man said this was something he would like . . . or . . . something beneficial! I remember that because I don't think Mr. White knew what the man was talking about. Then the other man seemed a little annoyed. He said something about having to come all the way out here again and that Mr. White was hard to find and something about a long drive in this terrible heat. I think the man was from the city," Cathy said.

"What makes you say that, Cathy? Terry asked.

"Well, the man sounded like it. You know, sort of NewYorkie. Kind of like Jimmy Cagney and some of the people who summer here," she explained.

Bless Hollywood, Terry thought but it provided at least an idea of this stranger.

Then Cathy mentioned the envelope.

"Yes, I saw him hand something to Mr. White and it seemed like he didn't want whatever it was, but the man said something like, "Ok, buddy, this is yours. I'm done now, or finished now, something like that," Cathy explained.

"Did Mr. White take whatever it was, did you see?" Terry asked.

"Well, the man turned then and went down the walk. Mr. White put the paper in his pocket I think and just started working again," she said.

"You didn't happen to see this stranger's car by any chance did you?" asked Bull.

Cathy thought she heard a car but couldn't add anything else. Still, it gave them a solid reason to consider the bits of paper as real evidence.

Terry and his boss were both having ideas of what and where to go next as they thanked the Romanos and went back to the station.

Father Boyle, the young priest from Saint Michael's, was walking toward the station as they pulled in.

"Morning, Father," Bull said.

"Chief Campbell, Deputy Kramer, I was just coming to see you," he said.

"Come in, Father, come in," Bull said as all three men filed into the police station.

"What can we do for you?" Bull asked.

"Father Hanover wants to know when Gaffer White's body can be released. He wants to do a simple funeral and Mass for the poor man and Franklin Brothers can supply a pauper's casket. I know that sounds rather sad, but it is actually quite a nice wooden coffin and there is a budget for it. He can be buried next to his mother too, it seems, since there were several plots reserved for the Wexler family and they have reverted to the church now," he explained.

"Well . . . that seems a good thing at least, doesn't it, Father?" Bull said.

Terry agreed and said he would contact Dr. Walsh to see when they could expect to schedule the funeral and let them know. He knew he and Joyce would attend and he knew it was possible the murderer would be there too.

Summers were slow at the Kentbury Public Library and Dolly Argyle was more than happy to aid the police in finding out all she could about two little pieces of paper. She loved research and puzzles in general. Bull Campbell had no qualms whatsoever about enlisting her help and knew that anything she found out or anything they discussed would be safe with Dolly. He did avoid telling her where the little clues were found, only saying they could be a lead in Gaffer White's murder.

While Bull Campbell said he wanted to spend the day in the office, Terry was happy to pursue a few ideas he had about finding the mystery man who gave Gaffer the intriguing envelope.

Why would anyone go to such trouble to find Gaffer White?

It sounded like this man was just a messenger, almost like a process server and that hardly made sense.

Who hired this guy and was it the murderer who snatched the paper out of Gaffer's trousers? Terry supposed Gaffer could have pulled it out himself, leaving a bit stuck in his pocket, but his gut told him this was an important lead. He began at the Pan About Town.

No one at the little town café had seen anyone answering the description they had from Cathy Romano. Terry went to two other eating places in town, including the drugstore, the Five 'n Dime, and Fred's Variety Store. Finally, wondering why he hadn't started there in the first place, he got a little information at the post office.

Yes, a man fitting the description did come in asking if they had an address for a Mr. Augustus Peter White. There was a White family that lived up Prescott Avenue but the new-on-the-job clerk this stranger spoke with never heard of an Augustus Peter White. The clerk referred the man to the Malcolm Whites—maybe they knew.

Mrs. Malcolm White greeted Terry, offering ice water. She was happy to finally meet the new deputy and understood that he was in a bit of a hurry. Yes, she remembered this man who inquired about Augustus White and since they were often asked if they were related to Gaffer, she assumed that was who he was seeking. They were not related, but Mrs. White told him about the odd jobs Gaffer did and by chance, she knew that her friend, Nancy Romano, was employing Gaffer that very day.

5'10" tall, slim, plaid sports jacket, funny hat, sunglasses, definitely a New York accent, said his name was Smith. Mrs. White had offered him ice water which he declined. He thanked her and she thought his car was a Ford, she wasn't sure, but it definitely was black.

Cathy Romano had done well. Mrs. White's information added to the description, but "Mr. Smith" had said nothing about why he was looking for Augustus Peter White.

Terry went back to the Pan About Town, ordered a sandwich to go and ate it in the car as he visited the two gas stations in town and then found his way to the Sunoco station near the highway.

"Yeah, I remember that guy, Deputy. Filled up. 1949 Ford, yeah, it was black. Definitely a NY plate. Sorry, didn't get the number."

Terry got back to the station in time to join the interesting conversation going on between his boss and Dolly Argyle. *If Dolly were a dog, she'd be a bloodhound*, Terry thought.

"Terry! Dolly's actually made some progress on these bits of paper. If she keeps this up, I'm gonna have to swear her in and put her on the payroll," Bull teased.

As Terry listened to the way Dolly began her queries, he thought the chief was right. Dolly had a good, logical mind and they were lucky to have her on the team.

Dolly began by taking the two pieces of paper to the upscale stationary store in Clinton. There she found out that the weight and color were expensive quality, usually used by high end businesses, doctors, lawyers, the kind of stationary you used when you wanted to make an impression. The Clinton store carried similar stationary which they showed to Dolly. Using a magnifying glass, the manager showed her just the hint of a watermark. He didn't think he could identify it, but he said it was definitely expensive and the ivory/yellowish color was not the most popular, if that helped. The manager gave Dolly three possibilities that he knew of.

When Terry related his small success regarding "Mr. Smith from New York," Dolly volunteered to start contacting stationary stores in Manhattan, but everyone realized what a daunting prospect that would be. Still, armed with the names of likely paper companies, Dolly thought she could at least give it a try. Bull hated to stretch their small budget for long distance phone calls, but he could hardly expect Dolly to use the library phone, so he told her to please use one of the police station phones to make her calls.

"Well, I've thought about that, Bull," she began, "and if it is all right with you, I can contact a friend from college who works at the New York Public Library. She loves a good puzzle as much as I do and she's right there, so big savings on phone calls. What do you think?"

Dolly was a treasure. Bull and Terry both thought it would be just fine and told Dolly as much. So, that part of the investigation was in good hands.

TWELVE

"Etta Marx speaking, may I help you?" Etta took the phone call in Nelson's office. He returned this weekend and she'd have to move back to her own desk, but for now she continued to enjoy the privacy of the editor in chief's office.

Ten minutes later, Etta was on her way home. That was a pretty interesting phone call. Maybe she was on the right track and the caller would be able to provide the answers she was looking for about Gaffer White and the Wexler family. She'd bathe and change and head out to the little restaurant at the bus stop in Clinton where the caller wanted to meet. That was fine. Nelson would be proud of her and that Bull Campbell would be standing on his head to apologize!

Etta was just drying off when there was a knock at the front door. Hardly anyone came to the front, but she quickly wrapped her hair in a towel and went to see who it was.

Look at this bitch, apologizing because she just got out of her stupid bath. Spending all that time in a bubble bath while decent people are working for the price of her perfume. I didn't think I'd have to do this again, but she deserves it and I have to make sure Greg will be safe. We do what we have to—God understands and these people are trash. Everyone knows Etta Marx is a whore. The world will have one less now.

"Miss Marx, I hope you don't mind, but I can't meet you later in Clinton, so I'm stopping by now. I can tell you what I know and you can tell me how you made a connection to my name and the Wexlers."

The day went quickly. Other than a horrific murder to solve, the rest of Kentbury was behaving itself. While weekends might bring a traffic accident, domestic squabble or something else needing police attention, Bull and Terry always took turns being on call. They would both be available this weekend, but they also had social obligations. Bull and Lou were having the grandkids for the weekend and Terry and Joyce were going out to dinner on Saturday night. Terry's thoughts were back at the office as he pulled into the drive and stared, wide-eyed at what sat on their little front porch.

Torn between embarrassment and laughing, Terry decided to laugh as Joyce told him the story of how two antique wicker chairs made it from a trash pile on Prescott Avenue to their porch. She was delighted with her find and did not share his embarrassment at all when he told her he knew exactly where she found them, and that he had wanted them too, but would never have asked.

"Well, Sweetheart, I think that just shows what good taste you have. These chairs in the city would be fifty dollars or more—each! I could sell them with one phone call, but I love them. I'll repaint them, make new cushions, you'll be so impressed," she said with an impish smile.

"I'm always impressed with you, Mrs. Kramer," he said, pulling Joyce along to sit on his lap in one of their new chairs and spending a few minutes in playful necking before going into the house.

Saturday morning Terry did a routine patrol around town, rode into East Kentbury, past Lake Raynard, on to the gorge and came around to the top of Prescott Avenue, down Red Hill Road then back into downtown. Nothing seemed amiss and he headed home to be with Joyce until they had to leave to meet the Skinners for dinner in Clinton. Gaffer White's murder was foremost in his mind, but for the moment at least, he and the chief were doing as much as they could. It didn't take Joyce long to get his mind off the murder to concentrate on the night out they were both looking forward to.

With a history as rich and diverse as Kentbury's, Clinton boasted two historic mills on the banks of the river with a stone dam just below the mouth of Spruce Run. It was not uncommon to still see farmers drive a horse and wagon into town, to stop at the feed store at the end of Main Street and with the variety of shops, including two dress stores and a bakery, Clinton was a hub for shoppers. On a leisurely walk across the little bridge from Main Street to West Main, one was easily enchanted by the history, the gurgling waters dotted with ducks and geese in a bucolic setting, much appreciated by townsfolk and visitors alike. The Red Mill, especially, was immortalized again and again in renditions by local artists.

In place since the 1700's, the beautiful Coach House Inn and Tavern, just across the bridge, was Joyce's favorite. A family-owned business for generations, the many-roomed restaurant was quaint and inviting. In the winter guests were warmed by fireplaces in each room. This summer night, ceiling fans whirled and breezes from the river kept enthusiastic patrons comfortable. With the soft lighting and candlelight floating over hand-hewn beams and wide-planked floors, it felt like stepping back in time. They had driven separately and the Skinners were already seated. As usual, Joyce turned heads as they walked to their table. Both couples were young and attractive and a pleasure to look at, but Joyce had a certain air, a presence. Terry never could put his finger on it, but he was always proud to be with her.

The Kramers and Skinners were enjoying each other. Joyce and Gloria had enough in common and were easy to be with. Mike Skinner was a little more reserved but that was ok, he was a banker after all, but he had been in Europe during the war with the Army and the women were pleased to see their husbands finding things to talk about. Joyce may have cautioned them, but Terry appreciated that no one brought up the murder investigation. Instead, they were sharing stories and getting to know each other better.

"Duke Ellington's Band was playing that night. She walked in and I thought they were playing for her—*Satin Doll*. I thought she stopped the music, but it was just me. Everything stopped when I saw her," Terry said, holding Joyce's hand and telling the Skinners about the night they met at a USO dance in New York. It was a bit out of character for Terry and Joyce suspected it was that second whiskey and soda but she was pleased he was relaxing for a change and she loved hearing his version of that special night.

"Excuse me, sir. Mr. Kramer? There's a call for you in the office," the young waiter said to Terry.

Terry made apologies and appreciated Joyce saying she would go home with the Skinners so he could take their car. All he said was that Chief Campbell needed him. Don't worry, just police business, but a little buzz ran through the dining room as Terry rushed out the door. At least he had enjoyed a lovely meal but dessert would have to wait.

THIRTEEN

The Kentbury jungle drums were beating loudly this warm August night as Terry pulled into the drive alongside the chief's car at Etta Marx's house on Taylor Street. Neighbors stood on lawns and porches and there were a few onlookers on the sidewalk. The rescue squad was there, but no lights were flashing and two of the volunteer responders were keeping folks away from the house. There was already an unmistakable odor wafting through the house as Terry went in and found the chief and Dr. Walsh in the bedroom.

Etta Marx lay in a pool of congealed blood by the dressing table in the corner. There was spattered blood on the bed and onto the floor. There was blood on the dressing table and mirror. Terry knew that pathologists and medical examiners studied blood patterns and it could tell a lot, but he was not versed in that science. A green cotton robe fell open to a white slip, the murdered woman's long, well-shaped legs splayed out in an unnatural-looking pose. A lace doily and items scattered on the floor near the body suggested Etta had reached out toward the vanity when she was hit from behind.

"Terry!" Bull said when his deputy walked in. "Poor woman. I've said some mean things about her and I thought she deserved to be put in her place about that damn article, but she certainly didn't deserve this."

"Nobody deserves this, Chief. What the hell's going on? Is this connected to Gaffer White's murder? Could it be?" Terry asked.

"Could be . . . probably . . . I don't know," the chief said. "Looks like the same kind of bludgeoning. No murder weapon in evidence. Terry, go take a statement from Minnie Lester. She found the body and is pretty upset, you can imagine. I'll finish up here with Marvin. You can meet me back at the station for a quick recap, but we'll get an early start tomorrow."

Terry nodded to a State Trooper coming in as he was going out but he did not see the detective who had been there the day they found Gaffer White.

Minnie Lester's Arts & Crafts bungalow sat in front of the small cottage Etta Marx had called home, a gravel driveway going past Minnie's widening to the left in front of Etta's. Minnie was Etta's landlady and Terry could not imagine what this was going to do to the sweet old lady, let alone her rental property.

A life-long resident, everyone knew Minnie, appreciated her kind nature and readily forgave her a few eccentricities which included a mild paranoia about being burglarized. Minnie lost her fiancé in the Spanish American War, never married and shared her home with several canaries. Terry was searching for the right words to use as he entered the house.

Several neighbor ladies were there. A half-empty sherry bottle sat on the coffee table and each lady held a glass of the golden liquid. Minnie looked tipsy.

"Miss Lester, how are you doing, ma'am? If you're up to it, I'd like to ask you a few questions," Terry said, half apologetically, half bemused to see this proper lady somewhat in her cups.

A slight, genteel woman, Minnie Lester brushed wisps of soft, white hair away from her face as she focused on this intruder. Squinting, lips pursed, Terry thought she looked a bit like a pixie. After a few seconds, she finally recognized him.

"Oh, Deputy Kramer, this is so awful. Thank you for coming. Would you like a glass of sherry?" she asked

Terry declined the sherry and after a little persuasion, the two neighbors went into the kitchen while Terry attempted to get a statement. The neighbor ladies did not think there was anything they could contribute, but he assured the women that all the neighbors would be questioned but probably not tonight.

"Was it the burglars, Terry? My doors were locked, but do you think they were coming here and just went down the drive to Etta's?" Minnie asked. She was not quite herself and Terry knew he would have to come back tomorrow to clarify things, but eventually, after some gentle persuasion and patiently listening to Minnie's Lester's concerns for the town, the state of the world and her canaries, Terry got a general idea of what transpired and how Miss Lester made the gruesome discovery.

Dr. Walsh was guessing the murder took place some time Friday afternoon. With the summer heat and only a few fans going in the cottage, the body was already decomposing when Minnie made her way to Etta's door about nine o'clock this Saturday night.

Because the houses shared a driveway, it was common for Miss Lester to hear or see Etta drive in and out. According to Minnie, Etta drove in at two o'clock Friday afternoon. Minnie was quick to say that had Nelson Hunt not been away, Etta would have bathed, changed and driven out again between five and six. Everyone accepted the "arrangement" Etta and Nelson had, none of their business, but every time Etta's car was at Nelson's overnight, the gossips made sure it was known at least. Some people found it scandalous, most didn't care.

"It was the security light you know," Minnie began explaining. "I always turn it on from the back porch switch before dark. Etta appreciated it as much as I did and it wasn't coming on, Deputy. I thought the bulb might need changing again. Etta's car was there, so I called her to see if she could please have a look. Her phone rang and rang." Minnie sipped her sherry. She looked reflective and Terry saw tears coming to her eyes. Eventually, she went on.

"Flora kept trying her, but finally I thought I just had to go see for myself," she said, explaining that Flora, one of the telephone operators, had been ringing Etta's phone from about eight o'clock onward, and it was Flora who had put the shocked Minnie through to Chief Campbell at his home. Considering her concerns about safety and burglars, Terry was surprised she had gone to the cottage at all at that hour.

Minnie was beginning to slur her words. Terry ended the interview, thanked her, told her it would be ok and that he would be back tomorrow if that was all right. He actually thought she would have been even more upset than she was, and suspected there might be more strength and sense in Minnie Lester than most people realized.

Terry spoke briefly with the neighbors who were going to stay the night, providing comfort and, no denying it, a certain excitement, but Terry was glad for the arrangement. The rescue squad had taken the body away, and the State Troopers were getting people to disperse after spending a good deal of time dusting for fingerprints, taking their own photos, along with the ones the chief had already taken, but apparently leaving the overall investigation with the Kentbury Police Department . . . all two of them. A barrier was placed in the driveway yet anyone determined could just walk in from the joint backyards, but Terry hoped that would not happen.

Terry called Joyce as soon as he got to the station. He was glad to hear the Skinners were still there, but he was anxious to get home.

Chief Campbell kept the meeting brief. He was tired, accepted that the weekend was shot, but he still wanted to get back to Lou and the grandkids and get a half decent sleep before continuing the investigation tomorrow. He'd make early Mass if he could. He'd need The Lord's help more than ever right now. There was nothing like this in his memory. Murders happened in the cities. Towns like Kentbury made do with a few robberies, arson once, years ago, and the weekend domestic fights. Two murders, probably connected, was beyond anything they ever experienced.

"I'll go back tomorrow, Chief," Terry was explaining about his interview with the tipsy Miss Lester. "Poor lady, everyone is pretty upset but finding a body like that . . ."

"I know, Terry. Her friends will make sure she's all right, don't worry about that, but we've got a mess on our hands. I'm not sure how much we can rely on the State Police either. They've got their hands full at the moment and I think we'll be pretty much on our own except for use of their labs if we need 'em. The detective who showed up at Gaffer White's crime scene has been reassigned, they're down two detectives—one retired, one with a divorce or some damn thing, anyway, just so you know," the chief explained.

Twenty minutes later, both men were driving home. Terry went over in his mind what he had learned from Minnie Lester. He would file a formal report, but not until after he talked to her again tomorrow.

Joyce was still asleep when Terry left the house a little before eight. He opened up and had coffee going when Lou dropped her husband at the office after church. Divesting himself of tie and jacket, Bull told Terry a few of the theories he heard this morning at Mass.

"People are scared, Terry. Who can blame 'em? Most folks are pretty respectful of what our job is, but there's always a few who think they know more than we do," he said. After running through a short list of people whom Bull considered potential problems and pains in the neck, he did impart a few things that might prove valuable.

Bull told Terry that Father Hanover spoke to him after Mass, about Etta Marx coming to see him shortly after Gafffer White's murder.

Perhaps a better reporter than Bull had given her credit for; she was tracing the dead man's life much as Bull had done when he searched the records at Saint Michael's. Father Hanover saw no reason to deny her access to the records, but he had not let her take the copies Bull now had, so she had diligently made notes, asked the old priest some questions, thanked him and left. He just wanted the police to know, that was all, and Bull said it was much appreciated. But there was more.

The next morning Etta was back, asking if she could see the church records again. Father Hanover didn't mind. Etta was not a parishioner, but he knew her from the reporting she did on church events and weddings. She asked about other Catholic churches in the county and he referred her to Saint Paul's in Califon and Saint Ann's in Hampton. She was surprised there were only two others in the county at the turn of the century and wanted to know how long they had been there and did Father Hanover know any of the priests who would have been in place in 1901? He told her what he could and she left. He had not given it much thought until hearing of Etta's terrible death and decided he had to tell the police. Bull thanked him and said it was important to know as much as they could.

"Hmm, that is interesting," Terry said. "I wonder what she was pursuing. Califon and Hampton, huh? Do you think Etta Marx was killed because she knew something?" Terry asked.

"Or thought she did," Bull answered. "Listen, Terry, I'll man the phones today and I want to get our reports started. People won't expect anyone to be here, so I hope it will be quiet," Bull said.

Even though the State Troopers had the place fingerprinted last night, it could take weeks to make a match and then only if those prints were on file. It wasn't the most promising path of inquiry.

"You go back to Minnie Lester's, talk to the other neighbors— apologize for bothering them on a Sunday, but I'm sure they'll understand. Oh, and have a look around Etta's house. See if you can find those notes, Terry, there could be something there."

Minnie Lester was expecting Terry. Greeting him warmly, her demeanor was a surprise. He expected her to be nervous. She was not. She did not appear feeble, frightened or confused. Actually, in the time he had been on the job and answering her calls about burglars, this was the most confident he had seen her.

"Oh Deputy Kramer . . . such a terrible, terrible thing. Poor Etta. Who could just murder someone like that?" she asked.

Minnie's neighbors had gone to church and were seeing to their own homes. They planned to take turns staying with their friend, but while glad for the company, Minnie stated that she was no longer afraid because her fiancé, as he would ever be, dear, sweet Clarence who died so long ago in Cuba, was with her last night.

"Clarence convinced me there was no point in being afraid, Deputy. I do dream about him, of course, but last night . . . I know it sounds strange, but last night he was really here. He told me not to be afraid. He said no one wanted to hurt me and that he was always watching over me. I can't explain exactly how that felt, but it was very comforting. Then he said whenever I saw a butterfly, I would know he was nearby. I asked him what about in the winter, you know . . . and he said that it didn't matter, whenever I needed him, I would see a butterfly. First thing this morning, there were two . . . right there by the porch. I knew it was Clarence, and I'm not afraid anymore."

Terry had nothing to say. He digested it all and decided that if butterflies made this sweet old lady feel safe, then that was just fine. He knew from past visits that Clarence, only twenty years old, had been one of the thousands to die of malaria in The Spanish American War. Miss Lester was only eighteen, and he could not quite fathom such a young girl remaining devoted to a memory for so long. It made him sad and admiring at the same time. A picture of a nice-looking young man in an Army uniform sat on the living room mantle. He had seen the scrapbook she kept, and her canaries were always named William and Teddy after William McKinley and Teddy Roosevelt.

"Miss Lester . . . that's . . . that's great, really. Uhm, but I do think you need to remain cautious, keep your doors locked, make sure you have a few lights on at night, you know," Terry cautioned, "but it's good not to be afraid. I'm glad for you," he said with sincerity.

They spent another twenty minutes discussing Minnie discovering the body. Tipsy or not, her statement last night did not change today, but she did add a few things. Terry doubted they were relevant, but he dutifully took notes and would make them part of his report.

One thing that did catch his attention was Minnie saying that Etta had been gardening in the late afternoon on Friday. Depending on what

Dr. Walsh told them about the time of death, it could be important. Terry wasn't sure.

By two o'clock, Terry had interviewed the immediate neighbors, several around the corner and had a few more facts, but nothing that seemed significant. Finally, he made his way to Etta's cottage to look over the crime scene again and see if he could find any of her notes.

I could have been a policeman. Who do they think they are? This little hick town deserves what it gets, I'd say. That whore Etta Marx: I'm glad she saw me. I'm glad she knew that I was the one giving her what she deserved. News reporter? Not news, gossip and I have those notes now. I wonder how long Greg will have to wait before they notify him about his estate, but probably not too long now. God, I'm tired.

Terry felt that too many people had been tramping around last night, but that's the way it seemed to work. Police, coroner, photographers, sometimes hysterical relatives and often well-meaning friends might parade around, touch things, move something, never realizing those actions could destroy evidence. But Terry did not think anyone other than Miss Lester and the required professionals had been through the house—anyone else except the murderer, of course.

Etta had done a cooking column but the kitchen hardly looked used. The living room, extra bedroom and her bedroom showed piles of magazines, a knitting basket, books everywhere and while not exactly messy, kind of cluttered and certainly lived in. He wondered who would be hired to do the cleanup. He studied the blood spatters and knew the chief had taken photos last night. They could prove valuable but right now he appreciated being able to see everything first hand.

Terry spent almost an hour checking in drawers, closets, even the knitting basket. He found several large notebooks that looked like outlines for columns Etta might be working on, but nothing remotely connected to Gaffer White's murder. On the little enclosed back porch, Terry found evidence showing Etta's interest in gardening; well-used tools, odd clay pots, a smock and a pair of gardening gloves that looked brand new. The yard and a few small flower beds looked well cared for. Terry took a quick look around but found nothing pointing to how the murderer might have entered the house. There was no sign of a break in but in August, most homes would have at least a few doors and windows open. If there had been any footprints, they were lost in smashed grass and the traffic from last night when a few neighbors had gathered there before Bull and the rescue squad arrived and the curious onlookers were asked to leave. At least they had not entered the house.

Etta's blue Pontiac sat in the drive to the left of the house and Terry couldn't believe it was open. Someone should have locked it. Certainly Bull and he could have seen to that. He chided himself for the lapse. The search of the car revealed nothing but a magazine, a few hairpins and an empty Coke bottle under the seat.

When he got back to the station, Bull was getting ready to leave after getting a good start on the paperwork and answering the few phone calls that came in, including one from Nelson Hunt on his way back from North Carolina. The newspaper editor would probably be in late tonight but said he would meet Bull at the station first thing tomorrow.

"He's understandably upset, Terry. Spoke with Etta a few times while he was away, mostly about newspaper stuff. Dr. Walsh will have some kind of more accurate time of death and he'll let us know tomorrow, I hope. In the meantime, I want you to get Etta's telephone records. Do that first thing tomorrow. Nelson said he spoke with Etta Friday afternoon, very likely shortly before she was killed. Let's see who else she might have talked to," Bull said with a surprising touch of drama.

FOURTEEN

Joyce was in the kitchen making potato salad when Terry got home. Every fan they had was on and thanks to the giant shade trees surrounding their little house, it wasn't too bad, but Terry was anxious for a cool bath and had a few ideas about how to spend the rest of this summer Sunday.

God, he missed a shower, but the bath was just what he needed. Towel around his waist, he found Joyce still in the kitchen, setting the table for a leisurely meal. She had changed into a cotton dress showing bare legs, bare feet and, as he had hoped, nothing underneath.

"Ah, Tarzan, there you are! Me Jane," she said with that wonderful, playfulness he loved.

Terry did a little Tarzan call and chest-pounding as Joyce raced him to the bedroom while Terry made sure the doors were locked. It had been four whole days since they made love and both of them realized that was just too long. They spent the next hour in a delectable haze of affection and excitement.

Joyce slipped quietly out of bed as Terry enjoyed a well-deserved nap. It was just getting dark when he awoke. Throwing on pants and a shirt, he joined his beautiful wife at their small antique table for a candlelight dinner. Joyce made him a whiskey and soda, made herself a Tom Collins and Terry shared a few of the less-dark things about the current investigation. Joyce rarely asked but knew her scrupulously professional husband would tell her what he could if he thought it appropriate. Her favorite stories were about the larger-than-life characters he seemed to encounter in his job, like the Crisp sisters and people in town she wanted to know, and others she would not.

"Butterflies, can you imagine?" Terry asked after relating his visit to Minnie Lester.

"Oh my. My goodness," Joyce said softly, tears in her eyes. It was a touching story and would eventually add to Minnie Lester's reputation for being eccentric, but most townsfolk who heard it would find it charming and endearing.

They were just finishing dinner when Joyce's mother called. Terry did not dislike his mother-in-law, but he never felt totally comfortable with her either. She did not try to hide the opinion that her beautiful, talented daughter could have done better. Joyce's dad, full of admiration for the former Marine, was pleasant and easygoing, but Terry was happy they lived two hours away.

"She really wants us to go to The Cape, sweetheart, but I told her how busy you are right now," Joyce explained when she hung up. His in-laws had a nice house at Cape Cod where they usually spent their summers away from Manhattan. But, while Terry did get two weeks off, he would not even think of taking a vacation with so little time on the job and certainly not while Kentbury was mired in murder. He wanted Joyce to go, but was selfishly pleased when she said she wouldn't think of going without him.

Both Terry and Bull were renewed by their mostly relaxing Sunday and by 9 a.m. Monday morning the police office was buzzing with phone calls, reporters and concerned citizens. Fred Browning was there answering phones, filtering information and generally using his professional calm that allowed Terry and his boss to meet with Nelson Hunt in the private little office at the back.

Nelson Hunt came to Kentbury after an equitable divorce but he wanted to get out of New Brunswick where his ex-wife and her new husband still lived. A seasoned newspaper man, the editor in chief job at *The Kentbury Kaller* was just what he wanted. Fifteen years later, he was a respected, well-liked Kentburian.

At 6'2, the 45 year old Nelson was an imposing figure. Soft-spoken, he conveyed a casual elegance and never lacked for female companionship, but he did seem to avoid a serious commitment, coming closest with Etta Marx. As he sat now with Chief Campbell and Deputy Kramer, he was surprisingly direct about his relationship and feelings about his murdered friend.

"I know Etta rubbed some people the wrong way," he began, "but she was fun. She was fun to be with, let me relax, didn't demand a lot. Oh, I know what people said. Listen, Etta and I are—were—certainly old enough to keep our business to ourselves, but we helped each other out," he said.

Terry appreciated that Nelson Hunt was not the kind of man to use cheap language about the relationship he had with Etta but the word "love" was not in evidence. Nelson was being honest which was what they needed right now. He was sad, upset, even perhaps angry—all acceptable reactions to the horror now assaulting their little town.

"Yes, I spoke with Etta around four o'clock on Friday. I agreed with you, Bull. Inky Grange called me about that article Etta took liberties with," Nelson explained, referring to the Kaller's typesetter, Donald "Inky" Grange. "I'm sorry to say, the last words I had with her were angry words and I planned to come see you first thing. Well, I am here first thing, aren't I, but for such a different reason." There were tears in his eyes. Terry went to get them all fresh coffee. None of the men wanted too much emotion but all were feeling it just the same.

"Did she say anything about what she might have been looking for, or may have found, dealing with Gaffer White's murder, Nelson?" the chief asked.

"I didn't give her much of a chance, I'm afraid. She seemed surprised that I did not consider her article fine journalism but said she was pursuing something about Gaffer White being baptized in another church, not Saint Michael's, and I told her to wait until I got back. I really don't know much more than that," he said, shaking his head and looking very sad.

"Mr. Hunt," Terry began, "we also have reason to believe Miss Marx was following an idea about Gaffer White, maybe a connection to Saint Mike's or another Catholic Church. Father Hanover said she took notes, but I did a search at her house and didn't find anything. Would it be possible to have a look at the newspaper office?"

Both Bull and Terry half expected some First Amendment comment or privacy thing from the Kaller's editor, but were relieved when he said that would be fine. They could go right now if they liked and search Etta's desk. Terry would go and also check in at the telephone company office to get Etta's phone records.

Marvin Walsh called Bull first, then Father Hanover to say that Gaffer White's body had been released and Franklin Brothers was preparing him for burial. Bull stopped in at Saint Michael's to talk to Father Hanover, wondering how he and his deputy were going to handle two murders, all the investigating, reporters, funerals and the frightened citizens who could barely understand what was happening in their little town.

"Tomorrow, Father?" Bull asked when the priest told him there would be a Requiem Mass at two tomorrow for Gaffer.

"It will be a small group, I'm sure, Ernest, but the Newberrys wanted to be informed so they could send flowers and they plan to attend as well. I know there could be some who will come for the wrong reasons, but I doubt there will be many people here. Also, doing this quickly and quietly, I'm hoping we can avoid having any newspaper people in attendance," Father Hanover said.

"Lou and I are coming and I want Terry to be there. I don't want to frighten you, Father, but it's quite possible the murderer will attend," Bull said.

"No, I'm not frightened about that, Ernest. At my age, I've seen and heard things you could not imagine. I already thought of that and perhaps something will make itself known . . . I'm praying for that, of course, and praying for the poor soul who can take lives so easily. What torment they must endure," he said.

"You're very generous, Father. I suppose a murderer is a tormented soul. I guess it's your job to save 'em, but it's my job to stop 'em," Bull said.

"Quite right, Ernest. You know I'm praying for you too, Son," the old priest said, comforting Bull in a way that surprised him. They would surely need more than prayers, but he could not imagine life without the solace they brought.

Terry and Nelson Hunt searched Etta's desk to no avail. While he was there, Terry took time to talk with two others who shared office space in the Kaller's little newsroom. Everyone was visibly upset at what happened to their co-worker and Terry was surprised that apparently Etta was more liked than he had thought. So, she wrote a dumb article and called him an "ex-Marine." Big deal. He felt like a rat. No one at The Kaller had anything valuable to add to the investigation, but they did say that Etta was excited about starting a gardening column.

Terry thought he might get Etta's phone records without a warrant, but he was actually pleased that Irene Rice, the supervisor for the Kentbury telephone office, knew her legal responsibility and would be happy to get Etta's phone records. They would be ready and waiting as soon as she saw the warrant. Good enough. Terry promised to be back that afternoon.

Chief Campbell called Judge Boone for the warrant and he and Terry were having a Pan About Town lunch in the back office while Fred Browning took care of things out front. The office was quieter now and they were finally going to be able to compare notes and pursue the leads they had so far. Bull informed Terry about Gaffer's funeral tomorrow.

"It's hard to say who will attend; there's sure to be some curiosity seekers, but the murderer could be there, Terry, and . . ."

"And maybe he'll have a big drooling grin or a black hat and we can pick him, out," Terry interrupted.

"Funny. I wish it would be that easy, but something might stand out . . . someone acting nervous, over interested, we might spot something, deputy," Bull said.

"I'll plan to sit in back and make note of who attends, if that's ok, Chief," Terry said.

"Good idea, Terry," Bull said, once again appreciating his young deputy.

"Oh, just so you know," the chief said, changing the subject, "Leonard Smith dropped in. Said he was available if we needed him. God help me, Terry, but I almost said yes. But let's see where we are, Son," he finished, taking a bite of his lunch, and appreciating the look on Terry's face when he mentioned Leonard Smith.

Terry had the most to report since the chief was spending his time doing paper work, filtering phone calls and handling more newspaper interviews. All the county newspapers now wanted their own story and Terry and Bull were surprised but grateful that the city papers were not showing any interest. If the murders got too much publicity, the State Police would be more in evidence; headlines and promotions seemed to go hand in hand.

"I guess two murders anywhere is news, but in our little town . . . well, people like a good murder mystery, don't they?" Bull stated, somewhere between disgust and amusement.

"Mystery's the right word, Chief," Terry said. "Let me tell you what we know, and then I'll tell you what I'm thinking."

Terry spent the next hour filling his boss in on all of the interviews he had conducted, filtering very little, but appreciating that Bull Campbell was way ahead of him on who was providing useful information and who just wanted to get some attention.

Finally, they began discussing their ideas about what the hell was going on. Even though they had the coroner's report, there was all the church connection that needed looking into, and they were waiting for results from the State Police labs about blood and fingerprints, as well as the crime scene photographs they expected to have today. Both men were anxious to get their ideas out there and see if their theories carried any weight.

The chief began by showing Terry the official coroner's report.

Etta died from blows to the head and while it did not say definitively the weapon was a baseball bat, the coroner told Bull he found the same kind of ash splinters with the same varnish on both victims. Very much like Gaffer White, Dr. Walsh deduced the first blow was to the back of the head which sent her flying into the dressing table where she grabbed onto the dresser scarf, pulling everything to the floor. The second blow, delivered when she was face down, was the one that killed her, crushing part of her skull. But unlike Gaffer White, the killer hit Etta four more times, delivering blows to her shoulders, back and buttocks.

"There's some kind of real rage there. Seems pretty personal, doesn't it?" the chief asked.

Terry agreed. They speculated about who would hate the poor woman that much, but if it were related to Gaffer's murder, what kind of connection could elicit that kind of violent anger?

"Ok, let's assume, for now, a baseball bat. I searched the woods by Gaffer's, through the house, even went along the water and both sides of the road for about a mile. Nothing. But now it looks like the same weapon, or at least the same kind of weapon, was used to kill Etta Marx, apparently in broad daylight. I did a search at Etta's yesterday, nothing. So, here's my question: Who the hell is running around with a bloody, damaged baseball bat?" The image was compelling and there was no answer, at least not yet, but they gave it a shot.

"Gaffer's attack was in a remote place. Nobody would have heard or seen anything," Bull stated.

"True, Chief. But think about this: because it is so remote, did the murderer get there in a car? Park it where? On the road? Did they walk up that rocky hill, through the woods? Old Gorge Road is narrow, most of it has a ditch along the shoulder, a car sitting there might be noticed, but path to Gaffer's cottage isn't in one of the spots where people park to fish or swim," Terry said.

"Yeah, but there are enough other spots to park along there where people walk through to the creeks and pools and if they knew the way, it wouldn't be much of a hike to get to Gaffer's place. Did you check with any campers who might have been there that week? Bull asked.

Terry said that was one of the first things he did once the investigation began, but the only campers he found were a few miles from Gaffer's and no one had seen anything.

"Right," Bull said, knowing his deputy would have covered as many bases as he could.

"But Miss Marx—that's a whole other situation. Broad daylight, people around," Terry was saying, "and I don't think Miss Lester had her nose out the window all the time, but she would have heard or seen a car, probably would have heard or seen a man going to Etta's cottage, wouldn't she?" Terry asked.

"Most likely. Unless they came in through that little patch of woods and just went to the front of Etta's cottage, Minnie wouldn't have seen anybody then," the chief said.

Terry was picturing the backyards that ran together from Church Street in the front, Mitchum Road parallel to Church, and Blair Lane which ran parallel to Taylor. There was a small patch of woods which sat between Mitchum and Taylor and Bull was suggesting that someone could have gone that way to avoid being seen. It would have still been daylight though, but Terry would go back for another look, talk to Miss Lester again and this time he'd check out the woods. In the meantime, he and the chief were still going over their notes.

"All right, here's the case as I see it so far," the chief said, showing his deputy the rough chart he had started.

After almost an hour, they were connecting dots but not getting a real picture. Some of their ideas could make sense but there were lots of pieces missing. Terry would be doing most of the leg work to find those pieces and both men agreed there was research Dolly could handle if she was willing.

"Ok, so far we've got some guy from New York, we think, tracks down Gaffer White and gives him some kind of letter or document that the poor guy doesn't want and doesn't understand, but it could be why someone waited for him, killed him, stole the paper and set him on fire," Terry stated.

"Why set him on fire? And what about the pants thing?" Terry asked. The State Police thought it could be some weird sex thing, with the way the groin area was mutilated. It was a piece of evidence they were keeping to themselves but the rumors hinted at it, making it even creepier.

"Why not set the whole place on fire?" Terry asked.

"Maybe they thought the whole place would go up—didn't count on that rain," the chief speculated, but it wasn't making a lot of sense.

"OK, but how would this person even know about the paper? Do you think Gaffer showed it to someone? Or . . ." Terry's question trailed off. That made him think of something to ask Dr. Walsh. He made another note on the "Leads to Follow" page of his notebook.

"Let's retrace his last days again. Someone may know something they don't realize could be important," Bull said, then continued.

"So Etta Marx finds something, or thinks she finds something, and it's connected to Gaffer White being baptized?"

"Yes, ok. Let's suppose she did find some kind of connection for all of that. The big question to me is, how would the murderer know it and how the heck could, whatever it is, be important enough to kill people for?" Terry wanted to know.

"Money. Sex. Power. Revenge. Love Gone Wrong. Those are age old motives, Son, barring the possibility that it's just some crazy maniac running around," Bull said.

Kentbury had its share of characters, but nobody in the crazy maniac category popped out.

"What about Millard Kent?" Terry asked.

Millard Kent and his sister, Thelma, lived a rather strange and sad, legend-filled existence in a rundown mansion secluded by woods, but right in town. The sad descendants of Kentbury's founding family were weird, but Bull Campbell dismissed the idea that they were at all involved in these murders. Nevertheless, Bull could understand why someone might think of Millard when the word "crazy" was used. Bull said he would make a call there though, just to see how they were doing.

FIFTEEN

While Bull Campbell was interviewing Millard and Thelma Kent at the once-beautiful Kent Mansion, Terry was back talking with Minnie Lester. Going over his notes, he wanted to know anything at all that she could remember about that Friday, as well as Saturday when she discovered the body.

"Miss Lester, Dr. Walsh thinks Etta was killed sometime late Friday afternoon or early evening. There were windows open. I think you told me the screen door was closed but the inside door was open. Did you hear anything—voices, the radio even?" Terry asked.

"Oh, now that you say that, Terry, I remember thinking Etta must have been in a jolly mood because I heard Glenn Miller, one of those jitterbug songs. Etta played her records a lot and I could hear it sometimes, you know, with the windows open."

"Would you possibly remember what time that would have been, ma'am?"

"Oh yes. I was going to get a peach pie out of the oven, so it was just five o'clock. That's when I noticed the music. It really didn't bother me, but I was surprised it was so loud, but then it just stopped. Etta was gardening that day too. She looked so cute in her smock and little hat. She was a good tenant, Terry. I know people talked about her and Nelson Hunt, but that really wasn't anybody's business," she said, surprising Terry with her rather modern outlook. He was also surprised to learn that Minnie was not worried about renting the cottage after it was cleaned up. She said she already had two inquiries about it but she was not in a hurry to get a new tenant.

Terry took a minute to look out Minnie's kitchen windows. There was a good view of the back of Etta's cottage, the little drive to the left where her car still sat. Terry could appreciate what the chief said about the front of the little house being so private. Facing the patch of woods that ran through to Blair Lane and up to Mitchum Road, you couldn't see anything unless you actually went to the driveway. After Mitchum Road, the terrain was a grassy hill that was part of the Commons that school kids cut through on their way up and down Prescott Avenue.

As soon as Minnie Lester mentioned hearing loud music on last Friday, Terry wanted to check something out. He thanked Minnie for her time and left with a promise to come whenever he liked. "And do remember me to Ernest," Minnie said, referring to Bull by his proper first name.

A nice Philco radio-record player sat in the corner of Etta's living room. It was a little older than the one he and Joyce bought last Christmas, but it was nice, in good condition. Terry lifted the lid. The record sitting on the turntable was Glen Miller. She had an extensive collection and took good care of the player; she wouldn't have left that record on the turntable. Did the loud music allow the murderer to sneak into the cottage? Was he invited in?

Terry locked up and made his way through the front yard to the patch of woods abutting Taylor Street, Blair Lane and Mitchum Road. A hundred feet of the little woods ran to the side of the large Victorian home where Dr. Sullivan lived and practiced medicine. While the doctor's house faced Blair Lane, the office entrance was on the side, facing Mitchum Road. Terry noted that Mitchum Road and Blair Lane both had cars parked there that probably belonged to the doc's afternoon appointments.

Just before emerging from the woods onto Mitchum Road, Terry spied something in the dense bushes and weeds. An empty pack of Lucky Strikes, a book of matches and candy bar wrappers suggested that some out-of-school kids were doing just what he remembered doing at about thirteen . . . trying to jump-start adulthood by smoking. If he could only tell 'em—he was struggling with quitting and wished he had never started. Terry gingerly put the cigarette pack, Clark Bar and Milky Way wrappers in his handkerchief to take back to the office. He doubted it had anything at all to do with Etta's murder, but if children frequented these woods, they might have seen something, and kids using these woods probably lived nearby.

A cool bath, fresh clothes and Terry was looking forward to dinner and a quiet night at home when he heard a car pull into the drive.

"Sorry to bother you, Joyce," the chief was saying as Terry came from the bedroom, "I just need to run something by that smart husband of yours."

Joyce offered drinks which were declined, then went into the kitchen so the men could talk in private.

"Well, of course it made sense what you said about setting the whole place on fire when Gaffer was killed, but Doc Walsh had lunch yesterday with a friend of his who's an insurance investigator and a few things were said that made the doc go back and have another look at Gaffer's clothes and the body" the chief began. "Marvin took pictures of this particular area, but I went to Franklin Brothers to have a look for myself before the funeral tomorrow."

Bull had Terry's undivided attention.

"There wasn't any question that Gaffer was doused with kerosene. It was handy and it's unlikely the killer brought it with him. Gaffer used kerosene heaters and an empty can was found in the corner. So it wasn't premeditated, right?" Terry asked.

"Right, I agree. But it must have been pretty soon after when the skies opened up and that heavy rain put it all out. So whatever was going to be hidden, well . . ." Bull trailed off in his narrative.

"But this is the interesting part," he started to say, but Terry interrupted him.

"It was concentrated. Is that it? It was all on the lower half of the body?" Terry asked.

"Now, how the hell did you know that?"

"I didn't, but when we started talking about burning the whole house down to hide something, I kept trying to picture this guy throwing accelerant around. Number one, he specifically wanted to burn the body, not just burn up the body in the house, and number two—that little bit of paper escaped because it was in a jacket pocket, above the waist. The jacket was hardly singed," Terry explained.

"Right. Now it gets really interesting," Bull said. "You'll see for yourself. There were knife marks on Gaffer's left inner thigh. Marvin was pretty upset with himself for missing it, but with the burned flesh there and all those cuts, he didn't see it" Bull said, not surprised by the look on his deputy's face.

"See what?" Terry asked.

"Gaffer White had a birthmark that sat at the top of his right thigh, sort of oval shaped and there were a few cuts around that too. It's one of those ugly purple things, Terry. Uh, people call it a port wine mark."

"Well, what the hell could that have to do with anything?" Terry asked.

Terry looked reflective. It was crazy but nothing jumped out to explain such mutilation. He'd be anxious to see the photographs.

Terry walked Bull to his car and they spent another ten minutes going over their plans for tomorrow. When Terry returned to the house, dinner was on the table. He shared a little of what Bull told him with Joyce, then asked if she wanted to attend the funeral tomorrow.

"Do you want me to go?" she asked.

"Yeah, I kinda do, Honey, if you're ok with it," he said.

"I can take notes, if you like," she kidded.

"I plan to sit toward the back and do just that . . . you can help if you like," he said, surprising her again with this plan.

Well, tomorrow would be an interesting day Joyce realized and turned her thoughts to what she was going to wear. What does one wear to the funeral of a murder victim?

Getting in early, both Bull and Terry managed to get caught up on office duties, answer phone calls and even take care of a fender-bender on Red Hill Road. No one was hurt in the minor accident and by noon, Fred Browning was in to take care of things while the two policemen went home for lunch so they could change and attend Gaffer's funeral out of uniform.

Terry and Joyce sat in the back of the church, notebooks in hand, surprised at the number of people dotting the pews. Terry knew most of the people and made note of the few he didn't recognize. Nelson Hunt was there and he suspected a few of the unknown faces might be other newspaper reporters. People Gaffer had worked for were there, a few shopkeepers and Dolly and her mother were just coming in. Bull and Lou sat toward the front behind Mabel and George Newberry, and the beautiful flowers on the altar were probably from them.

Rather than trying to make a list of people she didn't know, Joyce was making notes about how people were acting. Just sitting in a church pew obviously did not demand a lot of activity, but she found it interesting that while some people just sat quietly, others fidgeted, fussed with things, looked around and generally kept busy in spite of the surroundings.

The closed wooden casket sat at the altar. There was music, flowers, the Requiem Mass and more mourners (if that could be the right word) than a lot of people might expect. Father Hanover spoke eloquently about being present for Augustus Peter White's baptism fifty years ago, and about God's plan . . . simple, short and touching. A very small group went to the graveside; only Fathers Hanover and Boyle, the Campbells and Kramers, Dolly and her mother, and Nancy Romano.

Bull commented that the casket was surprisingly nice for a pauper's casket and learned that it was a special deal worked out between Franklin Brothers and Raymond Newberry. That was a surprise . . . Raymond Newberry was thought to be rather tight but perhaps kindness trumped frugality.

There was nowhere to go and nothing planned for after the funeral. Joyce thought that was sad but the chief and his deputy went back to the office while their wives went home. The gravediggers began the task of filling in the grave and the thud of dirt echoed through the peaceful cemetery as the small group walked to their cars. No one noticed the hidden figure, still and watchful, standing at the far end of graveyard.

Well, that's done. Greg's being stubborn again. He doesn't understand what I'm doing for him. We can finally have the wealth and recognition we deserve . . . all those years of being denied. It's funny . . . I don't feel anything really . . . did we really have the same mother? He didn't look anything like me—he had the mark though. I wonder . . . they said we had the same mother, but they lied so much, maybe that was a lie too. That stupid family, those horrible doctors . . . I was too little, how could I stop them? Greggie did though; he knew. He knew I tried, but I was scared. I'm not scared now.

SIXTEEN

The police radio in the house went off just as Bull Campbell was finishing breakfast. He could hear the sirens as he rushed down Prescott Avenue. He and Terry arrived at Saint Michael's at the same time and got to the back of the church just as the volunteer rescue workers were lifting Father Hanover into the ambulance. Father Boyle was rushing out the church office with what Bull knew was the kit used for Last Rites. Before Father Boyle jumped into the ambulance with the crack volunteers and their patient, Bull and Terry tried to get some kind of statement. The young priest yelled something they could not quite understand, but they did not try to stop the ambulance as it raced off to the Cool Springs Clinic, just a few minutes out of town off Route 69, in Glen Gardner.

"I'll follow the ambulance, Terry. Go secure the area . . . don't let anybody in there. Make sure it's locked up. We can look at it together later, but I want to get to the hospital. I'll be back as soon as I can, or I'll call in. I don't know what the hell is goin' on, but attacking an old priest is the limit. The limit!" Bull said as he hurried back to his car. Terry agreed and hoped his boss wasn't going to be a casualty as well from getting so riled up!

As the ambulance and the chief raced off, sirens blaring, Terry thought about how lucky Kentbury was to have such dedicated volunteers. Most of the small towns in the area managed with unpaid responders who devoted hours to training, and then were there whenever they were needed, giving back to their communities in such a direct and practical way. Terry remembered it always being like this and knew some of the larger towns were beginning to have paid fire and emergency departments, but he doubted they would be any better than the men and women in Kentbury.

Terry had to make his way through a small crowd of concerned citizens who were gathering at the church. He spent a few minutes talking to them but, while there was a great deal of speculation, no one seemed to have anything of value to contribute. He had a quick look at the area where Father Hanover was attacked, took the required pictures, and carefully picked up the bloodied marble bookend they would turn over to Dr. Walsh. While the church's front doors were always open, he made sure all the doors that led into the office area were locked, then finally got to the police station where a few more concerned citizens were waiting.

The phone was ringing as Terry entered the office. It was Dolly. She would be there shortly, if that was ok, and did he know how Father Hanover was? Joyce called right afterwards. She was still asleep when he flew out the door at 7:15 when he got the call from Bull, but she wanted to know how he was and how was Father Hanover? *Kentbury didn't really need a newspaper.* He wondered if Nelson Hunt knew that.

By nine o'clock, Terry was able to take care of the anxious townspeople and have two cups of his own good coffee, but still no breakfast, so he was more than appreciative when Dolly showed up with not only her findings about the paper, but with a plate of her scrumptious home made crullers. Still warm, sprinkled with powered sugar, Terry devoured one before they even sat down.

They spent a few minutes talking about the funeral yesterday, about poor Father Hanover and what craziness was going on, and Terry listened attentively Dolly said she made a little progress on the bits of paper she was tracking down.

"Well, we think we've found the company that produced this stationary," Dolly began. With the chief's permission, Dolly had taken the precious pieces of evidence into New York on the train a few days ago, happy for the excuse to visit her old friend from college, and readily understanding the responsibility she had in guarding the promising evidence. Starting with the information she gathered from the store in Clinton, she could hardly believe their luck on the very first day when the owner of the second store they tried, sent them to Mr. Bertram Tandy, an expert on paper and watermarks, who was sure it was made by the Putnam-Defoe Company in East Greenwich, Rhode Island.

"At first, we thought this heavy cotton paper could only be Crane. I think they're the oldest in the country, you know," Dolly was saying. "If that had been the case, I'm not sure we could ever track it down, everyone uses Crane. But Mr. Tandy is sure, because of the weight and color, and part of the watermark he detected, that it is from Putnam-Defoe."

Terry was impressed but he had to wonder where it was going to lead, but Dolly, bless her, had more.

"He just picked up the phone and called the company! Told them it was part of a police investigation—which was all we had told him, Terry—and he was just wonderful! A Mrs. Cunniff will be sending a list of the stores in Manhattan who carry it, and I guess we'll just go from there," Dolly said with deserved satisfaction.

They knew it was an amazing lead and amazing luck that the paper was somewhat rare, but unless they could find the sender, it would be a lead that went nowhere. Terry didn't hesitate to thank Dolly though and tell her how impressed he was.

"You know I'm happy to help, Terry. Just call or come up if you need me. I'll be in all day," she said as she left.

Terry was on his second cruller when the phone rang. Two minutes later, he was out the door and radioing the chief about some kids who found an old baseball bat with blood on it!

The Brewer Clan, as they were widely known, consisted of the hard-working father, Ned Brewer, his harried but always-cheerful wife, Tilly, and their seven tow headed children, aged sixteen down to Baby Penelope Marie, the cherished two year old girl with six big brothers!

The "Brewer Ranch," the chief called it, was out Mitchum Road going toward the gorge, in an area called Gin Fields. Terry knew the legend: in the 1800's, someone there was making a kind of moonshine and calling it gin. He knew where the place was but he had only been here once years ago, when it was owned by Old Man Sutter. When Mr. Sutter died, the place sat empty for a while until the Brewers bought it, sometime during the war. Pulling off Mitchum Road onto the dirt lane going into the property, Terry could see why his boss called it a ranch.

The original long, low, stucco and log house dated from 1820 with newer additions going in several directions. A wooden tub of red geraniums sat beneath a giant wagon wheel hanging on the long front porch, the word "Welcome" painted on it. A beautiful stone barn stood to the left of the house in a small field where an old grey horse and Shetland pony grazed, looking up for a moment when the black police car drove in. Odd bits of junk sat around and an old car was rusting in some bushes but, by and large, the area by the house was neat and attractive, complete with flower beds and a healthy-looking vegetable garden on the side. Terry was impressed.

As soon as he stopped, a wave of blond children came to greet him. Tilly Brewer had called the police and was waiting on the porch with a curly-haired little blonde girl in her arms. Terry had a flash of some kind of painting. It was all rather charming.

"Oh, Deputy Kramer," Tilly began, "thank you so much for coming. Now, my boys are good boys and they just didn't realize . . . they're always bringing things home, but that's boys, you know. You don't suppose this horrible thing was really used to kill someone, do you?" she asked, with obvious concern.

"I'm not sure, ma'am, but I will need to see it and talk to the boys as well," Terry answered.

Tilly put the toddler down to play on the porch and organized her sons.

"Boys! Attention!" Tilly yelled, producing a quick row of boys from tallest to smallest, who were now being presented to a bemused police deputy who thought maybe Tilly had been a Marine.

Beginning with the oldest, Terry was duly introduced to Russell, Edmund, George, Henry, Victor and four-year-old Charlie . . . and Penny, playing on the porch.

"I do want to talk to the boys, Mrs. Brewer, but I'd like to see the bat first please," Terry said.

As Tilly Brewer led the way to the side of the porch to retrieve the bat, Terry was being bombarded with everyone's opinion and explanation.

". . . just cuz it was layin' right there," said nine-year old Henry.

"It looked ok to me," from George, age eleven.

"I knew it was blood right away," from the oldest, sixteen year old Russell.

"I told 'em we had to show Mom!"

". . . wait 'til Dad gets home and . . ."

"Not me, I didn't do it!" a blanket denial from little Charlie. Not to be left out, Penny began screaming for fun and Terry was glad he and Joyce were waiting before starting a family!

Terry played baseball in high school, always loved the game, even played in the Marine Corps, so he immediately appreciated the nice old bat. White ash, wrapped handle that showed lots of wear, but well-balanced, the hand-turned bat was top of the line, probably early 1900's from the Reach Company in Philadelphia. His dad had one. He wondered what became of it, but he knew it wasn't this one.

The Brewer Clan watched in silence as Terry examined the bat, then carefully placed it on a tarp in the trunk of the police car. They would check, of course, but he held little hope of finding any useful fingerprints. It did look, however, like there was ample blood evidence smeared all over the old bat. He thought there might even be flesh and hair embedded in the chips and cracks, but did not mention that to the Brewers. He was grateful Russell intervened just as the bat was about to be washed and thanked the young man for being so astute.

Forty minutes later, after George and Henry showed him just where they found the valuable artifact, Terry was on the way to Dr. Walsh's office in Clinton with three more pages of notes, maybe a few answers but, like everything with this mess so far, lots more questions.

At about the same time Terry was interviewing the Brewers, Bull Campbell was talking to Father Boyle at the Cool Springs Clinic. X-rays showed Father Hanover had sustained one hard blow to the back of the head which Dr. Sullivan said was not life-threatening. The biggest problem was the old priest's age. A vicious blow like that could incapacitate him for a while, and on top of a mild concussion, there was a hairline crack on his right arm, probably from the fall.

"His spirit is tough," Dr. Sullivan was saying, "but the man is seventy-four. I've seen this kind of injury send someone straight into dementia. I hope that won't be the case here, but we'll want to keep him here for a few days to see."

Bull was relieved to hear Father Hanover would recover, but he would be out of it for a while, and the police chief would have to come back. Right now at least, he could get Father Boyle's statement about what happened.

"He's always up and out at dawn in the summertime, Chief Campbell. Puts me to shame, but he likes to see the sunrise and prepare for Mass. I'm usually not too far behind him, but he's usually there first," Father Boyle explained.

"Do you both always conduct the morning Mass?" the chief asked,

"Usually Chief, which you would know if you came more often," Father Boyle couldn't resist adding. Bull smiled.

"So tell me about this morning, Father," Bull asked.

"Well, we always walk down the side path from the Rectory to the side door of the church and come in that way. The door was open as usual, and as soon as I got inside I saw Father Hanover lying on the floor a few feet down the hallway, by the door to the office. My first thought was that he had a heart attack, then I saw the blood and the bookend. I knew it wasn't an accident." Father Boyle took a deep breath and went on.

"I felt for his pulse, but I didn't want to move him. I ran to the phone in the office and told the operator it was an emergency and to send the rescue squad. Then I got a towel from the bathroom and placed it on the wound to stop the bleeding, but it seemed it was just a few minutes and then the ambulance arrived, you arrived . . . ," Father Boyle trailed off, shaking his head in disbelief that someone could do such a thing.

"Oh, yes, and Chief Campbell, I'm really not sure because everything was so rushed and crazy, but I thought I heard someone go out the other side of the church, onto the parking lot area," he said.

"That's the door off from the choir area, Father Boyle?" Bull asked.

"Yes. It goes out to the parking area, by all the trees," he answered.

"Do you know if anyone was in the church at that time?" Bull asked.

"Uh . . . I'm not sure. There are a few folks who attend regularly, but it's a bit different in the summer. I'll give you the names of people who might have been there, but it was a little too early I think," he said.

SEVENTEEN

Bull was waiting for Terry at Dr. Walsh's home office on Leigh Street in Clinton. Dr. Walsh performed the few autopsies required in Kentbury at Franklin Brothers and sometimes at the hospital in Flemington, but he could do routine lab work here at his office where he balanced a family practice with his work for the county. He had office hours today, but ushered Terry through the waiting room to a small laboratory in the back. Terry turned over the bloodied bat as well as the marble bookend that was used to assault Father Hanover. Dr. Walsh would get to that as soon as he could, but it was the bat that now demanded their full attention.

"I'll be damned," Bull said as they all looked at the antique bat resting on an examining table like an important patient.

While Dr. Walsh did a cursory examination, Terry filled them in on what he learned at the Brewer's.

It was not a surprise that all the Brewer boys had chores and responsibilities at home and when they could, found work to add to the family income and have their own pocket money. Russell, the oldest, worked every afternoon at McRae's Grocery on Main Street, and Edmund and George took turns delivering *The Kentbury Kaller* on Thursdays while 9-year old Henry averaged fifty cents a week collecting bottles to return for the deposit. Always on the lookout for a discarded soda bottle or something to restore or sell to the junkman, it was eagle-eyed Henry who spotted two empty Coca-Cola bottles in a ditch along Mitchum road at the top of Taylor Street on Saturday afternoon, only yards from where Etta Marx lay dead in her bedroom.

Terry explained that when he got Tilly Brewer's permission to take Henry and George back to the spot where they found the bat, he considered it a great bit of luck that the candy wrappers and cigarette pack he collected earlier were still in the car. When he showed the boys, after promising not to tell Tilly, sure enough, they admitted to using this secluded spot to just hang out and occasionally smoke.

"I hope you read 'em the riot act," Dr. Walsh said.

Terry assured him that he had, but doubted it would do any good.

"They have a couple of spots, like most kids, I guess. They just happened to be at that one at a pretty important time. It was mid-afternoon. They went there after lunch, walked downtown for candy bars, got the cigarettes from an older kid, so I am estimating they were in that patch of woods between two and three. They didn't see anything unusual," Terry explained.

"The bat was concealed. It wasn't just thrown in that ditch. According to Henry, he spied a bit of the black handle sticking out from grass and leaves and debris that was there. I did a quick search there, Chief, but obviously could have looked harder," Terry said apologetically.

"Sounds like it wasn't meant to be found. I would have missed it, Deputy," Bull said and was complimenting Terry on the good work when Dr. Walsh interrupted with his findings on the baseball bat.

"I think we've got the murder weapon, gentlemen," he began. "I'm not sure if I will be able to type the blood, but it is blood, for sure, and you were right, Terry, there's hair and tissue here as well. I'll be sure and send all of this along to the State Police lab in Trenton, but I've got enough already to tell you a few things. Give me until dinner time. I've got some patients to see, but I can get to this in a few hours."

Before they went back to the office, Chief Campbell and his deputy needed to examine the crime scene at Saint Michael's.

As soon as the police cars pulled in to the parking area in the back of the church, Mrs. Richards was coming from the Rectory to meet them. Arlene Richards, a no-nonsense but pleasant woman, was the housekeeper for the Rectory, coming daily to cook for the priests and keep general order in the large brick house that was built a few years after the church was completed in 1898.

They could tell Mrs. Richards was anxious to help. She already knew that Father Hanover was going to recover, and quickly informed Bull and Terry that she and two of the ladies from Saint Catherine's Guild were going to the clinic as soon as they could.

"What on earth is going on, Bull?" she asked with expected concern, but other than the platitudes they had been giving out since Gaffer

White's murder, there was little they could tell the worried citizens of Kentbury.

"We're on top of it, Arlene, don't worry. Now, you can go ahead and tell your friends that and I know you pray hard, so keep that up, please, we need all the help we can get," Bull said, one practicing Catholic to another.

Arlene did not usually attend church during the week but got to the Rectory in time to have a nice breakfast waiting for the priests after Mass and Holy Communion. She had actually been a little early this morning, walking from her home a few blocks away, but Father Hanover was already up and out and Arlene had not seen him. No, she had not noticed anything unusual but was distressed to realize that the dear old priest was probably lying there when she arrived at the Rectory. She had said good morning to Father Boyle who was just going to the church when she arrived.

"He could have bled to death, couldn't he? Thank the Lord that Father Boyle was up and out early today," she said. "I'm going to see Father Hanover now, unless you need me, Bull, but when it's ok, I want to be the one to clean up in the church," she said.

"We appreciate that, Arlene. We'll let you know, but for now no one should go in there," Bull explained.

Bull understood that Terry had been in a hurry this morning and did not properly examine the inner office which held desks for the two priests. They took their time now, trying to understand just what had transpired.

In a small alcove around the corner of the large office were file cabinets and church records. One drawer was open and files were spilled onto the floor. It was the drawer marked "W," and it was not a big jump to wonder if the assailant was looking for something connected to Gaffer White, since Father Hanover told them of Etta's interest in those old records.

"There's nothing here on anyone named White, Chief. You'll have to ask Father Boyle, or if Father Hanover knows, but at least we have the records at the office Father Hanover gave you," Terry said. "If there were any copies, they're not here now," Terry finished.

"This damn baptism stuff is giving me fits, Deputy!" the chief said, exasperated by the constant suggestion about possible connections but they just had pieces and still couldn't see the whole puzzle.

"Nothing here for Wexlers either. They were Catholic, weren't they? Where are their records?" Terry wanted to know.

"Well, that's another question for the priests," Bull sighed.

Poor old Father Hanover. I should have been in and out before he came in. I'm glad he didn't die. Well, God was looking after him, wasn't He? I'm not sure there was anything useful there after all. Those records would be in Califon or at Saint Ann's in Hampton. Maybe I worry too much. I think everything is going to be just fine. If everyone will just keep doing what they're doing, it will be settled soon. Maybe I should leave for a while and let nature take its course. People believe what they want to. They believe some kind of monster is on the loose, but I'm not a monster. I just want things to be right . . . that's all.

Back at the office over sandwiches, the two policemen were exchanging information. Bull wondered if the two of them could handle all the leads they were getting, but he hoped with Fred Browning manning the office and Dolly on the team, they wouldn't have to ask for outside help. While the State Police were being kept informed, they didn't have the extra manpower for Kentbury's problems, which was fine with Bull and Terry.

"But how did those kids know the baseball bat was the possible murder weapon we were looking for? Who knew it was important enough to call us?" Bull wanted to know.

"C'mon, Chief, this is Kentbury. I know we weren't putting it out there, but someone . . . maybe one of the rescue squad guys, someone at the Sheriff's Office—Leonard—it wasn't really a secret that we were considering a baseball bat as the possible murder weapon. Russell Brewer said his friends were talking about it and good thing too. He's a smart kid. You saw what that bat looked like. It had all that goo and mess, dead ants stuck all over it, not normal. Luckily, young Henry was proud of his find and showed it to his big brother before he went to wash it," Terry explained.

"Ok, but that was Saturday wasn't it? Why didn't they call it in until today?" Bull asked.

"Well, it seems Henry put it in a shed to show Russell when he got home from work on Saturday. He stashes things there so the other kids don't mess with them, but he just forgot it until this morning. As soon as

Russell saw it, he showed his mother. She thought it was disgusting and would have washed it herself but Russell convinced her to call us," Terry said.

"Ask him if he wants a job," Bull said, only half kidding.

Terry filled his boss in on all that Dolly had learned, and that was promising but they were excited to now have the murder weapon that should get them closer to finding the killer. They were adding notes to their case board when the phone rang.

"That was Nelson Hunt, Chief," Terry announced. "Etta's sister wants to claim the body and arrange for the funeral. Mr. Hunt asked if you would call and talk to her," he said, handing the chief the sister's number.

"Ok," Bull sighed. "I hate this part, you know; talking to the family. Nelson told me a little about it already though. Etta wasn't close with her family, but the sister wants to take care of things and the funeral's gonna be in Bernardsville. They've made arrangements with a James DeMaio, the director at the Bridgewater Funeral Home, and they'll come get her as soon as we release the body," he explained.

EIGHTEEN

The next few days were spent in the often tedious, sometimes boring police work that Terry accepted went with the job.

He went over Etta's phone records that showed routine calls but there was one to Mary VanHaven, a call to Saint Ann's in Hampton, Saint Paul's in Califon and a very intriguing call to the Diocese in Newark. Terry turned the list over to Dolly who, as always, was happy to help. Boy, if they only knew what Etta was on to. It had to be something important and probably that something is what got her killed.

Thursday afternoon found Terry having a welcome break as he and Joyce drove to Princeton to interview Sharon Newberry. Chief Campbell was happy to give his permission for the young couple to make it an outing. They had to take their own car and that was just fine with them. Sharon was expecting them before lunch and they planned to eat out, then have a leisurely drive home. It was definitely an unexpected treat.

Sharon Newberry, now Mrs. Hamilton, wife of prominent surgeon, Dr. Philip Hamilton, greeted Terry and Joyce like long-lost friends. In a way, Terry was since he had been a few years behind her in school, but she was just as warm and welcoming to Terry's pretty wife as she invited them into her imposing colonial home in the heart of historic Princeton. It struck Terry how different Sharon was from her rather rigid mother. Sharon was relaxed and poised in a white cotton dress, looking even whiter in contrast to her fashionable tan. Her chestnut hair was swept back and up and she was certainly older, but just as pretty as Terry remembered her. He chided himself for mentally comparing Sharon to Joyce but Joyce won, hands down, at least in his happy assessment.

After the expected pleasantries and after the maid served iced tea, Terry finally turned the conversation to the reason for their visit.

"So, is this like Nick and Nora Charles? Joyce, do you often help Terry with an investigation? That's pretty exciting," Sharon said, referring to the famous Hollywood detective team in the Thin Man movies.

"Never, Sharon," Joyce laughed, calling Sharon by her first name as she was invited to do. "Terry asked if I wanted to drive to Princeton and we'd have lunch out and visit that wonderful flea market I've heard so much about. How could I refuse?"

"Well, I'm delighted you could come. Everyone in Kentbury talks about the glamorous city gal Terry married, now I know it's true," Sharon said with a smile.

Joyce liked the lovely woman and suspected Terry wanted them to meet. She knew when Terry was showing her off, but she always saw it as a compliment.

Other than echoing what they consistently heard when talking about Gaffer White—that he was a sad figure—Sharon could only say that she saw him briefly when she was at her parents. He helped her move a trunk out that the Salvation Army was going to pick up, but she really could not think of anything unusual that he said or that occurred that weekend.

"He seemed to live for lunch and any snacks Ona might come up with. Mother always sent him home with groceries. I think she gave him a ride that day, didn't she?" she asked.

"Yes, she did," Terry said.

"Well, poor old Gaffer, but I have to admit, I thought this was going to turn out to be some petty theft or even some kind of accident, but then Etta Marx is murdered. What on earth is going on in little Kentbury, Terry?" Sharon asked, her voice full of concern.

Even if Terry had known what was going on, he could hardly tell Sharon about it, but he reassured her as best he could.

"Did you know Etta, Sharon?" he asked.

"Oh, a little. She interviewed Mother a few months ago about her garden, but I don't think the story was finished. I remember Mother saying she asked lots of questions that had nothing to do with gardens and she stayed a long time, but she was always quite nice when I met her," she said.

Sharon promised Terry to call if she thought of anything, then recommended several restaurants in town where they could have lunch.

Before they went to find a restaurant, Terry made a detour onto Mercer Street.

"Oh my God, Terry . . . that's him isn't it?" Joyce couldn't believe it when Terry told her where they were and they were both dumbstruck to glimpse the white-haired gentleman on the porch. Joyce waved. The gentleman waved back.

"I can't believe it . . . wait 'til Daddy and Mother hear I waved to Albert Einstein . . . and he waved back! Mother will be on the phone for hours!"

Lunch was great. Joyce got to buy an antique vase at the flea market and the ride home was memorable when Joyce, playful and relaxed, sat next to her husband like a teenager, almost causing him to run off the road when she began to caress his leg and more.

"I could arrest you for that, you know!" he laughed, surprised but also pleased with her boldness. She kissed his ear in response and they both knew what was going to happen when they got home.

The ninety minute drive did provide a quiet time to talk about the investigation. More and more he was appreciating his wife's input, even if it just helped him to develop his own ideas. He still avoided being too explicit about the crime scenes but more than once he had to correct crazy rumors that seemed inevitable when horrific things happened in a small town.

"No, Honey, nothing was cut off anybody. Poor Gaffer and poor Etta Marx were killed with heavy blows, but that was it," Terry said in response to Joyce talking about rumors that the victims were dismembered.

"It's funny, really. From what you have told me, it's horrific enough without having to make it worse," she said.

"People like mysteries I guess. I think all the crazy stuff might be a way of facing some of the fear everybody is feeling right now. I hope you're not afraid, Sweetheart," he said.

"Well, not really. I'm a city girl, don't forget, but I do live with a big, strong, handsome policeman who is also a former Marine," she answered and did not admit that the little town she was trying to get used to was even less appealing with people getting murdered left and right.

Not only was Terry refreshed and renewed by the day out and the more than satisfying evening with his wife, but he had several theories about the murders and was anxious this sunny morning to share them with his boss. It was only a little after eight, but Bull and Dr. Walsh were already in the office when Terry arrived.

"Terry, good, you're just in time to hear what Marvin's found out. Some pretty interesting things. Oh, and what did Sharon Newberry have to say, if anything?" Bull asked.

Terry told them it was fairly routine and other than giving them a quick description of Sharon's beautiful home, he hadn't learned much from the outing. He did tell them about Joyce waving to Albert Einstein, which everyone agreed was something to tell the grandchildren.

Terry and Bull gave Dr. Walsh their undivided attention as he told them his findings.

"I was able to type the blood, A+, the most common type, but that's what Etta had. If there was any of Gaffer White's blood, it was too diluted and messed with the other, so if it was the only evidence, I couldn't say for sure it was the same weapon . . . except," he paused for dramatic effect, "the hair evidence is pretty interesting."

The part-time coroner explained that there was actually quite a bit of hair and tissue imbedded in the cracks of the old bat. The long auburn hair had to be Etta's. It was a match under the microscope, so he was confident about that, but there were also shorter strands of coarse grey hair. It seemed a very reasonable assumption that those hairs belonged to Gaffer White.

"They look to be a match under the microscope too. I'm making the findings official in my report, but I wanted to tell you first," he explained.

"That is great!" Bull said. "Good work, Doc. Good work, Terry. I feel like we might actually be getting somewhere."

They were talking about informing the State Police as a matter of protocol, when the phone rang.

"That was Chief Riggs. Wants to know how things are going—heard we found the murder weapon and wants to know if we need Leonard," Bull said with raised eyebrows and a little grin. "Leonard's making noises again about kids being involved since he heard about the baseball bat and kids finding it. God, how the hell does this stuff get out there so fast, will you tell me, please?" Bull said, obviously exasperated.

It was pretty much a rhetorical question. Bull lived here all of his life and understood there was little else on everyone's mind these days. Rumors flew high and wide, and all the local lawmen were understandably interested and would help if they could. Then there was Leonard Smith who was probably going nuts because he was being kept at arm's length.

"I'm going to see Sheriff Zimmer later and Harvey's gonna meet us at the diner in Flemington. We'll have some lunch, I'll fill 'em in, and I hate to say it, but we might have to at least talk to Leonard. I'm about positive it was Leonard who gave Etta Marx all that crap she put in the article about Gaffer, and maybe she told him something important," the chief said.

Dr. Walsh left, saying he'd have the official report by the weekend. Dolly popped in to say she was still waiting for the list from the paper company in Rhode Island. Terry took several routine phone calls, including one from Ethel Crisp, just wanting to know what progress was being made. He was able to say they were making headway and he would try to stop by today or tomorrow. It actually did fit in with a few ideas he was having about motives for the murder and the Crisp sisters could be a source of information. He felt Mary VanHaven was another source and he had a flash idea of taking Joyce along so she could meet these wonderful ladies he had been telling her about. He would not want to appear unprofessional though. When he ran the idea by his boss, Bull thought it would be fine.

"Lou did some investigating with me years ago. Nothing like this mess, but it was a pretty bad arson case, back in '28. You were just a little guy, but you might remember that horrible fire at the chair factory out by Drew Heights? Lou and I went all over the county on that and she was not only good company but was a big help too. Anyway, I trust your judgment, Deputy. If Joyce wants to go with you on these friendly calls, go right ahead," he said.

Terry appreciated his boss more and more. He did remember that horrible fire. He was only in kindergarten and it turned out to be set by the owner for insurance money. Luckily there were no deaths from it, but he remembered going to the ruins when he got older and kids telling creepy stores about the place being haunted. Not murder, but for a small town, Kentbury eventually seemed to experience almost every kind of crime there was.

"Oh Lord, Terry," the chief was saying as he hung up the phone. "Get down to the bank right away. That was Miss Copley. She says there's some kind of animal in the night deposit box and to bring your gun in case you have to shoot it!"

Terry remembered Miss Copley being at the bank since he was a kid. *She must be a hundred,* he thought, but she was first to open up this morning and heard strange noises coming from the large bin that was there for night and weekend deposits. If an animal did somehow get in there, the slanted, stainless steel box would be hard to escape. Terry had no intention of shooting anything, but he hoped it wasn't a squirrel; they could be cagey and nasty as well.

As soon as he got to the room where they accessed the deposit box, he knew it wasn't a squirrel, and it hadn't gotten in their by chance. When Terry saw other employees coming in as well as Mike Skinner, he quickly made an announcement.

"We've got a kitten here, folks. Any takers? She's pretty cute," Terry announced to an interested audience. But while there were some oohs and aahs, some cooing and a few laughs, no one stepped up to take the little cat.

"What the hell is that?" Bull asked when Terry walked in with a tiny black and white kitten, scrawny and full of fleas, but purring its head off.

As he quickly poured milk for the demanding baby, Terry was wondering if Joyce might want it or maybe even Lou Campbell, when Dolly popped in. That was it.

"Oh you poor little thing," Dolly said. "This baby should still be with its mama. What is the matter with people?" Dolly exclaimed.

Just like her mother, thought Terry. Dolly didn't miss a beat, but scooped up the kitten with the promise of a bath, a visit to the vet and love forever. She managed to say that she had only stopped in to say they were still waiting on the list from the paper company and she would get to Etta's phone records this afternoon, but the most important thing right now was this little waif that was, by the way, a he, not a she!

Bull sat at his desk chuckling. "Good work, Deputy. Now, if all our problems were solved that easy . . ." he said. They knew the kitten was in good hands and they knew they'd get reports on him since Dolly made them immediate godfathers as she went off to take care of her newest project.

Finally, an hour before Bull was leaving for his appointment in Flemington and lunch with the Sheriff and Chief Riggs, Terry got to tell him some of the theories he and Joyce were exploring.

"That mess with the trousers pulled down and the knife slashes on the body," Terry began, "Joyce wondered if the murderer might have been trying to castrate the poor guy."

"Well, I'd say a real sicko might do that, but they sure as hell don't know their anatomy very well!" Bull said.

Terry suppressed a chuckle at that but went on with more theories.

"I keep thinking that Gaffer might have heard or seen something that he shouldn't. You know, he was all over town doing his odd jobs.

People never paid any attention to the poor old guy—he could have been in the wrong place at the wrong time. But . . . that would not explain the slashing stuff," Terry said.

"What did Doc say about the kind of knife that was used—anything yet? Bull asked.

"I have that in my notes to ask him, but haven't heard anything yet. Thanks for reminding me," Terry said.

"Then, there's the murder weapon. We need to find out where that came from, don't we?

"Not a gun, not a knife. And if he had a knife, why the bludgeoning, why not just stab him? I could be wrong, but these murders were planned. The murderer knew what he was going to do, but he uses a weapon that we usually see with a sudden rage. You know, domestic stuff, frustration, even kids," Terry concluded.

"Well, I see those weeks of training we sent you to are coming in handy, Deputy," the chief commented. "I agree with all of that, but still no conclusions. Where are you going to go with this, Terry?" Bull asked.

"Not sure yet, Chief," he had to admit.

"We have to wait to see what Father Hanover or Father Boyle might be able to tell us. I'll stop at the hospital on my way home. Doc Walsh is still waiting to hear about fingerprints, but I don't see much hope on that. We're assuming Etta was killed because of something she knew or found, but unless we can find her notes . . . all that interest in Gaffer's baptism and other churches. That would be an outing for you and Joyce, check out those other churches. I don't know what the heck you'll be lookin' for, but without Etta's notes, we'll have to see if we can find out for ourselves what she was on to," Bull said.

Fred Browning was attending to the office phones, Bull was at lunch in Flemington, Terry was going back to Minnie Lester's and Dolly was searching for the kitten that already explored the whole library, knocked books off shelves he tried to climb and was fascinated with the cup of pens and pencils Dolly kept on her desk. And the really funny thing was that the whole while he was whirling around the library, he was making an incredible purring-motor kind of sound. He was just an ordinary black and white kitten, a dime a dozen, but Dolly could tell he was special. The vet pronounced him only four to five weeks old. Yes, he should still be with his mother, but he was a tough little guy and ready to eat whatever Dolly put in front of him. He didn't like the bath, but was small enough for Dolly to control. He didn't like anything the vet did, but that was all forgotten now as he ate the last of his food, drank some water and impressed Dolly to no end when he used the kitty box she provided. Finally, rid of all that joyous energy, she found him sleeping soundly in the bed she made for him behind her desk.

Names ran through her head—Banker, Dollar, Bull, Terry, even Chief, but she wasn't in a hurry. Dolly didn't want him to be a library cat since he would have to be alone too much, and she already called her mother to say she was bringing home a new baby. Even though Dolly and Neal talked about getting their own home one day, they were quite happy living with Mary, especially so right now, while Kentbury was in the grasp of a crazed murderer.

Dolly was cataloguing the new National Geographic and several other periodicals that arrived today, when she realized there was an envelope stuck in one of the magazines. It was from the Putnam-Defoe Company in Rhode Island! Slicing open the heavy, rich-looking envelope, Dolly quickly read the letter from Mrs. Cunniff.

Dear Mrs. Argyle:

> *Enclosed please find the list of stores and suppliers who carry our premium grade letterhead, "High Tea," with matching envelopes, PD-A-C121, which is what Mr. Tandy decrees are the samples you have, and Mr. Tandy has, thus far, never been mistaken. He also believes the samples represent a particular run from October 1950. With that in mind, I have enclosed a sample and I have typed an asterisk by those particular suppliers who have paper from that run. The list also includes orders for this paper going back to 1949. You will note duplicate orders as well. However, knowing Mr. Tandy, I advise you to begin with those I have marked since it may help to narrow your search.*
>
> *I understand this is part of a police investigation and I certainly hope this will be helpful.*

Sincerely,
Miriam Cunniff
Head of Marketing

Dolly was impressed. She always admired efficiency and she certainly appreciated the advice and definitely appreciated Mr. Tandy. The three pages listing stationary stores included eight in Manhattan and only three had an asterisk. There were two in Brooklyn, one in the Bronx, one in Jersey City with an asterisk, and one each in Elizabeth and Newark. Mrs. Cunniff was nothing if not thorough. Well, lots of work lay ahead, but Dolly was excited about it and was anxious to show Bull and Terry the letter and the sample.

While she waited for them to return, Dolly got on with her library duties, taking a few minutes to look through the new National Geographic. She loved the magazine and, as she perused a colorful article entitled "Siam Is Thailand Again," she knew what she was going to name the kitten!

Something Minnie Lester said was nagging at Terry. As usual, she was pleased to see the young deputy and offered him refreshment.

Sipping iced tea, Terry asked again about the night Etta was murdered.

"Oh yes, Terry, I will certainly not forget that day. I'm not afraid, I told you that, but I do admit that I keep seeing that horrible mess and poor, dear Etta lying there like that, just awful," she said.

"Yes, ma'am. What did you tell me about Etta doing gardening? Didn't you say you saw her that afternoon? I'd like you to tell me as much as you can about that day, if you could," Terry said.

"Well, let's see . . . Etta got home when I was in the kitchen cutting up the peaches for the pie I told you about. So that was about two o'clock," she explained.

"You didn't speak to her then, I take it," Terry said.

"No. I did wave but Etta was fussing with something in her car and she didn't see me and then she just went inside" Minnie stated

"Could you see if she was carrying anything?" Terry asked.

"Yes, well . . . hmm," Minnie said, looking to her mind's eye for a glimpse of Etta on that fateful afternoon. "She had her purse of course, and I think she had a book or some papers and she went back and that's what she was fussing about in the car. It looked like she decided to leave some things in the car. Oh, and she locked the car. I remember that because it seemed odd . . . no one in Kentbury locks cars, but I remember she pushed the button and held it, you know, to make sure it was locked."

Terry checked his excitement. He had a few more questions and didn't want to alarm Miss Lester and sidetrack her from remembering. So far, she was doing great!

"So, she was gardening later, in that hot sun?" Terry asked.

Minnie Lester had a strange look on her face. She was pretty sharp and her reputation of being a bit loopy or "cuckoo," as Leonard Smith unkindly would say, was hiding what Terry suspected was a smart and discerning mind, in spite of butterflies and seventy plus years of age.

"I cannot remember Etta gardening on Friday. That was usually a weekend activity, especially Saturdays. Deputy Kramer, do you think that wasn't Etta at all and was likely the murderer?" she asked, obviously having the same thought Terry was having.

"Now, let's not jump to conclusions. But just tell me what you can remember about that. You said it was before you put your pie in the oven, which was at five o'clock when the music was so loud, is that right?" Terry wanted to know.

"Yes, I put the pie in at five. I saw Etta again before that though, and she was getting something out of the car. She didn't lock it that time and I . . . ," she stopped in mid-sentence.

"What is it, Miss Lester?" Terry asked.

"Oh, dear . . . I almost spoke to her. I almost went out to say hello, but by the time I got the pie in the oven, I didn't see her. Was it Etta, Terry?" she asked with obvious concern.

"It might not have been Etta, Miss Lester, but are you sure it was a woman, could it have been a man?" Terry asked.

"Oh, oh . . . a man? Well, let's see . . . she had on that cute new smock with the yellow flowers on it, and that big straw hat she always wore in the garden," Minnie said.

"What about the size, the way she walked, was anything different?" Terry wanted to know.

"Well, now that you say that, I almost think they were not as tall as Etta, but with the hat I can't be sure. I didn't think for a minute it was not Etta, but I hate to say it, that walk could have been a bit mannish. Etta was rather elegant, you know, not the prettiest girl but she carried herself like a model, at least I thought so," Minnie said.

Terry thanked Minnie, reassured her and also hinted that he would like to bring his wife one day to meet her. She thought that would be lovely and she waved to him as he once again went down the drive to Etta's house, armed with a few more ideas.

Terry searched everywhere but could not find a yellow smock or any kind of gardening hat. The little porch in the back held an old green apron, some sturdy gloves and a bucket with various gardening tools. Terry did another quick search of the grounds, the little woods and even the ditch where the Brewer boys found the bat, but the gardening clothes were nowhere to be found. The murderer disguised himself, probably got what he was looking for in the car, then went through the little patch of woods, hid the baseball bat in the ditch and . . . .

From the way the blood had spattered all over, the murderer would have been covered in it and there was no evidence of any washing up, but that thought gave way to another idea.

On the side of the house, Terry found a green garden hose with small smears and stains that he was pretty sure were blood. He carefully unscrewed the hose to take with him and noticed more smears behind the faucet. Against the white paint of Etta's house, it definitely looked like blood. Terry went to his car for the camera, duly took pictures, carefully wrapped the hose in a tarp to deliver to Dr. Walsh, and waved to Minnie who was watching from her window as he left.

Terry pictured the murderer. Miss Lester said he wore dark trousers. She did not see the shoes. But surely, a man wearing such a stupid getup would attract attention, wouldn't he? Maybe he was able to get to a car parked nearby without being seen. It's possible. It was a hot August Friday, not that many people around at that hour. But it was still taking a big chance. Terry was anxious to get back to the office, do a little paperwork so it wouldn't get out of hand, and get home early tonight. He wanted to run all of this by Joyce; sometimes a woman's perspective opened other avenues he might not think of. It did feel like they were actually getting somewhere, but it was still a puzzle with lots of missing pieces.

NINETEEN

Marvin Walsh was waiting for Terry when he arrived with the garden hose. There were no patients this afternoon and Terry appreciated that the coroner could get right to the new piece of evidence. While the doc examined the hose, Terry told him about the time lines he was considering, starting with 2:00 p.m. when Minnie said Etta arrived home.

"You haven't really read my report yet, Terry, but I have serious doubts that Etta was doing any gardening in that short bit of time between getting home and being killed. She had bathed and was getting dressed, I believe, when she was attacked," Dr. Walsh stated.

"Well, that could be right, Doc," Terry said, "but what if she did do some gardening and then just took a bath?" Terry wanted to know.

"Well, not impossible. But you take a look at Etta's bathroom. She was a girl who indulged herself. Bath salts, bubble baths, expensive soaps. There was evidence of that on the body. It is quite reasonable to believe that Etta was soaking and enjoying a leisurely bath after getting home from work, and it was awful hot that day, not a great time to do gardening. Oh, and she had washed her hair. It was still damp. Even lying there that long, it was humid enough that her hair didn't completely dry. She would have been fussing with it, getting ready to go out, perhaps, but I just don't think she would have been doing gardening," the doctor said.

Terry had to agree and mentioned that Minnie Lester said Etta was pretty much a weekend gardener. He did not have an opportunity to look at Etta's house last Saturday and he also realized that he needed to be more on top of his investigating skills. Neither the State Police nor the chief even mentioned the bathroom, but he was happy to be learning from the seasoned coroner.

"Wow, I guess you certainly know what to look for and I guess you're right about a lady indulging herself like that. Joyce certainly enjoys a long relaxing bath," Terry said.

"Well, quite right. I'm basing this theory on years of experience and more importantly, having a wife and three daughters," Dr. Walsh said with a smile.

Terry got back to the office before his boss. Fred Browning had left for the day, leaving a few notes but nothing requiring immediate attention. Getting a root beer out of the old fridge they kept in the back, Terry heard the office door open, then a funny meow, and he knew Dolly had come in.

"There's your hero, Tuk-Tuk. Tell Uncle Terry thank you," Dolly said, holding the kitten and a manila file.

"Who? What's a Took Took?" Terry wanted to know.

"He's just like a little Thailand taxi, zipping around, making putt-putt sounds, full of beans—a tuk-tuk! Pronounced took-took, but spelled t-u-k, t-u-k," Dolly said with authority. She then explained about the National Geographic article on Thailand and knew immediately that this special little boy would have a special name. It suited him. She was adamant and that was that!

"Ok, Tuk-Tuk, I'm glad you've got a good home, and I'm really glad you got rid of those fleas!" Terry said.

Bull came in just as Dolly was about to show Terry the letter from the paper company and also report what she had found out so far about Etta's phone calls. Bull said he didn't mind if Tuk-Tuk ran around the office, but if he had an accident, Dolly was responsible for clean up!

Dolly wanted to show Bull and Terry the letter and paper sample before going ahead with calls to the stationary stores on the list. She wanted to make sure she had the authority to say it was a police investigation, and how much should she tell them? Once that was clarified, she said she would begin with phone calls this afternoon, but since it was already Friday and getting late, she might not be able to make any headway until Monday. Then she brought out her notes she made dealing with Etta Marx's phone records.

Of course Dolly started her inquiring with the call Etta made to Dolly's mother, Mary VanHaven.

"Mother said Etta was hoping to look at more photos. She was especially interested in a group Mother put together dating from 1902 to

1908. This was after that awful article came out, but Mother relented and said Etta could come around on Saturday, but of course she never made it," Dolly said softly.

"Well good. We'll definitely have a look at those photographs, Dolly, even though we don't know what the heck we're lookin' for," Bull said.

"There was a call to St. Ann's in Hampton. I spoke with Father Ellis who said he spoke with Etta about a baptismal certificate for any Wexlers, Whites or Farmers," Dolly told them.

"Farmers?" Terry asked.

"Oh, I think we are assuming the name Farmer, not the occupation," Dolly answered.

"I don't know that name around here, do you, Chief?" Terry asked.

"No, no, but I think there might have been a Farmer family in Flemington years ago," Bull said.

"I can check through old census records if you like, and Mother might know too," Dolly said, "but as far as St. Ann's in Hampton, Father Ellis was happy to speak with me and said he told Etta there was a White family there, but they moved to Hampton in 1948, from Pennsylvania, and Etta thanked him but said she was looking for records from the turn of the century."

"Ah, well that's something isn't it?" Bull said with interest.

"Yes, I guess. Now, Father March has only been at St. Paul's in Califon for about six months. Sounds like a nice young fellow, I must say, and said he thought perhaps he should call the police himself when he realized the Kentbury murder victim was the woman he had recently spoken with. He wouldn't tell me much, but said he would like to talk with you, so I told him Chief Campbell would call him. Here," Dolly said, handing Bull the note with Father March's phone number on it.

"Good work, Dolly! I wish we could pay you, but we couldn't afford you anyway, I'm sure," Bull said good naturedly.

Dolly said she made a list of all of the calls Etta made from her home phone, but were they going to check calls she may have made from the newspaper office? Bull said that Nelson Hunt was doing that and while a bit unconventional, they trusted him to do this, and it was not going to require another warrant. He promised to give them what he found, probably early next week, after the funeral.

"Where exactly is it going to be?" Dolly asked.

Bull explained that Etta's family was from Connecticut, and they were just not close. Her sister, though, was married and lived in Bernardsville. She was making arrangements and the funeral would be at an Episcopal Church there and Etta would be buried there as well. It was going to be on Tuesday.

"Lou and I are going to attend. It makes sense to see if anyone of interest might be there, but I have to tell you, I feel awful about the way I spoke to her—seems the least I can do is pay last respects," Bull said.

TWENTY

Bull had duty this Saturday, but that just meant he got to answer any calls. Both he and Terry would be actively looking at evidence, and working with unpaid overtime to solve this horrific case. Things were so crazy these past few weeks that Lou was starting to worry out loud. Bull promised he'd try to rest, but how could he? They both did appreciate though, that having Terry Kramer on board was making even these hectic times much easier.

"Joyce is just like you, Honey," Bull was saying to Lou, "she's going with Terry today to see the Crisp sister and Mary Van Haven. It'll be interesting to see what they find out." Lou readily agreed.

Terry was out of uniform, wearing khaki slacks and a cotton shirt for what he expected would be a pretty interesting day. Joyce, gorgeous as ever, wore a black and white cotton dress and open shoes with no stockings. "Too hot, darling," she had declared, "but from what you tell me about the Crisp sisters, I doubt they will be shocked."

Joyce had seen Lake Cottage from afar when Terry gave her a grand tour shortly after they moved to Kentbury, but she was enchanted now as they drove up the winding drive to the elegant home they called a cottage. Jimmy Doolittle was there to greet them. Joyce loved dogs as much as Terry, but they didn't want to get one until they had their own house.

"Well aren't you a special boy!" Joyce said to the handsome collie that was escorting them to the house.

An hour flew by as Joyce and Terry enjoyed not only the iced tea and lemon cake, but the interesting and informative conversation. Terry could tell that Joyce was delighted with the Crisp sisters and they with her. Without telling them exactly why he wanted to know, Terry was able to ask the unofficial historians things that related to Etta's possible leads about the Wexlers.

"You know, we were away from here for years. Oh, of course we visited and Mother always made sure we knew what was going on in town. That whole unfortunate business when Agatha White got pregnant, well, you can imagine it was a scandal," Ethel said.

"Oh yes, and the poor girl would never say who the father was, although it was even wondered if she knew," Madeline added.

"Things were so different then. A girl like Agatha White was not much better than an indentured servant. So much of a servant's life depended on a good employer. A bad one could make their life . . . well . . . hell," Ethel said apologetically.

"But it seems the Wexlers were quite good to her from what I've been able to learn," Terry said.

"Yes, yes, they were I guess, which was somewhat of a surprise if you think about it."

"Why is that, Mrs. Barrow?" Joyce asked.

"Well, not only was it considered a disgrace but the Wexlers were, well . . ." Ethel trailed off.

"They were not really very nice, Terry," Madeline stated with conviction. "Oh, they were wealthy and had lots of influence and control over not only goings on in Kentbury, but Califon as well where the dairy was. Our parents knew them socially, but Father said to always avoid business dealings with them, and he did," Madeline said.

"Actually, Antonia Wexler, Magnus's wife, was lovely, and I always thought a little sad. But it was that controlling thing: Magnus Wexler wanted to control everything, including his family. The two daughters were rather snobbish, but I think that's the way their father made them. Mrs. Wexler, Antonia, was much nicer but, as I said, a little sad," Ethel explained.

"Then Jerome was killed in that hunting accident and that seemed to take the wind out of Magnus. It wasn't long after that the family moved to Philadelphia. Is that right, Ethel?" Madeline asked.

Terry and Joyce could hardly consider this work, but they both realized that the Crisp sisters were a treasure trove of information. Before they left, the sisters graciously gave the couple a tour of their home.

"It's like an art gallery, isn't it, Honey?" Terry said.

The beautifully appointed home was full of treasures from a rich life, with souvenirs from their travels in almost every room. A bit dated and showing age and wear here and there, Joyce was, nevertheless, appreciative of the traditional good taste, and impressed Ethel and Madeline with her knowledge of decorating, interior design and antiques.

"You know," Madeline said, addressing Joyce, "we have been thinking that the cottage could use a bit of perking up. You know . . . new drapes, and the rug in the dining room needs replacing, and I would love to have my bedroom freshened up. Joyce is just who we need. What do you think, Ethel?"

Joyce was thrilled and Terry appreciated that perhaps his wife's expertise was a viable career after all, as long as you could find the right clientele. With a promise to come back to talk about this exciting development, Joyce and Terry left to grab some lunch and then go on to their appointment with Mary VanHaven.

They would later say this was one of the best Saturdays they had in a long time. Even with the reason behind it being as much business as pleasure, the young couple was sharing an unusual day, meeting colorful, engaging people, learning new things about her husband, not to mention the prospect of a paid decorating job!

Luckily, Joyce liked cats. Terry had told her about Mr. Dickens who was in residence at the library when he was a kid, and of course she knew all about the night deposit box kitten, Tuk-Tuk, who was already part of family, curled up on a chair next to another black and white cat, along with Jane Austin, Mark Twain and T.S. Eliot, all comfortable and content on the back screened porch that looked out to the gurgling creek flowing down below Lake Raynard. Mary VanHaven was telling Joyce the story about issuing Terry his first library card, and Terry was waiting for an opportunity to turn the conversation to Kentbury history, when Dolly and Neal Argyle joined them in the relaxing, feline-populated setting. Joyce had met Dolly before, but this was the first time she was meeting Neal.

A little taller than Dolly, the 6'4" man was immediately likable; nice looking, open and friendly and just rather sweet. Joyce thought they were a great couple. Neal worked at The Boathouse in Califon, where his hand-crafted canoes and paddles were prized throughout the country, and some even found their way to Canada and Europe. Dolly was quick to tell them that one of Neal's canoes was recently crafted for none other than baseball star Ted Williams, an avid fisherman, and an order for six was being completed for the US Park Service for use at the Grand Canyon. Dolly was going on about certain movie stars wanting Neal's canoes, when he stopped his proud wife, a little embarrassed by her bragging.

"Ok, Dolly, the Kramers don't want to hear my life story," he said.

"But that is pretty impressive, Neal. You should be proud," Joyce said.

Neal said he enjoyed his work but there was always room for improvement. In the meantime, there were two canoes sitting here at the little dock if Terry and Joyce ever wanted to take them out.

"That would be great, wouldn't it, Honey?" Terry said, half expecting his city-bred wife to balk at the idea, but she surprised him with enthusiasm for the idea and Terry immediately wondered if they could use such an opportunity to have a romantic interlude in one of the many secluded spots dotting the whole beautiful area.

Finally, after all the friendly conversation, more lemonade and biographies of the various cats, it was Joyce who brought the conversation around to getting a look at the old photos and more Kentbury history.

Terry and Joyce sat together looking through the catalogued albums, paying special attention to the albums Etta was interested in, dating from 1902-1908. Conversation flowed freely with Mary, Dolly and Neal all contributing. Terry and Joyce were learning a lot and every now and then, Terry asked a question.

"But I didn't come to Kentubry until 1920. The town was even smaller then and being married to a VanHaven, as well as being the new librarian, I suppose I did get to know people and learn things, but I really never knew the Wexlers. They were already gone by the time we moved here. Oh, I did see Agatha White and poor Gaffer sometimes, but I just knew the story everyone told. But you know, everyone said Agatha was slow, or retarded, but I never thought so," Mary said.

"Why is that, ma'am?" Terry wanted to know.

"Hmm, well, it happened when the library was still in the old building up the street. It was almost closing time on a hot day. I guess I remember it because I was fairly new here then and still trying to get to know people. This woman came in, a bit shabby looking, but there was something fey about her you know, other-worldly almost. I didn't want to tell her she had to go just because I wanted to close early—I was expecting Dolly then, and it had been a long day," she said, looking at her daughter. "But I was polite and I asked if I could help her."

"I like to look at all of the books," she said. "I asked her if there was one in particular she might want and she said the funniest thing; I think that's another reason I remember it so well. She said 'Oh, I like them all. I used to dust them at the big house, you know. Bobby can read a little but I can't,' she said."

"It was just so sad. My first reaction was actually to offer to teach her to read, but I didn't say that. Instead, I asked her if she would like to look at any of the picture books, and it was just awful, but she looked hurt. I knew that I had insulted her, but of course I hadn't meant to," Mary explained to a quiet and rapt audience.

Joyce broke the silence. "Then what happened?" she asked.

"She thanked me and turned to go. I felt terrible, you can imagine. I told her to please come back any time and I said that I was Mrs. VanHaven, the librarian. She said, 'I know. I'm Aggie White,' and she left," Mary said.

"Bull said she called her son Baby and later Bobby, never Gaffer I guess," Terry said.

"Yes, I believe that's true. She came several times after that and would just wander up and down the rows of books. She brightened when she looked at them, and I still wonder what she would have said if I had offered to teach her to read. But Dolly finally arrived and I was off for several months. Miss Worley filled in for me and mentioned that "Weird Aggie" had come by, but she told her the library was not for loitering, and I never saw her there again, although I would see her in town once in a while," Mary said with a bit of sadness.

The old photos were wonderful. There were enough to picture most of Kentbury all those years ago. Some showed the churches in place but the trees were small or non-existent and the streets looked bare compared to now. There were more horses, wagons and carriages and the photos progressed to show the automobiles and trucks creeping in to displace the beloved pleasure and draft animals everyone used. The Tyler-Sykes Mill was in several photos and there was one special album Mary had put together with just Kentbury sons who had served in the Civil War, the Spanish American War, World War I, World War II and Mary observed that she would have a separate one for the mess in Korea. Four boys from Kentbury were already there, and she told them the Blake family had a daughter there as an Army nurse.

There was a short interlude with everyone being very serious when they talked about President Truman, General MacArthur and the concern that Terry and Neal would feel compelled to return to active service. Neal had served with the 7th Army and was among the first Americans who liberated Dachau, one of the notorious Nazi concentration camps. Everyone appreciated that it was not something easily talked about, but more than once Mary told her gentle son-in-law that he should document his experiences.

"My parents have Jewish friends, the Bergmans, who took in several relatives who somehow survived the Auschwitz camp. It's hard to believe some of the things we heard. It's hard to believe human beings can do these things, isn't it?" Joyce said softly.

It was Dolly who turned the conversation to a lighter note, and it was not long before everyone went back to talking about local history and then the always-lurking stories everyone told about the famous Lindbergh Trial that took place in Flemington in 1935.

Flemington had a foundry, glassworks and bigger population than Kentbury but it was still a country town and county seat that went through a kind of madness when Bruno Richard Hauptman was tried and convicted there for the kidnap and murder of the Lindbergh baby. Little Flemington became a household name around the world then, and everyone had personal stories to tell, from the locals who served on the jury, the local prosecution team and just those who were here to see the spectacle in person.

"When we lived in Flemington, the first thing my parents wanted to see when they came to visit was the Courthouse where the trial took place," Joyce said. "I was in grammar school when it was going on, but it was all everyone seemed to be talking about. I certainly remember that!"

Another half hour went by and when Terry and Joyce finally left, it was with a wonderful feeling of new friendship, a promise of getting together soon for dinner, the enticing offer to have a canoe trip and picnic, a tour of the canoe company in Califon, and the loan of the antique album Terry wanted to pore over, looking for what he was not sure.

TWENTY-ONE

Terry got to the office early Monday morning, but his boss was there an hour ahead of him. *Bad coffee* was his first thought, but he'd had two good cups at home, thank goodness.

The chief reported a reasonably quiet weekend with a few phone calls and one little domestic dispute that he easily took care of so, by and large, he had been able to relax and enjoy a leisurely two days with Lou. They attended Mass on Sunday and while there were the expected questions and concerns, nothing valuable popped up. He and Lou paid a visit to Father Hanover at the Cool Springs Clinic, but the priest was still a bit disoriented, yet aware enough to know it, and asked Bull to please come again, so he could give a proper statement. The old priest also said that something was nagging at him about Gaffer White's history, but he just couldn't think of it at that moment.

"That's pretty interesting," Terry said.

"Ho, tell me about it. I'm going back to see him again today. That's one reason I wanted to get in early, but I'm anxious as hell to hear what you might have discovered. What did Joyce think of the Crisp sisters?" Bull wanted to know.

Bull could tell that Terry and Joyce enjoyed a very pleasant visit at Lake Cottage as well as having a good time with Dolly, Neal and Mary VanHaven. He listened closely as Terry told him about the bits and pieces of information that could be useful, suggesting the young deputy make notes of it all.

"Already did that, Chief," Terry said. Bull should have known.

"Joyce and I spent a good deal of time going over the photo albums we borrowed from Mrs. VanHaven, and it's been great for Joyce to learn so much about Kentbury. So far though, nothing has really struck me that could relate to the murders," Terry explained.

"Oh, yes, almost forgot," the chief said. "Nelson Hunt was in first thing to tell me that Bridgewater Funeral Home came and got Etta. Of course he'll be there Wednesday for the funeral. It's at 1:00 o'clock, so you won't see me at all, but I'll call you when we get back. We're taking our car. You can appreciate I don't want to be there in a police car," he stated.

"Did Mr. Hunt say anything about phone records?" Terry asked.

"Yes he did. They were pretty much the same calls we found on Etta's home records—the Catholic Churches in Hampton and Califon and with the time and dates, they were the preliminary calls and she must have followed up with calls from home. Fortunately, any long distance calls had to be logged and Etta was good about that Nelson said. There was a call to the Catholic Diocese in Newark but everything else was routine, I'm sorry to say," Bull explained.

"Are you getting Dolly to follow up with the Diocese?" Terry asked.

"Actually, I asked Father Boyle if he would look into that and he said he would be happy to. He'll let us know if he finds out anything," Bull said.

Bull left just before noon to have lunch at home and planned to then go see Fr Hanover.

Terry spent the morning typing up his notes for the growing files dealing with the two murders and taking the few phone calls that came in. They were still getting calls from reporters but fortunately, the crime in the cities topped even two murders in little Kentbury. At least no one was coming around in person, so they didn't have to deal with that. Bull had just left and Terry was thinking about lunch when Dolly popped in.

After a few minutes of exchanging compliments about what a nice visit they had on Saturday, Dolly wanted to report an exciting lead she had on the expensive stationary they were tracking down.

"I started with the companies that were marked with an asterisk, and I realized that one, they were not that anxious to talk to me, and two, they were not so inclined to take the time to go through their records to see which customers would have this stationary. Then, and this is rather daunting, they were quick to tell me that anyone could walk off the street and buy a ream of this paper or even a few single sheets and they didn't keep records for that," Dolly sighed.

Saying she had a few more ideas, including possibly an ad in the classifieds, Dolly left Terry as he started to close up and run to the Pan About Town for a takeout sandwich so he could eat in and keep working.

He was almost to the door when Cathy Romano and another young girl burst into the office.

"Oh, Deputy Kramer, hurry, he's just leaving town! I'm sure that's him, hurry!" the excited teenager said.

"Whoa, Cathy. Who's leaving town, what's this about?" Terry asked.

"That man! The one who was talking to Mr. White that day! The one who gave him the letter, you know!" she stated.

Terry understood and even though he wanted to tear out of the office after the guy, he needed to know more, so he took the calmer approach, hoping his excitement was not showing through the police officer demeanor he knew was so important.

"Betty and I . . . this is Betty Norton," she began, introducing her friend. Terry nodded to the blonde girl and told Cathy to please go on.

"Well, Betty and I were just walking to the Five 'N Dime and I recognized the hat first. I thought it was him right away, but I wanted to get a little closer. We were across the street and he was getting into his car. I almost yelled to him, but then . . ."

"I told her he could be the murderer," Betty interrupted, wide-eyed and expectant and just a little taken with the handsome deputy.

"Right, ladies. Cathy, you're sure it was the same man?" Terry asked.

"Yes, sir. It was him, really!" she answered.

"So he was headed out of town, which way?" Terry needed to know.

A minute later, Terry was racing out of the parking lot, resisting using his siren since it would probably upset people and lead to even crazier rumors than were already circulating, but he definitely caused attention by screeching around the corner as he left Main Street headed up Prescott Avenue.

Going as fast as he could without being a danger, he lost a minute when a county road truck was in the way, but after ten minutes and after going through the little Bunnvale area and not seeing a thing, he turned around to ask the road workers if they had seen a black Ford with New York plates. They had not, but Terry wasn't convinced they would have noticed anyway. The guy could have turned off so many side roads, it would be impossible to guess which one to follow. Reluctantly admitting defeat, Terry returned to the office. A black Ford with New York Plates was parked in front.

No one was in the car. Terry immediately wrote down the plate number and rushed to the office. There was a note on the door.

**Chief Campbell or Deputy Kramer, Please come upstairs as soon as you get in.
You have an important visitor.
Dolly**

"Oh, good," Dolly said when Terry came through the library door. "I was just about to call Lou to see if she knew how to get in touch with you or the chief, but here you are. Mr. April, this is Deputy Kramer. Deputy, this is Mr. Rudy April from New York," Dolly said with great satisfaction.

"Well, I'm really pleased to see you, Mr. April," Terry said as they shook hands.

Terry quickly learned that, yes, this was the man who tracked down Gaffer White a few days before he was murdered and he came back today at the request of his employer, specifically to see the police and tell them what he could. He had no idea he and the important letter were already part of the investigation. Now they were going to finally start putting some of those elusive pieces in the murder puzzle. The young man was nice looking, as Cathy Romano had observed, and he did have a bit of city twang to his speech, but he was polite and eager to help if he could, explaining that he had been drafted and this was probably his last civilian job and he wanted to do his best.

Terry asked his visitor to please come downstairs to continue the interview. It was probably okay for Dolly to listen in, but there were several townsfolk in the library. Terry gave Dolly a thank you and a wink as they left, and unless there was something they had to keep under wraps, he was sure he or the chief would tell her as much as they could. He also apologized for not being reachable. The usual protocol was to call in if they had been away from the radio, but they had not scheduled a volunteer for today, but they should have.

Bull got back to the office after his visit with Father Hanover, missing their visitor by ten minutes.

"Well, don't you look like the cat that swallowed the canary," Bull remarked as he walked in.

"A big fat canary, Chief," Terry said, then spent the next half hour filling his boss in on the valuable interview he had with Rudy April.

"I'm doin' cartwheels in my head, Son, big, crazy cartwheels! I think our prayers are being answered."

Terry told his boss about Cathy Romano and her friend coming in, his unsuccessful chase up Prescott Avenue, not knowing that Rudy April had gone down Mitchum Road to the gorge and drove by the path to Gaffer's house, then turned around and came back to the police station. When the young man found the office closed, he went up to the library and found the best person in the world to wait with. His conversation with Dolly was only what anyone might have read in the newspapers, but Rudy April was anxious to hear about it, since he was unaware of the murder until yesterday. Dolly told him what she could and they had only talked a short while when Terry arrived.

"It's still not going to give us the murderer, Chief, but you won't believe who sent that letter and why," Terry said to his boss who was all ears.

"Lenore Wexler?" Bull asked, incredulous when Terry told him, but anxious to hear everything.

"This is what Rudy April told me," Terry began.

"Miss Wexler moved to New York from Philadelphia after her mother died in 1925. No one in Kentbury knew it I guess, but no reason they should. Rudy said he was hired by the law firm in New York that was handling Miss Wexler's estate, which I gather is pretty big. He came to Kentbury today to check all of this out, about Gaffer's murder that is, because his employer, this law firm, wanted to have the facts for themselves, then decide just how they should proceed from their end of things. The person who sent him to Kentbury to find Gaffer White is a Sherman X. Dumont, Esq., of Dumont, Trundell and Trout, Park Avenue attorneys," Terry explained, handing the chief the card Rudy left.

"When he finally tracked Gaffer down that day, which he said had not been easy, his instructions were to give him the envelope and explain that it would be good news for him and also that there was money in the envelope, two hundred dollars in cash! Two days ago, Mr. Sherman said his wife saw something about a murder in Kentbury, a name she had heard him mention. He read the story, just a little paragraph on page eight of an old Daily News and then asked Rudy April to come back here today, find out what he could and then go to the police. I have the information for Mr. Sherman, so you can call him," Terry said.

"Whoa, this might finally give us some answers. This young fella, Rudy, he didn't know what was in the letter, only about the cash?" Bull asked.

"He's tracked down a lot of heirs, but he doesn't know all the details. He knew about the money so he could tell Gaffer not to lose it. He was surprised it wasn't a check, but when he met poor old Gaffer, he suspected it was because he wouldn't have known what to do with a check and the cash would be appreciated. He knew it was an estate matter, so that's why he said it would be good news, but that's the little he did know when Mr. Dumont sent him to find Gaffer," Terry said.

"You'd think Gaffer would have wanted to see that money right away, but he didn't open it then. Cathy Romano said she saw Gaffer put the envelope in his pocket, then this Rudy fella left, is that right?" Bull asked.

"Yes, that's what he said too. He reported to the law office that it had been delivered, but that was pretty much the end of his involvement until he got that call from the lawyer about the murder," Terry said.

"Well, ok, let's do that phone call!" Bull said, picking up the phone and asking for long distance.

Fifteen minutes later, Bull hung up. What he learned was compelling and would certainly provide leads to follow but still nothing that pointed to who the murderer might be.

Bull found out that Lenore Gregson Wexler passed away just weeks ago on July 12th. She was seventy-six. Lenore never married, she was the last Wexler. Her parents were gone. Her brother Jerome died in a hunting accident in 1910. Her sister Margery, who married and had a son, passed away in a mental institution when the son, her only child, drowned and her husband took his own life. In what might seem a strange twist of fate, the old cottage that had been Gaffer White's home for all these years was owned by Lenore. Bull Campbell always gave credit to Howard Shore at the Electric Company for looking past bills for the cottage when it turned out there were regular payments made from this law office in New York. Howard only knew the bills were paid and was asked to never talk about how and from whom and he never knew about Lenore Wexler anyway, only the law office.

"Mr. Dumont, Sr. was apparently very friendly with Miss Wexler. Sherman Dumont is the son, his father died some years ago, but their firm handled everything for her and he was quite upset to hear about Gaffer being murdered. He can't imagine who the murderer might be, since he said if Gaffer had preceded Miss Wexler in death, the estate was being divided among various charities. But Gaffer didn't die first, and even though there will be money going to these charities, poor old Gaffer died a wealthy man. How's that for crazy?" Bull wanted to know.

"The law firm will be tracking down any of Gaffer's possible relatives, but I just don't think there are any. Poor Aggie, who knows? I told him we always thought there were Wexlers in Philadelphia and that's when he said he would very much appreciate it if we could come to his office and he would tell us more. You and Joyce want to have a day in New York?" Bull asked.

"You and Lou could go, Chief, that might be better, wouldn't it?" Terry asked.

"With my ticker, son, I'm not goin' into that New York oven. Besides, if you do this tomorrow, I can be here and then you can be here on Wednesday when Lou and I go to Etta's funeral. No, I'd really appreciate you doing that and besides, you could drop in on your in-laws while you were there," Bull said.

Terry couldn't tell if his boss was being a wise guy, but he knew Joyce would love to go with him. He called her right away and they would be taking the train first thing in the morning. Terry stopped by the train station to get the newest timetable and was happy to have a short chat with Verne Cooper, the stationmaster, and got meet his wife and young daughter, Ricky, who were there for a visit as Verne got ready to close up. The little girl asked the deputy where his police dog was. *Cute kid,* he thought. A police dog . . . maybe one day.

TWENTY-TWO

The Jersey Central Railroad came to Kentbury in the 1850's, and along with the important freight line conveying products from the steel mill and hauling produce from local farms, there was the busy passenger line that made a comfortable commute for local residents to have a pleasant country life paid for with New York City salaries. There were even a few notable commuters like playwright Luther Bibb and fashion editor, Trixi Feinberg, but Terry and Joyce didn't recognize anyone famous this morning on their ninety minute ride into Grand Central Station.

Terry wasn't crazy about the city, but Joyce was right at home, hailing a taxi and getting them to the Park Avenue law office a few minutes early for his ten o'clock appointment with Mr. Dumont. Joyce went on to do some shopping and they planned to meet at her parent's apartment by noon. Terry did not say that he was glad his in-laws were at The Cape, but he was.

The law office took up the whole top floor of the beautiful old building. Terry waited in Mr. Dumont's large office surrounded by eighteenth century furniture, enjoying the impressive view and sipping coffee from a Wedgwood cup.

"I'm sorry to keep you waiting, Officer Kramer. Thank you so much for coming," he said, shaking hands before sitting down at his desk. He reminded Terry of Joyce's father—tall, slender, silver hair and a smart little moustache. Like his office, Sherman Dumont was elegant, in dress and manner, but was quick to put his visitor at ease which was also like Joyce's father.

"This is quite an awful business, isn't it? That poor man, and then this woman reporter who was killed. Are you sure the murders are related, Mr. Kramer?" Mr. Dumont asked.

Terry filled Sherman Dumont in on as much as he could, answered questions that came up and finally settled in to listen to the amazing story the lawyer told.

"My father and Lenore Wexler were trusted friends for many years. She was a very interesting woman, quite beautiful, but never married. I believe my father may have known much of what I have just recently learned, but I want to give you a summary of the facts as we know them from this end and maybe there will be some answers here for you as well," he explained, holding up a file with copies that he said Terry could take with him.

"My father died several years ago and Miss Wexler entrusted her affairs to this office, more specifically to me and I had dinner with her every few weeks or so. The last time I saw her, just two weeks before she passed away, she entrusted me with this rather long letter with instructions that it be opened upon her death. I'd like to read some of it to you if I may," Mr. Dumont said.

"Please," Terry said, transfixed with anticipation as Sherman Dumont began to read.

> *"Dear Sherman,*
>
> *"First, I want you to know how much your friendship and that of your father's has meant to me over the years. As you read this, I will be gone and I pray that there is a place where we are forgiven for our earthly transgressions. I have never believed in a vengeful God since I rather believe that we all do enough suffering on this earth. Your father understood and my Last Will and Testament, which you have at your office, will explain my wishes, but I want to tell you just why I want to dispose of my estate as I do. If you suspect guilt and forgiveness have inspired me, you would be right,"* the attorney read, pausing and taking a sip of his coffee before going on.
>
> *"I do not want to make this a condemnation of my father, but I will relate the facts as I know them, leaving you and others to make your own judgments. I made mine a long time ago.*
>
> *"My father was a controlling, harsh man. His success and proper Victorian manners gave him license to run the*

world as he saw fit. We were raised to believe we were better than almost everyone and while poor dear Margery and I secretly resisted this, our brother, Jerome, sometimes called Jerry, believed it wholly, doing as he pleased with almost no consequences or responsibility. My father's biggest rule was that we maintain dignity and our social standing, and all other matters were personal and private. One reason I rejected the Catholic faith after my mother died, was because I saw how easily my father used the confessional to absolve himself and Jerome too, I believe, of the many sins he committed, always believing he was right, never seeing or caring about the hurt and destruction their actions might have caused.

"Jerome's little 'misdeeds,' as my father saw them, were forgiven, covered up and somehow seen as nothing more than high-jinks by a spirited young man who would one day be head of the family. Our dear mother, strong and determined as I remember her growing up, was eventually worn down by my father's harshness, his indifference to Jerome's behavior and the demanding rules he imposed on all of us, including her. After my brother died, my father saw only his own grief and things became unbearable for my dear mother. This eventually drove her to move to Philadelphia, where she was from originally. Divorce was out of the question but when my father, more out of keeping up appearances than any love or devotion, also made the move to Philadelphia, expecting what I am not sure, the large home they shared there became a cloister for my mother who kept to her own rooms, seeing as little of my father as possible. Even though she survived my father by five years, she led a confined life, mired in her faith and never fully recovering from the terrible secrets that broke her spirit and broke her heart."

Terry realized there were explosive things being revealed and knew they had something to do with the crimes in Kentbury. He couldn't believe this amazing letter would solve those crimes, but it was hard not to make that leap. Sherman Dumont went on as Terry gave him his undivided attention.

"My brother Jerome was not killed in a hunting accident. He was killed while in the woods hunting, but was shot by the father of a young woman who lived in Glen Gardner. Jerome had been courting her but, believing anything he did was allowable and apparently tiring of waiting for what would be condoned in marriage, he eventually just took what he wanted. This happened at the end of 1909. The poor girl's life was ruined but it was several months before she told her mother who then told the girl's father. Jerome was killed on February 17, 1910, in woods adjoining Brookside Farm which is in Kentbury Borough but with land that runs into Clinton Township. The man who killed my brother died in 1918, and there would be nothing gained now by telling you his name.

"If my reaction to my brother's murder seems cold or harsh, it is because in 1897, just before I turned nineteen, Jerome assaulted me. He was fifteen. I never told anyone, but I hated my brother and my father as well, from that time onward. My survival came from my revenge which resulted in breaking off my engagement to a man my father wanted me to marry, to fiercely protecting my younger sister, Margery, from suffering a similar assault, and to never again be afraid of my father. It is ironic that my lack of fear became a crutch for both of us. We accepted the mutual contempt as a kind of truce, but I am not sure my father ever did realize the degree to which I hated him or just what it stemmed from, until he lay dying in 1920, at the house in Philadelphia.

"My mother and I spent a good deal of time in New York in those days, having acquired the house I still live in now. My mother was more content here and was thinking of staying permanently, but we dutifully returned to Philadelphia when word came that my father was dying. Margery was there too. She and her husband and son lived nearby and it was expected that we would all be in attendance at the end but no one, not even Margery, could know that my reasons for wanting to be there when Magnus Wexler died, had nothing to do with propriety or daughterly affection. I came to him then and told him that Jerome had been murdered and I knew because it was I who told the girl's father that Jerome would be alone in those woods that day, and that I had done that because of what happened to me those long years ago. I believe my father died with a great deal of shame and perhaps guilt, but I had

the satisfaction of seeing self-doubt on his face, perhaps for the first and only time in his selfish life.

"Jerome saw young women as prey—no young girl was really safe with him and while I have suspected that Wexlers dot the county because of Jerome, I am sure of only one terrible instance with that poor young girl, Agatha White, who came to work for us when she was only thirteen years old. Everyone said she was slow and perhaps she was, but she was shy and uneducated and no match for the handsome young son of her employer. I believe my father actually knew that Jerome used this poor girl for his own evil pleasure and it eventually resulted in a pregnancy," Sherman read, pausing again to sip his coffee and appreciate Terry's reaction.

"Wow," Terry said, shaking his head. "That's all pretty shocking, isn't it? Sounds like some dark novel or a movie kids couldn't go to." Sherman Dumont agreed and went on with the letter.

"Oddly enough, for once, the Wexler women—my mother, my sister and I, were willing to confront my father on behalf of this poor young girl who had been with us since she was almost a child. Because of our intervention, Aggie was allowed to return to our home and employment along with the baby that is, quite ironically now, the only living Wexler grandchild and my nephew."

Sherman Dumont stopped, shaking his head and looking very serious. "There is quite a bit more and you can read this at your leisure. The file I'm giving you has this letter and a few other pertinent items we've copied for you. When I sent young Mr. April out to Kentbury to find this Augustus Peter White, who was apparently known as Gaffer White, Miss Wexler explained that he was slow, worked as some kind of handyman and she felt she should have done much more for him over the years. We paid the small bills associated with the house he lived in, but I don't think Miss Wexler ever realized how bad the house was, from what you've told me. She refused to go there and apparently had not been in Kentbury since 1911, when she moved with her mother to Philadelphia. I will also say, and this is just a personal assessment, that Lenore Wexler became much softer, if that's the right word, in just the last six months or so, after she was diagnosed with cancer. She does not state it in this letter, but there was a separate note to me regarding the Will and there's a copy of that here which you can read later," he explained.

"Well, Agatha White died in 1935. I gather they were at the Wexler Estate in Kentbury for a long time, sort of caretakers or something, and then after that fire they moved to a kind of boarding house, but somebody had to pay for things all those years. Was that Miss Wexler?" Terry wanted to know.

"That's correct. She had a little information that my father would pass to her from a fellow who worked for us, something like what Rudy April does, but we now suspect this man was not so honest and his information was not reliable and the money he should have passed on over the years to Agatha White and her son, was not always delivered as it should have been. He is dead, by the way, so we'll never know for sure, but we do believe that's the case," Sherman said.

Did Agatha or her son actually know who was taking care of them all these years?" Terry asked.

I believe Agatha White did know, but it was an unusual arrangement. I think the Whites took it for granted in a way, having been looked after to some degree all those years and when Agatha White died, it was actually quite a while before Miss Wexler was informed about that and by then young Mr. White had left the boarding house. When he was tracked down, it was at that house owned by the Wexlers! I guess there's irony in that, but I do not believe Mr. White ever knew who owned the house he was in, but there we are. Actually, the house was originally inherited by Margery Wexler and then passed to Lenore when Margery died," Sherman said.

"So, that letter Rudy April delivered from you was telling Mr. White about his inheritance. But now what happens? Miss Wexler is dead. Gaffer White is dead, who gets her estate now? There are no relatives anywhere, I gather," Terry asked.

"Yes, that letter did deal with the estate and there's a copy in the file I'm giving you and I am very concerned that you think it was stolen. You are sure it wasn't consumed in the fire, or just lost?" Sherman asked.

"I suppose both those scenarios are possible, Mr. Dumont, but Chief Campbell and I feel whoever killed Gaffer White took that letter and we even wonder if that could have been the actual motive. One big question though, is how would he have known about it in the first place?" Terry said.

"This should be fairly routine since Mr. White died so shortly after Miss Wexler, the Will can stand as it would have if he actually died first.

We are required, and will of course, make every effort to find any living relatives, but we are fairly confident about the Wexlers, the Ballards, which was Mrs. Wexlers family and then Agatha White's family, but according to Miss Wexler, Agatha White was an orphan. It seems hard to believe that there isn't some direct relation, but right now it appears that these families are gone. Some were lost in the First War, several are documented as dying in the Spanish Flu pandemic and the last we knew of was a cousin who died at Pearl Harbor in 1941," Sherman said, shaking his head at the sad fate of the Wexlers.

"There is a two page document here from Miss Wexler that deals with Agatha White, the birth of her son, his baptism and so forth. It is not really a letter, more of a summary, but I'm sure you will find it interesting and possibly helpful in your investigation. It also seems unlikely that Mr. White fathered any children . . . ," he trailed off.

"But Miss Wexler suggested that her brother might have fathered other children in Hunterdon County. What about them?" Terry asked.

"Well, I agree that it is certainly a possibility, but how likely would it be that any of these people would come forth? Or would they even actually know that their ancestor could be Jerome Wexler? And if they did come forth, what proof would they have? Sometimes we advertise for heirs, but this is rather tricky and we will probably begin with private enquiries. Unfortunately, Rudy April will not be available to help with the investigation since you know he's been drafted, but if we need to send anyone else to Kentbury, I'll be sure and let you know," Sherman said.

Terry assured him that Chief Campbell would share what he could when appropriate and that this new information could surely be the key they needed to unlock the mystery, but the burning questions were still unanswered: who killed these two people, how were they connected and just where did all of this Wexler history and all the church stuff fit in?

Terry called his boss from his in-laws large apartment near Central Park. He couldn't begin to convey all the new information in a phone call, but since Bull and Lou were attending Etta's funeral tomorrow, expecting to be back late, Bull suggested they get in early Thursday morning to go over the compelling new material from Mr. Dumont. Terry and Joyce were planning to catch the 5:30 commuter train, giving them plenty of time for a leisurely lunch and a little shopping.

The train left on time and Terry and Joyce had an end seat to themselves as they pored over the letter and other amazing bits of information contained in the precious file. Only one car away from the lounge, Terry was having a hard time ignoring the cigarette smoke drifting by, but he had his last drag almost a week ago, determined to conquer the habit Joyce hated so much. He popped another Lifesaver. It helped.

It was still light when they got home and it was a landmark day for lots of reasons, including Joyce nodding a hello to Trixie Feinberg, the fashion editor, who Terry wouldn't know in a million years, but Joyce was thrilled. Kentbury was still just a little sleepy town, but lots of areas in Hunterdon County seemed to attract these New York celebrities, and New Hope and Bucks County, just over the county line in Pennsylvania, boasted artists, novelists and noted Broadway stars, and sometimes they took the train from Kentbury. Joyce said it was definitely a day to remember!

Dinner was an impromptu buffet Joyce arranged on the little dining table. Terry sat there, piling his plate with all the wonderful treats from their favorite New York deli while Joyce took her plate to the coffee table so she could sit on the couch and pore over the papers that, more and more, were reading like a gothic novel.

"Terry, look at this," she said, holding a paper from the file marked, "Miscellaneous Correspondence. "I wonder if Mr. Dumont saw this. It's some kind of ledger, but there are notations in the margins that relate to Aggie White . . . listen," she began.

"It's not exactly an accounts ledger, but it makes note of something titled 'Special Expenditures' dating from March 1 to July 1, 1901. There are dates and amounts, then in other columns marked <u>Item</u> and <u>Notation</u>, there are mostly initials and a few odd words that really make me think this has to relate to Aggie and her baby. Here, what do you think?" Joyce asked as Terry came to sit beside her.

"Hmm, yeah, Honey, you could be onto something," he said. "Like this . . . 'March 1 is the first entry and it just states Train Fare—75c, Room & Board—$2.00, then way on the right margin is AW . . . not a real leap to assume Agatha White," Terry said.

"Exactly! And these entries for $3.00, Doctor Visit, that's in early June and more entries for room and board, and only one more mention of a Doctor on June 15, the day after Gaffer was born and it's for $5.00, then in the next column $200! What's that about?" Joyce wanted to know.

"A bribe?" Terry said. "Something about Aggie and the baby? But it wasn't exactly a secret, was it?'

"Aggie being pregnant wasn't a secret, but maybe this doctor knew who the father was," Joyce speculated.

"What are these few payouts to cousins?" Terry asked.

Joyce ran down the columns that cited payments for room and board. Most of them had a notation to the right which read, "Cousins."

"Aggie didn't have any family, maybe it's Wexler cousins. But, look, here's one for room and board and the notation says 'Farmer'," Terry noted.

"I don't know, Sweetheart, but I think we have to see what cousins we're talking about and . . ." Terry cut her off.

"Well, Farmer is a name that came up in Etta's investigation. She inquired about the name with Father Hanover, but he didn't have any records with that name. Dolly mentioned it too. I think we've got some real leads and . . . beautiful lady . . . I will get to that tomorrow," Terry said with a sigh that turned into a yawn.

"I don't know about you, but the city did me in. You up for an early night?" he asked with what Joyce called his impish grin.

"Depends. Are you planning on just sleeping or what?" she asked, following her husband to the bedroom, unbuttoning her blouse along the way.

TWENTY-THREE

Fred Browning was taking care of routine things out front while Bull and Terry were sequestered in the back office with stacks of documents, coffee cups, and remains from lunch, testifying to the almost four hours they had spent so far going over what they knew, what they learned, and what leads they would pursue. Terry used an old bulletin board to arrange a map of sorts for the crimes, of who what and when, impressing the chief anew with how sharp and how smart his deputy was.

Today's *Kentbury Kaller* lay on the table with a front page tribute to Etta Marx written by Nelson Hunt and showing some very nice photographs of Etta he must have gotten from her sister. Nothing in the article made reference to why Etta might have been killed which the Kentbury policemen appreciated.

Bull reported there were about fifty people at the funeral, more than half from Kentbury, including Minnie Lester and the friend who drove her, but no one he would consider suspicious. It was a nice service, Lou cried and they were both glad they had a chance to meet Etta's sister and convey their condolences.

The first thing Terry showed his boss this morning was the copy of the letter which was delivered to Gaffer by Rudy April. Terry and Joyce read it three times, now Chief Campbell gave it his undivided attention.

Dear Mr. White:

I represent Miss Lenore Gregson Wexler who passed away July 11, 1951. It was Miss Wexler's wish, as reflected in her Last Will and Testament, that a portion of her estate be conveyed to Augustus Peter White, residing in the Borough of Kentbury, County of Hunterdon, in the state of New Jersey. It would be beneficial to you if you could come to our offices to sign papers and very importantly to verify that you are indeed the rightful heir, born on June 14, 1901, to Agatha White. A copy of your birth certificate and any other documents you possess would also be helpful.

Enclosed you will find $100 in cash to pay for your travel to our office and for any other needs as you see fit.

Please feel free to call me with any questions and I look forward to meeting you and moving forward with your inheritance.

Congratulations and all the best wishes, I am,

Most sincerely,
Sherman X. Dumont

Bull finished, shaking his head in amazement. "I guess he didn't have a clue to who he was dealing with. I can't believe Miss Wexler didn't tell him that Gaffer wasn't gonna hop a train and find his way to this Park Avenue law office, let alone 'call with any questions!'" he said.

"He's a lawyer, Chief. This is lawyer talk. I guess he thought it was all pretty routine, but once Rudy April reported what Gaffer was like, Mr. Dumont realized he would probably have to come out here to get things rolling, but before he arranged any of that, poor old Gaffer was murdered. Sherman Dumont is a nice guy, but he just didn't know," Terry explained.

Bull read Lenore Wexler's letter first, punctuating almost every new shocking paragraph with some mild expletives and a few not so mild, but who could blame him? Terry read it twice again since Tuesday and still found it shocking. Terry was quick to tell his boss that Joyce was privy to the file and Bull's comment was, "I share most things with Lou, son. This kind of stuff needs to be talked about and a wife is a trusted listener—or should be. I know lots of cops who hardly tell their wives the time of day, but that's their problem I guess," he said.

"I made a special point of thanking Dolly, by the way, for all the good work so far. All that time and effort to track down that damn fancy stationary and then the answer walks in the door, but Dolly does good work and she says this Mr. Tandy is someone good to know."

Terry agreed. Bull said that Lou suggested some flowers for the intrepid librarian would go a long way in saying thank you. Terry agreed with that too.

Stupid, stupid kids! I couldn't take the bat with me, I had to hide it. It was the only thing I could think to do. Now the damn police have it. Well, there really is no way to link it to me, is there? There's no way to know who took it or where it came from. Greg will get everything now. He's the rightful heir now. These people don't matter—they could never understand. I would love to just smash those stupid, nosey Brewer brats. I could. I could just get that Henry kid and push him down one of the mine shafts. That's a pleasant thought. Oh well, tomorrow's another day. We'll just see what opportunities might arise.

Now it felt like they had too much information. Terry still had not made it to Califon to talk to Father March but after their pleasant visit with Dolly and Neal Argyle, he was hoping to have another outing with Joyce and stop at The Boathouse after the official visit at the church.

Friday afternoon found Terry and Joyce having a counter lunch at the Califon Drug Store. The sandwiches were good, but the Wellman's Dairy ice cream cones they enjoyed while strolling along for their two o'clock appointment with Father March, were outstanding! The Wexler Dairy was bought by a dairy family in Flemington and eventually became Wellman's, known locally for its fine ice cream.

"Well, at least they didn't have to get new monogrammed towels," Joyce said, making one of her designer jokes that Terry loved.

Hints of fall were beginning to show on two maple trees gracing the lawn in front of Saint Paul's. The old stone church was small, chapel-like, with well-tended grounds and abundant flowers in neat, colorful medleys. A smiling Father March stood in the doorway waiting to greet the young couple walking up the cobblestone pathway.

"Welcome, welcome!" A rim of reddish hair circled the young man's balding head. Combined with the cossack he was wearing, it was no great leap to see him as a 14th century monk greeting visitors to his monastery. Medium height and build, brilliant blue eyes sparkled with an infectious enthusiasm. Joyce had a flash of being in England—there was something old worldly about the moment and Father March could be stepping out of a Gothic novel.

After a few moments spent admiring the old church, they got to the reason for the visit.

"Miss Marx wanted to know about any records from 1900 to 1910 that dealt with the name White or Wexler. I told her I would be happy to look for something, but I am ashamed to say I was more interested in tending the gardens than looking through the old records which, frankly, are a terrible mess. I've been trying to make order of the current records since I've been here, but I just didn't think they were that important," Father March said, somewhat sheepishly.

In spite of a sincere eagerness to help, the young priest had little to show the Kramers but did promise to make a real effort, especially since it could relate to a murder mystery of all things. He promised to call if he found anything. He liked the Kramers and Joyce told Terry she thought he was happy to meet some young people his own age.

"Yeah, nice fellow, but we're not Catholic, so . . ." Terry commented.

"You know my parents' old friend, Monsignor Picard? He was a parish priest when they first met and I think it's because they weren't Roman Catholic that their friendship grew. They had enough in common, like fishing and fine dining, that their friendship grew from that, with nothing to do with religion," Joyce said. So it was agreed they might have a new friend, and Terry was hoping it would begin with valuable information from the church records.

The Boat House was enchanting. Terry and Joyce agreed, when talking about it later, that it could be a museum people would pay to tour. Scattered around the imposing wood and stone buildings were canoes in various sizes and varieties, many with tags denoting where they were going; others sat in different stages of creation. Some were just beginning to be recognizable as a canoe or boat while others waited for final touches of paint or design, but each was a work of art. The unique scent, wood shavings and sawdust mingled with odors of paints and glue, with a top note of river smells, was invigorating; a little primeval, evocative and memorable. There was a peacefulness here, no one around, but Terry and Joyce followed scraping sounds through to the second building, finding Neal Argyle at work on a large canoe. They watched quietly for a moment, admiring their new friend.

"Terry, Joyce, I'm so glad you could make it!" he said, looking up from his project to greet the couple. "Let me give you a tour!"

An hour flew by as Neal introduced them to a few co-workers, regaling his visitors with the history of the company, enhanced by the dozens of framed photographs hanging on the grand pillars and wooden walls of the beautiful old buildings. They were delighted to watch a young man working on a duck decoy, appreciating the craftsmanship of the beautiful ducks, geese and fish that sat on shelves and display cases scattered throughout. Several workers were making the important paddles, attractive enough that Joyce thought they would be perfect accents in the right décor.

Originally started by returning Union Soldiers in 1866, the first Boat House was destroyed by fire in 1871. They rebuilt, this time with two large buildings sitting on the banks of the river, and in 1873, in a bit of brilliant marketing, they presented a canoe to re-elected President, Ulysses S. Grant. Every U.S. President after that would get a canoe, some then being donated to a charity or The Boy Scouts, but in 1904 Teddy Roosevelt promoted the company with unabashed enthusiasm for such a fine gift and, while never an exclusive supplier, the little company in Califon had, every year since, sold their hand-crafted products to park services around the country. Hanging proudly by the office wall was a picture of Teddy and two of his children in the 1904 canoe, along with a letter from the President on official White House stationary. As Terry and Joyce admired the photo, a petite woman, wearing dungarees, white blouse and a silver Indian necklace, popped out of the office. Her silver grey hair was done in a long, single braid and Joyce's immediate impression was that of an artist.

"Naomi, I want you to meet some friends from Kentbury—Terry and Joyce Kramer, this is my boss, Naomi Cousins," said Neal.

During the prescribed greetings, smiles and handshakes, Terry and Joyce exchanged looks, realizing what this could mean. Naomi Cousins caught the look.

"What's the matter—not used to a woman in Levi's?" she said with a chuckle.

"No, ma'am," Terry said, already putting on his police persona, "it's just that I'm the Deputy Chief of Police in Kentbury and . . ."

"And you're investigating those horrible murders!" she interrupted.

"Yes, ma'am, that's correct. And we have been looking at a lot of old records, some going back to the turn of the century. I'm wondering, Mrs., uh . . ."

"It's Miss, Terry, but you call me Naomi and that will just make everything more comfortable, wouldn't it?" she asked.

"Fine, ma'am . . . uh . . . Naomi," he said while Joyce looked on with a little grin. Naomi was a character, a very likeable one.

While Neal excused himself to get back to work, Naomi invited the young couple into her office. A fan was whirling overhead. Richly-aged wood-paneled walls were full of more photographs and testimonials, a Navajo-style rug graced the floor and Terry and Joyce were more than comfortable in soft leather chairs. Naomi's antique desk sat in front of a large window that looked out to the river and Joyce not only admired the good taste, she realized it was the kind of office to readily appeal to The Boat House clientele.

"So, am I a suspect? I sure hope not, I've got too much work to do," Naomi stated.

"Well, no, of course not," Terry began, "but in looking at old documents which could have a bearing on the murders, we've seen notations for "cousins." We've been thinking it meant a relative, but the name is connected to Califon and meeting you now . . . well . . ."

"A light bulb went off," Naomi Cousins said. "Well, how can I help you, Terry?"

After twenty minutes of focused conversation, they learned that Naomi's family settled in Califon in the early 1800's. She had a brother living in Millville, Pennsylvania and a few Cousin cousins lived in New York, but she was the last of the family in Califon. No, she had not immediately thought about any connection when she heard about Gaffer White's murder but she remembered family talk about a pregnant girl staying with the people who worked for her family way back then.

"How old was this poor man who was murdered?" Naomi asked.

"Mr. White was born in 1901," Terry said.

"Hmm . . . well, I came along a few years later, but my brother, Jonathan, the one who lives in Pennsylvania, is the oldest. He might remember some of what was going on then. I can give you his address and telephone number if that would help," she said.

"That would be very helpful . . . Naomi. But tell me, do you know who was working for your family in 1901?" Terry asked.

"Oh, certainly. That was the Farmer family. Binnie, the mother, was the cook. Her daughter, Violet, did the cleaning I think, and the husband was kind of the handyman, but I believe he might have worked at the dairy too. There was a cottage on the property then, and they lived there. By the time I came along, my parents employed a family named Lusk. That's who I first remember. Then there were the Quinns. They still live in Califon, but they're not house servants anymore. Patrick Quinn works here and his son, who's still in high school, works weekends with us but he wants to go to college, then come back and buy me out!" she said with a chuckle.

"Do you happen to know what became of the Farmers?" Joyce asked.

"I think they went to New York, but Jonathan will probably know," Naomi said.

"You have been very helpful, ma'am . . . Naomi. I may need to speak with you again if that's all right," Terry said.

"You come any time, Terry, and bring your pretty gal too," she said.

"I think she's seen too many westerns," Joyce said as they were walking to the car, but they liked the very direct woman and agreed that it was another fun and productive day. They decided the weekend could be spent going over more papers and looking through the photo albums, especially now with some definite names to work with. First though, they made a stop at the office to make a long distance call to Jonathan Cousins in Millville.

TWENTY-FOUR

Terry was up and out early on Saturday to do a quick patrol of the town. He and Bull were taking turns several times a day to be visible, covering most of Kentbury in about an hour. Joyce did grocery shopping, prepared lunch, planned dinner, did a little housekeeping and just when she thought she could get to files and old photo albums, her mother called. Fifteen minutes later, Gloria Skinner popped in to ask if Terry could help get their cat out of a tree, so the day flew by. After drinks and dinner, Terry had definite ideas about how to spend the rest of the evening and the case, old letters, old photos and new information, were all put on hold while the young couple took a welcome break.

Sunday morning, refreshed and renewed, Terry left for patrol right after breakfast. All the churches seemed well attended and the rest of Kentbury was peaceful and quiet, at least it appeared so. It was hard to believe there was someone out there who was a murderer—someone they must know, and would they strike again? The murders cast a pall over the little town; the dark shadows of fear and mistrust seeped into every home, every life—it was an evil cancer they had to stop. He reached for the pack of Camels waiting smugly in the glove compartment, but squelched the urge and popped a stick of gum instead.

While Terry was on patrol, Joyce was curled up on the couch with the albums and photos they borrowed from Mary VanHaven. Halfway through the oldest album full of sepia-toned cabinet photos and even a few tintypes from the Civil War era, Joyce found herself looking at a small newspaper clipping from *The Kentbury Kaller* dated 1904, talking about an annual employee picnic hosted by the Wexlers at some park near the dairy in Califon. Joyce added that to her notes she was keeping, hoping something would click and the bits and pieces might come together to provide answers or at least some insight. As a history buff, it was a pleasurable task; she was enjoying the intimate knowledge about Kentbury and its colorful past.

When Terry got back, Joyce was surrounded by piles of photos, he took care of a few house projects, then offered to make lunch, appreciating his wife's dedication and not wanting to interrupt the important research.

"Honey, look at this," Joyce said between bites of her sandwich. "I think this is the Farmer family you're looking for. Didn't Jonathan Cousins say the family came back to visit in the summers?"

"Yeah, he did and he was just a little kid, but he remembers his mother saying they moved from Califon to New York. He said he was eight or nine the last time he saw them, probably sometime around 1905. Apparently Mrs. Farmer liked to get out of the city and spend a few weeks in the country, but he said there was some kind of problem and his mother asked Binnie to please not come back. Unfortunately, he doesn't know why, but says that's what he remembers," Terry said, again relating part of the conversation he had with Naomi's big brother.

He was anxious to tell the chief about it first thing tomorrow, and if he and Joyce could gather other bits and pieces, even better.

Terry studied the old photo showing a rather large woman in a long print dress and big straw hat, flanked by a young boy in knickers and a young girl with a toddler on her lap. Terry thought they looked uncomfortable but people rarely seemed to smile in old photos for some reason. Scrawled in ink on the back was "Binnie," but no other notations.

"Yeah . . . Binnie Farmer would be my guess. Are there anymore?" Terry asked.

"Wait a minute!" Joyce said, jumping up and retrieving the detailed letter Lenore Wexler wrote to Mr. Dumont.

"Look, this is what I thought—it's just one word, but it could mean a lot," Joyce said, scanning the letter for the word she mentioned. "Here, here it is: *'Because of our intervention, Aggie was allowed to return to our home.'* Return, Terry, not stay at our home, but return," she said with great satisfaction.

Terry was impressed. He should have picked up on that but thanks to his amazing wife, that tiny clue would seem to confirm what Jonathan Cousins said about Agatha White spending time in Califon, staying at the cottage with the Farmers but obviously with permission from the

Cousins who employed Binnie Farmer. Resisting the impulse to bother the chief with the promising clues, he and Joyce spent the next few hours looking through the old photos. There was a small pile dating from the late 1890's, which they wanted to go over with Mary VanHaven, or anyone else who might have knowledge about the long-ago images.

Reading another letter from Lenore Wexler, they learned that even though Aggie White and her child were residing at the Wexler home in Kentbury, Jerome apparently had no interest in the boy and spent more and more time away.

My mother made sure the little boy had proper care and Aggie proved to be an attentive mother, but the child was slow and my father ignored him and discouraged any attention to the child from us. It seems cruel when I look back, but we easily fell into a belief that we had done as much as we could and at least they were not abandoned. I now realize there was so much more that we could have done, but we had pushed Father to his limit, as it were, and there really were times when we could almost forget that this forlorn little boy was in fact a Wexler.

It was hard to imagine such a strange arrangement, but everything about the Wexlers was strange it seemed. It did give them more insight into what a sad life Gaffer must have had, and Terry felt more determined than ever to find the person who made the end of Gaffer White's life as miserable as the beginning.

The weekend was pleasingly quiet for the Campbells and the Kramers. Lou even persuaded Bull to go see a movie. Monday morning, however, brought so many leads and directions to go, even Terry was thinking of asking Leonard Smith for help.

"Terry, I'm going to see Chief Riggs. Leonard has some damn idea he wants to tell me about, so I'll be out of the county for a while. I hoped to see Father Hanover, but he's having tests or something, so maybe tomorrow, but I want us to meet back here—by four if you can, and we'll compare notes. You need to go see what the heck is going on at the Brewers. It's all right with me if you want Joyce to go see Father March, and somebody needs to see what Raymond Newberry called about!" Bull said, almost out of breath reading the day's roster.

Joyce was more than happy with an assignment to go see Father March in Califon; Terry began his day at the Brewers, then would go on to the Newberrys, and the chief headed for a visit with Chief Riggs in Warren County. Monday was off to a running start!

Tilly Brewer met Terry on the porch and invited him inside. With thick plaster walls and a fan whirling away in the corner, the interesting old house was surprisingly cool inside. Baby Penny sat in her playpen but the boys were not in evidence. In contrast to his previous visits, things seemed unusually quiet. Terry politely declined the offer of coffee or lemonade, but was impressed with the immaculate kitchen, again admiring this busy lady's abilities as a homemaker. Before he could ask, Tilly explained that the older boys were at their jobs and the others were cleaning out the barn, cautioned not to disturb her until she called them.

Terry took a seat at the long wooden table as Tilly produced an envelope from her apron pocket. "This is what I wanted you to see, Deputy," she said, gingerly handing him the note she found this morning. "I walked down the lane to put in a letter to my sister and this was sitting in the mailbox," she explained.

Terry inspected the plain white envelope. It had little to tell. Addressed only to "Mrs. Brewer," it was printed with red ink in large block letters, as was the sinister note inside.

YOUR NOSEY BRATS SHOULD DIE

Tilly looked at Terry with pursed lips, hands on hips, showing more anger than fear it seemed to him, but obviously looking to the deputy for answers.

"What time did you say you found this, Mrs. Brewer?" he asked.

"It was early. I wrote my sister last night and walked down to the mailbox after Ned left for work, a little before eight. Our mail comes early and I didn't want to miss it," she explained.

The Brewer's mailbox sat at the end of their long lane. With the winding drive, it was not really visible from the house, so the note could have been put there anytime.

"I suppose you wouldn't hear a car from here would you?" Terry asked.

"With the windows open at night to bring in the cool air, we do sometimes hear a car but I honestly can't say that we heard anything unusual," Tilly said. "But what I want to know," she went on, "is this real or some stupid kids trying to scare me?"

"Well, even if it is kids, it is a very nasty thing to do. Does anyone come to mind who might play a prank like this?" Terry wanted to know.

Tilly Brewer could think of no one that mean and jumped to the logical concern that it might come from the murderer plaguing their town.

"I can't say it isn't, ma'am, and I'll need to take this with me, if that's all right, but let's do this," Terry said, hoping to reassure Tilly and cautioning her at the same time. "Let's take this seriously, better to be safe, keep the boys close if you can but don't scare them. I assume they're smart about talking to strangers, getting in cars, that kind of thing," he said.

"Oh, they're smart enough, Deputy, but they all have that independent streak too. I'll think of a way to keep them around and I'll tell Ned when he gets home, then we can both tell Russell and Edmund, they're old enough to understand and to help keep the others in line. Henry and George are the ones who wander wherever they please and they're the ones who found that hateful baseball bat. Don't worry, I'll keep a special eye on them," she said.

Terry admired Tilly's staunch resolve. She was a formidable lady but hardly a match for a menacing murderer. Terry's mind was whirling with what this really meant if, in fact, it was the killer who wrote the troubling note: just what kind of maniac were they dealing with? Most criminals want to stay in the shadows and don't write notes to call attention to themselves, especially notes that threaten children. Terry was anxious to show the note to Bull and Marvin Walsh as well, but the chief was out of the office, so Terry went up Prescott Avenue to the Newberrys.

Raymond Newberry met Terry at the door, using his cane but determined to greet the deputy properly, ushering him into his home office. The house was quiet and the retired banker explained that Mrs. Newberry was out and Ona Birch was running errands. Terry took a chair, admiring the well-appointed, welcoming room, more den than office he thought.

After a few pleasantries, Raymond Newberry gave the reason for his call this morning.

"Terry, it's possible—and I hate to even think it—but I'm concerned that the baseball bat we've been hearing about as the murder weapon could be mine," he said.

Terry gave Mr. Newberry his full attention, nodding for him to go on.

"Look here," he said, handing Terry an old photo of a young boy in knickers proudly holding a brand new Reach baseball bat. "This was my ninth birthday. I've always been a baseball fan, as was my father. I was so proud the day I got that bat and would never have gotten rid of it, but somehow I think it wound up with the things in the garage and went out with the trash for that last pick up day we had," he told Terry.

Terry immediately thought of the wicker chairs he coveted that now sat on his front porch, thanks to his shameless wife. He realized that if the bat was inadvertently thrown away, anyone could have come by and claimed it. The trash men could have taken it and if it did make it to the dump, it could have been claimed from there. But the timing was off. Terry had lots of questions.

"Mr. Newberry, I assume you asked Mrs. Newberry or anyone else in the house, Mrs. Birch, Sharon, if they had seen it?"

"Oh yes, of course, and I even wondered if poor old Gaffer could have taken it, but no one seems to even remember seeing it," he said.

"Sir, we do believe the bat we have was used for both murders and that would mean it would have to have been taken at least a week before the clean up day. When is the last time you actually saw it?" Terry wanted to know.

"It's funny. I had it in this room for years, sitting there in the corner. Last Christmas Mabel was decorating and asked if she could please put the bat somewhere else until after the New Year. I didn't see how it could be in the way, but she asked and so I agreed. I thought it was going in the hall closet but I forgot about it until this murder business and it wasn't in the closet, it wasn't anywhere! I asked about it and no one knew anything. Mabel said she didn't even remember asking about it last Christmas. Now, honestly, how ridiculous is that?" he asked, obviously agitated at the loss of a childhood treasure.

Terry saw tears in the dignified man's eyes as he began to speak.

"My father gave me that bat, Terry. It was a kind of noble thing to me, and I cannot believe it could ever be used for such foul purposes, you know?" he said.

Terry was struck again by just how far reaching these terrible crimes were. So many people were being touched by the evil events and he knew it would change them, and Kentbury, forever.

"Mr. Newberry, was there anything distinctive about the bat—markings, carved initials, something that would allow us to identify it as yours? What about the handle, was it wrapped? Terry wanted to know.

"Oh, yes. It was wrapped with cloth tape—pretty worn, but still there. It was well used, lots of memories on that old bat. No, I never carved my initials in it. There were scratches and dings and some of the logo was worn away, nothing really special. Oh, expect maybe a long blue stain near the top where my cousin scrapped it along a stone wall. I was pretty upset about that, but it made that mark, didn't really hurt the bat, thank goodness. That's all I can think of Terry. If you can, please let me know what you find out," he asked. Terry assured him he would.

TWENTY-FIVE

Triple-wrapped in brown paper bags, Joyce was hoping the Wellman's Ice Cream would make it home without melting. She couldn't resist the opportunity to surprise Terry with it, along with the valuable information she and Father March uncovered.

"Great!" Joyce said aloud when she placed the two pints of precious ice cream in the small freezer, still hard after the drive from Califon. Joyce called the office and left a message for Terry to call her if he got a chance. No, it was nothing urgent.

A cool bath, change of clothes, she was preparing dinner when Terry called back.

"Well, it's just an idea, Honey, but I would love to see that baptismal certificate you said you had for Gaffer White. No, I want to tell you my theory in person . . . I want to see your face," she said, almost playfully and slightly annoying Terry, but only for a second.

"Ok, deal, but there's a penalty for withholding evidence," he said, being playful himself.

"Oh, I hope so," she said

The mood was set for the evening it seemed, but Terry said he could not be sure when he would be home, explaining that he was on his way to see Marvin Walsh in Clinton, and that Bull was still with Chief Riggs and Leonard. The plan was to meet back at the station to compare notes, but he hoped to get home before dark, so Joyce put dinner on hold, something she was getting good at.

There's that horrible Brewer brat. Look a him! Snooping around in the garbage like some rat . . . all those kids . . . that family breeds like rats. I bet I could offer him a ride . . . promise a box of soda bottles, he wouldn't hesitate.

Oh for god's sake, who's that? That fat librarian. She thinks she's so superior, so educated. See you later, Henry. See you later, fat Dolly!

Dolly barely noticed the old Dodge pull away from the parking lot as she went to her car. She was closing early today but took a moment to talk to the young Brewer boy who appeared intent on searching the trash cans sitting in the corner by the old building.

"Henry?" What on earth are you looking for?" she asked.

"Look, Mrs. Argyle!" he said, pointing to a small pile of treasures which included soda bottles, wood blocks and an old picture frame.

"Now how are you going to carry all of that, young man?" Dolly asked, amused and somewhat admiring of the boy's enterprise.

"Oh, I got my bag," he said, holding up a small canvas bag with "HENRY," painted on the front in big black letters.

"Henry, are you supposed to be out here alone?" she asked, not knowing about the threatening note, but generally concerned for any child in Kentbury at the moment. About to offer him a ride home, George Brewer appeared with his own bag of treasures, and while the boys tried to convince her they were fine and planned more treasure hunting on their way home, Dolly insisted on driving them, and ten minutes later deposited them at their lane.

"I'll just wait until you turn the corner," she said, making sure they actually went home.

"Thank you, Mrs. Argyle," they said, admitting they were hot and thirsty and tomorrow was another day.

TWENTY-SIX

"If you can fit in a trip to Princeton, Terry, Dr. Appleton can see you today or tomorrow. Here's his number, you can make the arrangements," Marvin Walsh said.

Terry was pacing in the part-time coroner's little office, thinking about a hundred things at once, but appreciated Dr. Walsh taking the time to refer him to an old friend who was a noted psychiatrist. Terry wasn't sure about the science that was usually the topic of jokes and jibes, but he also knew human nature was an unpredictable, complicated thing. What made a criminal? Why did people commit murder, and why would they write weird notes to taunt a poor mother? He couldn't be sure if the murderer wrote the note to Tilly Brewer, but his gut told him he had. His instinct to take the note to Dr Walsh proved right. The doctor agreed it had a sinister aspect and could have been written by the murderer. He also appreciated that this young policeman was far thinking enough to realize the ramifications of such an important clue and ask for his help.

"Now to the bat, Terry. Let's have a look," the doctor said, lifting the murder weapon onto the examining table in the small office laboratory.

"I'll be damned!" Terry said.

There it was. There was the long blue stain he hoped would not be there. A little hard to see with the blood stains dominating the wood but, knowing what to look for, Dr. Walsh was able to find the older, bluish mark.

"Are you sure, Doc, it's not some other kind of mark, like ink or something?" Terry asked.

"No. It's consistent with what you told me and besides, what are the odds that there would be another blue stain on a Reach bat, just where Raymond Newberry said it would be?"

149

Terry had to agree. This was so important. But if no one could say who took the bat or when, he wasn't sure just what kind of clue it provided. What if Gaffer took it? But he wasn't known to steal things. Who would take it out of the hall closet? Mrs. Newberry, Sharon, Mrs. Birch? That was a pretty unlikely suspect list.

Terry knew he would have to deliver the troubling news to the bat's owner and he understood what that would do to the poor man: not only was it used to kill two people, he would never see it again—it almost felt like another murder.

Fred Browning was happy to stay as long as he was needed while the chief and Terry compared the day's findings. Terry got back first and added to the outline on the case board they put together and after studying the growing bits of evidence and information, he thought there could be a few things starting to connect the dots, but so much seemed hardly believable and definitely disturbing.

When Bull returned and apprised Terry about his meeting with Chief Riggs and Leonard, "disturbing" was definitely the word Terry was thinking, and this potential new piece of the puzzle came by way of Leonard Smith, making it even more unpalatable.

"We agree Leonard's a pain in the ass, but he's a policeman after all, and we can't discount what he saw. He had the license plate numbers which I ran and the first one is hers, the other one belongs to Tony Rothman. Leonard said as much because he saw them, but I wanted to be sure," Bull said.

"Jefferson, McCloud & Rothman?" Terry asked, referring to one of Clinton's oldest law firms.

"The same," Bull said. "Seems the first time he saw the cars along by the gorge was late May. He didn't think much about it since summer was here and he knew folks were spending more time there, fishing, picnicking and besides, it was in Kentbury, Hunterdon County, not his jurisdiction, but you know Leonard . . . the second time he saw the same two cars in that parking area, he saw them walking back together. He recognized them of course and knew he was seeing a rendezvous. His word, not mine," Bull said.

"Near Gaffer White's cottage?" Terry asked.

"You know—that pretty spot where all the trees come together by the rock overhang. It's not a place everyone knows about, not that easy to find, but the locals know it and it's what . . . couple a hundred yards from Gaffer's place?" Bull asked.

"OK, fine, but what was Gaffer going to do, blackmail 'em?" Terry asked.

"Oh, I agree. I don't think the poor old fella ever paid any attention to visitors and tourists. He kept to himself."

"But he might have recognized the car and . . . what . . . said hi or something?" Terry suggested.

"Hell, I don't know. Look, let's do this: you're going to Princeton tomorrow to see this head doctor, so you can make a visit to Sharon Newberry at the same time; make sure she's available. We want to keep this very quiet until we know just what we're talking about," Bull cautioned.

"Hamilton," Terry said.

"Pardon?" Bull asked.

"Sharon Hamilton now, formerly Newberry," Terry explained.

"Well, fine, but she's Sharon Newberry to me," Bull said.

Terry had a hard time believing the new information. There was probably some logical explanation, but he knew what the chief was suggesting: Tony Rothman and Sharon Newberry Hamilton were having an affair.

It was a rare thing when Terry could not put everything in the back of his mind to spend a pleasant evening with Joyce, but he couldn't stop thinking about Sharon Newberry and what it could all mean. He had a quick bath, changed and was glad for the whiskey and soda waiting for him. He was anxious to hear what Joyce had found out, so he sipped his drink and gave her his full attention.

"All right, Deputy Kramer, this is what Father March and I discovered today," she said with just the right touch of drama.

"Poor Father March . . . he was still sorting through the mess in the church office but was pleased to find a few boxes with old files going back to the Civil War up until World War I," she began. "He admitted he kept putting it off and jumped at my offer to help.

"He was only looking for the names Wexler and White, he didn't know about the possible Farmer connection. As soon as I told him, he found old records for them. They did attended St. Paul's but there was nothing for any births, then I found a box that seemed to record specific occasions—you know, weddings, funerals, baptisms. Father March said that is the way he was expected to keep records, but what he found so far was so mixed up he wasn't sure where to look for what. However . . ." Joyce said, pausing for effect and holding up a few old papers, "this was in the file box for baptisms."

Putting down his drink, Terry studied the papers Joyce handed him. Not quite as lovely as the certificate for Gaffer that Bull got from Father Hanover, this was, nonetheless, a hand-written, scrolled record on heavy parchment, documenting the birth of one baby boy born April 9, 1901 and baptized on April 14, 1901, as Francis Gregson Farmer. Joyce then handed Terry Gaffer's baptismal certificate she asked him to bring home. She then pointed out the name on one of the documents from the New York lawyer showing the name—Lenore Gregson Wexler.

"So?" Joyce asked.

"So . . . what are you thinking?" Terry asked.

"I'm thinking there are two sets of records in different churches showing baby boys with the same birthday and one of them has the middle name Gregson," she said.

"Yeah . . ." Terry said, looking at Joyce for ideas and having a few of his own starting to form.

"Terry, I think Gaffer White was a twin!" she announced.

"Shit," Terry said.

"Is that an official response?" Joyce asked.

"Honey, this is . . . this is good, really good. I'm not sure what it means, but I think we have to track down the Farmer family," he said.

Breaking the usual protocol when he was home and off duty, he did not wait to tell his boss about Joyce's theory. Hoping she would not notice he was using the phone instead of the radios he and Bull both had at home, he asked the operator to ring the chief's number. If he used the radio, Joyce could hear what was said; if Bull mentioned Sharon Newberry and Terry's trip to Princeton tomorrow, Joyce might want to go and he did not want to explain why she couldn't.

"Well, I'll be damned," was Bull's first response. "Are you sure, though?"

"Same birthday, the Farmer connection to Agatha White and then the name Gregson. Pretty darn coincidental, wouldn't you say, Chief?" Terry asked.

Bull agreed. But both men realized that instead of narrowing the investigation, the path was getting wider. One led to Gaffer White, the

Wexlers and a small fortune and the other to a possible secret affair. Could it be two different murderers with two different motives? That might be true if the murder weapon wasn't the same.

"We'll know more tomorrow, Terry. In the meantime, take a break, Son, enjoy your dinner. Lou and I are going to watch our new television and get an early night. Call me when you get back from Princeton. I'll see you at the station and we can see where we are then."

Terry appreciated the advice. He and Joyce talked more about the case during dinner . . . it was hard not to.

"We have to remember how different things were back then," Joyce was saying. "From what we know from Lenore Wexler's letters, her father was pulling most of the strings—I can see him separating twins, can't you?" she asked.

Terry really could not imagine that, it was in the category of weird and bizarre as far as he was concerned. He wanted to deal in facts but the deeper he got into this case, the stranger things were. Terry tried to imagine two little babies . . . two innocent little lives. He knew what became of Gaffer—could the other baby, if there was another one—have had a better life?

"Why would someone do that?" Terry asked.

"Yes, I know . . . maybe . . . maybe he didn't want the responsibility of two children in his home. It doesn't sound like Magnus Wexler had a lot of compassion, we know that," she answered.

"Maybe the other baby died," Terry said.

"Uhmm . . . maybe. I can ask Father March to check death and funeral records if you want me to," Joyce suggested and agreed to call him first thing tomorrow.

By the time Joyce brought out her surprise dessert from Wellman's Dairy, the talk shifted to the job she was doing for the Crisp sisters.

Terry was happy for her. Joyce needed to use her talents and education and what better place to begin in Kentbury than Lake Cottage? She started to lose him when the talk turned to damask and chintz, but it relaxed him enough that the day ended the way both hoped it would, safe and sated, lost in each other's arms.

TWENTY-SEVEN

Terry was ten minutes early for his appointment with Dr. Appleton. The drive to Princeton was uneventful; hardly any traffic and the threat of rain matched his mood. He called Sharon Newberry Hamilton and planned to see her after his visit with the psychiatrist.

Oliver Appleton was a pleasant surprise. In spite of himself, Terry was expecting some bow-tied eccentric, looking down his nose at a mere policeman and full of psycho jargon he wouldn't understand. He could not have been more wrong.

"Deputy Kramer, may I call you Terry?" he asked, extending a hand and ushering Terry into his comfortable, bright office in a imposing old building near the university.

Dressed in khakis and an open-collared oxford shirt, the middle-aged doctor would qualify as handsome. Silver grey hair, bright blue eyes, looking fit and tan, he quickly put his visitor at ease, anxious to help his old friend Marvin Walsh. He took a moment to show Terry a picture of two young men, one himself and one Dr. Walsh, when they were undergraduates at Columbia, and after a few pleasantries, he was ready to give Terry his undivided attention.

The doctor had lots of questions and Terry answered as directly as possible. It was gratifying, too, when he realized Dr. Appleton consulted on many criminal matters, not just those related to the insane, and Terry appreciated being complemented on his modern thinking that brought him here today.

Dr. Walsh suggested bringing the crime scene photographs along with the note, and Terry sat quietly while the doctor took several minutes examining them. Finally, he put them back in their folder and addressed his visitor.

"We've come a long way in understanding criminal behavior and I daresay we have a long way yet to go, but while many in our field believe criminals are born with a defect which makes them predisposed to crime, I'm in the camp that believes they are created by the circumstances in which they are born and raised," the doctor said.

"But we do see very disturbed little kids—kids setting fires, torturing animals, aren't they born that way?" Terry wanted to know.

"A good point, Terry, but one which actually supports my views. Most of who and what we are, come about from the very important first years of our lives. Now, I'm not discounting an inherited insanity which happens, or an injury which can affect behavior, but a young child who is stealing, setting fires and hurting animals and even other children—you look at their environment, and in most cases there is something very wrong. It can be abuse, neglect, obsessive and aggressive behavior on the part of the parent or guardian and that has a direct impact on development and future behavior. You would be surprised at the number of children under twelve who are institutionalized. We psychiatrists do not always agree about it, but I look first to the parents, especially the mother and, more and more, people in the mental health community are finding evidence to validate these ideas," Dr. Appleton said.

"Ok, but I see a lot of poor kids, and their situation usually has to be pretty bad for us to interfere, but most of them don't grow up to be criminals, do they?" Terry asked.

"No, thankfully they don't. But a good number of them will have brushes with the law, and how many of these children have successful lives? How many pass along exactly what they have learned and been taught by example?

"Marvin tells me you were a sergeant in the Marine Corps. I'm sure you know men and something about what they respond to. A sergeant is an authority figure, someone to look up to. I daresay you could teach me a few things if we had time to discuss it," Dr. Appleton said.

Terry thought it would be easy to spend hours talking to this interesting man, and he did appreciate what he was learning, but he felt they were getting off track.

"That's an interesting prospect. Sure, I hope we can talk again. Anything I can learn about human behavior is a valuable asset in my work. But, Doc, tell me what you think about the note," Terry said.

"This killer has a lot of rage. That suggests some hatred or resentment that seethed and festered over a long time. Bludgeoning someone to death is a personal attack, the murderer doesn't shoot and run away but gets to be up close and watch his victim suffer and die. Did you say there is no connection between the victims?" he asked.

"Nothing we can prove as yet, sir, but we have a lot of new leads to follow, but it's mostly Chief Campbell and I, so unfortunately it takes time," Terry said

"Well, I hope I can help. The mutilation in the first murder is significant," the doctor said.

"Is it some weird sex thing?" Terry asked.

"Well . . . it's probably not the kind of weird sex thing you would expect. I take it the woman, the second victim, was not mutilated in this way?" he asked.

"No, sir. She was bludgeoned, pretty badly as you saw in the photos, but nothing of that nature was done to her," Terry explained.

"I'd really have to know more, but my experience tells me the attack on the man represents not only something very personal, but could suggest impotence on the part of the killer. Was the victim likely to have had an affair with someone's wife or ever involved in any kind of assault on a woman or even a child in Kentbury?"

Terry didn't laugh, but he could have. He took a few minutes to explain just what kind of life Gaffer White had led, positive that he was not fooling around or attacking children.

"Ah, the poor man. He sounds like a very sad individual. Even stranger. He doesn't sound like someone to incur this kind of wrath. If the woman had also been attacked in this way, you could be looking at a compulsive killer, someone like . . . well . . . Jack the Ripper," he said.

Terry looked skeptical.

"Sorry, I usually go for the dramatic, but my point is that Jack The Ripper, and you know he was never caught, was consistent in his method, type of victim and mutilation. In this case, a man and a woman killed, but in such a violent, over-kill way . . . I will suggest that there is a connection, at least in the killer's mind," he stated.

"Doctor? In the killer's mind? Does that mean there might not be a real connection?" Terry asked, looking for clarification.

"There's already a connection and I hope it is one you will uncover before he kills again," he said.

"You think that is likely?" Terry asked, a question he posed to himself more than once.

"There was a case several years ago in Upstate New York in which three people were murdered before they found the twenty-nine year old man who killed them. It was not a small town, more of a small city, and this person worked in the local bakery. His three victims were stabbed dozens of times, he undressed them all as one final act of humiliation but there was no real sexual motivation.

"The first victim, a woman who worked in the library, had refused to let him take out a book because he had two that were never returned. The second, a mechanic in a local garage, humiliated this man in front of his peers by making a harmless joke, but in the murderer's sick mind, it was enough to get the jokester killed."

Terry sat quietly, finding it hard to believe overdue library books could result in murder. He thought of Dolly. Not greed or jealousy as the chief once suggested, but it could be some kind of revenge. He might buy that as a motive to kill Etta Marx, but Gaffer? He couldn't imagine it.

"The third victim," Dr. Appleton continued, "was a young woman who refused to go out with this man. It was a normal, natural thing, but to this man, it made her an enemy who needed to be taught a lesson. None of these people knew each other. There was no obvious connection except as the killer saw it."

"So how did they catch this guy?" Terry wanted to know.

"A person like this can become delusional. He started acting weird at work, saying things about the murders that didn't make sense—things suggesting the victims somehow deserved to be killed and talking about a woman who worked at the bank who might deserve the same kind of fate. When this man's boss told the police of his concerns, it was enough to get the man taken in for questioning. They could tell he was disturbed but they had nothing other than suspicion, so they called in a colleague of mine from Cornell to evaluate the suspect. It was his findings that led to the man's confession. It has become a textbook case.

"And the only connection was this guy feeling insulted, is that right?" Terry asked.

"Essentially, yes. It was discovered that his father abandoned his family when the boy was only four. The mother was not physically abusive to the boy, but humiliated him in various ways and the years he should have had love and nurturing were years of stress and emotional trauma. He was not bullied in school, but almost worse, he was ignored. His mother died shortly before he started killing. You might think he would have been free of her, but she was all he knew and he just exploded. The years of anger, loneliness, lack of social skills and no real friends, he didn't know where to go with his feelings and they came out in rage and murder," the psychiatrist explained.

"Wow, that's pretty complicated stuff. I don't know, Dr. Appleton, I can't quite imagine something like that being like these murders, but . . ." Terry said, trying to fathom such behavior.

"What happened to that man?" Terry asked.

"Well, his attorney pled not guilty by reason of insanity, but because it was easy to prove he knew that killing was wrong, he was convicted and executed," the doctor explained, shaking his head.

"You saw it differently?" Terry asked.

"The man was most certainly mentally ill and more would have been gained from studying his case, but the law is not very broadminded on this kind of crime, but it may be one day. Most of the police I work with are very skeptical, but interestingly enough, the U.S. Justice Department and the FBI are using our methods to their advantage; it is a growing science. Europe is way ahead of us, but we learn more every day. I daresay your case could be very interesting once it comes to a conclusion," the doctor said, pleasing the deputy with his optimism.

"Let's talk about the note," the doctor began. "Based on my experience I am inclined to think the killer did write this. I'll tell you why," he stated.

"I would rule out kids—it's too sophisticated," he said.

Terry was surprised. "Well, how is it sophisticated?" he wanted to know.

"First, the paper and envelope are good quality stationary. The printing is precise and neat, even perhaps a little obsessive in its neatness. Then, the wording itself. Does this sound like kids to you? It does not to me and if not kids, then do you really have the kind of adults in Kentbury who would go out of their way to send such a sinister message as a prank to a poor mother, knowing how disturbing it would be?"

Terry appreciated what the doctor was saying, but he found flaws with all of it.

"Well, a kid could get the stationary from his parents, some kids print pretty neatly. I don't entirely see why the wording is sophisticated, but . . ."

"Oh, I realize you are more familiar with the case than I am, Terry, but this is what I feel. But, more importantly, let me tell you what I think about the murderer, assuming any of my cockamamie ideas are correct," he said with a little laugh.

"Oh, sir, Dr. Appleton, I didn't mean to imply . . ." Terry said, feeling his face redden and wondering if the psychiatrist was a mind reader, since "cockamamie" was just the word that popped into this head.

"Let's just assume this note is from the murderer. Only someone with an incredible, over-exaggerated idea of self-importance would have the audacity to write something like this, knowing that it will most surely be seen by the police, but not caring because he feels smarter than you. He probably feels he is smarter than most people. He feels superior and yet has been overlooked all of his life.

"Now this is where I will bring in my idea of early development. I would say the person who committed these murders would be in his late thirties to middle fifties. They are organized and disciplined, something that comes with maturity. I can't be sure about the first murder, but the second was clearly something planned and thoughtful. Committing it in broad daylight speaks of boldness and even hubris and that could eventually be his downfall. They would have to be reasonably fit from the way you described the crimes and, as I said, this kind of rage does not happen overnight. Whatever the motivation is, it is something that has been growing inside this person for years, most likely beginning in childhood," he stated.

"And . . . don't rule out that one or both of the victims could represent a perceived evil or threat to the killer," he told Terry.

Terry was impressed. He hoped the note was written by the killer if that would mean this description was correct. No one came to mind at the moment, but he would be anxious to go over everything with his boss. The chief knew the town better than anyone; he just hoped the psycho stuff would really help and that Bull would be receptive to it.

"So what kind of childhood stuff are we talking about, and what kind of threat, Dr. Appleton?" Terry asked.

"All right, let's imagine the murderer was born between . . . oh, 1895 and 1920, making him thirty-one to fifty-five or so today. We look back through these past fifty-plus years as an amazing time in human history. Along with the impressive strides in science and technology, we've seen two world wars, atomic energy, child labor laws, economic growth but not until we suffered the Great Depression did we see the widespread, abject poverty that touched everyone. The studies on that continue today and . . ." he stopped, seeing the perplexed look of his visitor.

Terry was getting a little lost. He liked history as much as anyone, but he couldn't imagine what Dr. Appleton was getting at. *What the hell did this have to do with anything?* he wondered.

"Forgive me, Terry, I put my professor hat on there for a moment, but what I'm trying to say is we don't know, and you won't until you catch him, what influences have shaped this person. What kind of people raised him? What traumas or tragedies might he have suffered—things like combat. You know better than most how that affects people. So imagine a child, someone naïve and innocent, needing nurturing and love and getting neither, or suffering a great loss at an early age. I'm sorry, I've probably made things more confusing, but when you do catch this person, and I feel that you will, I believe you will uncover what I've been talking about. I'll be most interested, of course, to hear about it if you would be okay with that," he said.

Terry assured Dr. Appleton that he would look forward to it, especially if what he predicated about the murderer proved accurate. Getting inside a criminal's head was an emerging science and a valuable tool for the policeman who knew how to use it. Maybe psychiatry wasn't quite the voodoo people thought it was. As he was leaving, Terry couldn't help but wonder what the doctor would think of his nightmares, but the last thing he wanted right now was having to see a head doctor.

TWENTY-EIGHT

"Terry, welcome! You didn't bring Joyce? I was hoping you two could join me for lunch, but I hope at least you can stay," Sharon said as Terry entered the stately home.

Sharon was looking as lovely as usual and an expensive scent drifted by as she led the way to the living room. Terry was hating this. He didn't feel right about starting off asking if she was having an affair, but since he was here, it made sense to ask her about her father's baseball bat and then tell her what he found out. He knew her reaction would be important and he would have to go from there.

The maid came in offering refreshment. Terry declined and Sharon seemed disappointed when he said he couldn't stay for lunch, but she quickly caught his mood. She could tell he was here for something serious and immediately thought of her father.

"No, Sharon, he's ok . . . well he is going to be upset when I tell him what we found out about his baseball bat, but . . ."

"What about his bat?" she asked her voice full of concern.

Terry related what transpired yesterday after her father called the police station. He told her about their visit and then the confirmation from Dr. Walsh about the blue stain. There seemed no doubt that her father's beloved Reach bat was used to kill two people.

"Oh, poor Daddy! How awful, how disgusting!" she exclaimed.

"Sharon, when is the last time you remember seeing it?" Terry began, but Sharon was still trying to absorb the horrific revelation.

"God, I played with that bat. Daddy and I loved it because Granddaddy Newberry gave it to him. I even used that bat and got a home run with it when I was a senior and the girl's baseball team played Clinton. This is just awful, Terry!" she said, almost in tears.

Terry felt her reaction was appropriate and genuine.

"I'm sorry, Sharon. I haven't told your father yet, but I think he's prepared for the bad news. After all, he did call because he heard the rumors about a bat being the murder weapon and his was missing. Can you remember the last time you saw it?" Terry asked again.

"Oh gosh," she said with a sigh, "I've been going home a lot since April, but I seem to remember it when I was up there for Mother's birthday in June. Yes, it was. I put her presents in the guestroom closet and I remember thinking that I should get it out and put it back in Dad's office. I guess I forgot about it, but I don't remember seeing it there when I was up for that last clean up day, just before Gaffer was murdered, but I wasn't looking for it either."

Terry made note of her comment about more frequent visits since April and wondered if that might have anything to do with Tony Rothman.

"But that doesn't make any sense. Nobody would throw it out. Mother certainly wouldn't. Have you asked Ona? I don't think she'd just throw it away for heaven's sake," Sharon said, getting more upset as the whole idea sunk in.

"I haven't spoken to Mrs. Birch yet, but I plan to. We have to wonder if Gaffer might have taken it. Your dad thought it could have been thrown out for pick up day, but it would have to have been taken before that," he explained. He felt a knot in his stomach but forged ahead with the questions he came here to ask.

"Sharon, I will apologize before I ask, but please understand that I have to and you have to tell me the truth. If you don't, I can't promise what will happen as our investigation progresses and if the State Police jump in, well . . ." he thought that was a good beginning, but Sharon was looking at him like he was from Mars.

"Terry, I'm sorry, what on earth can I possibly tell you?" she said, obviously perplexed.

"Sharon . . . oh, God . . . I'll just say it. Sharon, are you having an affair with Tony Rothman?" he finally managed to ask.

For a second Terry thought she might faint, then he thought she was going to hit him, then she started to cry. It was awful. Terry wasn't good with women's tears, especially beautiful women he used to have a crush on, but he only stared, waiting for her to calm down and was happy that she had a handkerchief in her pocket since his was in the car.

Finally, with a look between anger and humiliation, she faced Terry and asked how the hell he knew and what on earth could it have to do with the murders?

"You have to appreciate that these are devastating crimes, Sharon, and even though it's mostly just Chief Campbell and myself investigating, the State Police and all the surrounding counties are on high alert and something that would have passed as unimportant before is now a potential clue or lead. Your cars were seen on Old Gorge Road, not far from where Gaffer was murdered, and the police officer who took notice actually saw you and Tony Rothman. He took the plate numbers, that's all," Terry explained.

"It wasn't you? Who was it?" she wanted to know.

"You know, I don't see how that matters. You seem to be confirming the truth of it, so I would appreciate your telling me what I need to know," he stated with enough authority in his tone to make her understand how serious this was.

Sharon was pacing. She stopped by a window that looked out to the garden, taking a moment to compose herself. Finally, she faced her accuser.

"All right. Yes, I've been seeing Tony since late March. He's divorced, you know," she said, pulling on her handkerchief and not looking Terry in the eye.

Yeah, he's divorced, but you're not, Terry couldn't help but think.

Taking a deep breath, Sharon did look Terry in the face and began to explain. Terry hated hearing it, but he listened quietly, hoping Sharon did not think he was judging her. He wasn't—he was just disappointed.

"Phillip is teaching now as well as having his busy practice. He's gone so much, I guess I've been lonely, but I'm sure that's not enough of an excuse, is it, Terry?" she asked.

Funny how quickly someone can fall off their pedestal, Terry thought, but he didn't care why she was having an affair, he only cared about what, if anything, it had to do with the murders.

"Sharon, please, unless this is somehow connected to the mess going on in Kentbury right now, your personal life is your own, but you've got to understand why I'm asking," he told her.

Wiping her eyes, she took a deep breath and waited for his questions.

"Your cars were seen on Old Gorge Road at least twice. Is that a place you go often?"

"We met at his place in Pittstown a few times but it's not a very private house and he was worried about nosey neighbors. We've never met around here, I'm too well known but when we could, we'd have a day in the city," she explained, referring to the anonymity they enjoyed in Manhattan.

"Tell me about meetings at the gorge," Terry asked.

"That was my idea. I used to go there to swim when I was in high school. It was always a special place, private and not a lot of people knew about it. But even fewer people know about the passage in back of the overhang, you know, the one that comes out into that secret grotto and little pool and waterfall. You must have been there, haven't you, Terry?" she asked.

Terry had to admit that he did not know about the secret grotto but he would check it out, almost blushing with the thoughts he had about taking Joyce there, but he was getting off track. "Sharon, did you ever see Gaffer White there? Did he ever see you . . . speak to you perhaps?" he asked.

Sharon stared at the deputy for a moment and he could almost see the wheels turning as she tried to make sense of his question. It was cool in the large home, but she looked flushed and uncomfortable.

"No. I never saw Gaffer there. I doubt that he saw me, but he certainly never spoke to me, Terry. Just what are you asking anyway?" concern heavy in her voice.

"I will be very straight with you, Sharon. It appears the murder weapon for both Gaffer and Etta Marx was your father's baseball bat that somehow went missing from your house. You've been having an affair you hope to keep secret but you've been meeting in a spot near the first murder site and if Gaffer White did happen to see you there . . ."

Sharon interrupted.

"You think that I killed that poor man because he saw me with Tony? Are you crazy?" she asked in a heavy whisper, tears welling again in her eyes.

"No, Sharon, I can't see you doing any such thing, but what about Tony Rothman? You know I'm going to have to talk to him," he told her.

"Oh God, this is a nightmare," she said, standing abruptly. "I'm not in love with Tony. I've been stupid and foolish and I need to end this. Tony's fun to be with, he's handsome, romantic but he would never, ever do something so terrible. Terry, does any of this have to become public? Please tell me it doesn't," she pleaded.

"Sharon, look, Chief Campbell will have to know everything, but unless there's a reason to pursue this line of inquiry, no . . . there's no reason anyone will have to know, but . . ."

"But what?" she asked.

Terry was thinking of Leonard Smith.

"You know Leonard Smith, don't you?" Terry asked.

"Oh, please, don't tell me he's the one who saw us," she said.

"I don't know what to tell you, Sharon. Leonard is . . ."

"Leonard is an idiot!" she said.

Terry agreed but didn't say so. He tried to reassure her.

When his visit finally ended, he left with a feeling of loss. He lost the idyllic memory of a beautiful woman he'd known most of his life, and he felt he had lost a friend. It seemed even he was a victim of this mess and it needed to end.

TWENTY-NINE

J oyce spent the morning at Lake Cottage. She left at noon with a whole briefcase of notes, swatches and magazine photos that her charming new clients wanted her to study before they made any final decisions about redecorating. It didn't take long for Ethel to decide that if Madeline was getting her bedroom re-done, her room could use refreshing too. Even Jimmy Doolittle got into the act when Ethel suggested a custom-made dog bed for the sweet old boy. Joyce was thrilled that each lady had enough good taste and personal style that the job would be anything but boring. It also occurred to her that a trip into Manhattan would be necessary and maybe Terry would come along to find out what he could about the Farmer family. Before going home, she decided to stop by the police station and run the idea by her husband. She had to admit, it was all pretty exciting!

Fred Browning was such a nice man, Joyce was thinking as she left the police station after finding Terry was out. She was on her way up to the Kentbury Library to say hello to Dolly when she heard her name.

"Mrs. Kramer! This is fortunate," said Father March. "I was going to leave this with your husband, but now I can give it to you in person. I think you'll find it important."

Joyce called the priest before she left the house this morning and he promised to look through the death certificates for anything that might relate to any Wexlers, Whites or Farmers. He found several that he put aside but when he found the last one, he decided to take it to Kentbury right away.

Father March could not join Joyce for lunch but she thanked him profusely for driving all the way down from Califon, and he was right . . . his find was interesting and when Joyce got to study it at home, she was amazed at just how interesting!

While Terry was driving back from Princeton, Bull was on his way to Glen Gardner to see Father Hanover. Doc Sullivan called to say the Father was doing surprisingly well and the police chief could come any time he liked.

Bull could hardly find the elderly priest amidst the get well cards and flowers. The remains of breakfast sat on a nearby tray and the patient was sitting up and looking much improved from just a few days ago.

"Good morning, Father! I see your appetite is back and I have to say, you look almost your old self. How are you feeling, Father?"

"Ah, Ernest, thank you, thank you," he said, being one of the few people in the world to use the chief's proper name. "The Good Lord doesn't want me yet, I guess. I am feeling much better. Young Father Boyle thinks I need to recover at the new Catholic home in Camden, but I just want to go home," he said.

After a few minutes of small talk, Bull began asking the many questions he had.

"Now, Father, you tell me the minute you feel tired or need to rest. I do have a lot to ask you, but we'll do just as much as you feel up to, ok?" Bull said.

"Could you please tell me all you can remember about the other morning . . . even the smallest thing, starting from the time you left the house? Did you notice anything unusual?"

"Ah . . . well, we're pretty predictable, Father Boyle and I. We're both early risers, but I'm usually the one out first. I remember thinking what a fine day it was going to be, maybe not too hot for a change. I was even hoping to find time to do a little fishing at the gorge," he said.

"Did you happen to notice, Father, if there were any cars in the parking lot?" Bull asked.

"I'm sorry, Ernest, there may have been, but I can't say for sure."

"Well you just go ahead and relate everything as you remember it, Father, and I'll ask you questions after that," Bull said.

"Yes, fine, fine. My thoughts were on trout, God forgive me, more than the morning Mass, but I went in the side door, like every morning and peeked into the church, didn't see any one that early, but I always look," he said.

"That's important, Father. Do I assume the front doors were open, as usual?" Bull asked.

"Of course. Our Lord doesn't lock anyone out, there's no reason we should," he said, not noticing the grin Bull suppressed as he made notes.

"I was walking toward the sacristy and . . . oh dear . . . it's so unpleasant, but it was like a bomb crashing down! Everything went dark. I didn't see anyone," the old priest said.

"That's fine, Father. Did you possibly hear anything or maybe just feel like something was wrong?" Bull asked.

Bull couldn't deny disappointment at Father Hanover's negative response, but he turned the line of inquiry to the church records and history that seemed to permeate everything so far. Bull was surprised when he realized the priest did not know about the mess in the church office.

"So you hadn't been in the office yet that morning?" Bull wanted to know.

"My goodness! Yes! That is exactly the last thing I saw before I was bashed on the head—I'd forgotten that! I was not quite to the office door but I thought I saw papers on the floor and I smelled something odd!" he said with excitement and satisfaction. Bull waited to hear more.

"Yes, I saw those papers and I wondered what on earth papers were doing on the floor. I was about to go in and see, but just before I was hit," he said, closing his eyes and wincing at the memory, "this kind of chemical scent was there . . . heavy, almost like kerosene, but not quite. I recognized it and found it very disturbing because it is something I had noticed before . . . it is a scent I associated with Etta Marx.

"What kind of chemicals?" Nelson Hunt asked.

The newspaper editor was sitting at his desk, shirt sleeves rolled up, looking over copy for a feature article when the police chief popped in with a rather odd question.

"Just a lead that's come along. I know it sounds strange. It might not be anything," he said, but his mind was racing with possibilities. He made the decision to tell Nelson Hunt what Father Hanover said about a scent, with the hope that something would click with the unusual clue.

"I don't know, Bull, unless you're talking about the printer's ink. You've noticed that, I'm sure. Go downstairs and see Inky—you'll see what I mean," Nelson said.

"Yes, Chief," Inky said when Bull walked into the room with the printing presses, overseen for two decades by the capable Donald, "Inky," Grange. "We have all complained over the years about going home smelling like printer's ink. It's sort of like cigarette smoke . . . you don't necessarily notice it yourself but other people do. It gets into your clothes, your hair—kind of like farmers who always smell like the barn," he said.

The presses were not running, but Inky was busy setting type for the next edition, and the unique smell of printer's ink was quite evident.

It probably wasn't much of a lead anyway, Bull had to admit, but it just nagged at him. He'd follow his nose, he decided, then laughed to himself at the terrible joke.

When Fred Browning left, Bull locked the office doors so he and his deputy could finish sharing the information each had gathered, and there was hell of a lot of it.

"Lord, Terry, I feel like we're going around in circles. We keep learning things, but it just makes more questions and no damn answers. I guess it's just going to take time to check on all of this. I'll call Mr. Sherman to see if Rudy April is still available to do some investigating. He's right there in the city and could look into finding this Farmer family—just find 'em, we can take it from there, but that would be a big help," the chief said.

Joyce called as they were winding down and told Terry about some very interesting information Father March found. Terry promised to be home shortly. The phone was ringing as Terry was going out the door.

"You go ahead, Son, I'll get it. It's probably Lou wonderin' where I am," Bull said.

It was only a five minute drive from the office to his house. With a thousand different things whirling in his head, Terry was looking forward to a cool bath, dinner with Joyce and learning about what Father March found. Joyce was sitting on the porch when he pulled in but before he could even greet her, he got a radio call.

"What?" Terry shouted into the receiver.

"Yes. Yes, sir. Ok, yes, I agree," he was saying.

Joyce waited patiently, wondering. "*What now?*" She expected Terry would tell her, but she would never ask. The call ended and she waited to hear what was going on.

"The phone was ringing when I left the office," Terry began. "Bull thought it was probably Lou, but it was Chief Riggs calling from the hospital in Flemington. Leonard Smith's been shot. They don't think he's going to make it."

Bull said there wasn't a thing either of them could really do, but he had the immediate same thought Terry had which involved Sharon Newberry and Tony Rothman. After that, they had to wonder if there was a possible connection to the murders in Kentbury and if so, what? But a gun is a long way from a baseball bat. Convinced a good night's sleep was going to be more valuable than interfering with Chief Riggs and Sheriff Zimmer—Riggs's deputy and Sheriff Zimmer's territory, Terry had a whiskey and soda with Joyce, told her only part of what had transpired during the day, then went to take that cool bath.

Halfway through dinner and a second drink, he apologized to his beautiful wife.

"Honey, I shouldn't have told you like that. I don't know anything at all yet, but you do understand how rare this kind of thing is, don't you?" he asked, referring to the shooting of a policeman in the quiet environs of Hunterdon County.

"I know, Sweetheart," she said, looking sad, hurt, he couldn't be sure. "Does it have anything to do with the murders here?" she asked.

"I can't see how," he said, determined not to tell her anything about Sharon and Tony Rothman.

"I'm so sorry," Joyce said. "I know you don't like Leonard Smith, but I also know you would never wish this kind of thing on anyone. Let's pray he comes through. You'll know more tomorrow, but at least it's not your case, Terry. Let me show you what we've discovered," she said.

"I called Father March before I left for Lake Cottage this morning and he promised to have a look in the death records for any infants who died around that time. He found several, but when he found this one, he thought it was important enough to bring here in person," she said.

Terry studied the Record of Death for an infant boy named Francis Gregson White, born April 9, 1901, Mother: A. White. But . . ." Joyce said, holding out another old church document, "there was this note in the same file stating that the baby was to be buried at St. Ann's in Hampton.

"Father March thought that seemed strange and called Saint Ann's. They had a record there for the death of the same baby and the note in that file stated the baby's funeral and burial was in Califon!"

"What the hell is that about?" Terry said, trying to connect the crazy dots.

"Wait . . . there's more, it gets crazier," Joyce said.

"Father March tried to find a grave, or at least record of where a grave could be. He couldn't find anything. He said sometimes, in those days, if a family was poor, an infant might be put in a coffin with someone else if they had another burial at the same time, but he couldn't find a thing," she said, finding the information interesting but macabre.

Terry appreciated the diversion and after a few minutes he and Joyce were throwing out one theory after another, trying to find a plausible explanation for how it could possibly connect to the murders.

"Terry, I've had a little longer to think about this than you have and I wonder if, for whatever perverse reason, Magnus Wexler could have manipulated the records to erase the birth of two babies," Joyce said.

Terry looked thoughtful.

"Honey, I should probably put you on the payroll," he said.

Joyce looked surprised. She threw out the idea but was the first to admit that not only would it be bizarre, but the question of why loomed heavy in the air.

"Ok . . . I'm impressed with myself, I guess, but I'm afraid I don't know where to go with my brilliant theory," she admitted.

"Yeah . . . I don't either, but something about it almost makes sense. Suppose Old Man Wexler did do this, how do you get the two churches to go along?" Terry asked.

"Money," Joyce said. "New carpeting, stained glass windows—churches always need funds."

"Yeah . . . you could be right, but what happened to this other baby? Or did it really die, but if so, why the goofy stuff with the burial records?" Terry puzzled.

"What about the town or county records, Terry? Wouldn't they have this information?" Joyce asked?

"I thought of that and I'll get Dolly on it if she has the time. She's great at research and she's discreet. I'll clear it with Bull, but I'm sure he'll be ok with it," Terry said.

"Hmm . . . I wonder how much Father March would be willing to help," Joyce said.

"Yeah, he's been pretty helpful so far," Terry said thoughtfully.

"I hate to bother Father Boyle or poor Father Hanover, but . . . Father Hanover was here back then. We'll get the chief's help with this and now I really need to find someone from that Farmer family. They apparently took care of Aggie White. They could have a lot of answers," Terry said.

Joyce told Terry that her work for the Crisp sisters would require a trip to Manhattan. That suited him just fine. If Rudy April had any luck tracking down the Farmers, assuming they were even in the city, they could make it another productive day together.

"I guess they could have moved or all be dead or . . . boy, talk about a mixed up mess," Joyce said with sympathy for her hard working husband.

"Nothing about this has been simple or easy, but I feel like we're getting somewhere," Terry said, trying to sound positive, but there were still more questions than answers.

THIRTY

Leonard Smith didn't make it. Bull called Terry at home to tell him and said they had to get their questions answered right away regarding even the slightest connection to Leonard's death and the so-called affair poor Leonard stumbled on.

"I hope we can eliminate Tony Rothman, and Sharon as well, Terry. I don't want to have to involve them if we don't have to, but it's pretty damn coincidental. You tell Sharon about Leonard discovering their affair and Leonard's shot the same night. I don't like it. I don't like it one bit," Bull said.

Terry didn't like it either, but he doubted very much that Sharon Newberry Hamilton drove from Princeton to find Leonard and shoot him. He did assume she would have let Tony Rothman know about his visit with her, but Rothman actually had less to loose than Sharon. It might make for some gossip if their affair became public, but that seemed par for the course for the lawyers he knew; half of 'em were fooling around or doing something scandalous to fuel the lively gossip mills.

He also had to consider that Leonard was a victim of their very own murderer. Leonard had put forth theories and ideas and maybe the poor guy actually did know something and needed to be silenced. Still, two murders with a baseball bat, where did the gun come from? And if they had a gun, why use the bat?

On the short drive to Clinton, Terry mentally inventoried the little they knew of Leonard Smith's ideas about Gaffer's murder. Leonard was obviously feeding Etta ideas about kids. He had a thing about teenagers all being potential delinquents which clouded most of his police work. It drove Bull crazy when Leonard brought out his list of boys in town, age twelve upward, whenever there was a break in, vandalism or anything else Leonard could pin on them. Of course sometimes he was right, and that just encouraged his slanted thinking. More than once the chief had to smooth things over with ruffled parents and kids whose only crime was being a teenager.

Terry knew Bull was going to ask Chief Riggs if there were any notes in Leonard's papers that might relate to the case. They hadn't found anything useful from searching Etta's things; maybe they would have more luck with Leonard's.

Terry arrived a little after nine at the old colonial building on Main Street in Clinton, which served as the distinguished offices for Jefferson, McCloud & Rothman. Dreading the unenviable task of questioning Tony Rothman, not only about a possible connection to the Kentbury murders but also about his whereabouts last night, he steeled himself for meeting the man who was sleeping with Sharon Newberry.

"Deputy, have a seat," Tony Rothman said, ushering him into the large office with rather funky modern decor. A large abstract painting dominated one wall and Terry wondered what Joyce would think of it.

"Cigarette?" the lawyer asked, holding out a pack to his visitor.

Good looking, confident, he probably saw why Sharon would be attracted to him, but Terry wasn't impressed.

"No thank you," he said, dying for a drag but damned if he would give in now.

"So, what can I help you with?" Tony Rothman asked.

"I was coming here today anyway, Mr. Rothman, about another matter, but I also have to ask you where you were between six and eight last night," Terry stated.

"God, Kramer, Sharon called me after your visit yesterday and I thought, like most everyone, that Leonard Smith was a fool, but I did not shoot him," he replied, impressing Terry with how quickly he caught on.

"I'd like to take your word for it, but would you mind telling me where you were last night between the hours of six and eight?" Terry repeated.

Manicured, five dollar hair cut, expensive suit, Tony Rothman stared at his inquisitor for several seconds. Not about to lose this kind of pissing contest, Terry stared right back.

"I was here until almost six," he finally answered. "You can ask Bob McCloud, he was here when I left, and you can ask our accountant, Mrs. Dilwood. I walked across the bridge to the inn and sat at the bar for a while, talked to oh . . . Lee Pierce, Otto Subbe . . . uh . . . Milton Hines.

A couple of us went into the dining room and had dinner. I had a steak," he said, looking at Terry with a half grin. Terry was not amused, but if his alibi checked out, and Terry was going to definitely check it, he could eliminate Tony Rothman as a suspect for Leonard's murder. That still left the questions he had about Gaffer White's murder.

"Look," Tony began when Terry asked about the cars at the gorge and his involvement with Sharon, "we never saw this poor old guy who was murdered and I'm a lawyer for chrissakes and . . . I'm divorced. Sharon's a great girl but I'm not about to commit murder to protect her reputation," he said with smug confidence, but enough logic that made sense.

"I can see the logic to that, Mr. Rothman, and there is certainly nothing other than a few odd coincidences to connect you or Mrs. Hamilton to the murders, but you appreciate that I have to follow every lead we get," Terry said.

"Do you own a gun, sir?" Terry asked.

Reaching into a drawer, Tony produced a .45 Colt and laid it on the desk.

"Hmm, may I?" Terry asked.

"Go right ahead, Deputy."

Terry was familiar with a weapon traditionally used as a military side arm. He could tell it had not been fired recently and learned this morning that Leonard was shot with a .38. This was certainly not the weapon used to shoot Leonard Smith.

Tony Rothman was imposing: handsome, graying hair and that "I'm a Harvard attorney" air, was gnawing at Terry's confidence, but the former Marine sergeant would be damned if he let it show!

"You know, Kramer, if you ask your questions the right way, assuming you'll check out my alibi for last night, no one has to know you're asking about me. It wouldn't take long for the gossips to put two and two together that you're inquiring about the murder last night, and after that, I don't know . . . but you don't want a defamation suit on your hands, I'm sure," he said.

"*There it is!*" Terry thought. The bastard put on his lawyer hat and the condescending tone was loud and clear.

"I've already thought of that, sir, and I have no intention of being indiscreet. My questions will not involve you specifically and that is in consideration of Sharon, not you. I know how to do my job," Terry shot back.

Tony Rothman's alibi checked out as Terry suspected it would and his questions were general enough that he doubted anyone would figure out why he was asking. He said he was checking on information regarding recent burglaries and no one seemed the wiser.

The leads flying in about Leonard Smith's murder were keeping the state police and police departments in two counties busy but, thankfully, Chief Campbell and his deputy were able to keep their focus on the horrible crimes in Kentbury. There was the obvious question that Leonard's murder could be linked to those murders but, for the time being at least, Terry and his boss were the only ones actively pursing that possibility. Chief Riggs knew there could be a connection but he was occupied with his own investigation and helping Leonard's family with the funeral. He was happy to let his colleagues in Kentbury do the footwork, knowing he would be kept informed.

Before Terry could call Sharon Hamilton in Princeton, she reached him at the office around lunch time.

"I suppose you need to know where I was last night," she said.

"I have to ask you, Sharon, but I appreciate your call. Where were you last night, then?" he asked.

"Right here. Phillip was home for a change. We had dinner, watched some television, had an early night. I would ask, Terry, if you have to check on that, that you would question Mrs. Pratt and Effie first. I was out in the morning but they know I was here the rest of the day and night," she explained, talking about her cook and maid.

"I don't need to talk to anyone, Sharon. I believe you, and I'm sorry if I upset you yesterday. I . . . ," he said.

"Listen, I won't pretend I am not embarrassed but, Terry, I'm glad really, and I'm glad it was you who came to see me. I am grateful for your discretion, it means a lot. I told Tony it's over. I'd like to say he was upset, but he was only upset for himself I think. I've been very foolish, but I do love my husband and I'm going to work on that," she said with a catch in her voice.

Well, Terry thought when he hung up, *maybe Sharon has a foot back on her pedestal.* He hoped it was the end of any involvement on her part, but he still had the murder weapon coming from her parents' home. How the hell was this going to shake out and who was this evil person among them? A stranger would stick out, so it was someone they knew . . . it had to be.

THIRTY-ONE

L ou Campbell was as disturbed by the horrible murders as anyone in Kentbury, but she was flattered and pleased to be accompanying her husband to see Minnie Lester and inquire about, of all things, perfume and cleaning products!

"Why, Lou, I haven't seen you in ages. How are you, dear?" Minnie asked.

Bull knew a little time would be spent on small talk, but after almost fifteen minutes of it, he brought the conversation around to the reason for their drop in. He could have just gone into Etta's cottage, but he not only felt Minnie Lester deserved consideration about any police visits, he also needed to ask some questions of Etta's landlady before he and Lou had a look around.

"Well, Ernest," Minnie began, being another of the few who addressed Bull by his given name, "I told young Terry Kramer that Etta was a rather elegant lady. She liked her luxuries, but she deserved them, you know. She worked hard, why shouldn't she have a few indulgences?"

"Nothin' wrong with that, Miss Lester. I'm just wondering if Etta's sister took any of her things. We explained about how the cottage looked and it was still a crime scene, but the State Police released it for clean up," Bull explained and immediately felt terrible to think of Minnie having to deal with that. "Did Etta's sister happen to contact you about packing things, getting rid of anything or sending someone to do it?" Bull inquired.

"Oh, yes . . . I think she said her children might come to do that, but I haven't heard from her. I've left everything just the way it was. I know I'll have to go there eventually but Terry has been back you know, so I was not about to disturb anything until this is over. There is a cleaning service in Flemington who will take care of things when we're ready," Minnie explained and Bull was glad to hear it.

A few minutes later he and Lou were entering the charming little house and he was warning his wife about the unpleasant scene she was going to see in the bedroom.

"That poor, poor woman," Lou said as she stood in the bedroom doorway, too easily imagining the woman who died there. Since no cleaning had yet been done, Lou saw the spattered blood and several large stains, now dried and ugly, testifying to the horrible death that occurred here.

"Are you ok, Sweetheart? You don't have to do this, Lou," Bull said, thinking perhaps this wasn't such a good idea after all, but he needn't have worried.

"I'm a farm girl, Bull, and I've raised two children. I've seen blood before. Now what do you want me to do?" she asked with a bit more bravado than she actually felt, but determined to help if she could.

"Just take a look at the woman stuff here, Lou, the perfumes, things in the bathroom, you know," Bull said, already seeming perplexed by a world he knew little about.

"What are you looking for exactly, Bull?" Lou wanted to know, recognizing that look her husband got when he was trying hard to solve a puzzle—whether a crime or rewiring her favorite lamp. "I thought we were looking for a chemical smell of some kind," she said.

"Well yeah, we are. We'll look in the kitchen too, but it occurred to me that Father Hanover couldn't be sure what the smell was but he associated it with Etta. So . . . ," he said.

"So you thought about how you think some of my perfumes smell like bug spray and wondered if it could even be something like that?" Lou asked.

"Exactly, Mrs. Campbell. I don't pay you that high salary for nothing it seems," he chuckled.

Bull followed silently as his capable wife scrutinized the dead woman's bedroom and then the bathroom for the magic potions and scents all females understood and all men found just a little mystical.

"Etta had expensive taste, didn't she?" a rhetorical question from Lou after finding opened bottles of fragrances by Worth, Chanel and Guerlain, along with pricey bath soaps and oils, all used.

Thirty minutes later, after looking at all of the possibilities of scent that could be related to Etta Marx, ranging from costly perfumes to household bleach, Bull wasn't sure why he thought they might find some real answers; did the elusive clue point to a woman wearing perfume? Did it point to someone who worked at the Kaller? A list of people ran through Bull's mind and he realized he was becoming suspicious of everyone and he hated the feeling.

"C'mon, Chief, you promised we could go see Father Hanover, then you can take me to the Acme so I can pick up something for dinner," Lou said.

Bull hated to take time away from real police work, but maybe that's just what he needed—for a little while at least.

"Ah, Louise, I see Ernest has you working for the police now. I hope he swore you in properly," Father Hanover said, happy to see Lou and anxious to help in the investigation. In spite of a bandaged head and his arm in a sling, Lou was pleased to see how well the old priest was doing and that his sense of humor was intact.

An hour flew by with as much talk about church activities as the ongoing investigation, but when they left, Bull felt more relaxed and looked forward to helping Lou do a little grocery shopping.

"I'm getting so tired, but Greg finally understands now. He thanked me, just like he used to do when we were little. I'll probably have to leave Kentbury, but that's ok—it won't be long now, just a few things to take care of and those church records won't matter; I shouldn't have been so worried. "Well, hello there. You're a Brewer aren't you? I've got a couple of soda bottles here if you want them. Oh, you're welcome. I have some more, I'll save them for you. See you later!"

"Russell, you and Edward are going to have to keep an eye on Henry and George. We told you why and how important it is, but they're still running around collecting their junk and they don't know how serious this is. I can't watch them every minute," Tilly Brewer told her eldest son.

"I'm sorry, Mom. I know it's important. School starts next week; that'll keep 'em home more and I bet the police are gonna catch this guy. Don't worry, Mom, it'll be ok," Russell said, trying to reassure his worried mother. Stupid kids. Poor Mom, she has enough to worry about. I guess it's up to me to read 'em the riot act, Russell told himself.

"You're nuts!" Henry said when Russell told him and George that the murderer was out to get them.

"No, I'm not. Mom got a note and gave it to the police. You have to be careful, do you understand? Mom can't be worrying about you and wondering where you two are all the time," he said, hoping some of his words would sink in.

"I bet you wrote the note," said George.

"Don't be stupid. You know I would never do that to Mom, so just do what she says—stay here and don't be running all over the place. There's a bad person out there, don't you understand that?" Russell asked.

"OK, you're right, Russell. We're sorry," said Henry.

"Yeah, I guess . . . we're sorry. But it's against our nature!" George had to add.

THIRTY-TWO

Chief Campbell took the call from Mr. Dumont relating the information Rudy April gathered on the Farmer Family. The lawyer told Bull it was their young investigator's last job before he reported to Fort Dix and he spent considerable time and effort to do his best. Bull said to please be sure and tell him how much they appreciated the good work and to wish him luck.

Rudy April's investigation found that the senior Farmers were deceased, but there was a daughter living in Jersey City. Terry had an appointment with her the next day. With a little planning, he and Joyce took the train again and while Terry backtracked across the river to his appointment in Jersey City, Joyce went on to get what she needed for Lake Cottage. Terry would get back to Manhattan as soon as he could but they expected to have a few hours together in the city and be on the evening train back to Kentbury.

Rosemary Farmer Byrd was Binnie Farmer's youngest child. There was an older brother who was deceased and her older sister, Violet, passed away only a year ago. Terry was not sure what he expected, but he was pleased to meet the middle-aged woman who met him at the door of a large Victorian house. In spite of a rather sad expression, Rosemary smiled a lot and did not hide her curiosity about why a policeman from Kentbury wanted to talk with her. She had not been back to Hunterdon County since she was little and did not know about the murders.

"How awful. Those poor people. I remember hearing about Aggie White but more really because of Greggie, but he left when I was little. I didn't know her son or the woman you mentioned," she said, referring to Gaffer and Etta Marx.

"No, you wouldn't have known Etta Marx, but if there is anything you can tell me about Agatha White staying with your family in Califon

181

when she was expecting, it could be really helpful. Do you have any recollection of that? You mentioned 'Greggie,' who is that, Mrs. Byrd?" Terry asked, notebook in hand.

"Oh dear, you know . . . family stories can be so strange, can't they? I will tell you what I remember, Mr. Kramer, but it's a child's memories all mixed up with family history," she said.

"Whatever you can tell me will be helpful. Right now we have lots of ideas but most of it doesn't make sense," he said.

"Well . . . I'm not sure any of this will make sense, but I was just a toddler when Aggie White came to stay with us in Califon. You know, my family worked for the Cousin family and we had this nice little cottage on their property. I have a few memories of that time, but I remember most from after we left and went to live in New York. I thought Greggie was my real brother until I was almost six and he went away," she told Terry.

"Went away?" Terry asked.

"Well . . . that's what I was told. I had just started first grade and always said good-bye to Greggie and couldn't wait to see him when I got home, but one day he was there when I left, but was gone when I got home. I never saw him again. We had a neighbor whose baby died and I thought maybe Greggie died too, but my mother said he went to live with another family and was better off. I was heartbroken but I never spoke of him again, not to my mother at least and as I got older, I thought he probably was better off wherever he had gone, at least I hoped so. There were arguments and my father said my mother was being harsh or cruel but she said there was something wrong with him, he was a freak and she wasn't going to raise 'that bastard,'" she explained.

"I didn't know what a freak was . . . I thought it was a nationality, like French or Italian, but Violet explained it to me and I didn't understand," she said.

That might have been endearing, Terry thought, but it was too sad . . . too terrible.

Terry knew he was learning something important and waited for her to go on.

"I'm ashamed to say it, but my mother was awful to that baby. She seemed to hate him or something and my father, who was really nicer to us than my mother ever was, spoke to me once about it when he saw how unhappy I was. He told me Greggie was going to be with a family that didn't mind how different he was, but I didn't see how he was different. I think he was talking about the birthmark, but it never bothered me, but," Terry interrupted.

"What kind of birthmark, Mrs. Byrd?" he asked.

"Oh . . . I remember it bothered my mother; she commented on how ugly it was, and no wonder they paid to send him away, something like that. It was one of those dark purple things—funny, I thought it was pretty. It was on his thigh, sort of roundish I think. Poor little thing. He couldn't help it, but my mother was not a kind person and she found it ugly," she said.

"Your father never intervened?" Terry asked.

"My father tried, Mr. Kramer, but he drank, and I guess I didn't blame him, but he just sort of retreated as I got older. It was easier to ignore things than fight all the time I suppose. My mother wore the pants, as they say, and our home life was not always pleasant. My brother was not treated as poorly as my sister and I were, and Violet left when she was seventeen, married a fireman. I left when I was sixteen and was very, very lucky to marry Mr. Byrd," she said, pointing to an old photograph of a nice little family . . . herself with an affable-looking man and two little girls.

"Well, do you know what happened to this baby?" Terry asked, once again mesmerized by the history they kept learning about the sad life of Agatha White and her children . . . which he was now convinced included Gaffer and a twin brother.

"I can tell you what things were said over the years about it, and some of it had to do with money. This is what I believe happened, Mr. Kramer," she went on.

"My father worked for Mr. Wexler at the dairy in Califon. I did know, after I got older and understood these things, that Mr. Wexler's son, the one who was killed hunting, I think, got Agatha White in the family way. I don't really know why, but some arrangement was made for her to stay with my family. My father got a promotion at the dairy and there was money paid for Agatha to stay with us even though my mother made her work. The babies were born at our house in Califon. I don't remember that really, but I remember hearing about it," she said.

"So . . . there were two . . . twins, is that right?" he asked, excited to confirm what they already believed.

"Yes, well . . . yes, I guess that has to be the case, but honestly, and I know this sounds strange, but nothing was ever really said about this other child and when Greggie left, I remember some big argument about money, but after that one little conversation with my father, he was never mentioned again—at least not to me," she said, sadness in her voice.

"Mrs. Byrd, I want to show you a photograph if I may," Terry said and placed the photo Joyce found of the people they thought was the Farmer family.

"Oh my goodness. Yes, that's my mother, my brother, and I'm sitting on Violet's lap," she said, taking a long moment to study the old picture.

"Mrs. Byrd, we have some confusing church records that show the birth of two babies, at least with the same birthday, but then there's a record of birth for this baby with the last name Farmer, but then a death for a Francis Gregson White, only a few days old. Do you know anything at all about that?" Terry asked.

"I'm afraid I don't, except everything about poor little Greggie was strange. You said a birth certificate with one last name, and death certificate with another, but probably the same baby?" she asked, confusion showing on her face.

"Yes, ma'am, that's what we have found. We have a few theories about it, but we are trying to find out as much as we can. It's possible that Mr. Wexler arranged the death certificate to hide the existence of one of the babies, but we're not sure and certainly not sure why," Terry said. He could tell Mrs. Byrd was digesting this strange possibility and he waited patiently, hoping she was remembering something valuable.

"Well, I do know when my parents left Califon it seemed very quick and I was quite little, but even then that memory is that one day we were there, and all of a sudden we were on a train and that night I had to sleep in a new place. I do know my parents left with a good deal of money, and it was Mr. Wexler who arranged my father's new job as a supervisor at a cheese factory. We always had lots of cheese to eat," she said with a little laugh.

"I remember my sister Violet telling me about an argument she overheard when Greggie went away—she said my mother was telling my father that there was no reason Mr. Wexler had to know Greggie was gone and they deserved that money. I guess there was money every few months from Mr. Wexler, and when Violet and I were older and talked about it, we put two and two together and figured my parents were being paid to take care of Greggie, but . . ." she stopped and Terry saw tears in her eyes.

"But he was gone," Terry said.

"Yes. I'm sorry . . . I loved that little boy and I always hoped he was somewhere having a good life," she said.

"You have no idea what happened to him; who took him, or . . . ?" Terry asked.

"No, I'm afraid I don't, but . . . ," she said, a quizzical look making Terry hopeful that she remembered something.

"But Violet and I did have a conversation once about a year after she left home to get married. We were older then, and I told her I had seen a young boy I thought could be Greggie. That's when she told me that a year after Greggie left, at Christmas time, she went with my father to a Catholic orphanage in Brooklyn, and my father gave one of the sisters a package and some money. When Violet asked about it, my father swore her to secrecy—never to tell my mother—but something made Violet think it had to do with Greggie," she said.

Terry's mind was whirling. Could Gaffer's twin have grown up in an orphanage in Brooklyn? If he did, did he somehow come back to Kentbury to murder his own brother, and if so, with what purpose?

"You never looked into that? Do you happen to know which orphanage, Mrs. Byrd?" Terry asked.

"No, no . . . by then I was caught up in finding my own life, anxious to leave home. I had just met Calvin, Mr. Byrd, and it just got lost, you know?" she said, with sadness.

"Yes, ma'am, I do, but you've been very helpful. This is my number in Kentbury if you think of anything else, anything at all," he said, handing her a card as she walked with him to the door.

"Oh, one thing, and I don't really know why, but when we left Califon, I don't think it was on very good terms with the Cousins. My mother did not speak well of them and I had the impression my father blamed her for whatever was wrong, but I don't know what happened I'm afraid."

There were plenty of seats on the early train back to Kentbury and, while it made a few more stops than the later train, it gave Terry almost two hours to go over his notes with Joyce and see just what they could make of it all. The seats opposite were piled with bags and boxes from

Joyce's shopping, and enough good deli food for the next few days, including gourmet sandwiches and salad Joyce said would be dinner.

"An orphanage? How horrible would that be? This gets worse and worse, doesn't it?" Joyce observed.

"But, Terry, have you thought about the fact that if this twin brother is actually running around Kentbury, someone would recognize him, wouldn't they?" she asked.

"I know," Terry said with a sigh, "I've thought about that too but maybe they were the . . . what kind . . . fraternal . . . you know the kind that don't look exactly alike," he said.

"Yes, I suppose that could be the case, but . . . you think this Greggie is the Francis Gregson White, Francis Gregson Farmer . . . all the same baby with a birth certificate and a death certificate?" she asked, then lit up with another possibility.

"Terry, what if there were actually three babies . . . triplets?" she asked.

"Oh, Honey, please . . . this is crazy enough without triplets, but . . . ," he said, actually wondering if that was possible and if so, what would the implications be?

"Well, actually, I don't suppose that is the case, but it just looks like someone did a lot of fiddling with records to make this baby disappear. It doesn't sound like Lenore Wexler knew about it, but Aggie White . . . surely she knew if she had twins," Joyce said.

"Look, you said yourself how different things were back then. Mr. Wexler, for some reason, didn't want this other baby. I can't imagine it was because of the birthmark but maybe he saw it as some kind of shame or something," Terry speculated.

"Shame? There was already enough shame I'd say, and faking a baby's death, giving him away, having him grow up in an orphanage, I'd say that's about as shameful as it gets!" she said, the outrage evident in her voice.

"I know, but this is all still just speculation. I'm going to get Dolly to find that orphanage; if anybody can find it she can," Terry said.

"What would you do without Dolly? I think we are definitely having Dolly and Neal over for dinner, or at least our treat at the Coach House, don't you think?" Joyce asked.

"Yeah, you're right, Honey, and I'm going to share some of this with Dr. Appleton if the chief gives me the ok. It's getting into some pretty complicated territory," he said. Omitting his visit to Sharon Newberry, Terry had finally told Joyce about consulting the notable psychiatrist in Princeton. She applauded her husband's modern thinking and agreed that it was a valuable science that just might shed light on the strange happenings in Kentbury.

While Joyce put away the packages and got their deli dinner ready, Terry took a few minutes to call his boss. Bull was impressed, said they would certainly ask Dolly to research the orphanage angle, and agreed that any ideas from Dr. Appleton would be welcome.

It took Dolly and her friend Myrna who worked at the New York Public Library, the rest of the week to track down Saint Brigid's Children's Home in Brooklyn. Begun shortly after the Civil War, the institution was still in operation with a current population of ninety-seven children, ages four months to sixteen years. Dolly appreciated what she learned from her friend who had all the resources available in the city, and then made her own inquiries with a few phone calls. First thing Monday morning, notes in one hand, crullers in the other, the intrepid researcher found the two policemen anxious to hear her findings and appreciative, as always, of the delicious homemade treats.

"You remember my friend Myrna, the one who helped with the bits of paper we tracked down? Well, she was the one who helped with this too," Dolly began, giving full credit to her old college friend for finding the orphanage. "She assumed this had to do with the same case, but I only told her we were looking for a child born April, 9, 1901, with the last name White or Farmer, who may have been sent there in 1904 or 1905. I guessed at the dates from the information Terry got from Rosemary Byrd, and that proved right at least," she said.

"I spoke with a very nice lady at Saint Brigid's who said the records were confidential and repeated just what Myrna had learned, that a three year old child with that birth date, named Francis Gregson Farmer, was placed with them in the fall of 1904. But when I told her this was a police investigation, she seemed eager to help and said we could get a release and request the information through a judge or a doctor," she told them.

Terry was on the phone to Dr. Appleton before Dolly got out the door. Bull thought Dr. Walsh could also make the request, but Terry convinced him that Oliver Appleton not only had more clout, but they needed a psychiatrist more than a coroner right now.

"Hell, Son, I'm gonna need both if we don't get this solved, but I will give Marvin a call so he knows what's going on," Bull said.

THIRTY-THREE

"A s terrible as this is, Bull, I'd say it's good news for you and Terry; it's also a story more suited to one of the city papers than the Kaller, but we'll do a front page obit after the funeral," Nelson Hunt said.

"Yup, you're right, Nelson. We had to look at it as a possible connection to the murders here. This whole thing is crazy enough, but at least now we don't have Leonard's death in the mix, and that's off the record, you understand," Bull said good-naturedly, knowing he could say things to Nelson and not expect to see his remarks in print.

"Leonard would have been ok eventually—he just had some growing up to do, but he just . . . I don't know . . . I certainly won't speak ill of the boy. I do feel sorry for his parents; the Smiths are nice folks," Bull said.

The men were talking about the news burning up the phone lines and whirling around two counties since early this morning, when a jealous husband from Phillipsburg was arrested for shooting Deputy Leonard Smith.

Terry came in just as the Kaller Editor in Chief was leaving. "So it's true? Leonard was killed by a jealous husband?" he asked.

"Afraid so, Terry. Apparently Widow Thacker wasn't the only female Leonard was seeing," Bull said.

Bull and Lou attended Leonard Smith's funeral at the Presbyterian Church in Annandale. The chief understood when Terry volunteered to stay on duty after Fred Browning said he would be going to pay last respects and could not watch the office. Both Bull and Terry hoped the day was coming when it wouldn't matter if the office was closed for a few hours, or even a whole day, the way it used to be before the murders, but Terry used the hours at the office to update the case board with new information.

Not for the first time, he had a strange feeling about the Newberrys. Looking at the boards covered with the crime scene photos, time charts and question-marked notations, he could not ignore the baseball bat belonging to Mr. Newberry; Mrs. Newberry driving Gaffer home that day; Etta having been to their home and, even though Sharon had nothing to do with Leonard's death, there was still that connection of her rendezvous spot on Old Gorge Road being yards away from Gaffer's cottage. And the flowers for Gaffer's funeral, and Raymond buying the casket . . . was it kindness or guilt? But even with the vague and tenuous connections, none of it made sense.

Bull got back to the office later than expected. He told Terry Leonard's funeral was well attended, full of police, as would be expected, and three of the mourners were yet more of Leonard's lady friends. "Poor Mrs. Smith—I think she was mortified at her son's behavior, but she is heartbroken too," he said.

"It's sad all around, Chief, but at least they have the person who did it with a clear motive," Terry commented.

"Yeah . . . I know . . . you remember the first detective that was at Etta's crime scene, Walter Dent?" Bull asked.

"He was there?" Terry asked.

"Yes, and he apologized that he couldn't stay with the case, but appreciated the updates we give and he says the gossip around the barracks is that we're a pretty impressive team. He thinks you should apply to the Troopers, Terry, and I said I'd pass that on," Bull told him.

"I guess that's a compliment . . . I don't know . . . I'm hoping to get back to take some night courses, maybe at Rutgers if I can. The GI Bill is a great thing and I can take advantage of that, but don't worry, Bull, I'm not going anywhere too soon and if I did, it wouldn't be to the State Police," he said.

THIRTY-FOUR

I t took only two days for Oliver Appleton to have the records from Saint Brigid's Children's Home in hand and make an appointment to meet Terry on his turf at the police station in Kentbury. It was a pleasant fall day and with the children back in school, the little town was quiet and charming—hardly a backdrop for horrific murder and intrigue, which Dr. Appleton commented on when he arrived at the station a little after ten Wednesday morning.

"Thank you so much for coming, Dr. Appleton. I think we're pretty good policemen, but this case has gone in directions we just can't seem to make sense of. I give full credit to Deputy Kramer here who asked you for help . . . God knows we need it," Bull said, shaking hands with the eminent psychiatrist.

"Well, I have to confess, Chief Campbell, that I find this case extremely interesting. As you know, I do consult for the FBI on occasion, but we just don't see this kind of thing very often in a little town like Kentbury. I really do want to help, and I appreciate your letting me come here and see things first hand," he said.

He could see why Terry liked this man. Bull was immediately at ease and anxious to see not only the information from the orphanage, but to see what the doctor could make of the evidence and material he and Terry put together over these four long weeks of the investigation. The newspapers weren't saying too much, thank goodness, but they got calls every day from worried citizens, most of whom were grateful to the hard-working chief and deputy, but a few others who suggested they were over their heads. The mayor and town council put on a little pressure, but Bull held his own with them; still, it was time to catch this evil person and get their town back. He was a little uncomfortable with the psychiatry angle,

191

but between Terry and Marvin Walsh thinking it was ok, Bull would keep an open mind.

Bull, Terry and Dr. Appleton met in the privacy of the back office, letting Fred Browning man the front and take care of the phones.

"Impressive, Terry . . . yes, yes," the doctor said after studying the charts and photos on the boards Terry had set up. "I'd like to study this, if that's permissible, but I have some unusual information here, so let's start with that and if I get too technical, just stop me," he said, addressing the rapt audience of two.

"This child, Francis Gregson Farmer, was three years, seven months old when he was left with the sisters at Saint Brigid's Children's Home in Brooklyn in November of 1904. In the summer of 1905, the child was placed in foster care with a family who was apparently abusive. He was back at the orphanage for a while then, in September of that year, he was again placed with a foster family where he stayed until he was almost eight. When he returned once again to Saint Brigid's, he was only there a very short time and then sent to the Angels of Mercy Home in Manhattan, and this is very strange," he explained, glancing at the file notes.

"In those days, and still today actually at some institutions, children were separated by gender after a certain age. Angels of Mercy is a home for girls," he said, appreciating the look on the faces of the chief and his deputy.

"Well, what the hell is that about, Doc?" Bull finally asked.

"I'm not sure, Chief, but several things present themselves. First, it is possible it was a clerical error, and an error that just appears on paper, or perhaps an error that actually sent this poor child to the wrong home. But there is a little more information, then nothing.

"The Angels of Mercy Home was closed in 1940 and absorbed into Saint Mary's on Long Island. A lot of the old records were lost but I was able to contact an administrator there who sent me the only record they had on this child," he said. Terry and Bull were silent, the mystery of it all heavy in the air.

"This is a form for placement, fairly routine, requesting a place for F.G.Farmer to go to one of the factory homes. The date is April 1911, making F.G. Farmer ten years old. Sadly, it was not uncommon to send orphans that young to what would be the equivalent of a workhouse where they where housed and fed and, while there was some schooling, these children were almost like slaves. This record indicates that the child was sent to the J.S. Mason Corset Factory in Hoboken. There was a terrible fire there in 1912, with nineteen people perishing and the company never recovered. I met a dead end looking for any kind of records, but there is a record of those who died in that fire but no one with the name Farmer or White is on it," Dr. Appleton said.

"That's a lot of work, Dr. Appleton, in such a short time no less. Please know how much we appreciate your help," Bull said with great sincerity.

"Oh, I appreciate the opportunity to help you with this. I suspect most of the crime in Kentbury is pretty routine, as they say, and this is anything but routine. But let me get to what I found next.

"The last thing in the file was a short, handwritten note from a doctor whose name I can hardly read, but might be Dodge or Hodges . . . just not sure and I could not find a doctor with those names in any references for that time. Doctors were not always on regular staff at orphanages and it's even possible this doctor was an intern or part of a rotation system, so I don't think you'll find him, but what he writes is compelling. If I may," he said, getting a nod from Bull to go on.

Just before he began to read, a familiar voice interrupted him.

"It's about time you got here, Oliver, these poor fellows definitely need help," Marvin Walsh said with a chuckle.

"Marvin, glad you could make it. Just in time to hear this," Dr. Appleton said to his old friend. They got together regularly but it was several months since their last visit and both doctors were pleased when Bull suggested Marvin should join them this morning. Quickly apprised of the findings so far, Dr. Walsh made his way to the coffee pot and a comfortable chair as his friend and colleague began to read.

"Pay attention, Marvin, you will have something to add to this, I'm sure," he said, immediately intriguing everyone in the room.

"Now, it is an old note with some staining and a few illegible words, and the bottom is missing, I think torn away on purpose. I have made a typewritten copy of the note for you, so this is what I could make out." When he finished reading his copy of the strange document, he handed it to Bull and Terry to read for themselves.

22 October 1910
F.B (or T) Dodge . . . Hodges, M.D.

The child known as Francis Gregson Farmer has been in the (something) system for over six years during which time s/he has been in three different foster homes and back and forth at Saint Brigid's and Angeles/Mercy. (illegible).

While all of the placements were made aware of the child's unusual problems, very little is known about this rare condition, seen in approximately one out of two hundred or so births, but because of the embarrassment and social stigma associated with this (illegible), it is suspected that number could be higher. Degrees of the condition vary, causing different problems, different in male and female, often exhibiting dramatic changes in puberty. (Ink stains, next line not legible).

(not legible) . . . . emotional and personality defects, characterized by uncontrollable anger, feelings of hate and per . . . (I believe this word could be persecution), a lack of worthiness and . . . .

The note ended there,

Terry and Bull were looking at each other, a million questions written on their faces.

The two medical men were staring at each other too, but their expressions were more knowing. Bull finally broke the silence.

"So what the hell are we talkin' about here? And the 'she/he thing'— are you tryin' to tell us this twin is a girl?" Bull asked.

"Well . . . that's very perceptive of you, Chief Campbell, and the real answer is that I don't know, but let me tell you what I suspect. Marvin, it's not your field or mine, but I have touched on it in my work and I know it was briefly mentioned when we were in medical school, so jump in if you have any ideas, please," he said.

"You have probably heard stories about babies being born with genitalia that were neither exactly male or female, or just some confusion about it . . . Johns Hopkins in Baltimore has made the latest advances in this area and a Dr. Lawson Wilkins . . . ," Marvin Walsh interrupted.

"I know that study, Oliver, read about in JAMA I think. You're talking about adrenogenital syndrome. The adrenal gland cortisol connection, is that right?" he asked, referring to the Journal of the American Medical Association most doctors read.

"Exactly, Marvin," he said.

"Dr. Appleton, Dr. Walsh, I think my deputy and I are reasonably smart guys, at least I know Terry is, but you need to speak a little plainer, please, for those of us who didn't go to medical school," Bull said.

"Yes, I'm sorry, Chief Campbell. I'll try to keep it simple.

"We know a lot more today than we did in 1901, but sometimes a baby is born with mixed up sex organs. A girl child may appear to have a male organ and a male child may be unusually small. Severe cases cause vomiting, diarrhea; there can be early development, poor skin, girls producing too much testosterone can develop facial hair. As I said, doctors at Johns Hopkins and folks at the Mayo Clinic are making great strides in understanding this, but you can think of it as a glandular problem. Some studies suggest it was the mother but a wider view is that both parents need a recessive gene to . . ." he could tell he was losing them again.

"Sorry . . . I think this baby born in 1901, had this problem. It is rare in twins, but not unheard of and the birthmark you mention, as far as is known, is not directly related to this—two different things, but these children were definitely dealt a very poor hand I would say," he explained.

"Marvin, you did not see any evidence of this when you autopsied Mr. White?" Dr. Appleton asked.

"I'm afraid not. The groin area was mutilated, heavy stabbing wounds and slashes, then the lower half of the body was set on fire. But I have to say, this could explain why there was so much attention to that area of the body. I wish I could say I saw something unusual, but there was no reason to be looking for it, and what I did find presented as normal male genitalia," he said.

Bull had his hand over his mouth, staring at Dr. Appleton. Terry had seen the look before and knew his boss was having a hard time making sense of it all, or perhaps just a hard time seeing how it could be relevant. Terry already made a few leaps though and was deciding if he wanted to share this with Joyce; he thought he probably would.

"So you're telling us that this baby was a girl . . . but everybody thought she was a boy . . . and she/he got shuffled around, having what sounds like a pretty rotten life, but somehow comes back to Kentbury fifty years later to murder her twin brother?" Bull asked, actually making sense of the crazy theory.

"Yes, that's a possible scenario, Chief," Dr. Appleton said. "If this is what that doctor was talking about in the 1910 note, then we have to understand what it would mean back then."

"There was a family in Frenchtown a few years ago whose little girl was born with just this problem," Dr. Walsh volunteered. "The father wanted to place the child in a home, the mother was ashamed but loved the baby, and there are treatments now and even surgery that can help these children. These parents divorced but the last I heard, the mother and little girl were doing well."

"Exactly! Even now, over fifty years since the birth of the children we're talking about, there is a great stigma and often shame attached to it, so just imagine what this child must have endured that long ago," Dr. Appleton added.

"All right . . . let's suppose you're right about this," Terry began, "why kill Gaffer? Why kill Etta Marx?"

"This is speculation, but it is based on what I see more of in my field than you do in yours. First, you have to understand that this person would be very damaged, very disturbed. I could even say it would be unusual not to be disturbed with this kind of background. Killing the sibling who had a normal life, at least the killer would see it that way, was a kind of revenge, even a cleansing. Fire has always been used as a way to erase, expunge . . . sweep clean. As for the woman reporter, perhaps she somehow discovered a connection and put herself in the killer's sights," Dr. Appleton explained.

"But you're not absolutely sure this is what we're looking for, are you?" Terry asked.

"Right!" Bull said, a little red-faced and exasperated with the strange conversation. "And if any of this is true, if any of it has to do with the murders, we will not . . . I repeat not . . . make it public. The murders are about all Kentbury can handle and we're sure as hell not going to tell people it's all because of some weird sex stuff! And, Doc, I have to ask, if this proves right and connects to the murders, what are we supposed to do, go around asking people to undress?" Bull asked, clearly perplexed with this strange scenario.

Marvin Walsh suppressed a grin, anxious to hear Oliver's response, but Bull Campbell made a great point.

"Well . . . I doubt that would get a lot of support, but once you find your murderer, a medical examination will certainly be warranted and that would benefit people in my field more than yours, I'm afraid. But, Chief," the psychiatrist said with that hint of drama Terry had heard before, "I hope you realize that the person you're looking for lives here and you probably know him . . . or her."

THIRTY-FIVE

This would have been so much easier if those horrible kids didn't find the bat. I was working at their age, earning my way; all they do is run around nosing in other people's stuff and making trouble. Greg even agrees with me now—he knows God sent me that brat this morning. I was leaving, but he was right there with his stupid bag, right in front of me, like a gift. He couldn't wait to see what I had in the trunk. He'll be bones if they ever find him . . . but they probably won't. It's just too bad his stupid brother wasn't with him, but it's good . . . I feel good . . . . I don't even care about the money anymore . . . Greg can have it, he deserves it.

When the doctors left the office after the two hour meeting, Marvin Walsh agreed to give his colleague a quick tour of Kentbury, then go on to lunch together in Clinton. Bull's plan was to get lunch sent in so he and Terry could keep working.

Looking at the evidence so far, now with a perspective neither men were completely comfortable with, Bull and Terry were re-thinking everything: they had been looking for a man, now they might be looking for a woman, but not necessarily . . . and what kind of woman? Ugly, weird, hairy?

"Chief, even if all of this is true . . . we never talked about the money. The timing is interesting, isn't it?"

"Meaning?" Bull asked.

"Meaning . . . is it just a coincidence Gaffer got killed as soon as he was notified about being the Wexler heir?" Terry answered while adding a notation to the bulletin board.

"Well . . . I'll tell you . . . I would love this mess to be about money and not men who are really women or vice versa," Bull said, visibly frustrated by all the strange evidence coming their way.

Terry never told Bull about his thoughts concerning the Newberrys but that connection seemed less likely with all they learned this morning, but he'd at least mention it. He was forming his ideas when Fred Browning knocked on the door.

"Chief, Ned Brewer's on the phone. Henry didn't make it to school and he's saying something about a note. He's pretty upset and says his wife is a nervous wreck," he said.

"Tell him we're on our way, Fred," the chief said as he and Terry raced out the door. Terry didn't think the morning could get much stranger, but apparently it could.

Ned Brewer met the policemen at the door, ushering them into the large kitchen where his distraught wife was watching Baby Penny who sat in her highchair, pushing bits of food into her mouth, happily unaware of the unfolding drama.

"I told them . . . I told them not to wander off, to stick together. Russell spoke to them; he even told them about the horrible note, but now . . . oh, God, where can he be? Please find him, please!" Tilly said on the verge of tears.

"Honey, c'mon, you know how he is. Remember last year when he skipped school because he had that arithmetic test? He's probably just . . ."

"Stop it, Ned! I know something is wrong. Tell him, Deputy Kramer, tell him about the note!" she said.

Ned already knew about the note, but they were discussing its possible implications when Russell, Edmund, George and Charlie burst into the room, all talking at once. Ned left work when Tilly called about an hour ago. Finding her almost hysterical when he got home, he called the school and asked that his children be sent home right away, making sure they would come together. Now Bull and Terry were trying to pick out anything useful that might help them to track down the missing boy.

Getting everyone calmed down, they learned that Tilly got a call from the school secretary around eleven o'clock, saying that Henry was not in school and wanting to know if he was sick. In spite of their free-spirited roaming, the Brewer children had good attendance records and Henry's truancy happened only once. Still, it was school policy to check on absent pupils.

Tilly explained that her immediate thought was the evil note, but she only told the school secretary that yes, Henry was ill. She wasn't sure why she lied, but she didn't want to start some kind of big problem if her son was just playing hooky, but it only took another minute for Tilly to feel panic and call Ned who said he was coming right home and would look along a few roads on the way.

"That's why I didn't call you that minute," Tilly said, addressing Bull and Terry. "I kept thinking he'd walk in the door with Ned and he'd be in big trouble, and . . ." she was gulping back tears, trying to be brave and everyone felt helpless.

"We had our bags, Mom, but I thought we were going to look for stuff after school on our way home, then Henry said to go ahead 'cause he wanted to check that big trash barrel in back of the church. I had to go to set up for show 'n tell, so I left him . . . I just left him. I'm sorry, Mom," George said, tears running down his face.

"George, this isn't your fault, and you've already helped a lot," Bull told the distraught boy. "Terry, get yourself down to the church and have a look around. Talk to Reverend Jeffries, he may have seen or heard something. I'll go to the school.

"George, when Henry went to the church and you walked on to school, do you remember if there were a lot of others around . . . other children, maybe teachers or parents? Bull asked.

"Yeah, I guess . . . we were a little late though, so most of the kids were ahead of us. I think there were some cars, but I'm not sure . . . I'm sorry," he said, chocking down more tears.

Ned comforted his son while everyone looked on. Russell and Edmund were feeling like they let their mother down, George was guilty and only little Charlie wasn't quite sure what all of it meant, but each wondered what they could have done differently. None of it felt right . . . where was their brother?

Terry wasn't sure what he expected to find in the trash barrels behind the Methodist Church, but amidst the paper, odd bottles, cans and some actual garbage, his heart fell when he spied the corner of a canvas bag stuffed down into the barrel. Gingerly pushing aside the trash piled on top, he pulled out the soiled bag to see HENRY painted on the front in big black letters. His mind raced with what it meant and the sticky red splotches on the bag left no doubt that Henry Brewer was in trouble.

The new walkie-talkies they carried did not always work, and almost never if too far away, but if Bull was at the school, only a few blocks up the street, Terry hoped to get him and not have to leave what he was sure was a crime scene. Bull got there in less than three minutes.

"What the hell . . . Jesus, Terry, what kind of maniac are we dealing with?" Bull asked when Terry showed him the bag.

The gravel parking lot in back of the beautiful old church was small but could accommodate ten or twelve cars and on Sunday mornings, worshipers parked along Church Street and on side streets. The minister's old Pontiac was often in the parking lot but was not there this morning. While Bull got on the radio to contact the State Police about what they now considered a kidnapping, Terry walked methodically about the area looking for anything unusual. As soon as he could, he would track down Reverend Jeffries and start knocking on doors. He was hoping the Troopers had some men to spare when he heard the sirens, then he wondered who was going to tell the Brewers.

Three State Police cars and one unmarked Ford were parked on the street by the church after Bull stopped them from going into the parking lot that was possibly a crime scene. Terry was telling them what he had found and was happy to see Walter Dent, the detective he met that night at Etta Marx's. One of the troopers was taking photos while Bull made notes and Sgt. Dent took Terry aside to get his account of what they knew so far.

"You're sure this kid's in trouble and you think it's connected to the murders?" Walter Dent asked.

"Yes, sir. The note is back at the station if you need to see it, but this is the boy who found the murder weapon. We're now working on the assumption that the murderer could be a mentally ill person and they have some kind of grudge against this kid for finding the baseball bat," Terry explained.

"Most murderers are mentally ill the way I see it, Deputy, but you mean what . . . some kind of real crazy guy?" the detective asked.

"Yeah . . . well . . . I actually took the note to a psychiatrist, a very good one, and he's the one who thinks the note is genuine and the person who wrote it is yeah . . . crazy," Terry said. He would not, unless he had to, talk about any of the theories Dr. Appleton suggested. When they caught the murderer, and if the doctor's ideas proved right, they would probably have to make it known to police officials, then let the prosecutors and lawyers deal with the rest of the mess, but he wasn't about to bring it up now. Besides, their immediate concern was finding Henry Brewer.

Bull asked the Troopers to block the church driveway when curious neighbors began to appear and kids on lunch break gave up recess and dancing in the gym to enjoy the excitement of all the police activity at the church. When Bull became aware of the buzz running through the crowd that they found some kid's body in the trash bin, the Chief made a quick announcement that there was no such thing and unless they had something to tell the police, they were to leave immediately. A few adults lingered, but most of the youngsters and teens found their way back to the school.

"Terry, I'm running up to see the Brewers before they hear something they shouldn't. I'll come back here as soon as I can. We need to find out if anyone saw anything. I hate to do it, but we might need to get the kids in an assembly to see if anyone saw Henry or might know something. I don't get it: it's secluded down here I guess, you can't see the parking lot from the street but still, broad daylight, lots of people around on the streets . . . make sure we check all the backyards, go down the hill and check the railroad tracks," Bull said, referring to the Jersey Central line that paralleled Church Street, literally defining "the other side of the tracks," country towns were known for. "Check the bushes around the church. Is the church open? Check that too," he said as he ran off with the unenviable task of telling the Brewers their son was possibly kidnapped, which would be the better scenario—the blood on the bag Terry found could mean it was even worse.

THIRTY-SIX

While Bull Campbell met with Ned and Tilly Brewer in their living room, with Russell watching the other children in the kitchen, Joyce was on her way to Lake Cottage. She heard about Henry Brewer when Gloria Skinner came by, thinking Joyce might have more information and was disappointed when the deputy's wife said she knew nothing about it.

Joyce knew better than to call Terry and probably couldn't reach him anyway, but she quickly made the connection to Henry Brewer and the murder investigation that was driving her husband crazy. She thought Madeline and Ethel might know more than she did and met Madeline and Jimmy as she pulled into the drive.

"Yes, dear, I'm afraid there's another crime—this young boy is missing. Ethel heard about it from Cousin Velma, who lives on Church Street. Lots of police cars by the Methodist Church, she said. We just don't know what could be next it seems; but your poor husband . . . it must be quite upsetting for you," she said sympathetically.

"Well, Terry and Chief Campbell can handle it, I'm sure," Joyce said, realizing what a pat response that was, but what else could she say?

"I was just taking Jimmy for one of our big walks," Madeline explained. "Ethel won't be back for a while, why don't you come along, the leaves are so beautiful now and Jimmy is anxious to go. Besides, it would be lovely to have company. I'm not really afraid, but things certainly are strange lately," she said.

"Well . . . yes . . . that would be nice, thank you," Joyce said, pleased she was wearing slacks and comfortable flats.

The big dog, free of a leash, raced down the drive with a joyful woof as soon as his mistress said, "Let's go, Jimmy!"

"You do get a different perspective walking, don't you?" Joyce commented as they trekked along the lakeside road, approaching the gorge area. The oak and maple trees were beginning the autumn redecorating, as she always thought of it, but she was inspired by the season changes and did appreciate how much more dramatic they were in the country.

Joyce was used to walking miles in the city but instead of shop windows and elegant restaurants to look at, she was enjoying Mother Nature's window dressing that included busy squirrels, noisy birds and a large rabbit that sent Jimmy running until Madeline called him back. Joyce was keeping up though, impressed with her guide's energy and stamina. As always, she found the company charming and entertaining; they talked only briefly about the murders and the missing boy, then happily turned the conversation to town history and decorating.

"Now, Jimmy and I always go a little way onto Old Gorge Road, and I let him chose left or right," Madeline said when they came to the crossroad.

Joyce watched with amusement as Jimmy looked to the right, then did two barks and turned left onto the dirt road that ran along the beautiful gorge. She was enjoying herself but was thinking they should get back soon so she could show the ladies the fabric samples she had, then at least drive by the police station. Even if Terry wasn't there, she might learn what was going on. In spite of the scenic walk and good company, it was hard not to worry about her husband and wonder what was happening. They heard sirens several times but neither lady speculated on what they might be for.

"Jimmy! Get down here!" Madeline shouted. The collie was barking furiously at something in the woods and his mistress was worried he might have a confrontation with a wild animal and be hurt, or worse. She began to enter the dense wooded area when Joyce stopped her.

"Let me go, Madeline, I'll get him," Joyce said, as Madeline continued calling the dog.

Joyce followed Jimmy's barking, hoping whatever it might be was small and non-poisonous.

When Jimmy saw that a human was finally paying attention, he ran to Joyce and sat down, but before she could grab his collar he took off again, this time barking and looking back at her. *"C'mon,"* he seemed to be saying, so Joyce followed, negotiating the rocky, leaf-strewn path until she found the dog sitting by what looked like an old well.

"What is it, Jimmy? What have you found?" she asked, approaching the dark stone structure that looked like it had been there forever. Moss-covered and nearly hidden by overgrown bushes, Joyce doubted she would have seen it if the dog didn't lead her to it. Jimmy was whining now and anxious for Joyce to get on with it, but she was not so eager since all she could think of after entering the woods were snakes.

Gingerly approaching the four foot high wall, she peered with one eye closed into the dirt-filled well. The horror and shock Joyce might have felt if she indeed had found a snake, paled now as she looked upon the small, curled-up body of a tow headed boy!

Detective Dent and most of the State Troopers left the church area to begin canvassing the nearby houses, leaving one car and two officers at the church until school was out and curious children were in their homes. When Reverend Jeffries finally arrived, he explained to Terry that he had an early meeting in Lambertville, and it was Mrs. Jeffries who had called him at the meeting to tell him what was happening. The minister was horrified at what may have transpired here, but he had left from the parsonage this morning, three doors down from the church, and had seen nothing unusual. Of course he would pray for the Brewers, he'd go see them. The family attended here and he knew them well.

Terry was getting ready to leave when he saw the school principal walking toward him.

"Deputy, can I have a minute, please?" Mr. Woodward called out.

Terry told the concerned man what he could, affirming that it was Henry Brewer they suspected may be a kidnap victim, and suggesting the best thing would be to follow routine and continue with a normal school day.

"I'm going to make sure each class is cautioned at least, make sure they will not be walking home alone . . . I'm already getting calls from parents, you can imagine," he said.

They spent a few more minutes talking about how best to handle things, finally deciding school would remain open tomorrow, the State Police would assign two cars to patrol during school hours, and Terry was impressed when Principal Woodward explained that they had an emergency telephone tree in place, but had not had to use it since hurricane season in 1948. There was something touching about that . . . not needing it for so long . . . and both men appreciated this as a different kind of emergency, but just as menacing, just as threatening.

"Oh, and Mr. Woodward, keep an eye out for anyone who might have seen something. This probably happened at a pretty busy time, maybe someone saw a car, maybe heard something even," Terry suggested.

The principal promised to call if anything came to light.

Terry was getting in his car to leave when the radio went off.

"Who gave you this message? My wife is where and she said what?" Terry asked Fred Browning when the part-time volunteer reached him.

"It was Mrs. VanHaven, Terry. She called and said Joyce borrowed her car and went back to Old Gorge Road to wait for the police and the rescue squad. I already called them," he told Terry who thought he heard the sirens in the distance. He digested as much as he could of the strange message and took off toward the gorge, still on the radio. "Fred, call the chief and tell him what you told me. He's at the Brewer's, but don't say anything to them, just tell the chief and he'll know what to do," Terry cautioned, signing off and putting the siren on as he sped down the road.

What the hell was she doing on that road, in Mary VanHaven's car no less, and was this boy Henry Brewer?

It took Terry less than four minutes to get to the spot where Mary VanHaven's old Nash was sitting on the side of the road, in front of the ambulance that had just arrived. The men on the rescue squad were getting a stretcher out as he pulled up.

"Glen, Johnny, let me have a second before you move anything!" he shouted, running past the two Kentbury citizens who were among the small group of dedicated volunteers Terry so admired.

When Joyce peeked into the old well, which was part of a bygone home no longer there, she was steeling herself to see something unpleasant, but it took her mind several seconds to adjust to the sight of a young boy, bruised and bloodied, lying curled up on top of dirt and shale, surrounded by leafy debris.

"Madeline! Mrs. Stone, there's a boy here, Jimmy found a boy!" she shouted.

Madeline was already negotiating her way into the woods when she heard Joyce's call. Jimmy came rushing up, barking and escorting his mistress to his important find.

"Is he . . . alive?" Madeline asked when she looked into the old well.

"I think so . . . I'm afraid to touch him, but . . ." Joyce said, deciding to lean over the side of the thick stone wall, mindful to keep her balance and stretching as far as she could to touch the poor child who lay almost five feet down into the rocky, dirt-filled prison.

"Careful, dear," Madeline said, impressed by her young friend's response to such an awful thing. The girl had spirit, but she knew that.

His face felt cold and clammy. Gently placing her fingers under his chin, Joyce felt a pulse.

"He's alive," she whispered, tears in her eyes.

Quickly taking off her light jacket, she carefully placed it on the boy and told Madeline what they would do.

"Madeline, are you all right to stay here with him, you and Jimmy?" Joyce asked.

"Yes, Joyce. Don't worry about that, but you're younger and faster, so hurry dear, I don't think we could lift him out of there, but I also don't think we should move him," she said.

"You're right. Where is the nearest house, a telephone, do you know?" Joyce asked.

"The two closest houses are just summer people and they'll be gone by now. Go back the way we came. That cute yellow bungalow we passed belongs to Melvin Falk, but I'm honestly not sure he has a telephone . . . if his big old truck isn't in the driveway, he's not home anyway. You might have to go on a little further, but Mary VanHaven is probably there and if she isn't, you just go in and use the phone, now hurry!" Madeline instructed.

Joyce almost fell running down the path. There was no truck at the yellow house and she sprinted another quarter mile to Mary VanHaven's, bursting in the front door and scattering some surprised cats in the process!

"What on earth, Joyce . . . what is it, dear?" Mary said when her out-of-breath visitor popped in.

Joyce explained quickly. In a few short minutes, she was easing Mary's old car onto the road while the retired librarian made the very important call to Fred Browning at the police station. Once sure that her message was on its way, she called her daughter at the library.

Only minutes had gone by since Joyce left, but every minute counted for that poor child. Prayers ran through her head as she parked and ran back to Madeline and the boy. She knew Mary told them approximately where along the road they were and to look for the car; she thought she heard a distant siren above Jimmy's greeting.

"Oh, Joyce, he hasn't made a sound," Madeline said when Joyce got back. "I tried to feel his forehead, but I'm afraid I can't reach over that far," she said. Joyce was touched to see that Madeline had taken off her cardigan, resting it on top of her jacket. All they could do it seemed was to keep him warm, but just when Joyce was wondering if she could hoist herself up and over and into the old well, the rescue squad arrived along with her husband.

"Joyce! Where are you?" Terry shouted.

"Terry, I'm here," she said, running back toward the road, accompanied by a barking Jimmy.

Everything happened very fast once they reached the well. Terry identified the boy as Henry Brewer and jumped into the would be-grave to assist in getting him out and onto a stretcher. Terry accompanied them to the ambulance, and agreed when they said they should take the extra ten minutes to get the boy to the hospital in Flemington where they had a pediatric floor, more doctors and more equipment than the capable, but small, Cool Springs Clinic. The ambulance roared off down the lake road only minutes before Bull pulled up, followed by the Brewers.

"They think he's going to be ok, Mr. Brewer, Mrs. Brewer. They know what they're doing," Terry assured them, praying he was right.

"We have to go right now, Ned!" Tilly said when she realized her son was on his way to Flemington.

"We're going right now, Tilly. You follow me, I'll use the siren, don't worry," Bull said, rushing back to his car, followed by Terry who was hoping they could talk, but obviously that would have to wait.

"Deputy, you'll want to search this area and I've got to escort the Brewers to the hospital. Ned's doing ok, but Tilly's not going to be ok until she sees her boy; they'll get there a lot faster with a police escort and I want to hear what the doctors say . . . and, if Henry can tell us what happened, we might finally catch this maniac," Bull said. Just before leaving with the Brewers, he asked if he heard right—was it Joyce who found the boy?"

"That's right, Chief, but I don't know the whole story yet myself," Terry said

Joyce, Madeline and Jimmy had to give official statements to Terry and to Walter Dent when the detective and State Troopers arrived. When they could finally leave, Joyce drove Mary's car back, accompanied by Madeline and Jimmy.

THIRTY-SEVEN

Detective Dent and two Troopers joined Terry as they searched the area, eager to learn what they could and gratified to have the boy found so quickly. They didn't try to whisper their comments about what a looker Mrs. Kramer was, but Terry pretended he didn't hear. He certainly wasn't about to have a conversation about his wife with a bunch of cops.

"You know, unless it's just a kid fooling around, these things can turn out pretty bad. I'm glad this one didn't. You better put Mrs. Kramer on the payroll, Deputy," the detective said.

"She's a beautiful lady . . . you're a lucky fellow," Dent added, and that was ok—direct and respectful.

"Thank you, yes I am," he said.

Everyone agreed that finding Henry at all, let alone so quickly, was just short of miraculous, but with the strange coincidence of the deputy's wife finding him, Terry knew the story was well on its way to becoming part of police lore and legend. Still, both he and Joyce were making sure people knew they considered the real hero Jimmy Doolittle, the collie.

By the time Terry left the gorge, the sun was starting to set in the fall sky. It was cool in the woods and he doubted the boy would have survived the night; he even wondered if he might have fallen prey to any of the more dangerous animals populating the area, and that hardly bore imagining.

Tired and anxious to get home, Terry knew he'd be sorry if he didn't stop at the office to file a quick report and check for any messages. He was surprised to see all the lights on and Fred Browning still at his desk.

"Just thought I should wait, Terry. We've had lots of calls about the Brewer boy, you can imagine, and I told them that yes, he was found and is at the hospital in Flemington. Bull called earlier and said that was our comment for the moment. He also said the boy was unconscious but the doctors expected him to come around, but we're not going to say that. Bull said that for now, our only statement is that he is still unconscious," Fred told him.

Terry supposed Fred spent so much time volunteering for them because it filled the widower's days and he enjoyed it but, like Dolly, they could never afford to pay him what he was worth. He made a point of thanking Fred when he left, and maybe he and Bull could come up with something practical to show their appreciation.

Fortunately, there was no crime, domestic dispute or traffic accident to attend to and Terry called Joyce to say he would be home as soon as he could.

"I have a nice big T-Bone for you, Deputy, and we're saving the bone for Jimmy," she said. Terry realized they had missed lunch and that steak was just what he wanted, along with a whiskey and soda and a quiet evening with his heroic wife.

He was just turning out lights and locking up when Nelson Hunt came in.

"I saw the lights, Terry. I know you've had quite a day. How's the Brewer boy, can you tell me?" the newspaper editor asked.

Terry told him what he could, confirmed that, yes, Joyce and Madeline Stone, along with her collie, found the boy and that the State Police were handling an official statement. Did he think Bull would give *The Kentbury Kaller* an exclusive? Terry thought he would.

"Off the record, Terry, is this thing connected to the murders?" he asked.

"Off the record, Mr. Hunt, I'd say that there could be a connection and we're getting closer to solving this damn thing," Terry stated with more conviction than he felt.

He saw the candlelit table through the dining room window as he pulled into the driveway. Delicious smells greeted him when he entered the house where Joyce was waiting, drink in hand for him, wearing one of his white dress shirts and nothing else.

"You're a wicked, woman, do you know that?" he asked, putting the drink down and taking her in his arms.

Their urgent lovemaking began in the doorway, continued through the living room and ended in the bedroom.

"So, is this a new kind of hors d'oeuvre or what? I like it, I think we should have this every night," Terry said.

"I tell you what—you wash up, I'll get the steaks going but I won't change and we can have the same thing for dessert, what you do think?" Joyce said, getting a long kiss as an answer before she left for the kitchen.

After a quick bath and change of clothes, Terry was enjoying one of his favorite dinners—steak, baked potato and fresh string beans, while listening to Joyce's account of the day's events. "Wow . . . what are the odds that you would show up just then and agree to go for a walk?" Terry asked.

"I know . . . Madeline and Jimmy might have found him anyway, but my being there made it easier I guess," she confessed, shaking her head at the way things had come together. "Do you think God had a hand in it?" she asked.

Her question surprised him. Joyce and Terry were Protestants, attended church a few times a year, but did not consider themselves very religious.

"Yeah . . . maybe . . . why not?" Terry answered. "Bull is going to say that was the case, and who are we to say otherwise? Even if Henry didn't die from his wounds, he wouldn't have lasted long out there—look how cold it is tonight," he said.

"You said it's close to Gaffer's White's place . . . I didn't see another house," Joyce said.

"Yes, Honey, it's yards away from Gaffer's cottage through the woods that way, closer than if you were on the road. I don't know why, but the person we're looking for seems to have knowledge of that area," he said.

Tell me again about that property? What kind of well was that anyway?" Joyce wanted to know.

"That bit of land up there was part of some kind of early settler house. A little way from that well you can see an old foundation, but the well was filled in a long time ago and thank God for that," Terry explained.

"Do you think the person who put him in there thought it was going to be a deep well with water in it, but then just left him there anyway?" Joyce asked, horrified at the cruelty of such an act.

"Who knows, but from what we've seen, and assuming it is the same person who committed the murders, I doubt they would have cared . . .

they were probably disappointed it was filled in. I'd say Henry Brewer is damn lucky," Terry said.

After telling Joyce about the call from Tilly Brewer, his finding the canvas bag in the trash at the church and the ensuing events, he wanted to tell her about the visit from Dr. Appleton. Joyce got them each another drink, then was all ears. She doubted it could top the rescue of Henry Brewer, but she was wrong.

THIRTY-EIGHT

I *can't believe they found that stupid kid! Mrs. Kramer and a dog,*
a dumb animal. I can't think straight when I'm afraid, but I'll be
ok . . . I'll have to leave sooner than I thought, but if that kid wakes
up and tells . . . It was too easy . . . he was right there when I left the church.
God must have sent him to me. I asked if he wanted the bottles I had in the
trunk, he couldn't wait! He looked right in and wham! He just fell in the
trunk, but I was glad it didn't kill him, I wanted to dump him like the trash
he rummages around in, but he's lucky that kid. At least he's not awake . . .
Greg says that's good and I don't have to leave right away and besides, if I just
run, people will wonder why. I have to get the rest of my pay, and then I can
disappear in the city. Greg will know what I should do.

As much as Terry wanted to go to the hospital himself, there was no
real reason to. Bull kept him informed and the doctors would call if there
was any change. Tilly, not surprisingly, was staying at the hospital while
Ned's parents came from Bound Brook to take care of the family. Ned
was back at work and the boys back at school, but it was two days now
and Henry was making noises which the doctors said was a good sign,
but he was not yet fully awake.

In the office early, Terry was wondering how he could make time to
go to Princeton. He had learned that Dr. Appleton was still in Clinton
with Marvin Walsh yesterday when news reached them about the
kidnapping. Apparently, the psychiatrist had some definite ideas about
what might be happening and asked to be kept informed. Terry called a
minute before the doctor could call him.

"That's amazing, Terry! He is a very lucky boy. I doubt the person
who did this expected him to be found—at least not so soon and so that

214

would have made another murder. Thank God for that dog . . . and you said your wife was there—what are the odds on that?"

Terry listened attentively as the doctor told him he was pursuing a line of inquiry through old medical records but had no idea what, if anything, it would reveal. In the meantime, Terry thought of a line of inquiry himself.

"We have this great gal who helps us with research and I don't want to tell her about all of the things you suspect concerning this possible twin, but she might be able to track down people on the list you gave us," Terry suggested.

"Which list is that, Terry?" he asked.

"The one with the names of the people killed in the fire at the factory—you know, where those orphans were placed. There's no full record left of any of the children sent there, but if any relatives are left from the list of the people who died . . . ,"

"Terry, that's an excellent idea! It could prove just as fruitless as what I'm looking for, but you've got what is it . . . nineteen names there? It's quite possible you could find someone; by all means look into that, but it will take time. If we're lucky, we may have caught this person by then," he said.

Terry hoped he was right and found it interesting that the doctor was saying "we." The doc was on the team it seemed, and that was fine with him.

Dolly was happy to take the list, especially when Terry explained it could provide a name for someone connected to the murders.

"Can you tell me connected how, Terry? The murderer himself?" Dolly asked.

Dolly was smart and Terry knew he could trust her. He was not going to tell her about all the theories Dr. Appleton had, but he wanted to explain as much as he could.

"Dolly, we've been talking with a big shot psychiatrist in Princeton about this. Most people don't know, and don't need to know, but we're pretty sure there's a connection to what happened to Henry Brewer and the murders. We think the person who hurt him and dumped him in that well also wrote a note to the Brewers a few weeks ago threatening those boys because they found the murder weapon," Terry began.

"Oh, those poor children . . . and you think the murderer really did this?" Dolly asked.

"Pretty sure the same person. But the doctor who's been helping us thinks that someone actually related to Gaffer White . . . a twin possibly . . . could be behind it and this doctor is the one who found the connection to the orphanage you tracked down for us, and now there's this possible connection to the factory in Hoboken, but the only records left were just names of survivors from the fire," Terry explained.

"I see. Maybe a relative of one of the fire victims could tell us about this child . . . F. G. Farmer. I'd say it's a long shot, Terry, but I'll start with census records and see if I can find anyone that way. If I can find any old newspaper articles about the fire, there could be some names there too," she suggested.

Terry thought that was a great idea and told her so.

"You know how much we appreciate your help, Dolly, and I don't have to say this is all very confidential," Terry said.

"Terry, you did say 'twin,' didn't you? You think Gaffer White had a twin?"

"It's possible. There are lots of old records that seem to suggest that," he said.

"But a twin . . . I don't think I've seen anyone around that looked like poor old Gaffer, have you?" she asked with expected skepticism.

"No, I haven't. But you know about fraternal twins and people change a lot. It's strange, Dolly, that's for sure," Terry said.

"Well, strange is certainly one word for it, but I'll do my best, Terry. Tell Bull not to worry, I won't tell a soul, not even Mother," she said, taking the file Terry handed her.

Terry could hear the phone ringing as he went down the stairs from the library.

"Joyce for you, Terry," Bull said with a wink. Terry took the call at his desk.

"No, I'll do it, Terry," Joyce said when Terry offered to take the T-Bone treat to Jimmy Doolittle, but Joyce said she wanted to do it and combine her visit with Madeline and Ethel, hoping to get back to the decorating project that was, understandably, put aside with the events of yesterday.

In spite of being double-wrapped in foil and then put in a paper bag, the collie quickly detected the treat Joyce had for him.

"Yes, this is for you . . . you know, don't you? That special nose of yours saved a little boy, do you know that? What a good dog you are," Joyce told him.

Jimmy was prancing and barking all the way to the door, but Joyce wanted to make sure it was ok to give him the treat, when Ethel called from the side porch.

"Jimmy, behave yourself! I'm sorry, Joyce, just come in, I'll be right there," she said.

"Good morning, Ethel! I have a little reward for Jimmy and wanted to make sure it was all right to give it to him. I'll just wait here," she called back.

Finally, after explaining that they rarely gave Jimmy bones . . . but also explaining how seldom they had steak . . . and when they did they had fillets without bones, the patient dog received the special treat and ran off to the side patio to enjoy it in peace.

It was only natural that before any talk of decorating took place, Ethel wanted to hear Joyce's version of yesterday's events. She heard her sister's version several times by now, and once word got out that not only had the poor little boy been found, but that Madeline and Jimmy, along with Deputy Kramer's wife, were the ones who found him, the sisters had been inundated with well-wishers and gossip-seekers alike, in person and on the phone.

Ethel was hardly jealous, but you could tell she was sorry she had missed the excitement.

"Actually, God must have arranged for me to have that appointment yesterday. It was my day to take Jimmy and we never walk as far as when Madeline takes him . . . oh, I'm just so glad everyone is all right and dear, sweet Jimmy, we're so proud of him," Ethel said.

While Joyce was immersed in color charts, fabric samples and more talk about the rescue, Terry was on the phone with Detective Dent who had a few questions before he could submit his own report on the kidnapping. As soon as Terry hung up, a call came in from the hospital informing them that Henry Brewer was awake, but cautioning this was classified information and the official response had not changed—Henry was still unconscious.

Bull rushed off to Flemington, leaving Terry behind to meet with Dr. Appleton who should be there by ten o'clock. While the deputy waited for their newest team member to arrive, he went over the two bulletin boards, with a kidnapping now added to murder charts. Something was nagging him. What was he missing?

Fred Browning came in at the same time Dr. Appleton arrived. Bless Fred, he was apologizing for being late.

"Not late, Fred, just in time. Dr. Appleton and I will be in the back. Get yourself some coffee and relax," Terry said.

Terry was quiet as Oliver Appleton studied the bulletin boards. He watched the doctor purse his lips, raise his eyebrows, squint his eyes and make a few undecipherable sounds before finally turning to the eager deputy.

"I wish I could just connect the dots, Terry, but while I see a certain pattern, I'm inclined to think this second murder is the one that could be considered to have a 'normal' motive," he said.

Terry was disappointed. Did he really expect some great moment when the doctor would name the murderer on the spot?

"Meaning what exactly, sir?" Terry asked.

"This newspaper woman may have come upon information that threatened the killer. Miss Marx may have been planning to do some kind of story and that's what got her killed. But the first murder, Mr. White, I think the connection was very personal and the motive was an imagined one in a demented mind. Do you agree?" he asked, surprising Terry.

"Uh . . . yeah, I guess I agree. I mean I see what you're getting at," Terry answered, realizing the psychiatrist in the room would make more sense of it than the policeman in the room, but the policeman was learning.

"Terry, you make reference here to letters from a Lenore Wexler— could I possibly see them?" the doctor asked.

After almost an hour in which the doctor studied the letters and Terry took several calls, including one from the chief at the hospital, Dr. Appleton said he had a clearer picture of events so long ago and that this picture would support his theory about the Farmer child. But first, Terry had important news.

"Henry Brewer is awake, Dr. Appleton, but he doesn't remember what happened, can you believe that?" Terry asked, as exasperated as Bull sounded when he called in.

"Sounds like amnesia. The boy's mind is protecting him from what was a very violent and traumatic experience. His memory of events could come back, or he may never remember it," the doctor explained.

"That's just great I guess!" Terry said, wondering if they would ever get a real break.

"Does he know his family, does he know his name? His amnesia isn't total is it?" the doctor asked.

"No, I guess he knows those things. The chief said he was happy to see his mother and asked her what happened. Bull did get to talk to him and Henry said the last thing he remembered was walking to school with his brother," he said.

"Well, sometimes hypnosis could help, but this kind of amnesia can be dangerous, especially in a child. I agree, by the way, with not making it known to the public that the boy is awake. What are his injuries, by the way? It sounds like he suffered a concussion," the doctor asked.

"Yeah, a concussion—a big gash in the back of his head and a big bump in front. When I first saw him, he had all this dried blood on his neck and shirt. I thought he had been stabbed, but it was just from the head gash. The chief said he has twenty-two stitches and there's lots of bruising, probably from being dragged around, the poor kid," Terry said.

Dr. Appleton had to leave by noon but he hoped what he offered would be helpful. He promised to call the minute anything became known and of course Terry said he would do the same.

"This is my home number, Terry. Even if I'm not there, they know how to reach me. This person is very dangerous, make no mistake about that. Kidnapping a child and leaving him for dead, is vengeful and irrational. If you don't find him . . . or her . . . soon, they might loose all sense of reality and hurt more people. Just be careful, please," he said.

"I can't believe someone you think is this crazy isn't noticeable. I mean, how can they act normal?" Terry asked.

"That's part of the danger, I'm afraid. If I'm right in believing the murderer is this same child we're talking about, they have had years of learning how to fit in. They would have discovered early in life how to present a persona that people expected, all the while hiding their true nature, hiding the agony and torment they suffered, but something has made it come to a head now—something to do with Kentbury, perhaps even to do with the Wexler inheritance. Be vigilant, Terry, I feel strongly that something will happen to reveal who they are; I just hope it is not something that will result in another death," the doctor said.

THIRTY-NINE

Bull got back after lunch and listened to what his deputy was telling him with less skepticism than he had a few days ago.

"Marvin Walsh was at the hospital when I was waiting with the Brewers and we had a chance to talk. He told me Dr. Appleton is the top head doctor on the east coast, we're lucky to have his help. I guess I'm getting old, Terry, but we just never had stuff like this—if somebody broke the law, we caught 'em, tried 'em, they went to jail, period. Now somebody commits a crime and we have to find out if his mommy was mean to him or he was forced to eat spinach . . . I don't know . . . it used to be easier," Bull said. Terry appreciated that he was joking, but maybe not entirely.

"I'll admit, though, it scares the hell out of me to think we can't find him . . . her . . . and we have to wait until the next crazy thing," Bull said.

Terry agreed. The two policemen spent the rest of the afternoon going over the three cases and studying the crime boards until they were getting bleary-eyed. Tired, and with thoughts turning to home, Bull looked up to see Father Hanover and Father Boyle walking in.

"Father Hanover! I didn't know you were home. Father Boyle, why didn't you tell us?" Bull said, surprised but pleased to see the two priests.

"I didn't know myself, Ernest, but when I heard about that poor child being kidnapped, then the story of his miraculous rescue, I told Dr. Sullivan I needed to get back to Saint Michael's. The doctor agreed I was well enough and Father Boyle picked me up a little while ago," he explained.

"Don't worry, Chief Campbell, we're not going to let him do too much," the younger priest told them.

"Well, I think that suits me, Father Boyle, but Ernest, I remembered what was bothering me about Gaffer White's baptism all those years ago.

I can't be sure, but I seem to remember a baby dying and being buried at Saint Paul's in Califon. I'm afraid it's a rather vague memory and I don't know what it could mean, but I guess you could check on it," the old priest said.

"Father, your memory is fine. We actually know about that and we're not sure what it means either, but we're looking into it," Bull said, not wanting to reveal too much.

"Well, fine then. I know this is all very troubling. If this is over before it gets too cold, I was hoping we might get in a bit of fishing. What do you think, Ernest?"

"I think that sounds great, Father," Bull said.

Before they left, Father Hanover was told a little about the case and wanted to know if anything had come to light about why he was attacked and what the person who hit him might have been after. There were no real answers and Bull wasn't about to throw out the latest crazy stuff to a priest; maybe the Father wouldn't be embarrassed, but he would.

"Please look after him, Father Boyle, and we can use all the prayers we can get," Bull said as they left.

It was after seven o'clock when Terry got home. Rich aromas of beef stew welcomed him but he was disappointed to see Joyce in slacks and a sweater.

"So where's that white shirt you look so great in?" he asked.

"Never mind, I've had a busy day and I know you have too. Besides, the shirt is in the hamper," she said.

Terry washed up and got into more comfortable clothes. As expected, most of the conversation revolved around the case, but Terry enjoyed hearing about Joyce's visit with the Crisp sisters and about how much Jimmy appreciated his T-Bone treat. When Terry told her what Doctor Appleton's theory was after reading Lenore Wexler's letters, Joyce got excited.

"See, that's what I said, isn't it?" she exclaimed.

Terry had not been sure how much he was going to tell his wife about Dr. Appleton's theories, especially as related to the male/female glandular stuff, but when he began to tell her a little the other night, he wound up telling her everything. Joyce was intelligent, intuitive and maybe more broad-minded than he was. She was easy to talk to and he realized how much he appreciated her and how much he valued her opinion.

Joyce had said something similar to what Dr. Appleton was suggesting: that if this glandular problem thing was what the one baby had, given the Victorian attitudes of the time, Old Man Wexler would have rejected the infant as fast as he could.

Talk about the case continued as Terry helped Joyce clear the table and clean up.

"After all, Lenore Wexler's letter indicated he had to be forced into letting Aggie come back to work for them so they could take care of her and the baby, but he wasn't about to accept this other baby if he could help it, so . . . ," Joyce began.

"So . . . he pays off the Farmers to take the other baby and that's why they move so quickly to New York," Terry added. "Maybe the Cousin family knew something about it and that's what caused this rift we've heard about."

"Yes, could be, and he gets all the crazy stuff with the church in Califon to record the birth of each baby differently, then somehow gets Saint Ann's in Hampton to record a death certificate, gets the burial, or the record of a burial, to be in Califon, just crazy and complicated enough to confuse anyone who might have ever questioned anything," Terry said. "Then that thing you picked up on about the name Francis with an "i", and Frances with an "e", the boy/girl thing again," he said, referring to the different spellings of that name they found on the different documents.

"Yes, he wanted to erase that poor little baby, Terry. I wonder that he wouldn't have somehow arranged to murder it," Joyce said, with an expression as dark as her words.

"You know Dolly checked public records and didn't find anything for a birth or death of these babies. That wasn't so unusual in those days, especially in the country. Sometimes births and deaths got recorded months later if somebody got around to it, but Dolly didn't find anything," Terry said.

"Yes, I remember we talked about that. In those days, someone like Mr. Wexler would have had so much power, enough money to do what he wanted. Maybe he even thought he was protecting his family," Joyce said.

"Yeah, well . . . you're being very kind, Honey. I think the only thing he was protecting was himself with not the slightest concern about his grandchild, but I'd say he got some kind of just reward: loosing his son, estranged from his wife, hated by his daughters—I guess you do reap what you sow," Terry said.

"Well, I have sewn a delicious dinner, so what do I reap? Any ideas?" Joyce said, tiring of the shop talk and looking forward to bed.

Joyce went ahead to the bedroom while Terry made a drink and looked through some of the old photos they had from Mary VanHaven. He felt like little bits and pieces were floating around in his head and something would happen to make them all come together, giving him the answers he needed to find the person haunting the town. It felt like a haunting . . . creepy, vague shadows just out of reach. Tomorrow was Sunday and usually that meant he could sleep a little longer, but he and Bull would be in early. Terry finally turned out the light and went to the bedroom.

Joyce was asleep. He gazed upon her for a little while, thanking the God that helped dogs save little boys, apparently the same God that let him live and yet did not save so many of his fellow Marines, the same God that let an innocent little baby be turned into a murderer and yet, the same God that gave him this wonderful, beautiful woman. His grandmother taught him that having faith meant accepting things and not always questioning, but God's Plan, whatever it was, did not make a lot sense sometimes.

The phone was ringing. It was after ten. *Now what?* Terry wondered.

"Terry, I'm so sorry, I know it's late, but Neal and I were in bed reading and Tuk-Tuk was running around and making a mess—he loves to tear up paper and he jumped into the files I brought home with the list from the fire victims you left with me," she said. Terry knew Dolly would not call so late if it wasn't important, but he was anxious for her to get to the point.

"I really had not paid a lot of attention to the list as yet because I was waiting for a census book to be sent from Trenton and for the phone directories from Margaret at the phone company but . . . is it all right if Neal and I come over?" she asked.

FORTY

Joyce heard the phone and realized Terry was not beside her. Grabbing a robe, she thought he might be gone, which happened now and then after a late night phone call, but instead, she found him in the kitchen putting dishes away.

"What was that call?" she asked, giving into a big yawn.

"I'm sorry, Honey. That was Dolly. She and Neal are on their way over," he said, explaining the little of what Dolly told him.

Terry switched on the porch light and Joyce ran to throw on some clothes, getting back in time to welcome their late visitors. Coffee or drinks were declined; everyone sat down, giving Dolly their full attention.

"I told you I really only glanced at this list—I was waiting for the records and phone books before I started trying to find any people with these names, but . . . I don't know what it means . . . maybe it's just a weird coincidence, but Neal said you needed to see this right away. Here," she said, handing him the list of victims from that long ago fire.

The name jumped out at him halfway down the list. Terry could only stare while a thousand thoughts bombarded his brain. Lightening dots were suddenly connecting, but why would this person be doing these things . . . and this was a list of dead people.

"This can't be a coincidence, but these people are dead. This isn't a name of anyone that we thought could be connected . . . ," Terry trailed off as Joyce took the list to see whose name was such a surprise.

"I'm sorry . . . I don't see any familiar names. Who are you talking about?" Joyce asked, realizing she wouldn't necessarily know everyone Dolly and Terry did.

"God, I hate to call Bull this late, but I have to and I need to talk to Dr. Appleton," Terry said, as all eyes followed him to the telephone.

Lou answered on the second ring. Bull was asleep on the sofa but she knew if Terry was calling at this hour it was important. When Bull got to the phone, Lou listened to the exclamations and questions which conveyed little information, but she knew something serious was going on.

"I can't believe that, Bull . . . why on earth?" Lou asked when Bull told her why Terry called.

"What are you going to do at this hour? You're not even sure what it means . . . you can't make an arrest can you?" she asked, decidedly worried that her husband was going out and would possibly be confronting a demented killer.

"It's ok, Honey. Terry's calling Dr. Appleton right now and if we can get his opinion, that'll help us know how to handle this. I'll be at Terry's. We're not going to open the office at this hour, we want to be quiet about it, but we'll probably at least watch the house. Now don't worry, Lou, please. I'll call you when I can, but I might be out the rest of the night," Bull cautioned.

It was not the first time Lou watched Bull go out so late, but it was usually a traffic accident or a domestic problem . . . this was the first time he was going out into a starlit fall night to catch a murderer, and the first time she could remember him going out in old khaki pants and a plaid shirt; he wouldn't even take a few minutes to change into his uniform.

Saturday night in Princeton, especially once the fall semester began, meant any variety of receptions, cocktail parties, dinners and informal get-togethers for the fortunate residents of the beautiful historic town. Dr. Appleton and his wife were just finishing dessert with a rather stuffy group of academics when he got a message to please call Deputy Kramer at his home number as soon as possible.

There were whispers and polite questions when the good doctor begged forgiveness, but they would have to leave. *So sorry, absolutely lovely evening. No nothing wrong, just something needing immediate attention. Yes, we'll just have to stay longer next time.*

"Thank you, Oliver, now I can curl up with that Agatha Christie I'm in the middle of," Lydia Appleton said to her husband as they rushed back home where he could return Terry's call in the privacy of his den.

Terry was still talking with the psychiatrist when Bull came in. He nodded to everyone, thinking he should have brought Lou, but it was hardly a time for a party. That funny thought led to another though, as he pictured a real party when this was over, but they weren't there yet.

When Dolly quickly told him how she came to discover this unusual bit of information, Bull could only shake his head.

"Does anybody think it's strange how a dog, and now a cat, are having more luck solving this damn thing than we are?" he asked, and went into the kitchen with Terry, leaving everyone realizing his comment was more truth than humor.

"Yes, sir. Yes, I think we can do that," Terry was saying from the phone he had carried as far into the kitchen as he could, knowing everyone could hear, but appreciating a bit more privacy.

"Chief Campbell just got here, Dr. Appleton. He wants to talk with you," Terry said when Bull gestured that he needed to speak with the doctor.

"Yes, Doctor, that's right. No, there was no reason to suspect that at all . . . no, doesn't look anything like Gaffer that I could see," Bull said. The call ended a few minutes later and Bull walked back into the living room.

"Except for this name being the same, and that doesn't prove a damn thing," Bull began, "we have to go over everything; we have to find what links it all. So far everything I can think of is circumstantial. Doc says he can get here first thing tomorrow. Terry, by then we should be able to make enough connections to get a search warrant for the car and maybe the house too. I hate to call so late, but I'll get a hold of Judge Boone right away. Right now I want both of us to go to the house—we'll just watch for now. I want you to use your own car, no police cars. You can take the first shift, I'll get back to relieve you in my own car by five; that will give you enough time to catch a few winks and be ready to meet at the office when Dr. Appleton arrives," Bull explained.

"Look, Chief, I can pull the whole night, you can . . ." Bull cut him off. Terry was worried about his boss. It wasn't so much that he was old enough to be his father, but he was dealing with some heart problems and this case was pushing everyone too hard, but Bull was still in charge.

"No, we're going right now and I will be back there in time for you to get some rest. You're going to need it, Terry—we're all going to need it I think," he said.

"Is there anything we can do, anything at all?" Neal asked.

"Yeah, keep an eye on Joyce for me," Terry said rushing out the door after Bull.

"Terry, be careful!" she yelled after him.

"Joyce, would you like to come home with us?" Dolly asked. "We have plenty of room and Mother would love it," Dolly said.

"That's sweet of you, Dolly, but I want to be here when Terry gets back. I don't know if he'll be able to sleep, but he'll need a good breakfast," she said.

"We can stay for a while if you like," Neal said.

"I would like that. It's not even twelve o'clock . . . in the city we'd just be getting started. How about a drink?" she asked.

A peaceful night and a little extra sleep on Sunday morning was no longer possible. How could they go quietly to bed when they knew what was happening?

Time flew by as they talked about the case. Joyce was careful not to mention the latest theories proposed by Dr. Appleton concerning the she/he thing, but Dolly did know about a possible twin, so it was a lively conversation as ideas, theories and wild speculation flew about, reminding Joyce of a an improv class she took once when she was interested in acting. By one o'clock the amateur detectives were ready for sleep. Joyce watched Dolly and Neal drive away, then locked up, leaving a few lights on—she didn't want to be in the dark. She stayed dressed and curled up in bed, falling asleep thinking about Terry, trying to picture him alone in their car, sitting and waiting and watching . . .

Terry was parked in a wooded lane to the side of the house. He could see the Dodge parked in the drive, a dim light was on, but things seemed quiet. He dozed off a few times, but if a car started up he would hear it. He wished he had thought to bring along some coffee; he might have given in to the Camels in the glove compartment, but it was just as well they were in the police car. The quiet time gave him a chance to think of lots of questions—questions if they could answer might tell them if, in fact, this was the murderer and kidnapper. At 4:45 there was a tap on the window.

"All quiet I see," Bull said as he slid into the passenger seat. "I parked down by the next drive. I can see pretty good from there. I take it nothing has happened. I know you want to get going, but there's a few things I want to tell you first."

"Yeah, I want to tell you some things too. Why are you all dressed up?" Terry asked, noticing that his boss showed up in a suit and tie.

"Church, Son, it's Sunday," Bull said, pleased to see that his explanation made Terry look at him like he was crazy.

They spent ten minutes talking, and Terry appreciated why Bull came dressed for church when his boss told him about a second call from Dr. Appleton.

"Yeah, Terry, we like to say people don't always know what they know and after what the doc suggested, I realized we were missing things right in front of us . . . we just weren't asking the right questions," Bull said.

"You get going now, Deputy, you can still get a little sleep, but Dr. Appleton said he'd be here by nine. He's predicting she'll be in church and if we can get Father Boyle to go along, that will buy us more time to check on all the connections we need to get a warrant," Bull said, explaining that he got Judge Boone out of bed at midnight to ask for the warrant, but was not surprised when His Honor said they needed more.

The morning light woke her. Terry was not there. Trying to understand what that could mean, she found him asleep on the sofa. She studied him for a moment, pleased at what she saw, then tiptoed into the kitchen, shutting the door and quietly going about making coffee and a good breakfast for her hard-working husband.

"Oh, Sweetheart, did I wake you?" she said when Terry came into the kitchen to find Joyce at the little table, sipping coffee while bacon sizzled on the stove.

"No, no . . . I need to get going," he said, leaning down to give her a kiss. "Breakfast smells great. I'm going to wash up and get some fresh clothes. I have to meet Bull at the office, but I'll tell you all about it, just give me a few minutes," he said.

Joyce set the dining table by the windows so they could talk and look out to the pines.

"Even though Father Hanover is back, there's still only one Mass at ten o'clock. Father Boyle has been managing I guess, but it helps us with only the one service to worry about," Terry said.

"What if she's not there?" Joyce asked.

"Yeah, I know . . . and even if she is, we're not prepared to do anything just yet, but I think this is right, Joyce, lots of things make sense. I'm not sure what Dr. Appleton has in mind but even Bull thinks we're damn lucky to have him," Terry said.

"You said he called Bull at home, late—what did he say, do you know?" she asked.

"A little. Bull and I only spent a few minutes talking when he came to take over watching the house, but the doctor has an interesting theory about the name. He doesn't know how to prove anything yet, but I think Dr. Appleton is going to try to talk to her," he answered.

Dressed in grey trousers and white shirt, Joyce was surprised to see Terry grab a sport coat as he was leaving for the office.

"No uniform?" she asked.

"Not today. Bull showed up in a suit and tie but he's going to be at church," he said.

"And you're going to church too?" she asked.

"No, Honey, I'll be at the Newberry's, and I'm taking the police car, you can have ours now if you need it," he said.

When he left, Joyce took a quick bath, did her make up, picked out a suit and hat and then she called Dolly.

"I know it's early, Dolly, but I was wondering if you might want to go to church. No, not the Dutch Reformed, I thought we might drop in at Saint Michael's," she said.

FORTY-ONE

Terry and Dr. Appleton were going over last minute plans, but plans that involved Ona Birch showing up for Mass this morning. If she wasn't there, then they would hope she wouldn't leave Kentbury before they could get the search warrants from Judge Boone. Terry was listening to Dr. Appleton put forth his theory about the name Ona Birch being on the fire victim's list, when Bull returned from an early morning visit to Fathers Boyle and Hanover at Saint Michael's.

"Well, I never thought I'd be asking a priest to lie, and in church no less, but they're fine with it," Bull said, looking rather pleased with himself.

"Are you sure the Newberrys don't know why you're coming?" Bull asked.

"No, but Mr. Newberry is pretty sure it has something to do with the murders. I just told him that they were not to say a word to anyone until I go there. They'll be fine, Chief," Terry said, reassuring his boss about a plan that included civilians.

"Time to go, Doctor," Terry said.

"Right, you and Dr. Appleton go ahead, Terry. Lou insists she's not missing church just because of this, but that's good actually. We'll be there together like always. Doc thinks Ona could be extra suspicious right now and the more normal things look the better," Bull said.

"That's true, Terry. Paranoia is definitely part of this woman's personality but if she believes the Brewer boy is still unconscious she's less likely to bolt," the doctor said.

"I still don't understand how she can expect to get the inheritance, if that's what's driving her," Terry said.

"I don't know if that's the motivator, but if you can make an arrest, I think I can get permission to talk to her," he said.

"Ok, and you think she's going to go to church not because she's devout but because . . . ?" Terry asked.

"Because she's there every Sunday and Dr. Appleton believes it's a kind of habit she's afraid to break even though she hates what she thinks the church did to her," Bull explained, surprising Terry with not only his understanding of what the psychiatrist told him, but his apparent acceptance of something he resisted only days ago.

"So why try to kill Father Hanover?" Terry asked.

"I doubt she wanted to kill him. I think he must have come in before she could get out but, assuming we're right about her, most of our questions and ideas will have to wait until we get her in a situation where she feels comfortable enough to talk," the doctor said.

"OK, I've been thinking about this," Terry began, "she's Catholic, goes to church all the time, has she been to confession? Has she told a priest about this?"

"I don't think this woman goes to confession, Terry. I think she talks directly to God and feels a special relationship. I suspect that she may even believe God wants her to do these things, or at least condones them," the psychiatrist said.

While Dr. Appleton followed Terry up Prescott Avenue to the Newberrys, Bull and Lou were walking into Saint Michael's, going to their usual pew, halfway up on the right. A few minutes later, Lou Campbell nudged her husband when she saw Dolly and Neal Argyle, Mary VanHaven and Joyce Kramer sitting to their left, just two pews back from Ona Birch.

"Oh for God's sake," Bull whispered, kneeling again to pray that all would go well this morning.

Because of only one Mass these past Sundays since Father Hanover was in the hospital, the church was well populated. That suited the police chief just fine. Nothing appeared unusual. As always, Bull loved hearing the pipe organ played so beautifully by Lou's cousin, Nicholas, and the altar flowers were especially fine this morning in honor of Father Hanover's return. The senior priest wore vestments and sat at the altar, but Father Boyle officiated. When the homily ended, which today had dealt with commitment and forgiveness, Father Boyle took a moment to welcome Father Hanover home from the hospital, thank everyone for their prayers and gifts, announced a fortieth wedding anniversary for

Victor and Irene O'Hara, then went ahead with the lie Bull asked him to tell.

"We surely give thanks for the life of Henry Brewer who was saved so miraculously only a few days ago, but I will ask that you keep this innocent child in your prayers. I know there was talk of his recovery, but he has not awakened and has slipped into a coma. The good doctors are doing everything they can, and we too must do what we can, which is to pray for Henry and for his family."

When the service finally ended, Bull watched Ona Birch leave in the first wave of parishioners, while he and Lou held back to speak to Joyce and her entourage.

"Why do I feel like I'm six years old, Bull?" she said when her husband's boss asked her how she and her party just happened to be here this morning, giving her a very stern and serious look.

"Thank goodness Father Boyle doesn't know you, Joyce. I was really worried there for a minute when he was talking about Henry Brewer being rescued that he would somehow make reference to you, but thank goodness he didn't," Bull said.

"Oh, that poor child, and that poor mother," Mary VanHaven said. "I believe the Brewers attend the Methodist Church but that was certainly nice of Father Boyle to ask everyone to pray for him," she said.

Bull felt a little guilty deceiving everyone, but only a little. It was quite a small lie and with any luck, this one-woman crime wave was coming to an end.

They were almost the last to leave, yet a few people lingered, so Bull only thanked Father Boyle for a lovely service, leaving other thanks for later in private.

As they were walking to the car, Lou whispered something to Bull which gave him pause. It took him only seconds to realize how helpful her suggestion was and he called out to Joyce and Dolly as they were getting into Neal's car.

FORTY-TWO

"Yes, ma'am. Yes, the doctors said he could be in a coma for a long time, they just don't know. No, he didn't wake up yet. Yes ma'am, I'll tell her. Thank you for calling.

"That was her, Grandma, that was the woman Chief Campbell told us about," Russell said to his Grandmother Brewer when he hung up.

Well, that just proves it, doesn't it? God is protecting me, Greg said He would. Now I can at least collect my pay from everyone and leave when I'm ready. At least I've got what I need in the trunk, no reason to unpack. I guess that brat could wake up though. I suppose I could visit him at the hospital, but no . . . I need to leave soon, it's time.

"I still can't believe this, Terry," Mabel Newberry was saying as Terry and Dr. Appleton gave a censored explanation of why they believed Ona Birch murdered Gaffer and Etta and kidnapped Henry Brewer.

"Are you sure we'll be safe, Doctor?" Raymond Newberry asked, just as shocked as his wife when they heard the reason for this visit. Raymond was in his wheelchair this morning, looking frail, and Terry hoped they were not asking too much of the couple.

"If I'm right about this woman, she's fine as long as she's not threatened, and from what I have ascertained, neither you nor Mrs. Newberry has ever done anything to upset or demean her, is that right?" the doctor asked.

"No, Ona has been a good housekeeper and a good cook. We gave her a Christmas present, a bonus on her birthday; we were the only people who offered her a steady position. We thought she was a war widow, we felt sorry for her; now you say that it is unlikely she's ever been married!" Mabel was saying, getting more agitated as she went on.

"Mabel, do you think you can do this without showing that anything might be wrong?" Terry asked.

"Yes, Terry, I certainly can," she said, surprising Terry and confirming what Dr. Appleton suspected: that while Mabel Newberry might float through life acting like a helpless, genteel banker's wife, she was tough and determined and you wouldn't want to be her enemy.

"Please call me Oliver, Raymond," Dr. Appleton said. "You can introduce me as an old friend, but we'll drop doctor. I don't want to give even the slightest reason for her to be suspicious."

"Should I call now?" Mabel asked.

"Yes, go ahead, she should be back from church by now; I just hope she went home," Terry answered.

"Oh, I'm glad I caught you, Ona. An old friend of ours has dropped in and we've invited him for dinner. I was hoping you could come in today . . . make one of your chicken pies for us. Yes, that's right, and just a salad and we won't worry about dessert, Jell-O or something. I know this is last minute, but we'll pay you extra of course since it's Sunday. Yes, I think we have everything. Good, thank you, Ona! We'll see you shortly," Mabel said, hanging up and turning to her audience. "How was that?" she asked.

"Perfect," Oliver said.

"Ok, I'll need to get out of here," but I'll be right next door. I won't be seen through the trees, but I can see the whole side of this house. Remember, if anything seems wrong, if something isn't right, flip that switch for the floodlights and I'll be right here," Terry told them.

They were not expecting anything to go wrong. They were trusting Dr. Appleton. There was no reason for Ona Birch to see him as anything but an old friend of her employers. Mabel Newberry seemed more than up to the task of role playing for a few hours, but Terry was a little worried about Raymond.

"That woman . . . that terrible woman . . . my bat . . . using it for such evil. Well, I have this just in case," he said, taking out a .38 revolver from under the blanket draped across his legs.

"Oh, Raymond, for heaven's sake," Mabel said.

"Mr. Newberry, sir, I don't think that is a very good idea. Dr. Appleton will be able to control the situation; there's no reason to think you would need that, is there, Doctor?" Terry asked, looking to the psychiatrist for support.

"Well, Raymond, I think it might make everyone feel better if you put it someplace handy, where you can get at it if it were needed, but I really doubt you will need it. I appreciate that you have it though," the doctor said.

Terry admired the way that was handled. Everyone, including Raymond Newberry, seemed less tense after Terry put the gun in the drawer of a side table. "It's there if you need it, sir, but I do not expect that you will," Terry said.

Terry sprinted out the back door, racing down the stone walk and across the manicured lawn onto the neighbor's driveway where he had parked the car when they arrived. He didn't have time to think about where he would be hiding if the neighbors were not away, but it was starting to feel like they were finally getting some breaks. He was just getting comfortable when he saw Ona's old Dodge pull into the back of the Newberry's by the three-car garage. Their drive was on the other side, below the house, but he had a good view of the whole side of the Newberry property and a partial view of the back, but because he was parked on a hill with trees and bushes all around, he only had a very limited view of cars going up and down Prescott Avenue. Terry doubted he would be doing much more than just watching and waiting if things went the way Dr. Appleton predicted, but tonight or tomorrow they would expect to make an arrest. While Terry was talking to Bull on the radio, Dr. Appleton was meeting Ona Birch.

Mabel Newberry was fixing drinks, making them light at Oliver's suggestion, when they heard Ona's car, then the back door. Dr. Appleton thought his host looked nervous, but Mabel was fine. Going into the kitchen, as would be expected, she returned shortly, warming to the idea of an impromptu dinner party. We're in for a treat; Ona is making one of her delicious chicken pies," Mabel said, obviously feeling that everything seemed fine. They were making small talk when Ona came in with a cheese and cracker tray and a bowl of nuts.

"Oh, this is great, thank you!" Oliver said.

"Ona, this is Oliver Appleby, an old friend of ours. I told him how lucky we were to get you here today and we are certainly looking forward to dinner," Mabel said. Raymond shot her a glance when she used the wrong name, hoping it wouldn't matter. The doctor didn't blink an eye.

Years of experience, lots of letters after his name from degrees and certificates gracing his walls, still took a back seat to the old "gut reaction" that Oliver Appleton felt when he met Ona Birch—the hair on the back of his neck stood up and he knew this was the person they were looking for.

"Nice to meet you, Mr. Appleby," she said and returned to the kitchen.

"Appleton . . . Oliver Appleton," Raymond whispered to his wife.

"Oh . . . oh dear," she said sheepishly.

Mabel and Raymond were looking at their guest, expecting what they weren't sure, but he said not to worry and thought it best to calmly continue on with their simple plan and when the timing seemed right, he hoped to get Ona's reaction to some questions. In the meantime, Raymond was getting more relaxed, happy to tell Oliver his life story. Oliver interrupted . . .

"Yes, I remember that, Raymond!" he said with a raised voice, and making a gesture that Mabel picked up on right away.

"No," she whispered, shaking her head in response to the doctor wondering if they could be heard in the kitchen. Raymond seemed annoyed and was asking for another drink when Ona came in again.

"The pie is in the oven, Mrs. Newberry and I've set the table. Do you want to use that big cucumber for the salad?" she asked.

"Yes, that would be lovely, Ona," she said and Dr. Appleton saw his opening.

"Mabel was just telling me about the awful things that have been going on here; she actually drove the man home and she said you fixed him lunch that day. That's just terrible, I'm so sorry," he said.

"Yes, poor Gaffer. He was a sad man, you know, I don't know who would want to murder him," she said.

"Were you close . . . you know, from working together?" he asked.

Ona stared at him for a second, looked to her employers, then said that no, they were hardly close; he was just an old tramp really. Then, realizing what that must sound like, she qualified her snobbish comment.

"You know . . . he lived alone in that abandoned house at the gorge and I only saw him when he was here, which wasn't all the time," she explained. Before Oliver could think of another "innocent" question, Ona went back to the kitchen. He could tell she was insulted by the suggestion that she would be close to Gaffer and the psychiatrist was feeling that she was more dangerous than he initially suspected, and the thought would not leave him that she may have killed before.

"Now who is that?" Raymond said when they heard a car pull up to the circular drive in front of the house. Before Mabel could look out to see who it was, the front door opened.

"Hello, parents!" Sharon yelled from the entryway. "Happy Sunday! Phillip's playing golf, so I decided to come up for the day."

"Oh, it's our daughter. My goodness, we weren't expecting her," Mabel said, rushing to the hall to greet her.

"Is this ok?" Raymond asked, a worried look on his face, but before the doctor could answer, the attractive young woman came in, followed by her mother who was also hoping it was ok, and not seeing any reason it was not, until Sharon saw who was standing by the sofa.

"Well, my goodness, Dr. Appleton! What on earth are you doing here? Do you know my parents? Daddy, has mother flipped out and you need the most prominent psychiatrist in Princeton? You know, I just played bridge with Lydia last week, but I had no idea . . . is everything all right?" she asked, feeling more serious and more perplexed by the looks she was getting.

For one of the very few times in his life, Oliver Appleton was speechless. Raymond was scowling at his daughter when Mabel did her best to save the day.

"Sharon, I want you to help me with something in the bedroom . . . now, dear, please," Mabel said, ushering Sharon to the other end of the house, leaving the two men staring at the hallway that led to the kitchen.

Sound did not travel in the well-built home and they did not think it likely that Ona would have heard anything. Still, they couldn't be sure, and Mabel felt safe talking to Sharon behind closed doors in the master suite.

"Mother, are you serious? And Terry Kramer put you up to this— what the hell is the matter with him?" she said, her immediate reaction being protective of her parents.

"Sharon, no one forced us to do this, but we can help. Besides, Terry is right out there, watching," she said.

"Out where?" she asked.

Mabel explained as much as she could to her daughter and, doubting that Ona would have heard her, they went to join Raymond and Oliver, with a much more demure Sharon returning to the living room.

"Well, how wonderful to see you," she said to the doctor. "Daddy, how are you?" she asked, bending to give him a kiss. "What's everyone drinking?" she asked, going to the bar to get something for herself. "I need a lemon," she said, marching off to the kitchen before anyone could stop her. A few seconds later she was back.

"Ona's gone, Dr. Appleton. She must have heard me . . . I'm so sorry," she said, but she was relieved that Ona Birch was out of the house.

No one had heard her car, but then they didn't always and unless they were near the side windows, they would not have seen her leave.

"Mabel, turn on the floodlights!" Dr. Appleton said.

FORTY-THREE

When Terry first called in to the office, he told his boss that everything was in place and that Ona had just arrived, but he was not prepared for Bull's little surprise: thanks to Lou, she, Dolly and Joyce were there, making phone calls and trying to track down information that would turn their leads and suspicions into hard evidence.

"Well, like what?" Terry asked.

"Well, like your wife finding out that Ona was the part-time cleaning lady for the Kaller. The day she knocked out Father Hanover, she had been working there from five that morning but was not there when Inky got in at six, and she had to come back the next day to finish up. She probably reeked of that ink smell Father Hanover recognized," Bull told him.

Why was he surprised? Bull said they would fill him in later and to check in every thirty minutes. Terry just finished the third check-in when he saw the flood lights flashing! He realized Ona's car was gone—he must have been on the radio and did not see her leave!

He raced from his hiding place, parked behind Sharon's car in the front drive, and was in the Newberry's living room in less than two minutes. He could hardly believe what had transpired. What were the odds that Sharon would pop in on her parents and find a visitor who was a doctor, pretending not to be a doctor, who turned out to be someone she actually knew? It made some sense though: Sharon's husband was a prominent surgeon and they traveled in the same upper class circles of Princeton. People don't usually ask what a woman's maiden name was and there was no way Dr. Appleton could have guessed.

"Dr. Appleton, call Chief Campbell, tell him what's happening. Tell him I'm going to see if I can catch up to her," Terry shouted, rushing back to the car, torn between using the siren that would cause attention and spook Ona, but would be safer as he flew down Prescott Avenue.

Where was she? What if she had gone up Prescott, back to her house? But the doctor said she would be fleeing and going that would take much longer to get to a main highway. Terry slowed down at each crossroad, looking left and right, but he couldn't find her. Cars pulled over when they heard the siren, and the deputy was happy for the sparse Sunday traffic. The chief would have alerted the State Troopers. They could already be on the highways, but if Ona Birch was as cunning as Dr. Appleton suspected she was, she could be on any of the back roads going who knows where.

Before he knew it, Terry was crossing the tracks onto Main Street. Everyone in the police station heard him rush by. In a few short minutes, he flew through Rosemary's Corner on to Route 69. Finally, a mile past the turn off to Clinton, Terry saw a car he recognized.

"Turn around, Terry," the chief told him over the radio when he saw his deputy in the rearview mirror. "The Troopers will have more luck if she's gone up or down the main highways. Right now I want to get back and talk with Doc Appleton."

After making sure the Newberrys would be all right and assuring them that Ona Birch would not return, the doctor had rushed down to the police station. He was talking with Bull's three volunteer detectives when the chief and Terry rushed in.

"Jesus, Doc, can you tell us exactly what happened and where the hell she might be . . . is she going to hurt somebody, hurt herself?" Bull asked.

Dr. Appleton explained what had transpired at the Newberrys. Even with the short time he was able to talk to her, he felt confident Ona Birch was exactly what he suspected and yes, she was dangerous.

"The fact that she was willing to work today when Mrs. Newberry called, indicated that your ploy worked, Chief. She felt safe enough to do that, and she may need money. You said she did call the Brewer's house to verify what she heard in church?" the doctor asked.

"That's right. I had to tell the Brewers what Father Boyle was going to say this morning and I told them they might get that call. Russell told me they had several calls, but even though she made up some name, he knew Ona's voice from seeing her at the market where he works. I gotta hand it to you, Doctor Appleton, you've been right on the money so far, I just wish you could tell us where she is right now," Bull said.

"Maybe I can, Bull. Your impressive team here has been filling me in on some of the background of this case. I won't go into it all now, but it's possible she has gone back to the house where she murdered her brother."

"That's good enough for me, Doc. C'mon, let's go," Bull said as they rushed out the door.

Bull approached Old Gorge Road from the end where it met Mitchum, while Terry and Dr. Appleton took the road around Lake Raynard. They were not using sirens and Terry listened attentively as his passenger explained why Ona Birch might go to Gaffer's Cottage.

"It's a guess, Terry, a long shot really, but if she's running, she knows she's been found out and the stress and reality of that will push her over the edge. Her actions now will not seem logical or rational to us, but she may be neither at this point." He continued.

"I'm sure you understand that the worst crime we know is murder, and taking the life of a mother, father, and certainly a sibling, especially a twin, is among the most horrific," he said.

"But they didn't know each other, wouldn't that make it easier?" Terry asked.

"You might think so, but remember that Ona Birch . . . Frances Gregson Farmer . . . is, in layman's terms, a very mixed up human being. It's not my primary field, but studies of twins show remarkable attachment, even among those who have been raised separately. There are cases where they find adult twins, raised in different homes, many didn't even know they were a twin . . . they have wives with the same name, same kind of dogs, hobbies, even the same jobs—remarkable things that go way beyond coincidence," he said.

"That's pretty weird, Doc. So, she's sorry she killed Gaffer?" Terry asked.

"Well, not sorry . . . more remorse, depression, guilt, all mixed up with anger and probably a terrible longing from a very lonely and sad life."

Terry had a million questions but they would have to wait. Approaching the stretch of road with the path to Gaffer's cottage, they saw Bull just pulling up behind Ona's old Dodge.

"You were right again, Dr. Appleton. Pretty impressive," Terry said.

"God, I hope I can talk to her, make a case study," he said, catching the look Terry gave him.

"Forgive me . . . this is my field, after all, and the more we can learn from these poor souls the more we can help others and hopefully prevent tragedies like this," he explained.

Persuading the policemen that he would be safer and more useful going with them rather than waiting in the car, the three men were slowly climbing the rocky path when they heard a car start.

"Damn it!" Terry yelled, turning and running back toward the road, with Bull and Dr. Appleton close behind. Terry was in the car and pulling out after their suspect when Bull and the doctor reached the road.

"C'mon, Doc," Bull yelled, jumping into his car, setting dust and rocks flying as they joined the chase.

"Why the hell didn't we block her in?" the chief was saying, angry with himself and surprised at his deputy who was usually so careful. "I'm sorry, Doctor, please hold on," Bull cautioned as he turned on the siren, going faster than anyone should on the narrow lake road.

"I'm sorry, Greg! I know I should have just left but I wanted to go to that house one last time. All the times I went there . . . no one ever saw me. I needed to know . . . I needed to see where he lived. I hated that old bum . . . I never believed he was my twin, but he had it . . . he had the birthmark. But he was a man . . . they didn't give him away, erase him. Oh God . . . if I can just get to the crossroad . . . if I can just . . .

Two young couples having a leisurely Sunday stroll along the lake were jolted out of their romantic interlude by screaming sirens. Running toward the commotion, they arrived just in time to see a car fly off the road and crash through the trees, stopping two feet from the water!

No less than six State Police cars, along with the two official Kentbury vehicles, a fire truck and at least eight cars belonging to curious townsfolk, lined each side of Lake Road, where Ona Birch's car careened down the bank, almost to the water. The police were finally turning people away which meant most of them found a place to park, then walked back to the site of the crash, only yards from Mary VanHaven's house. Word was spreading quickly. A small crowd was gathering on Mary VanHaven's back porch, and Terry was not surprised to see Dolly, Lou and Joyce among the curious onlookers.

The tow truck was arriving and Terry expected that he and Bull would be here for quite a while. He took a few minutes to walk down to Mary's to talk to everyone and to see Joyce.

"No, she's alive. Dr. Appleton went in the ambulance with her. I think he wants to take her to Somerville, but I don't know what they'll decide," he told Joyce when they went inside to talk in private.

"Oh, Terry, I'm so glad this mess is over. I was so worried about you," she said, embracing her husband, wondering why she felt like crying and realizing she did not want her husband to be a police officer, but now was hardly the time to say so.

"It's ok, Honey, I'm fine, I'm fine. I have to get back, but I wanted to see you, make sure you're ok," he said.

It was well past dinner time when a semblance of normalcy returned to Lake Road. People went home with stories and gossip that would go on for months. Bull finally joined Lou at Mary's and they left for home, planning to make a stop at the Brewers on the way. Joyce left right after she talked with Terry. She didn't think he'd mind leftovers tonight as long as there was enough whiskey, and she planned on drinking a whole bottle of claret by herself.

Joyce bathed, changed and was on her second glass of wine when Terry finally came through the door.

"You are so beautiful, do you know that?" Terry said after a lingering kiss.

"So you keep telling me," she answered. "Why don't you go get comfortable, I'll fix you a drink," she said, knowing this was going to be a night of talking. Love making was always a happy, kind of celebrating they enjoyed and tonight felt too serious, almost sad. She decided not to tell him how she was feeling about his job . . . they were exhausted and she had her own work that would get her out of this gloominess. The claret bottle was half empty by the time they finished dinner and exchanged information.

"It sounds like Ona . . . Frances . . . worked all over the place. I wonder what kind of investigator I am, Joyce; I thought she only worked for the Newberry's, so did Bull," he said.

"Well, it sounds like the Newberrys didn't even know. These extra jobs of hers were at odd hours, it didn't seem to interfere with her working for them," Joyce said.

"Lou is the one who found out she had a job at the Methodist Church. She called Reverend Jeffries, just to get a little more information about the day Henry was kidnapped and asked if he knew Ona Birch. He told her Ona cleaned the basement where the Sunday school is and where they have social things, but she made her own hours more or less. He said it was possible she had been there that morning and he never thought to mention it," Joyce said.

"There's no question Ona is guilty and we'll get that search warrant now and have a look at her house. There were a couple of suitcases in the car, and they're locked up at the office—we'll search them tomorrow. Dr. Appleton thinks there's a lot more to learn. He says she's a certifiable cuckoo and shouldn't go to jail," Terry said.

"He didn't say cuckoo did he?" Joyce asked.

"No, of course not, but we'll know a lot more tomorrow I hope," Terry said. "In the meantime, Honey, I'm beat. Leave the dishes, let's go to bed. Joyce didn't argue, deciding she'd use the leftover wine to cook with.

FORTY-FOUR

Bull didn't know when Kentbury would get back to what could be considered normal, but two days after Ona Birch crashed on Lake Road, Henry Brewer got his memory back. When Bull and Terry took Henry's statement, they were reminded how resilient children could be: perhaps it was the security of a big, loving family but Henry did not seem overly traumatized by his ordeal, and one of his first questions was to Terry, asking when he could get his bag back!

Dr. Appleton was able to get Ona admitted to the hospital in Somerville where she was in serious condition. Since he had privileges at that hospital, and with FBI intervention, he arranged to be the consulting psychiatrist for her case. She would be assigned a court-appointed attorney if she recovered enough to be charged, but Dr. Appleton and two other psychiatrists expected to get her declared mentally unfit to stand trial.

As Dr. Appleton had suspected, a physical examination showed an ugly purple birthmark, always hidden under clothes, yet—he had no doubt—contributing greatly to a sad and lonely life. The physical also confirmed that Ona did suffer from the condition that involved the adrenal gland, resulting in confusing genitalia; a condition that was so embarrassing and misunderstood in 1901, that she was rejected by her grandfather, sent away from her adoptive family, shuffled around in orphanages and generally would have been considered a freak.

The morning after the crash, Terry and Bull, armed with a search warrant, went into the two-bedroom furnished house rented for thirty dollars a month by Ona Birch.

The small house was neat and clean with little evidence that anyone lived there. The landlord said Ona could be a pain, a bit uppity he said, but she paid her rent on time and that was all he cared about. He couldn't believe she was a murderer but his main concern was how long before he could rent the house again.

The search of the house was disappointing, but the items they retrieved from the car were not.

Two beat-up suitcases and a small purse sat on the desk in the back office. The purse had the usual things . . . a wallet with over two hundred dollars in cash, a bank book for an account at a bank in New York, driver's license, and in a zipper pocket, a large pocket knife.

"Ok, this goes to Marvin, Terry. This could be what she used to cut up poor old Gaffer," Bull said. The first suitcase they opened held clothes, some toiletries but nothing remarkable, expect perhaps a large bottle of Shalimar they suspected belonged to Etta Marx. The second suitcase was much more rewarding.

"Just more clothes," Bull said when the first thing they saw in the second, larger suitcase was a flowered smock.

"Wait a minute, Chief," Terry said, carefully lifting out the new-looking garment.

"I think this was Etta's and it's what Ona wore to get out of there in broad daylight . . . she would have been covered in blood, and that looks like blood to me," he said, seeing sinister red stains running into the pastel flowers.

"Minnie Lester thought it was Etta she saw, but remember, Dr. Walsh doubted Etta was gardening that day . . . I'll take this to Minnie later," Terry said, putting the brightly colored smock aside.

"OK, looks like all kinds of stuff in here, Terry," Bull said, holding up an envelope with a torn corner, knowing immediately it was the letter delivered to Gaffer by Rudy April. "I'll be damned," he said.

"I suppose . . . what . . . Gaffer had this that day and showed it to her?" Terry speculated.

"What have we got here?" Bull asked, holding up a registered letter, the same letter from the New York lawyer's office, but dated two weeks earlier and with a hundred dollar check, made out to Augustus Peter White.

"How the hell did she get this?" Bull wanted to know.

"We'll need to check with the post office. It's weird, Chief, just like everything with this damn case. I guess she couldn't cash a check, but she obviously took the cash from the other letter when she killed Gaffer," Terry said.

The large suitcase was proving to be a treasure trove of clues and tantalizing information.

"This looks like some kind of diary," Terry said, holding up a frayed sort of scrapbook. "Look at all the notations."

As the two policemen carefully turned the pages of the thick book, they knew they were seeing something important, but it might take Dr. Appleton to make sense of it. First, though, they'd give Dolly a shot with some of the obvious things they were seeing.

"Terry, take this up to Dolly. Show her where we want her to start, and no one is to see it but her," Bull cautioned.

"Not even that cat . . . Tuk-Tuk?" Terry asked.

"Very funny," Bull said.

While Lou was ready to return to her role as housewife, and Joyce had commitments to get the decorating job done for the Crisp sisters, Dolly was happy to find that she was still needed as the unofficial, chief investigator/researcher, looking for the many unanswered questions relating to the murders.

"Wow!" Dolly remarked when Terry showed her the scrapbook, immediately understanding how important it could be and said that on this slow Monday, she could get on it right away.

Terry then went to see Minnie Lester who confirmed that the bloody smock was Etta's. Terry answered the few questions she had but did not volunteer much; he doubted the sweet lady would understand half of it. As he was leaving, there was a beautiful butterfly by the door. Terry thought it was getting late in the year for them and when he looked at Minnie, she was smiling knowingly. He didn't say anything though . . . what could he?

Terry got back to the station and learned that Bull had a successful visit to the post office, where he found records showing that Ona Birch signed for a registered letter for Augustus Peter White, addressed to General Delivery, two weeks before he was murdered.

"Terry, you remember Alfred Young . . . turns out he's the one who gave this registered letter to Ona Birch and, as luck would have it . . . luck for Ona . . . that was Alfred's last week there before he retired. He moved to Florida to be with his daughter, didn't know a damn thing about the murders here. I just got off the phone with him and sure enough, he got this letter and thought he'd have to go hunt down Gaffer, when who comes in but Ona Birch," Bull said, shaking his head at yet another bit of irony.

"Alfred knew who Ona worked for and knew Gaffer did sometimes too, and when he asked her, she said sure, he was there now, and she'd be happy to sign for it!"

"What are the odds, Chief?" Terry asked.

"Yeah, I know," Bull said.

"So she opens the letter, and all this inheritance stuff is what pushes her over the edge?" Terry asked.

"Seems so. That's what Doc Appleton thinks anyway," Bull answered.

Terry spent the rest of the day completing the required paperwork while Bull was on the phone touching base with Sheriff Zimmer, Chief Riggs and Detective Dent at the State Police. Around three o'clock, Bull announced that he was walking down to Saint Michael's to see Father Hanover and Father Boyle to thank them again, and to tell him what he could about Ona Birch. He was gone only a few minutes when Dolly ran in, excited about something she learned from the scrapbook.

"There's some really strange stuff here, Terry, but I was intrigued by all of the old news clippings. Why where they important? I started to make a list of the names in the articles and a few are familiar. Farmer jumped out right away . . . a death notice for Binnie Farmer, death notices for several priests from parishes in New York and then clippings of some movie stars, almost like a teenager would keep," she said. Terry waited, he knew there was more.

"Then . . . this is exciting . . . here's a clipping about that terrible fire in Hoboken. Apparently the fire started in a pile of rags on the third floor, maybe someone smoking, but the only avenue of escape was a stairwell and doors that went out to a loading elevator—people piled up on the stairway that got quickly blocked and the doors to the elevator were locked. Most of the survivors were on the ground floor," she said.

Terry pictured the horrible scene that turned into combat in the Pacific. He shook it off, but he knew that those poor people had been in hell. He suspected Ona/Frances was lucky for once and had been on that lower level.

"Terry, are you ok?" Dolly asked.

"Oh, yeah . . . sure, just thinking about those poor people, mostly women and little kids, really sad," he said. Dolly agreed.

"Anything else?" he asked.

"Well, the dates might be significant. It appears that she had some idea of who she was, but any reference to here, to Kentbury, Califon and Hunterdon County, only started showing up in her notes about eighteen months ago. Didn't you say that's about the time she came here?" Dolly asked.

"No, more recently than that. She started working for the Newberrys a little over a year ago, but what are you getting at?" he asked, admiring Dolly's detective skills.

"I found this card in one of the back pages and it's for some kind of private investigator. She liked to date things and the date on it is May 12, 1949. Right after that is when references to Kentbury started to show up," Dolly said, handling Terry the black and white business card.

> R.S.Blane
> Private Investigator
> Estates, Heirs, Divorce Matters
> EV 5-3234

"And you've already called, I assume?" Terry asked.

"I did. It's Evergreen, a Brooklyn exchange and the number is for an answering service. Mr. Blane is deceased, apparently not long after the date on the card," Dolly said.

"That's great work, Dolly, we don't pay you enough," Terry said,

"You can't afford me," she joked.

"I know, but we'll pay for the phone call," Terry said.

Dolly left, promising to keep working on the scrapbook.

Terry was anxious to tell the chief about Dolly's success so far, but something was nagging him. They had been wrestling with ideas about how Ona/Frances might have found her way here in the first place and Terry had an idea.

Bull came in just as his deputy was ending a phone call to Sherman X. Dumont.

"Chief, I just talked with Mr. Dumont in New York," Terry said as Bull got himself a cup of coffee.

Terry told Bull about Dolly's finds so far and then explained the idea he got from the business card.

"R.S. Blane, Buddy they called him, was the investigator they used before Rudy April. I remembered Mr. Dumont saying they thought this guy was dishonest but that he had passed away. I never knew a name, but . . . I don't know . . . something just clicked and sure enough, that's his card Dolly found in the scrapbook," Terry said with satisfaction.

"That is some terrific intuition you have, Deputy," Bull said. "I guess it can explain how she found her way here . . . but wait minute . . . how did she find this guy? Did she go to him with what? It almost sounds like he found her, is that possible?" Bull asked.

"I know. He sounds like someone who might have been playing any angle and . . . I don't know, I guess he could have tracked her down. But even if he did, what sent him looking in the first place?" Terry wanted to know.

It was a huge question and once again, Dolly would find the answer for them.

FORTY-FIVE

Halloween came and went without a lot of problems, but Terry wasn't sure how he felt about a few smartass teen boys dressing up as Ona Birch.

"Just be glad they didn't dress up like you and Bull," Joyce said.

"Yeah, let's not give anybody that idea!" Terry said.

They were having a quiet dinner with most of the talk so far about Joyce finding just the right chair, the perfect painting, the right fabric, and how everything was coming together nicely for Madeline and Ethel. The sisters were even talking about having a holiday party if they could finish in time.

"So, tell me about Henry Brewer," Terry said.

It was not surprising that after Henry got back home and the family started to recover from the terrible event, they made a point of thanking Joyce and Madeline . . . both recipients of one of Tilly Brewer's amazing apple pies, and Jimmy Doolittle was suddenly finding that he had a new best friend.

"Henry comes after school when he can, and almost every Saturday. Jimmy gets walks and lots of attention. Madeline and Ethel love it, and . . . it seems Tilly is delighted because Henry has given up his life of trash hunting . . . not just because of Jimmy, but he's fascinated with learning about antiques! I've never known a kid like that," Joyce said.

"So, they're teaching him about antiques and stuff?" Terry asked.

"More or less . . . he asks me lots of intelligent questions too when I'm there, and he loves the history about where things came from, what they were used for; most kids are out playing cowboys or riding their bikes, but not him! George comes sometimes too—I predict that those two will go into the antique business someday—it wouldn't surprise me," Joyce said.

By the time they were clearing the table, Joyce was listening to Terry's day and the all-pervading subject of Ona Birch.

"We're planning to meet with Dr. Appleton at the hospital in Somerville tomorrow, but the big news is Dolly figured out how Ona/Frances learned who she really was and where she came from," he began, having his wife's full attention.

"Dr. Appleton says that scrapbook was like a Bible to her. He thinks most of her life story is in it and maybe some more sinister things, like news clippings about a couple of murders, and one of them at that factory in Hoboken, although that was always considered an accident" Terry told her.

"God, really? Is he going to investigate them?" Joyce asked.

"I don't know, maybe. But Dolly found some bills sent to a Miss Ona Birch at an address on the lower East Side in Manhattan. When she tracked it down, it turned out to be a boarding house that was still in operation," Terry said.

"And?" Joyce asked.

"And . . . Dolly couldn't get anyone on the telephone, so her friend Myrna, you know the one who works at the public library, actually went there. She found out that this Buddy Blane wasn't a permanent resident, but he stayed there a lot and . . . Ona Birch had lived there for several years," Terry told her.

"Wow . . . so he somehow discovered who she was, or what . . . ?" she asked.

"The landlady told Dolly's friend that she remembered very well Mr. Blane bragging about all the cases he handled and talk about this little town in Jersey he had to go to a lot, and then one night at the dinner table he mentions a place, this town and Hunterdon County, and Ona gets all excited. She said after that, they were together a lot. Ona seemed to have money, she worked in housekeeping at a fancy hotel, and this guy kept giving her information. One day she pays her board and ups and leaves in some old car she bought—and that's got to be when she came here," Terry explained.

"But then she finds a job so she can work with Gaffer?" Joyce asked.

"Apparently just another coincidence, but in a small town like this, with the kind of work she did, it wasn't hard to learn who Gaffer was and wind up working with him," Terry told her.

"Yes, but . . . my God, what are the odds of that happening?" Joyce asked.

"Do you know how many times I've asked that in this crazy mess? If I could get odds like that at the racetrack, I'd be playing the horses," Terry said.

Terry didn't like hospitals. The smells were like the medical units he remembered and none of that was pleasant. Dr. Appleton was taking them to a private room with a State Trooper sitting by the door. Frances Gregson Farmer, aka Ona Birch, had been officially charged with two counts of murder and one of kidnapping. Dr. Appleton doubted she would go to trial, but rather would be declared incompetent and sent to a mental institution, one near Princeton if he could arrange it.

She looked small. Her cast-wrapped leg was suspended in the air. Bandages bulged under a blue cotton gown. Bloody scrapes were healing on her forehead and around the bluish-yellow bruises under eyes that looked lively, suspicious, but not afraid. She gave Bull the creeps.

"Frances, I told you Chief Campbell and Deputy Kramer were coming today. They'd like to ask you a few questions, if you feel up to it," Dr. Appleton said.

She stared at them, looking annoyed, Terry thought. When she finally spoke, it was to the doctor, her tone dismissive, superior, Terry wasn't sure, but she was giving him the creeps too.

"I can talk to them, Oliver, but you have to stay," she said, surprising them with the use of the doctor's given name. He seemed fine with it though. Bull thought it was probably some head doctor strategy.

Yes, she killed Gaffer White. She and Greg were the rightful heirs, but Gaffer was an embarrassment, an old tramp, stupid. She did him a favor.

The mutilation—that was Greg's idea, not mine.

Fortunately, Dr. Appleton had told them who Greg was. Following his instructions, they were not questioning her about Greg, but Bull felt like throwing cold water on her.

No, she was not a war widow, she was never married and she never lived in Somerville, but everyone felt sorry for her. That was Greg's idea too.

Why kill Etta Marx?

She and Greg did that together. That idiot investigator, Buddy Blane, told Etta this interesting story about some old bum in town being related to the Wexlers, but he wanted money for more information and she wouldn't give him any. Etta thought she could figure it out herself. Greg was going to kill Buddy Blane too, but he died first.

Lucky guy, Terry thought.

"I'm tired, Oliver, they can go now," she said.

Bull and Terry left, waiting outside the room with the State Trooper while Dr. Appleton spent a few more minutes with his patient.

"Let's go to lunch if you have time, my treat," he said as they walked out of the hospital.

Seated in a booth at the Town House in downtown Somerville, the three men were enjoying the good food and pleasant atmosphere while they listened, once again, to Dr. Appleton's explanation of just who the hell Greg was. Terry seemed accepting of Greg's identity, Bull was struggling with it. It wasn't that he didn't believe him . . . it was just . . . well . . . it was just so damn weird.

"Oliver, please," Bull said, now on first name basis with the down-to-earth doctor, "you're telling me she actually believes this Greg person is real? And it's not one of those two people in one body thing they want us to believe . . . she knows she's Frances and was just pretending to be Ona, is that right?" Bull asked.

"That's right. Remember, she was very little when she was sent to that orphanage, but she was known as Greggie, being raised as a boy, and while Binnie Farmer, the very disappointing mother figure, did not nurture the child, she found love and acceptance from the Farmer girls. When she was sent away and started being known as Frances, a girl . . . which she was . . . Greggie stayed. He was there to protect her, kind of like an imaginary playmate, but much more real. She needed someone and Greg was there for her," he told them.

"And Ona Birch?" Terry asked.

"Frances was sent to that factory when she was ten. Ona Birch was a little older and became the child's first real friend. They were inseparable but Ona and Frances fell victim to a horrible man there, a manager of some sort, who used these children for his own pleasure. He could do what he liked . . . he was powerful, they were not," he said.

"God, that is so disgusting, so sad," Terry said.

"Yes, and he got what he probably deserved—they murdered him," he said.

"My God, those little girls? How?" Bull asked, trying to imagine something so bizarre.

"This man would take them to some unused room with a mattress in it. Apparently, when he discovered the unusual anatomy that Frances had, he got quite excited; it aroused him and he was bothering her more and more. By chance they discovered an old shaft in the room that had been covered up and one night . . ." he was saying, but Terry cut him off.

"They pushed him down the shaft," he said.

"Exactly. It was pretty easy. They didn't get caught and there was no regret. Frances tells the story like you might talk about a family picnic. They did not consider it wrong, they were only protecting themselves. Things were better after that, and it's possible that Frances still had a chance to have some kind of decent life, but just a month later, the fire happened and her only friend, the only person she could rely on, was killed," he told the two men who were sad and disgusted at what they were hearing.

"Frances was eleven then and in the chaos and mess that followed the fire, she was able to run away. She knew Ona was dead and she didn't want to be Frances anymore, so she became Ona Birch. She said it was Greg's idea," he explained.

Bull was looking less perplexed, but while he could understand about taking someone else's identity, the make believe friend was harder to accept.

"Look, you understand that if you cut yourself and that cut gets infected, the body has ways of fighting that infection, am I right?" he asked.

Bull nodded. Terry waited patiently, but he thought he knew what was coming.

"Well, this is the same kind of thing, only it's the mind that has been wounded and Greg was the mind's way of protecting itself . . . protecting Frances, a frightened, lonely little girl," he explained.

"I've been reading some about this, Dr. Appleton," Terry began, "and I keep finding something called skitz . . . skitza . . . .".

"Schizophrenia, Terry. I find it is very over-diagnosed these days, but it is a mental disease which fits most of what we have seen in this case—I just happen to think it is even a bit more complicated than that," the doctor explained.

They talked a bit about Magnus Wexler, reflecting on the string of tragedies he set in motion. His grandchildren, Gaffer and Frances, had tragic lives, and while the policemen didn't want to feel any sympathy for a murderer, they could feel sorry for the child she had been.

FORTY-SIX

"This is wonderful," Joyce said, taking her seat next to Terry at the elegantly-set table. Dolly and Neal sat opposite them and, with Mary visiting her niece in Easton for the weekend, the two couples had a chance to get together, not only for the great dinner Dolly prepared, but to talk about the fascinating case still so prominent in their lives.

When Terry told Dolly that the things they were finding out could not be discussed in front of anyone's mother, Dolly said her mother was going to be gone for the weekend and to come for dinner.

Dinner was delicious, the company great and while everyone would occasionally throw out a question or thought, Terry was the main entertainment as he filled them in on what he was learning about the case. There was no question that Dolly and Neal could be trusted with the sensitive findings and the Kramers appreciated having someone to share it with.

One compelling question was answered when Bull had a long phone conversation with Sherman Dumont about the inheritance to Gaffer from Lenore Wexler.

"Gaffer died just two weeks after Lenore Wexler, so the Will is being handled without any consideration to him or any heirs. Dr. Appleton said Ona . . . Frances . . . had some confused idea that she could step in and prove she was the heir, but it was all mixed up with this make-believe Greg person. She didn't come here for that specific reason, but when she saw that letter, Greg started telling her that should be their inheritance and it pushed her over the edge. I don't understand all of it, but I guess when a person is that crazy, it makes sense to them," Terry explained.

"OK, so where is all that money going to go now?" Neal asked.

"There's lots of charitable stuff but something kind of interesting too," Terry said, taking a bite of dinner while everyone waited for him to go on.

"Mr. Dumont had some discretion as to which charities would benefit, and Miss Wexler always talked about a scholarship, but she never put it in writing. He's setting up a committee that will oversee and support her idea and make a foundation that will give scholarships to medical students going into psychiatry. They're calling it the Augustus Peter White Scholarship and would you believe one million dollars?" Terry asked.

"Wow!" Neal said.

It was a staggering sum and they all realized that the generosity was so much more than just a million dollars; Gaffer's terrible, sad life would count for something after all.

"My goodness, a million dollars . . . what was the whole estate, do you know?" Dolly asked.

"Not really, but Dr. Appleton is going to be on the committee when they look for deserving students. It's got to be pretty big though, because they're also donating a half million to Johns Hopkins for research.

By the time they were enjoying coffee and dessert, Dolly and Neal were hearing the latest findings regarding Frances Gregson Farmer.

"So, she is ok with being called Frances after being Ona Birch for all those years?" Neal wanted to know.

"Apparently. Doc says she prefers it," Terry said.

"Well, how the hell did she survive, on her own like that, only eleven?" Neal asked when they heard about how she ran away after the factory fire.

"Frances is smart—she worked in a restaurant for scraps and a place to sleep and somewhere along the way learned to cook. She cleaned houses, dressed like a boy sometimes to get jobs cleaning out stables. By the time she turned fifteen, she could do almost anything. More than once she had to run from people who offered a life of prostitution, but she survived. She managed to save money, she only had a little schooling, but she could read and a great deal of her education came from the movies," Joyce said, taking over the story so her husband could get a few bites of dessert.

"The movies?" Dolly asked.

"Yes, one of her jobs was cleaning a movie theater. She got to see them for free and that's how this lonely, unloved girl, glimpsed a life she could never have. But she learned. Dr. Appleton said she learned better English, learned about things like clothes and make up. Sometimes she even pretended the characters in the movies were her friends and she'd tell people about them. She eventually elevated herself enough to get a good job at one of the New York hotels where she worked in housekeeping. She was never going to be really normal though, Dr. Appleton said. She didn't have friends, never had a real home and more than once she would spend the night in one of the suites that she knew was not being used, kind of a treat for herself," Joyce said, turning to Terry to see if he thought it was all right to tell the rest of what was a sordid story, perhaps not suitable for table talk.

"You told me you couldn't tell some of this to anyone's mother, Terry, but . . . nobody here is a mother," Dolly said with a grin.

"Fair enough," Terry said, letting Joyce tell the rest while he took a sip of coffee.

"One night, the assistant manager of the hotel had the same idea about this empty suite, planning to invite one of the maids to join him, but when he went to check it out, he discovered Frances, asleep in the giant bed. Even though Frances wasn't pretty like the girl he had in mind, the manager decided this one was right there, so he made advances. Greg told her to kill him, sort of cheering her on, protecting her," Joyce said in a dramatic whisper, appreciating the look on their faces, probably like hers looked when she first heard the story from Terry. There was only silence for a moment while everyone tried to concentrate on dessert.

When the Kramers finally said goodnight to the couple quickly becoming their best friends, it was after midnight. Joyce talked to several of the cats luxuriating around the house and Terry made a point of petting Tuk-Tuk and thanking the kitten for finding the list that essentially broke the case.

"Keep up the good work, Tuk, we couldn't have solved it without you," Terry said, and wondered if everyone knew just how close to the truth it was!

Terry was in by nine o'clock, Bull would get there eventually. Things had been so quiet that he and Bull were getting in later and leaving early. Fred Browning was visiting his daughter for the holidays and wouldn't be back until January, and that was fine. Terry sipped his own good coffee as he looked out to the decorations up and down Main Street, thinking about the antique earrings he was getting Joyce for Christmas. A light snow dusted the town yesterday, disappointing the kids who were anxious to get their sleds out, but giving the little colonial town a Currier and Ives look that Terry loved.

"You're in early," Dolly said, coming in with offerings of homemade cookies shaped like reindeer and snowmen.

"So are you, Dolly," Terry said.

"Well, I'm closing early today so I can pick up my dress for tomorrow. I'm sure Joyce will be a knockout, as usual," she said.

"She made me get a new suit—Neal didn't have to get a new wardrobe, did he?" he asked.

"Actually, yes. Neal lives in dungarees and flannel shirts, he was overdue for a new suit," she said.

"I guess this is going to be some party from what Joyce tells me. You know, Bull thought he wanted to do something like this, but when the Crisp sisters volunteered, Lou convinced him they could have a get together after the New Year if he wanted, and besides, everyone is dying to see the decorating Joyce did. I can't wait myself," he said.

"Are the Appletons coming?" Dolly asked.

"Joyce was told to invite anyone she wanted, so of course the Appletons are coming, but I think half the town is invited . . . I know the mayor and his wife will be there, our friends Mike and Gloria Skinner . . . oh, and Joyce invited Father March, and he accepted," Terry said.

"What about Nelson Hunt?" she asked.

"No, he's going to be away, but I don't think he would have gone anyway," he said.

"What about the Newberrys?" Dolly wanted to know.

"I'm not sure . . . some people see this as a kind of celebration . . . I guess a party is a celebration, but this is . . . I don't know . . . some way of saying thank you, and we survived . . . and we love our town and won't let bad things destroy that," Terry said, surprising Dolly with the little speech, but she loved him for it.

The day passed quietly and Terry left early to pick up Joyce's present in Flemington. Christmas was a few days away, but he was going to give her the earrings early so she could wear them tomorrow night.

FORTY-SEVEN

"I'm sorry, Mrs. Kramer, but I don't think you can go out in public . . . you'll cause a riot and I'd have to arrest you," Terry said with a grin when Joyce came into the living room. "God, Honey, you look fabulous!"

The dress was beautiful, but Joyce made it sensational. This was the secret dress she found at Bergdorf's a few weeks ago . . . he wasn't allowed to see it, which he thought was silly, but he had to admit that the thrill of seeing her now was like an extra Christmas present. The red velvet dress draped gracefully to show a hint of bare shoulders, a sweetheart neckline and it met her figure in all the right places; it was chic and elegant, like the lady herself. Her beautiful blonde hair was swept up, and her fine features and blue eyes did what Terry loved . . . they melted his heart.

Terry had to admit that the new suit made him feel good and Joyce insisted on giving him an early present too—an expensive silk tie, Christmas red, that looked great with the navy suit and white shirt.

Terry could tell Joyce was thrilled with her early present and he was more than pleased with himself when she said the garnet and pearl earrings could not have been more perfect.

"C'mon, they want us there early and that's probably a good idea; we can park by the garages, I know it's going to get crowded," Joyce said as Terry draped the seldom-worn but treasured mink stole over her shoulders.

They saw the lights a mile down the road. Brightly lit torches lined the drive, soft lights and candlelight enhanced the huge wreaths, poinsettias and gigantic arrangements with holly and mistletoe, several of which Joyce had done. The house was a fairy tale.

Jimmy Doolittle had gotten to know Joyce pretty well since she spent so much time at Lake Cottage, and the handsome collie greeted her and

Terry with great excitement, resplendent in a new collar and red satin bow.

"Well, Jimmy, how festive you look," Joyce said as they petted him on the way into the house.

"Oh, Joyce, this is so exciting, and who would have thought such a tragic thing would have brought us to this?" Ethel said when her young guests arrived.

Terry had not thought of it that way, but there was truth in it. It was only four months ago, yet seemed like four years since he came here to check on the fire they had seen at the gorge.

Terry had another pleasant surprise when Joyce told him the evening was going to be even more special because of the pianist booked through an agency in Manhattan. The unmistakable sound of soft jazz greeted them as they went in, and for a fleeting moment, Terry wondered if Joyce missed this . . . in the world she came from a high class party was not the rare treat it was here.

It was not long before the house was overflowing with enthusiastic guests, enjoying an evening the likes of which most would not see again for a long time, if ever. The catered affair would be talked about for years, and deservedly so. Men and women in black and white uniforms, offering delicate canapés on silver trays, a sumptuous buffet and a generous bar, was just not the every day Kentbury experience!

Joyce lost track of the compliments on what she had done to the beautiful old home and she had fun telling the story of how a little project turned into a huge overhaul. Was it true that Better Homes & Gardens was coming to do a story on Lake Cottage? No comment. It was actually American Home, but she was not saying anything until it was definite.

Bull and Lou couldn't get over it.

"Well, where did she find all this stuff?" Bull asked, as he and Lou took a tour.

"It's her job, Bull, she gets paid to know where to find these things," Lou told him.

"Yup, beautiful and talented, just like you, Sweetheart," he told his wife who smiled at the compliment.

Everyone got a kick out of the glowing reindeer bow tie Dr. Walsh was wearing, and Mrs. Walsh said she had nothing to do with it!

Raymond and Mabel Newberry did not make it, but Sharon and Phillip Hamilton did, driving up from Princeton with Oliver and Lydia

Appleton. Since the fateful Sunday when Sharon popped in unexpectedly at her parents, the Appletons and Hamiltons were becoming good friends.

Terry thought it was interesting that all the town's clergymen were here: Reverend and Mrs. Peebles from the Dutch Reformed, Reverend and Mrs. Jeffries from the Methodist Church and Fathers Boyle and Hanover in the dining room, testing the punch with young Father March. They were definitely having a good time but they would all leave before twelve, citing early church services, but it was nice to see them as just guests at a non-church function.

Ned and Tilly Brewer were enjoying themselves, especially so when Madeline and Ethel said how much they liked Henry and George and what fine boys they were.

Two guests were a big surprise: Terry couldn't believe it when Sherman Dumont and his wife came in, but he quickly learned that Sherman's father had actually gone to law school with Ethel's husband. When she learned about his role in recent events, she called him, and here they were!

"You're not driving back to New York tonight, are you, sir?" Terry asked.

"No, we have a room at that quaint inn in Clinton . . . the Coach House," he said.

Terry and Joyce both did a double take when Naomi Cousins walked in with Dolly, Neal and Mary VanHaven. Naomi Cousins was a . . . distant cousin . . . to the Crisp sisters. Why did that surprise them?

While Joyce was getting compliments about her decorating, Terry was trying to avoid questions about "The Ona Birch Affair," as many now thought of it. There were not a lot of people bringing it up, yet there always seemed to be a few. But when Oliver Appleton signaled that he needed a few minutes, Terry was eager to hear what he had to say. Bull joined them when they found a small sitting room off one of the bedrooms and closed the door so they could talk.

They knew the court declared Frances Gregson Farmer mentally impaired and with the overwhelming evidence, and her admitting to at least two of the crimes, she would likely be committed to a prison for the criminally insane. They also knew that Dr. Appleton and several like-minded psychiatrists were trying to get her sent to a hospital in Princeton where she would get better care, and where they could study and evaluate her unusual case.

"Frances was transferred to Princeton yesterday. She's in a secured wing, lots of locked doors, but no bars and I'll be able to see her, learn more . . . but Frances has cancer, she probably has only five or six months to live; that is largely the reason we succeeded in getting her sent to Princeton," he told them.

"Cancer. Does she know?" Bull asked.

"Yes, I told her and do you know what she said?" the doctor asked.

"She said Greg already told her and that God decided she had to suffer for the things she has done, so he gave her cancer," he said.

"I thought God wanted her to do these things?" Bull said.

"This is some kind of guilt, but this poor, damaged human being actually thanked me for getting her to such a nice place. She said it was the first time in her life that she felt safe," he told them.

"Isn't it hard, Oliver? You know . . . treating her, feeling sorry for her, but knowing all the things she's done?" Bull asked.

"Not hard, really, Bull. I have compassion for her, more than most people would I suppose, but make no mistake, she is insane and she could be dangerous. I never forget that," he told them.

"What about the other murders, Doc?" Terry asked. "Aren't you obligated to have her charged?"

"Actually, I'm not. Everything she tells me is privileged. You, however, discovered enough to suggest an investigation about those very old cases, but you'll have to decide if you want to start that now or wait until after Frances is gone," he replied.

Terry and Bull appreciated the sense of that, but they were officers of the law. It was definitely something they would have to discuss.

They talked a few more minutes then left the sad subject behind as they returned to the holiday festivities. Terry went to find Joyce and saw her near the perfectly-trimmed tree, talking with Lou Campbell and Minnie Lester. Making a quick stop to see the piano player, he was walking toward his bride when the opening bars of Satin Doll filled the air. Joyce looked up when she heard the familiar song, and the handsome couple joined a few others on the small dance floor at the end of the beautiful room.

Terry understood that Joyce felt like the third hostess tonight and they stayed until the last guest left, wishing everyone Merry Christmas and Happy New Year. Madeline and Ethel said the party was a triumph and gave Joyce credit for most of it. When the couple finally said goodnight, they left with a large tray of the delectable party food, looking forward to enjoying it for days.

Talk on the ride home was about how beautiful everything was, who wore what, who had too much to drink, who spilled punch on the rug and how wonderful the piano player was.

"You're a pretty romantic guy, Terry Kramer," Joyce said, grateful to Bull for taking the duty tomorrow so they could catch up on sleep and a few other things.

They were just going into the house when Joyce asked about the little meeting she knew took place with Bull and Dr. Appleton.

Terry told her what they talked about and she wasn't surprised to learn that the eminent psychiatrist was writing a book about the case, understanding that it would likely be a lofty, scientific offering, appealing to the psychiatric and medical communities.

"Well, guess what? Lydia Appleton is writing a book too . . . we had a nice chat by the fireplace," she said playfully.

"You're kidding? A book about the case?" he asked skeptically.

"No . . . not exactly. It's fiction, a murder mystery."

"She's not putting us in it, is she?" Terry asked, imagining what that kind of book, fiction or not, could do to their privacy.

"No, actually, she's making up a fictional town and I believe the hero is going to be a little old lady. She's even got a title," Joyce said, watching Terry's eyes narrow, waiting for the punch line.

"OK, so what's the title?" he asked.

"She's thinking of calling it 'Murder at the Gorge.' What do you think?" Joyce asked.

"Well . . . hmm . . . I like it. Yeah, I do, I like it," he said.

"So, did you say you had a special surprise for me . . . I mean other than the fancy necktie?" Terry asked playfully.

"Maybe . . . but it might put you on Santa's naughty list," she said.

"I thought we were already on it," he replied, lifting her into his arms and carrying her to the bedroom. It had been a long day but happily, tomorrow, they could sleep in.

CPSIA information can be obtained at www.ICGtesting.com
Printed in the USA
LVOW08s0108210214

374574LV00002B/86/P